FIRSTBORN DAUGHTER

Kat Gilks

Firstborn Daughter

Cover design: Meredith Hughes

ISBN: 978-1-997713-11-1

FIRSTBORN DAUGHTER

Kat Gilks

DEDICATION

To everyone who has supported me in my writing,
and especially to all of the cats that inspired Taggy.

PROLOGUE

It was a fairly normal March afternoon, with the sun hidden behind the clouds in such a way that there appeared to be no time at all. Only the gradually dimming daylight lent any clue that it was past noon. The wind blew lightly through the treetops, but on the ground, it was pleasantly warm and still. It had rained earlier and the ground was damp and muddy, but no one was deterred in the slightest. It was a beautiful day to be outside.

A young man who looked to be in his early twenties walked with a three-year-old girl past the new construction site on the village's main street. The man wore jumpsuit overalls with forest-camouflage patterns and carried himself like a soldier, while the little girl wore a dark blue rainproof coat and pale blue trousers. She also had on fluffy white mittens that stood out against the man's clothing as he held her hand.

The little girl skipped and hummed to herself as she hurried alongside the man, whose strides were naturally long. Every few steps, he would shuffle a bit backwards and she would run forwards and they would resume walking side by side for a pace before the cycle repeated itself.

The construction site they had just passed was full of workers who were all wearing identical grey jumpsuit overalls, safety vests, and hard-hats. They were building what appeared to be more townhouses to accommodate new arrivals who wanted to flee the city but not lose any of their amenities. The man was nervous about the village getting more crowded. He liked the quiet safety of the woods and the village with the small cottages beside the lake. The mansions at the other end of the lake were already too close for his comfort. He shuffled his daughter toward the store where they were heading to pick up their grocery order, not wanting to gaze long at the construction site.

"Look, Papa – hot chocolate!" the little girl cried out joyfully, pointing to a small kiosk at the edge of the store's parking lot.

The man took her to the kiosk and lifted her up toward the counter.

"Hello!" she greeted the server. "Do you have hot cider?"

The server smiled at her but shook their head. The little girl kept smiling.

"That's okay. I'll have hot chocolate."

The girl contentedly took her cup and held it tightly as the man put her down to pay. As he did so, the little girl thanked both him and the server. Once the man finished paying, the girl gave him a warm hug.

Suddenly, several police cars sped past them down the road through the village before doubling back past the construction site.

"Notice to all residents of Little Hobidigan! Notice to all park visitors! Security sweep is underway! Please comply with officers and all will be well. Keep calm and carry on! No one is in immediate danger! Please comply and we can all be on our way."

The mechanical voice blared through a loudspeaker from the police cars, which spread down the street. One of the cars stopped beside the kiosk and two officers jumped out.

"Identity card, please!"

The man complied, handing the officer both his card and the girl's. The server held out their card toward the officer, but he brushed them away as he turned his full attention to the young man.

"This is your daughter?"

“Yes,” the man replied, indignant at the question.

“Hmm, there must be a mistake. This can’t be you.” The officer with the cards looked at his partner, who was holding a scanning device. He passed the cards along to her.

“Good resemblance though, eh? Almost had me fooled.”

“The kid’s is genuine, it looks like,” she replied, shrugging.

“I assure you, that’s my identity card and she’s my daughter,” the man insisted. “No mistake!”

Another police car returned, having received a call for backup. Whatever the target of the security sweep was, they had found something new. Two more officers emerged.

“Separate them!” one of the newcomers ordered. “Here, take the kid!”

The girl was pulled away by the officer with the scanner, the force of which spilled her hot chocolate all over her. She screamed and burst into tears. One of her gloves came off in her father’s hand and he automatically clenched it in his fist.

“Sweetie, you okay?” he called out. “You fucking idiots! You could have burnt her!”

“She’s fine and she’s wearing a raincoat,” the officer hurriedly grumbled. “She’ll be fine. Come with me, sweetheart.”

“No! Papa!” the girl shrieked, reaching back toward the man in camouflage. “Papa, help!”

“Let go of her! She’s my daughter, okay? Do you want to do a DNA test? I promise you, she’s mine! I didn’t steal her. I’m her father and we live here. Ask anyone!”

“It’s true!” the server added, standing dumbfounded beside the carafe of hot chocolate. “She’s his daughter. They’ve lived here in the village all her life!”

“Shut up! This doesn’t concern you.” The officer holding the struggling toddler managed to aim her scanner steadily at the young server. “You leave this to us, you ungrateful snot.”

The girl screamed as she was shoved into the patrol car and belted into the seat that was much too large for her. The officer in charge of her bolted into the car after her and kept her device aimed out the window.

“Look, calm down, okay?” Two officers had grabbed hold of the man and he was still struggling to break free. They were not having any success securing him.

“Aren’t these supposed to have an off-switch or something?” one asked his partner.

“You want to start looking for it?”

“I don’t have a fucking off-switch!” The man panicked. “Let me go!”

“You’ve got a fucking barcode, so you’ve got a fucking off-switch, you fucking dumb robot!”

“It doesn’t work that way!” The man successfully freed himself from the officers and started toward the car the girl had been shoved into. “Give her back!”

“She’s not your daughter – leave her alone or I swear I’ll shoot you dead!” The device that the officer in the car held was not just for scanning. The man froze mid-stride.

“Stupid robots!” the first officer spat at him. “You are nothing but piece-of-meat machines taking our fucking jobs away. Do you know they’re adding robots to the forces now? Do you?”

The two officers managed to recapture him and threw him down on the sidewalk, kicking at him and venting their frustrations about the new robot police rookies.

“How could I know that?” the man screamed. “Leave me alone!”

The car with the girl sped away.

"Anna!"

"Leave her alone – she's better off without you. Robots don't have kids. Robots shouldn't be around kids because kids shouldn't learn to like robots! They're taking away their futures. What's going to happen to little Abby by the time she's old enough to work, eh? She's going to be on the fucking streets, that's what! And she's going to be outcompeted by robot whores!"

"Her name's Anna," the man muttered defiantly.

"Damn it, where's that off-switch?"

"Guess it's the same as everyone else's, you dummy," the man continued. "Beat me to a bloody pulp."

Suddenly, a man came running from the construction site. Instead of grey overalls, he wore black trousers, a white self-ironing shirt, a brown jacket, and a red tie under his vest and hard hat.

"Stop, stop! What's going on here? I've got a tour scheduled. Potential buyers! They take one look at this mess and I might as well set fire to this whole place."

"Sorry, sir!" The officers stopped beating Anna's father and pulled him up. "We'll take him into custody and be out of your way."

"What the hell did he do? He didn't seem to be causing any trouble."

"He's an escaped robot, sir. Had a fake ID and everything. Maybe kidnapping?"

"No!" the subject of the conversation insisted. "I didn't steal her!"

"Maybe she was lost and he was just trying to help her," the man in the sharp clothes suggested. "And he thought he'd be nice and buy her something to drink! Is that something that we usually beat people up for?"

"He's not people, he's a robot!"

The look on the sharply-dressed man's face was one of shock and concern.

"All the more reason not to beat him! Who does he belong to?"

"Don't know. Here, check out his barcode!"

The man in camouflage relented and held out his arm to the manager, who dutifully pulled out his phone to scan his barcode.

"It's coming up blank. Maybe he's a discard? Or there's a glitch somehow. All robots have owners, but his barcode says NOT REGISTERED. So he's probably not escaped – just lost himself."

"Well, if he's a discard, can we take him back to the station and let the real flesh-and-blood officers have at him?"

"No, because I will take him. I work for the Robot Rental Corporation. He's ours by default. We can always use more units." The manager brazenly turned away from the officers to the man. "What is it you do, RB14600218-36?"

The young man's face fell.

"I'm a mechanic, sir," he sputtered, tears and blood running into his mouth. "I fix things."

"We'll find lots for you to fix, don't worry! Vehicles or appliances?"

"Both, sir."

"You have any experience with plumbing? Electrical?"

The man nodded.

"Come with me. We'll get you cleaned up and sorted out."

Reluctantly, the officers accompanied the manager to the Robot Rental Corporation's waiting truck and shoved the young man into a chair in the cargo compartment.

"Thank you, officers! Now, I think you need to continue your security sweep elsewhere. My clients will be arriving shortly."

He closed the door of the compartment, leaving the man alone in the dark.

CHAPTER ONE

Tori and Patrick spent a lot of their evenings sitting in their living room, and in every way, this was a typical evening. The fireplace was turned on to the maximum setting, radiating heat to combat the rainy chill of a late March cold front. Their cat, Taggy, had settled into a tuck position directly in front of the simulated blaze, turning every so often to avoid getting too warm in one spot. Rain splattered against the windows and an errant tree branch knocked against the back porch railing.

Since neither of them liked working to music, the room was quiet inside as they stared at their respective screens. Tori had three different datapads in front of her as she went over her store's accounts, while Patrick set aside the datapad with his notes from his latest maintenance committee meeting to read a novel. Every so often, they stopped to say something if a random thought occurred to one of them. Tonight had been mostly silent, except when an ad popped up on one of Tori's datapads that she had forgotten to mute. Taggy's snoring was the loudest sound within the house.

"You'd think people wouldn't be buying so much stuff nowadays," Tori remarked as she closed the file showing her store's excellent sales. "Especially stuff they don't need, but we're doing as well at the bookstore as the second-hand clothing shop across the street and our upstairs café runs out of food almost every day."

"Well, people need to eat and you sell good-quality food." Patrick barely looked up from his book, sensing his wife wanted to start a full conversation.

"We hardly have anything to give to the shelters afterward. I feel bad about that."

"Your dad will be happy, though. He'd much rather you turn a profit than be overly charitable."

"Considering he thinks this is just a fun project to keep me occupied and give us the illusion of independence, does it really matter what he thinks? I never ask him for money!"

Patrick chuckled. "I love it when you sound like a rebellious teenager."

Tori sighed in frustration and closed her datapads. Wrapping her blanket more tightly around herself, she curled up into a corner of the couch.

"I'm still amazed how many people want to buy religious books and candles and cards and all our paraphernalia. I'm not surprised at how well our lending library is going, but why buy the books outright?"

"We sell escapism. Not to mention I haven't seen any of the books in our store anywhere else. Have you?"

"No, though that's partly because I take that into account when ordering."

"Is there a point to this?" Reading time is over, Patrick. He admitted he enjoyed their conversations, even if they were repetitive, and was not annoyed about being interrupted.

"Does there have to be a point to everything? Can't we just talk?"

Patrick delicately put his bookmark into the novel and joined his wife on the couch.

"Talk about what, milady?"

"Something? That tree branch is driving me crazy."

"I'll add it to the list for the Repair Squad. Someone in our co-op who is much better with power tools should deal with it."

"You're clumsy but a good organizer." Tori gave him a kiss.

Patrick was ashamed to admit he needed the compliment after a long, chaotic day. The heavy rain and wind had caused flooding in several of the houses in their cooperative block. Shingles had blown off roofs. The rubbish and recycling bins had toppled into a heap. One of the block's two vans had suffered a mechanical failure. There had been a lot of running around in raincoats between the houses. Children had chased soggy recycling across the shared yard. He had envied his wife being inside the store.

"I swear, running the Repair Squad is more arduous than my courier shifts. I'd rather drive around Alexandrina all day."

Tori burst into tears. "You trained as a journalist! You hate being a courier!"

"Not anymore, Tori." It was his turn to comfort her. "Once I took the job, I got used to it. Your dad runs a good company."

"Stop talking about my dad!"

Tori put her glasses on the end-table and buried her head into Patrick's shoulders.

"What's wrong with me? I should be happy that everything is going well."

She did feel like an angry teenager despite being twice as old as one. Waves of rage swept through her and she kept crying into her husband's sweater.

"Maybe my medicine is mixed up again."

"Would some music help?" Patrick settled himself onto the couch with a second blanket, kicking off his slippers to sit out his wife's latest bout of despair.

"No, nothing that would calm me down will drown out that branch tapping on the stupid railing. Everything will annoy me."

"Would it be better if we went upstairs?"

"Maybe later."

Tori breathed heavily and methodically into Patrick's shoulder, attempting to calm herself. She hated how unpredictable her cocktail of medicine made her feel. Between her medications and the ever-changing barrage of symptoms of her autoimmune disorder, she was ill more often than she was healthy.

"You didn't sign up for this," she whimpered. "I'm sorry."

"What do you mean? Of course I did. We got married."

"I wasn't like this then."

"You weren't any better. If that's what you think, you're remembering it wrong."

"At this rate, you'd have been better off as a single dad with kids. They'd be way easier

than me to take care of."

Patrick started to say something but realized quickly that what had sounded like a reassuring response in his head sounded patronising. He finally decided to change the subject.

"When I was left with several kids this afternoon – when we had to put all the bins back together after the wind blew them apart, I mean – it was exhausting! I wouldn't have had the strength left to get the kids supper." His overly jovial tone had the wrong effect on his wife.

"Oh, just stop it, please!" Tori let go of him and buried her face into her knees, sobbing anew.

Patrick picked up his novel again but otherwise did not move away from her. He would let her cry and he would be there if she needed him.

Meanwhile, Tori thought of how cute their neighbours' children were and how much she wished she could have had any. She no longer told Patrick about incidents at the store because she felt as though they were the same problem over and over again. The problem was hers. Her customers frequently asked her about her family and it would almost always end with her hiding in the storage room for ten minutes in tears once they left. It was usually an honest mistake on their part, thinking that a married Christian woman of thirty-five would be a mother in much the same way they assumed a child of ten would be in school of some kind. She would give customers book recommendations and they would innocently ask if her kids liked it. Such an incident had happened that afternoon and she felt terrible. The customer had expressed sorrow and pity for her, but that felt worse for Tori than being ignored.

This is your problem and will always be your problem. She owed her existence to her father wanting an heir for his businesses, but when it became clear she had inherited her family's recessive autoimmune disease, he had come to the realization that having children, while lovely, was not ultimately important, and he had raised her with that belief. She was his wonderful daughter and he would do anything for her health and happiness.

It was not as though Tori had nothing to do. She loved her store. She loved her community. She loved her faith. Most of all, she loved Patrick. The world was terrifying, but their home together was their warm refuge. Her illnesses seemed determined to destroy it.

Patrick had been both in lust and in awe of her when they had met. He had been willing to be as patient as possible with her as they fell in love. He had not predicted that ten years later, he would be awkwardly reading beside her on the couch while she inconsolably cried. He tried to feign Taggy's nonchalance.

A message came through from one of the neighbours reporting that another unit had flooding problems.

"I need to get to the Barkley-Lawleys'. Their crawlspace has flooded," Patrick muttered. "At this rate, we are going to have to replace the whole damn plumbing system in this co-op!"

"Good thing the store is doing well," was Tori's muffled reply. Most of the families in their block were barely making ends meet. "See you when you get back! Love you!"

Patrick kissed the top of Tori's head (which was by now the only part of her that was not covered by the fluffy quilt) and disappeared out the back door.

Eventually, exhausted from crying, Tori went over to the kitchen for a glass of water. Taggy followed her inquisitively, meowing excitedly and twirling around his food dish.

"It isn't bedtime yet, Taggy-boo," she admonished him, picking him up for a quick cuddle. Taggy squirmed slightly but obliged his food-giver her strange need to squeeze and kiss him.

Her phone started buzzing and she glanced at the incoming number in surprise. It was past the usual time for calling anyone.

"Why is Nellie House calling us so late in the evening?" she asked the cat, who responded with a plea to be let back down. "It's not like them to call us at all anymore."

Taggy trilled thankfully at having his paws on the floor again as Tori picked up the call.

"Hello? Tori speaking." She was not sure how to address them.

“Is this Victoria Lapoule Williams-Kirke?” the voice from Nellie House asked sharply.

“Yes.” From the tone of their voice, Tori inferred they were angry with her.

“We need you and your husband to come to our office in person immediately tomorrow morning. We open at eight in the morning and expect to see you there at that time.”

“Um, why? We don’t need your services. The government has made it clear we can’t really use you.”

“I’m sorry about that,” the voice on the other end of the call softened slightly, though it still sounded anxious. “This is Nala Amin Abbas, remember? I was your caseworker. I should have introduced myself again. This has just really thrown me off.”

“What has?”

“I can’t discuss it now. We have to meet in person. Our system says your phone is in the city, so you need to come tomorrow.”

“Both me and Patrick?”

“Yes, unless you have a contagious illness. This affects both of you. You might have to stay here most of the day.”

“Why?” Tori cringed at how panicky and confused her own voice had become.

“I wish I could tell you, Tori. I think there has been some weird mistake.”

“Mistake? Mistake with what? Is it something about the last donation I made? Were there stolen goods in it or something?”

“No, nothing like that. Like I said, this might be all a mistake. We’ll see you tomorrow.”

Tori shut her phone down and stared into the middle of the room in confusion.

"That did not make sense, Taggy. Our file has been closed for over a year."

She hurriedly sent messages to her employees to let them know she was not able to work the next day, which left only one person for the morning shift, and went back over her files from Nellie House. There was nothing but forms, medical assessments, and rejection letters. She would not be able to have children and the government had determined that she would not be able to adopt them.

"So what do they want now?" she wondered aloud. Taggy mewed in a way that she interpreted as him saying he did not know either.

Taking her water back to the living room, she curled up on the couch again and closed her eyes. She decided to make peace with the annoying branch outside and counted each rhythmic tap against the railing, reciting meditative prayers as she drifted off into a light doze until her husband returned.

"Feeling better?" Patrick asked as he took off his wet boots and raincoat.

"No, now I'm scared."

"Like, you feel scared instead of angry?"

"No, as in I'm scared because we got this weird phone call from Nellie House and we both have to be there at eight sharp tomorrow morning!"

"What the …?"

"My thoughts exactly. They sounded really upset, though. Like we're in trouble for something."

"In that case, I guess we should get to bed. I'll feed Taggy."

The cat was the only one unconcerned.

CHAPTER TWO

The rain had not let up all night and was still pouring down as Tori and Patrick arrived at Nellie House the following morning. So as not to arouse suspicion by their mysterious trip, Tori was cramped up in a tiny space in the back of Patrick's courier vehicle between parcels. Courier vehicles dotted the city and they often made multiple trips to the same locations in one day. They hoped no one would notice that the vehicle did not move for however long they needed to be at Nellie House.

Tori squeezed past the boxes and out the driver's door, balancing awkwardly on Patrick's lap as she activated her umbrella before hopping out into the rain. Her feet splashed onto the uneven wet cobbles and the fact that her shoes were waterproof did nothing against the cold. She hobbled over to the door and rang the bell.

A young assistant whisked them inside and immediately pulled them past the reception desk toward the back offices.

"Whoa, where are we going?" Tori asked, struggling to deactivate her umbrella as she walked through the dimly lit corridor. Only the emergency lights were on and the assistant seemed to be the only person there, even though it was nearly time to open.

"Nala's office," the assistant replied hurriedly.

"Have you had to downsize recently?" Patrick wondered, trying to make the interaction seem vaguely normal.

"Yes, incidentally, but we thought this issue would be better dealt with as confidentially as possible. We don't want the media hearing anything about this. So we gave everyone except me, Nala, and a couple caregivers the morning off. Said we had to deal with a leaky pipe."

"Why would the media be involved?" Tori practically shrieked.

"Nala will explain. I'm going to pretend to fix a pipe."

The assistant disappeared back down the dark corridor as Patrick pushed Tori into Nala Amin Abbas's tiny office. The office at least had windows that let in the gloomy morning light, illuminating a pair of stiff chairs they were expected to sit in.

"Good morning!" Nala greeted them with a sense of requisite cheeriness. "I'm sorry to drag you down here on such a terrible morning. Can I pour you some coffee? Energy cocktail?" She held out two carafes.

"Coffee, please," Tori answered automatically. She hated the taste of energy cocktails and they made her sick.

Nala poured them each a large mug of coffee before refilling her own with the hot energy cocktail. Tori watched as Nala's drink poured out as a purplish blue colour with an overpowering raspberry scent, making her queasy as she tried to figure out what they were there for. Patrick sipped his coffee noisily.

"Sorry – it might be a bit too warm to drink yet," Nala realized. "I just brewed a fresh pot. It has been a long night."

"I'm fine," Patrick coughed, having burnt his lips slightly.

"Um, could you explain why you called us in like this, please?" Tori asked anxiously. Her eyes darted around the room, looking for anything that she might vomit into if necessary.

"We have a difficult situation." Nala paused to sip her drink. "A week or so ago, the police brought us a child whose parents they couldn't locate. They brought her to us to see if we could do anything. We can care for a child and they don't. Makes sense."

Tori and Patrick gave the social worker looks of confused exasperation.

"That sounds like your normal job," Patrick pointed out.

"That's what we initially thought," Nala agreed. "But then we did a more extensive genetic search for her parents. It turns out we found them…but it makes no sense."

"What do you mean?" Patrick wondered, glancing at his wife. Tori could not talk at all.

"You two are the closest genetic matches for the child's parents."

Before Patrick could respond, Tori threw up her coffee and breakfast smoothie onto Nala's desk. The social worker nonchalantly grabbed a towel and handed Tori the empty recycling bin she had hidden behind her.

"Sorry," Tori whimpered. She slumped back into her chair.

"Are you okay? Did you even hear her?" Patrick demanded. He turned back to Nala, who was rearranging mugs around the towel. "What do you mean, we are the closest genetic matches for anyone's parents? We can't have kids. You know that."

"I heard her," Tori whimpered. "Maybe she means you?"

"Er, no, that's not what I meant. That would be more explainable. No, the results clearly show you, Patrick Matthew Semaganis Kirke-Williams, as the only option for the child's father, and you, Victoria Elisabeth Lapoule Williams-Kirke, as the only option for the child's mother."

"I'm no one's mother!"

"Considering when you have been on file with us, the timeline does not even make any sense," Nala continued. "This child was born on the 2nd of April, just under three years ago. I had a meeting with you four days prior to that, according to our records, so I can vouch that you weren't pregnant."

"You mean there's a three-year-old who is genetically related to us and who is without parents?" Patrick's tone was a mix of concern and confusion.

"Apparently, yes. I mean, one would assume she has parents. Someone had to gestate and give birth to her."

"Not me," Tori muttered.

"Someone had to raise her for nearly three years, considering her good health and how well she can talk, walk, and use the toilet," Nala continued, rather too matter-of-factly for Patrick and Tori's comfort. "But the police think she was abducted. There are no records of her in any system except her birth registration and occasional health visits. Her recorded parents don't seem to exist, so the assumption is they are aliases."

"So we've been brought here because…?" Patrick was slowly piecing together the narrative the police must have constructed.

"They think either your child was abducted from you, or you sold her illegally, or you abandoned her for some reason. There are officers in our meeting room waiting to question you."

"What?" Patrick screamed. "If I had a daughter, I would never sell or abandon her!"

Tori threw up into the recycling bin and grabbed the window ledge for stability.

"And if my daughter had been abducted, I would still be looking for her!" In his exuberance, Patrick accidentally knocked over his coffee onto the towel, soaking it from the other side.

“It would have been all over the news,” Tori added, realizing with horror why Nellie House had been trying to keep the media away. “The granddaughter of the founder of Ninja-Cowboy Courier getting kidnapped…they can’t think that happened…”

“That…that is why they think something worse has happened,” Nala admitted.

“But that doesn’t even make any sense!” Tori started to cry. “If I had a child, I wouldn’t have tried to get rid of it. My dad would have been showing us off as a perfect family.”

“Yes, I thought as much,” Nala reassured her. “None of this makes any sense to me. How about you two meet with the officers? They’ll want you to go in separately.”

“I’ll go first!” Patrick volunteered, gulping what remained of his coffee quickly and backing out into the corridor.

“Thank you. Please don’t get yourself arrested!” Tori called out after him.

“Love you, dear!” he shouted back as he spotted the meeting room and headed to it.

Nala began to fuss with the dirty towel on her desk and took another swig of her energy cocktail. Tori sat in place, still crying.

“Can I get you anything? Some water? Another smoothie?”

“Sure, water, please.”

As the other woman left to get water, Tori reluctantly took a sip of coffee and wiped her eyes with her sweater. Vomiting her breakfast had disrupted her medicine schedule and she anticipated a cascade of symptoms as a result. She was not sure she could keep from passing out if the police insisted on questioning her.

How is there a child out there that has me for a genetic mother? She had never even conceived a child that had died, let alone had one that was apparently a living, breathing toddler. Her genetic code was defective, so why would anyone steal and use it?

"How sick is this child?" she asked as Nala returned with water.

"As healthy as ever! No records of any visits to a hospital, just to a couple of local clinics for required vaccines and check-ups. She hasn't even picked up any sniffles from the other kids while she's been here."

"Then how can she be mine?"

"I don't know how that works."

"Yeah, me neither."

Tori would have been surprised if Nala had told them that Patrick had a child, but she would have understood how it might have happened. Most men of his age and education had donated genetic material in exchange for payment when they were younger. Even him having an affair would have made logical sense, though she could not contemplate him doing that. They could not have children together, however, so where did this child with both of their genetics come from?

Patrick was having none of the nonsense the police officers were trying to throw at him. They asked him about his motivations for marrying Tori, having decided he had thrown himself at a rich heiress to pay for nefarious habits. No matter how dark of a characterization they were giving him, however, they still could not adequately explain how his alleged daughter had ended up disappearing.

"For the last time, I would not have sold or sent my daughter away," he insisted. "I don't know how else to tell you that. I love my wife and if we had had any children, no matter if they had the same health problems, I would have loved them too."

"So, to be clear, you are suggesting that your child was abducted without you knowing about her existence?" the lead officer inquired. "How do you propose that happened?"

"I don't know. It makes no sense to me either."

He was soon dismissed and Tori dragged her feet into the meeting room, hoping she did not look like too much of a mess.

"Good morning, Victoria Lapoule Williams," the lead officer intoned, gesturing for her to sit down in the chair that her husband had just vacated. "I apologize for this ordeal. You look like you could use some rest."

"I'm fine," she lied. "What do you want?"

"You are the only recognized daughter of Michael Cruz Brettley Williams, the CEO and founder of Ninja-Cowboy Courier, right?"

"I'm his only daughter, yes. There's no one else."

"You're his only child with his legal wife, Cleo Elisabeth Lapoule Martinez, but are you his only child?"

"Yes! I had several siblings that died in utero or as babies, but sickly little me is the only one still alive. And no, my dad didn't have kids with anyone else."

"So you are the only daughter of one of the wealthiest men in Alexandrina, but you live in a housing cooperative and own a café bookstore in Goat Cove? Not exactly what most rich heiresses do, is it?"

"Yes," Tori replied with mild annoyance. "I guess I'm not like most rich heiresses."

"Are you estranged from your family?"

"No, not at all! We visit them often." My father thinks I'm playing at being an independent adult under his supervision.

"You have been married to your husband for how long?"

"Eight years. We've been together for ten."

"And no children? Was this by choice?"

"No, we would have liked to. I'm too sick. We never had any."

"So how do you explain a child having you for a genetic mother?"

"I don't know! I'm too sick for fertility treatments."

"Okay, more to the point, how do you explain a three-year-old being found alone with no family that happens to have the same DNA as you and your husband? Whose registered parents seem to be con artists? Seems to me like you paid someone off."

"Why would I do that? If I had given birth to a miracle baby, why would I get rid of her? I'm married to her father. If he hadn't wanted her, I'd have tossed him out."

"You're right, we aren't making sense. Your father doesn't go around spouting nonsense about 'family values,' and even if he did, he wouldn't be embarrassed by his daughter and son-in-law having a child. That's what's supposed to happen, right?"

Both Tori and the second officer nodded.

"Any chance you did get pregnant and someone abducted the zygote during some kind of health exam?" the second officer asked with curiosity. "I know they can do wonders with transplants now. My wife adopted an embryo directly from the biological mother and had it re-implanted into herself. It was a dreadful ordeal, but we have a healthy son. Now she wants me to take a turn."

Tori had never heard of anyone abducting unborn babies at any stage of development and the thought of anyone doing so – let alone to her specifically – made her gag. She managed not to spit water all over the table as she took her time contemplating the question. She did not remember any time when she could have had a zygote removed without her knowledge. Then again, if it had been without her knowledge, how would she remember?

"Um, well, I suppose…probably not, though. I really have not been pregnant. I haven't had any surgeries recently. Sounds like a really risky way to abduct children."

"I think we will put that down as a remote possibility but not worth pursuing further evidence at this time, even if it is the most likely explanation," the lead officer decided. "It is equally rare odds that both you and your husband had your DNA used without your consent to create the same child for the illegal adoption market."

His tone of voice indicated he was gearing up for a new line of questioning.

"That is also possible, though," the second officer interjected. "It seems clear to me that these two are clueless and surprised."

"Yeah, seems that way to me too. We seem to be left with possible but highly improbable scenarios. Nothing we can investigate right now. The Alexandrina Police and the Federal Cascadian Police will both close this file and leave it with Nellie House. You are free to go, ma'am."

Tori stood up and stumbled out of the meeting room.

"Wait, what do you mean, close this file? What will happen to the child?"

"As far as we're concerned, we found her parents. It's up to social services now."

Nala's assistant waited outside the door to give Tori another bottle of water and guide her back to the social worker's office.

The office now smelled strongly of cleaner as she sat back down beside the window. The rain had stopped and birds hopped excitedly around the nearby trees. Nala went out to talk to the officers, leaving Tori and Patrick alone to contemplate the morning. The clock on her phone read 10:52.

"Are you going to be all right?" Patrick finally asked. "Are we going to be able to go home? Are we under further investigation?"

"How should I know?" It was her answer to all three of his questions.

"This is ludicrous." He checked the buzzing on his phone and swore quietly. "More flooding. Pretty much the whole block at this rate."

Tori started giggling uncontrollably.

"What's the matter now?"

"We have just discovered we have a kid, genetically at least, and we have just spent two hours being questioned, and now you're back to your Repair Squad business."

"Hopefully I am not going to be delegating repairs from jail."

Nala returned to her office shortly thereafter as her assistant led the officers out.

"Well, that is thankfully over!" Nala shuddered. "I'm always uneasy while the cops are here. Glad they've left and none of us have gone with them!"

She sat down and poured everyone more coffee.

"Apparently, everything is fine from their end. Now it is up to us."

"Up to us or you?" Patrick asked.

"All of us. I have a not-quite-three-year-old in the playroom upstairs who needs a home. You two have one. I see no reason why she can't go with you. I'll prepare the necessary forms and then you can take her home."

"What?" Patrick narrowly avoided spilling his coffee again.

"She's your daughter, according to all the available evidence, so you have every right to take her home."

"You mean, just like a parcel?" Tori squeaked. "We don't have to prove anything to you? No tests or home visits or…?"

"You already did all of those. If it wasn't for your sickness, you would have passed with flying colours. You'll be great parents!"

Tori tearfully hugged her husband. "We have a daughter!"

It was Patrick's turn to be speechless.

"Where is she? Can we see her? What's her name?" Tori turned back to Nala, vibrating with anticipation.

Nala showed them camera footage from her phone of the children in the upstairs playroom. She switched between several camera angles so a little dark-haired girl was the central focus. The girl was alone beside a shelf of picture-books, gazing at the illustrations in one of them as she diligently turned each page. To Tori, it seemed like the girl was reading the words as much as looking at the pictures, but she pushed that thought out of her mind. The girl was barely three.

"She's adorable!"

"She loves books!" Patrick sputtered excitedly.

"Well, of course she does! She's our daughter, isn't she?"

"Her name is Anna Elizabeth," Nala answered Tori's other question. "I'm not sure it would be wise to try to change her name at this age. She seems very attached to it."

"Oh no, that's lovely!" Tori was mesmerised by the camera footage. "Can we meet her now?"

"I'll have one of the caregivers bring her downstairs. I don't want you catching anything from the other toddlers! The caregivers can pack up her things while you get acquainted."

"What sort of things?" Patrick wondered. "We don't exactly have any toddler things at home at the moment."

"We can go shopping!" Tori bounced back into her chair.

"She has some clothes that we got for her while she was here so that she wouldn't be stuck in the same dirty outfit. And then we give each child that comes through here a book and a stuffie. Hers is an elephant."

Tori watched as one of the caregivers delicately interrupted Anna's reading and took her out of the playroom. The toddler did not protest or even appear to be scared, unlike her new mother, who was still shaking in joyful terror.

Handing Nala back her phone, Tori glanced out the window again. Some of the birds were collecting sticks to build nests, while others were furiously pecking for grubs. She was almost sure she could hear peeping chicks in the distance.

Finally, it's my turn.

CHAPTER THREE

"Anna, this is your new mother and father," Nala introduced Tori and Patrick to their daughter. "They have come to take you home."

The little girl eyed her parents inquisitively, but with noticeable confusion and suspicion. She seemed to at once recognize them and yet clearly knew they were strangers to her.

Tori was stuck on admiring how gorgeous Anna was. She had an olive-brown complexion, bright blue eyes, brown-black hair that was curly despite being almost shoulder-length, and a soft round face. She was dressed in a matching sweater and trousers set: dark brown with light blue trim. Her caregiver had dressed her in a dark blue rain-proof coat that draped over her shoulders. The athletic shoes on her feet seemed well-worn for such a young child. Anna carried a plain black tote bag that had a stuffed elephant's head sticking out of the top.

"My new mama and papa?" she asked, turning to look at Nala skeptically. "They don't look right."

"That's because they are new. You have never met them before."

"Um…okay." Anna turned back to Tori and Patrick.

"Hello, Anna," Patrick managed to greet her.

"Hello!" The toddler smiled, eager to please everyone. "My name is Anna Elizabeth M-, I mean, Anna Elizabeth."

Her face fell upon stumbling over her full name, as though she remembered being chastened for saying it earlier.

"My name is Elisabeth too!" Tori answered impulsively, hoping to connect with her and brighten her mood. "I'm Victoria Elisabeth Lapoule Williams-Kirke."

"That's a pretty name," Anna answered. She turned to Patrick. "What's your name?"

"Um, Patrick," her new father muttered.

"So what's my name?" she asked, looking back at Nala. "Do I get a new identity card?"

"I'm just working on that now," Nala explained. "We'll get a temporary one printed off for you. Your name is Anna Elizabeth Lapoule Kirke now, and you'll be called Anna Williams-Kirke until you get older."

Anna let the sound of her new name replay itself in her head, seemingly satisfied.

"Where do you live?" Anna asked, looking at Tori.

"We live in Goat Cove. Have you ever been there?"

Shaking her head, Anna reached out and gave Tori a hug. Her new mother hugged her back, squeezing her eyes shut to keep from passing out. When Anna let go of her, she seemed to sense something was wrong with Tori, who had to grab the edge of the desk to stand up again. She turned to Patrick, holding out her arms and lifting her hands into the air.

"Up, Papa?"

Hesitating for only a brief second, Patrick swept Anna up into a hug. Despite the tears in her eyes, she latched onto him tightly, wrapping her arms and legs around him and dropping her head onto his shoulder.

"Take me home, New Papa and New Mama!"

As they left Nellie House, Anna burst into nervous giggles at the idea of riding in a courier truck.

"I'm sorry, this is against all safety regulations," Patrick apologized as he moved parcels around to accommodate her and Tori. "We didn't know you were coming home with us today, Anna, or we would have brought something more comfortable."

"It's an adventure!" Anna proclaimed.

"Well, I think the first stop on our adventure should be to get lunch! We must celebrate!"

"And I really need to eat," Tori added quietly, lying flat on a bed of parcels.

"What's wrong, New Mama? Are you having a baby?" Anna sounded matter-of-fact at that idea, as though that was the main reason anyone would be ill.

"No, I can't have any babies. I'm too sick. I've always been sick."

"Since you were little?"

"Yes, even littler than you."

"That's sad. I hope you get better!"

"Me too." Tori decided that such sentiment coming from an earnest nearly-three-year-old was worth smiling about. She usually hated hearing anyone else say it. It's a chronic illness – you don't get better. You just get worse. Will you get sick too, someday?

"I think we'll do the drive-thru," Patrick decided. "What do you like to eat, Anna?"

"Fruit!" When that was met with silence, Anna continued to list random grocery items. "Noodles, beans, rice, seaweed, veggie-tables, eggs…oh, and fish! I like fish."

"I suppose I should have asked before pulling into the drive-thru," Patrick chided himself. "I'd have picked somewhere else."

"Can I take your order, please?" the automatic voice beeped.

"Three veggie combos, please."

Tori sat up to eat as they continued to hide in the back of the truck. To any onlookers, Patrick was a courier stopping for lunch.

"What's this?" Anna asked, as Tori laid out a veggie burger in front of her. "How am I supposed to eat it?"

"It's like a sandwich. You bite it."

"What's a sandwich?"

Tori tried to demonstrate, but Anna was too small to properly grip the burger.

"Well, you bite it like an apple or peach."

Anna's eyes lit up and she attempted to bite it again, but the burger nearly fell apart in her tiny hands.

"Sorry, I thought ordering the child's size combo would be a bit suspicious," Patrick explained. "You never know who is watching."

Nodding, Tori pulled a multitool out of her handbag and cut the burger into quarters.

"Here, let me make smaller pieces for you. Now, hold the small burger in both hands so you don't drop it. Then bite it like a peach!"

Anna grimaced as she tasted her lunch.

"It doesn't taste like peach. It tastes like beans."

"No, it won't taste like peach. We can have peaches when we get home."

"I like it!" Anna decided. "Thank you, New Mama."

With mixed feelings of regret and relief, Patrick dropped Tori and Anna off at their front door and headed out on his actual courier run. He gave his new daughter a hug and promised to be home for supper.

Anna's eyes widened as she took in the sight of her new parents' house. It had two levels, two doors, and lots of windows.

"We live in this half of the house," Tori explained, gesturing accordingly. "Our neighbours live on that side. There is a wall in the middle. And then we have neighbours in each of the other houses in our block. There are lots of kids!"

"Why are there stairs?" Anna asked, as they entered the front hallway. "My old house didn't have stairs."

"The bedrooms are upstairs." Tori shut the door and wondered how many of their neighbours had noticed them. They would surely wonder who the little girl was.

"Why are the bedrooms up? You have lots, like at Nellie House?"

"Not lots. Just three bedrooms and a bathroom. They built our house so that it wouldn't take up much space on the ground, so they put the bedrooms upstairs on top of the kitchen and living room."

"Oh! Can I use the bathroom?" Anna struggled taking off her shoes, eventually sliding them off.

"Yes, I'll take you into the one down here. It's just past the stairs."

Tori was impressed at how well-trained Anna was at using the toilet and sink. All she needed to do as her mother was lift her up and down.

"So just us live here?" Anna did not let her need to go to the bathroom interrupt her questions.

Before Tori could respond, Taggy decided to introduce himself.

"Kitty-cat!" Anna gave him a mystified look, uncertain whether the animal was safe.

"This is our cat, Taggy," Tori introduced them, bending down to pet his ears.

"He lives here too?" Anna let the cat sniff her and rub against her toddler legs. Taggy left black furs on her brown suit.

"Yes, he lives here too. He thinks the whole house belongs to him."

"He scratches? Bites?"

"Only if he's scared or really excited. Would you like to give him a treat?"

Taggy decided that Anna was a worthwhile friend as she dropped treats into his dish. Anna quickly toured the ground floor and made her way back to the stairs.

"We don't have your bedroom ready," Tori apologized as they climbed to the upper floor. "We'll get it set up soon."

"My bedroom? Just me?"

"Yes, it will be all yours! Well, Taggy is sharing it too right now. As I said, he thinks every room belongs to him."

The cat had followed them upstairs and plopped himself onto the folding cot in what would soon be Anna's bedroom.

"Can I sleep with you?"

"If you want, if you get scared at night. We're just in the next bedroom."

"At my old house, we all shared." Anna clung to Tori with sadness. "My bed in your room?"

"We'll make it fit," Tori promised, despite having no idea how.

"Can we nap now? Like Taggy?"

"That is a great idea. We'll leave him here and go sleep on Papa's and my bed." Tori relished the idea of referring to her husband as 'Papa.'

While she was exhausted, Tori could not sleep like Anna and Taggy. After trying to rest her eyes for a few minutes, she pulled out her phone and started browsing. She could not resist going through all the toys and books in her store's collection, but then she turned her attention to Bargain Bonanza. Anna needed more clothes and shoes. They needed furniture for her bedroom, even if they were going to cram her bed into their room initially. They needed more groceries. Patrick could pick up their order as his shift ended.

What does she want? What does she like? Who is this little girl who looks so much like me, except with Patrick's facial features? What are her favourite colours?

She managed to doze off for a few minutes until Anna woke up to use the bathroom again.

Their first evening together as a family passed in a blur. Tori marvelled as Anna gobbled up a bowlful of canned peaches and still had room for a fish supper that Patrick brought home after his shift. Anna was mystified at the pineapples in the sauce, but determined they were delicious. Her parents were mildly confused as to why she had never eaten canned pineapple before, since the pineapple and the peaches were next to each other on the shelf.

"Maybe my old mama didn't like it," Anna offered. "But I like pineapples! Can I have more tomorrow?"

"If you want, sure," Tori answered before her husband could protest that they did not have any more pineapple in the cupboard.

While Patrick had picked up part of Tori's Bargain Bonanza order on the way home, Anna's new items were in an assorted pile in her new bedroom and not really useful for the night. Taggy took the opportunity to examine and sniff all the new parcels before he decided to sleep on the biggest box. Anna put on the blue pyjamas that Nellie House had given her after letting herself be bathed.

Why are you so compliant? Tori wondered. Are you just scared? Do you want to please us? Why are you so calm about being bathed by a stranger?

Anna's calm demeanour vanished upon her first experience with a hairdryer. She screamed in terror at how loud it was and cried that it was too hot on her head. She continued to cry as Tori put it away and dried her curly mop of hair with a towel instead.

Oh God, did I burn her scalp? Tori usually had her hairdryer on its highest setting and had never used it on a toddler before. I should just leave it and sort out her tangles in the morning. Or will that hurt worse?

"What happened?" Patrick called out from the bedroom. "Are you two okay?"

Anna wiped away her tears and resumed as stoic of an expression as she could while Tori gently combed her hair.

"I'm fine, Papa!" Anna whimpered. "I just got scared. I'm okay now."

Once she realized she was going to be sleeping in Tori and Patrick's bed again, Anna gleefully climbed under the covers and settled into the little spot Patrick had set up for her, including a makeshift railing out of a bookshelf. She snuggled her elephant and let Tori read the storybook from Nellie House to her. It was a fairly banal storybook, featuring a tale about a baby elephant learning to count, eating different plants, and meeting various animals. Anna's theme at Nellie House had evidently been "blue-brown clothes and elephant stuff."

"Are elephants real, Mama?" Anna asked once the story was finished. "Do they live near here? In the woods, maybe?"

"They are real, though they are endangered. That means there aren't very many of them left. They don't live in Cascadia, though. They live on the other side of the world."

"Oh," Anna sounded disappointed. "Can we go visit them?"

"We can't go see real elephants because they are too far away, but we could go to the zoo and see virtual ones. That's like a big storybook, where you can touch and smell them."

"Yay!"

"But they will be louder than a hairdryer," Tori warned. "And very big, even the baby ones. They are life-sized."

"That's okay. You'll protect me!" Anna hugged her tightly.

"Um, yes." Tori was unsure how to respond, having never taken a child to the zoo before. "Of course, I will protect you!" She hugged Anna back.

"Cause you're my Mama!"

After Tori and Patrick tucked her into bed with a goodnight kiss, Anna fell asleep on the assumption they would be joining her soon.

"At least she could tell us what she wanted, unlike a baby," Patrick reassured his wife as they started to get ready for bed themselves.

"I'm worried I hurt her with the hairdryer. It was on the 'hot' setting."

"She's got the thick hair that you used to have! The hot air probably never even got to her head."

Patrick immediately regretted his choice of words as Tori started to cry.

"Oh shit, what did I say? Was it your hair? It still looks lovely! Just not like the images of you at two."

"She's such a lovely little girl, isn't she? How is it she looks so much like us? She's so smart. I love her so much already! How is she mine? And what if they're wrong and she does get sick like me?"

"Then we will do our best to get her at least as good of care as you have. I love her too. I love both of you."

"This feels like a dream."

"I know, but it isn't." Patrick kissed her. "I'm looking forward to tomorrow."

"Me too."

"And apparently, you're going to send me out for more pineapple."

"Yes, and that was one of the most romantic things I've ever heard you say."

Annoyed at the humans making noise in the den, Taggy joined Anna and her elephant.

INTERLUDE 1

"Hungry, Mama, hungry!"

The toddler poked at his mother forcefully. She was curled up on the couch and her eyes were squeezed shut, though she was not sleeping.

"Wake up, Mama!"

Reluctantly, the woman opened her eyes and pushed herself up onto her elbows. She was seven months pregnant and tried to ignore how hard the baby kicked her.

"You just ate, Tyler!"

"No! Hungry! Dark!"

Looking around in a daze, the woman realized the light from the fireplace was the only thing illuminating the room.

"You're right, it's dark now. Let's go check the doors and windows again, okay? Then I'll get you something to eat."

Tyler toddled alongside his mother as she inspected every window and door in their cabin, which were all still locked and sealed tightly except for the one screen atop the bathroom window that let in some fresh air. His mother shut all the curtains and blinds so the outside darkness disappeared. When she turned on the kitchen lights, Tyler collapsed to the floor, burying his face into his knees.

"Oww! Eyes hurt!"

"Sorry, sweetie!" His mother picked him up for a snuggle and kiss before plopping him into his highchair. "Mama needs to see to get your supper."

She placated him with some crackers and went through the cupboards fervently. There was very little food left in the kitchen that could be used to make a decent meal. There was a random assortment of canned beans, rice noodles, and applesauce. The refrigerator was almost empty.

This is all wrong. I have nothing left. We're trapped here.

Her body contracted and she fell to her knees in pain.

"Mama!" Tyler shrieked.

"It's okay, sweetie!" she managed to respond. "Your little brother or sister is just scared."

The wave of pain having passed, the woman crawled back up into a standing position. Tears ran down her face and she poured herself a glass of water.

"Please stay safe, baby," she whispered. "You need at least another month yet."

"Juice, Mama?"

The woman slowly prepared a sippy cup of juice for Tyler, then sat down at the table.

"Supper?" the toddler asked. He looked at his cracker crumbs and sippy cup in bewilderment. "You hungry, Mama?"

She shook her head at that moment because she could not contemplate cooking or eating any longer. Her brain could no longer process the thought of being hungry. Despite her pleading toddler and the forceful unborn baby, she felt she was waiting to die.

"Please, Mama?"

Just because I can't eat doesn't mean he can't, she reminded herself.

"Did you eat all of your crackers?"

He gestured to the crumbs on his tray.

"Okay, Mama will make you some noodles." She returned to the cupboard with renewed resolve.

I don't really want to die. I want my family back! But I can't survive here alone and I have nowhere to go.

"We need to leave here," she consoled herself by talking out her thoughts to Tyler, who was much more mesmerised by his crumbs. "But here is the only place where your sister knows to come back to."

Of course, she is only three years old. If she does come back here, someone will have to help her. She might be gone a long time. It has been over two weeks, so if anyone was going to bring her home, they would have done it by now.

"Crying?"

"Yes, I'm crying because I missed your sister's birthday! She's three!" The jar of spiced apples that was supposed to be part of her birthday supper was still sitting on the counter.

Tyler started to sob sympathetically and his mother rushed back over to hug him.

"Oh sweetie, don't worry! Mama promises she won't let anything happen to you. I won't let anyone take you away from me!"

Still in tears, she returned to making noodles. As she waited for the water to boil, she scrawled a note on the jar of spiced apples.

FOR ANNA'S BIRTHDAY - DO NOT TOUCH OR OPEN UNTIL SHE COMES HOME

Not used to being forceful, she added "please" in tiny handwriting at the bottom.

CHAPTER FOUR

O the holly bears a berry as white as the milk,
And Mary bore Jesus all wrapped up in silk

"Don't you both look lovely!" Patrick exclaimed to his wife and daughter as he came rushing in the back porch door.

His hair was windblown and he wore an old rain-suit. Meanwhile, Tori and Anna were standing in the living room by the fireplace in their finest outfits. They smiled at him as he struggled to keep his dirty boots on the mat and not shake excess leaves and water everywhere.

"We were beginning to wonder when you'd get back!" Tori admitted. "The wedding is in an hour and we have to carpool with the Pike-Macraes. I just got a text from Aliya and they are almost ready."

"There was traffic backed up downtown over another protest. Put me behind over two hours and I still had to pick up supplies for the Repair Squad. But don't worry! I'll be ready right away."

"I'm happy to see you, Papa!" Anna delicately gave Patrick's arm a squeeze and he bent down to give her a kiss on the forehead.

"I'm happy to be home too, my sweet Anna!" He then surprised Tori with a kiss before dashing off upstairs to change.

"What is Papa going to wear to the wedding?" Anna asked as they moved into the entryway.

"A suit, just like for church. He's got a very nice one that I laid out on the bed for him."

"Is it sparkly like our dresses?"

"Well, no, but I did pick out a shiny tie that matches us."

Tori and Anna were both wearing red dresses with rain-proof wool cloaks and shoes that sparkled red and silver. While they were the same shade of red, their outfits were very different in appearance: Anna's dress was fluffy and frilly, reminding her mother of a cheerleader's pompom, while Tori had on a tightly-fitted gown with a billowing skirt. Tori's dress was several years old and did not fit her comfortably, so she moved awkwardly as they finished getting ready to meet their neighbours for the carpool.

"Are you all right, Mama? You took your medicine, right?"

Tori laughed at what she still felt was the ridiculousness of her three-year-old daughter asking her such a question. Anna was very diligent about reminding her mother to take her medication because she did not want her to get any sicker.

"Thank you! Yes, I did. My dress is just a bit tight. It's old because I've gotten fluffier since I last wore it."

"You look beautiful!"

"Thank you – and so do you!"

"My dress fits nicely. It's new!"

It was the second week of December and Anna had been living with her new family for over eight months. Tori was elated to buy her as many clothes, books, and toys as possible, even as she tried to restrain herself from shopping so as not to overspend their budget or appear to be showing off. Their friends and neighbours generally could not afford to buy lots of new things (and on their own, neither could Patrick and Tori), whereas Tori had been buying everything new her whole life. Her father consistently sent his heiress daughter monetary gifts to "get presents for my granddaughter," while her mother continued her pattern of being distant but indulgent. Anna helped alleviate Tori's guilt at spending so much by growing ten centimetres taller since March. She needed lots of new clothes and shoes, so Tori could justify buying them for her.

One of their neighbours, who lived a couple of houses down from them in their co-op, had invited them to their wedding and the occasion was an excellent excuse for Tori to buy her daughter a party dress for winter. The wedding would be Christmas-themed and include a visit from Santa Claus for the kids. Tori had rolled her eyes when their immediate neighbour, Aliya Pike-Macrae, had told her of the bride's plans.

"How am I supposed to explain to Anna that weddings don't normally have a strange old man bringing presents?"

"I like it – it'll be fun!" Aliya was a kind neighbour, but found the Williams-Kirkes disagreeable and aloof. "But you do have a point. Liam and Naomi are too young to understand, but Grace and Anna can be confused together, at least!"

Grace Pike-Macrae, Aliya's eldest daughter, was the same age as Anna and the two girls had become friends over the summer. Initially, Anna had been shy and reserved around others, preferring to accompany Tori to her store or be at home with Patrick. Gradually, she had started to play with the children in their housing block and the children of her parents' close friends from church, developing a bubbly, congenial personality. She no longer seemed like a toddler.

For their part, their neighbours and friends had embraced Anna as though Tori and Patrick suddenly having a three-year-old daughter was a normal occurrence. Parents encouraged their children to play with her, even if they were wary around Tori and Patrick, being unsure of what had happened and not wanting to ask too many questions. Nellie House suddenly letting them adopt a child when they had been adamant they would never allow such a thing before had raised eyebrows. A few neighbours had innocently asked about Anna's resemblance to them, wondering if she was their niece.

Gradually, however, everyone had come to accept that the Williams-Kirkes had a new daughter and that Anna was a lovely child, even if she was precocious and had received many lovely presents that they could not dream of affording for their own children. They had certainly noticed how happy Tori and Patrick were and did not want to spoil that joy.

Patrick came rushing down the stairs, wearing his suit and shiny red tie, and tripped on the bottom step. Tori caught him before he tumbled headfirst onto the hard floor.

"Okay, I meant to do that," Patrick joked, looking like Taggy did when he missed a jump. "Is the carpool ready?"

"Aliya texted that she's just buckled Grace into the van, so we should go over now. You have your essentials?"

"I'm clumsy, dearest, not forgetful!"

"Do I have my essentials?" Anna asked quizzically, holding out her empty hands.

"Mama has yours," Tori clarified. "You can carry them when you're a bit older. Your dress doesn't have any pockets."

They took a quick photo together in the entrance hallway before heading out to join the Pike-Macraes in the van.

"You three look so much alike!" Aliya gushed as Patrick buckled Anna into the last child-seat. "You all match! Like out of a catalogue."

"Figured we'd go with red for Christmas," Tori muttered, keenly aware of how much she and Anna looked alike.

Seeing old images of herself as a child only made Anna's resemblance to her more eerie. Unlike herself, however, Anna had not spent half of her third birthday in the hospital. So far, Anna had stayed healthy, but Tori could not fathom how a daughter of hers could not fall sick eventually. She did not want to be reminded that her new life as a mother was on borrowed time. She did not feel she would be able to watch her daughter grow up.

O the holly bears a berry as green as the grass,
And Mary bore Jesus who died on the cross

Patrick and Tori expressed relief to each other that the bride had chosen to decorate primarily with angels, musical instruments, stars, and animals, even if she had Santa Claus attend her wedding reception. The bride and groom had bought gifts for each child in attendance, which was a considerable expense. Grace and Anna had ended up with lamb stuffies and spent the rest of the reception playing with them together, except for a few times when they got up to dance. Patrick put his clumsiness aside and pulled Tori onto the dance floor.

"You look gorgeous dancing in that dress," he gushed. "The skirt twirls perfectly!"

"It compensates for me not being able to move above my waist."

"Why, are you all right?" Patrick disguised his concern by spinning her intimately close to him. "You seemed fine all evening."

Tori laughed. “Don’t worry about me. I just should have had it tailored and I’m not used to doing that. Age and meds made me chubbier than when I first got this.”

“You can still breathe?”

“Yes, and breathing hasn’t exactly been a problem for me. My lungs are fine.” For now, she mentally added.

Patrick spun her back out again.

The overly holly-jolly atmosphere was broken by the sounds of a woman screeching and of metal hitting the wall. Everyone stopped dancing, chatting, or playing (while the music carried on blissfully) and turned to stare at one of the tables near the kitchen.

“You stupid damn robot!” A woman was screaming at one of the servers. “I asked for tea! Tea requires hot water! Hot! Boiling hot! Not cold. That carafe was full of ice-water!”

“I’m…I’m so sorry, ma’am,” the server sputtered. The metal carafe in question was broken open on the floor, with water having splashed all around them. “I…I’ll get you some hot water right away. Just as soon as I clean this up.”

“Get away from me! I don’t want you near me! You’re a piece of trash!”

“I don’t want anyone to get hurt, ma’am.” Another server was already bringing a mop and bucket.

“I want a real person! No robots!”

“We aren’t robots,” the second server protested.

“Like heck you aren’t! You move like one. You talk like one. Well, that one does, anyway.” She pointed to the initial server.

“I’ll get you some hot water, ma’am,” was the only reply. “I can get someone else to bring it to you if you want.”

"Auntie, it's all fine!" The bride, Keziah, came running to the table. "People make mistakes sometimes. The kitchen is a busy place!"

"A robot would not make a mistake," the second server added as they mopped, seemingly to no one in particular.

"That's right," Keziah agreed. "Thank you all so much for making this such a lovely party! I'm sorry for my aunt here. She's had a bad run with robots."

"Haven't we all?" her aunt asked, genuinely surprised that her outburst had not been met with much sympathy. "They're ruining everything! Taking jobs! And they look more and more like people!"

"Auntie, you're the one who is ruining my wedding," Keziah insisted. "No one wants to think about robots right now."

"I just wanted tea! Why is that so hard?"

Keziah sighed and gave her aunt a reassuring hug.

"Here is your tea, ma'am!" The first server returned with a giant mug and a fresh carafe with steam rising from the spout. "Again, I am so sorry about the mix-up."

Keziah looked back at the guests, most of whom were still watching the scene from the dance floor and other tables.

"Okay, everyone, who is up for a line dance?" She returned to the floor and pulled her bridesmaids into something resembling a line.

Patrick and Tori were bemused. Neither retreated to their table, where Anna, Grace, and Liam had started to eat the breaded centrepiece.

The music started and Tori groaned as "Grandma Got Run Over by a Reindeer" blasted obnoxiously throughout the hall. Keziah and her friends danced wholeheartedly. Most of the guests joined in with reluctance. It was a bouncy, fast-paced arrangement of a terrible tune, but Patrick admitted to his wife that he thought it was the best version he had heard. It was mostly instrumental and increased in tempo as the song progressed, as though it had been specifically created for line dances at Christmas-themed weddings. When they returned to the table, they both agreed it had been fun.

"I thought reindeer were cute," Grace said as Patrick and Tori sat down. "Why would they be mean and run over a grandma?"

"It's just supposed to be a silly song," Patrick replied, glancing at Grace's parents, who were busy fussing with their younger two children and therefore unable to pay attention to her question. "Reindeer are lovely animals. But they are big! They wouldn't mean to run over anyone, but if they are running in the dark and it is slippery, they might hit someone by accident."

"And you're right, we shouldn't laugh at someone getting hurt," Tori added. "It isn't a very good song."

"I don't like it," Anna proclaimed. "I want happy songs about lambs and baby Jesus."

For emphasis, she trotted her stuffie across the table.

"Me too," Grace agreed.

"Us too." Patrick turned to Tori. "Let's head home soon."

O the holly bears a berry as black as the coal,
And Mary bore Jesus who died for us all

As Christmas approached, Anna was excited to decorate the house. Tori and Patrick dragged out their various baubles and Nativity scenes, determined to let their daughter enjoy them. For the first time in several years, they decided to put up a Christmas tree. Taggy found the new addition of indoor foliage to be intriguing but made sure to keep his exploration limited to dignified sniffs and swats of the ornaments.

"What does a tree have to do with Jesus?" Anna asked. "There are no trees in the story."

"The tree is a symbol of life," Patrick explained. "Trees give us air to breathe."

"Okay…" Anna remained confused, not yet understanding metaphors and symbols well. "But it doesn't say anything about a tree in the Bible."

"No, it doesn't," Tori agreed. "Do you remember at Easter how we talked about Jesus dying on the cross?"

"Yes!" Anna replied excitedly.

"Well, the cross is made of wood, which came from a tree. So we have a tree to remember that. But it is a pretty tree because babies are happy! Like how Naomi is so sweet and cuddly."

"Yeah, but she cries a lot too."

"She can't talk yet," Tori defended the baby. "When she learns to talk, she won't cry as much. You cried a lot too when you were little."

She realized how vapid that sounded, considering that she had never heard Anna as a baby. Tears welled up in her eyes as she felt a pang of resentment at having been robbed of her daughter's infancy.

"My baby brother cried a lot," Anna agreed. "I guess he's learned to talk now, maybe."

Patrick and Tori exchanged glances of surprise. Anna had never mentioned having a baby brother before. Did she mean another child at Nellie House? Another child that had lived with her before? Another child from their genetics?

"Do we have a son too?" Tori asked her husband after Anna had gone to bed. Their daughter no longer felt the need to have her bed in their bedroom and had settled into her own space.

Tori curled her body up under her quilted blanket in front of the fireplace. Even though they had spent the whole afternoon and evening decorating, she did not feel very festive.

"Wouldn't that be pushing our luck?" Patrick replied, pouring them each a glass of whisky. "We have a beautiful daughter."

His tone betrayed the fear and hope in his heart. He loved the idea of having another child, but if this son of theirs existed, was he all right? Was there indeed some kind of conspiracy against them? How many more children had been created without their genetic parents' knowledge?

"But we could, couldn't we? Maybe he looks like you!" Tori wiped her eyes.

"I promised you that I was fine not having any children together," Patrick insisted, handing his wife her glass. "I meant that. I am fine with not having a son. I don't need a legacy."

"But you'd want one if we had one!"

"Well, he might have other parents who love him. Anna said he might be old enough to talk. That's old enough to be attached to his family, no matter who they are."

"So was Anna."

"And I'm still skeptical about her other parents. The people who raised her. Heck, someone had to give birth to her! Or tend to her if she was in some lab somewhere, whatever. Somewhere, she has other people. She must have loved them. They must have loved her. I don't buy for a minute that she was just found one day."

“She’s so precious!” Tori whimpered. “I love her so much. I can’t believe she is ours! You’re right, maybe she really isn’t.”

“Oh, she’s our daughter, all right! Only, maybe we share her.”

“With whom?”

“Someone. Maybe we will meet them. In fact, I hope we do! Then, everything might start to make more sense.”

“But we could lose her!”

“We could lose any of us at any time.” He gestured to the photos on their wall that included his father, grandparents, cousin, and friends who had died within the past two decades.

“I can see why Anna likes songs about fluffy lambs and the baby Jesus. None of this loss and death stuff.”

“It is all part of the story.”

O the holly bears a berry as blood it is red,
And we trust in our Saviour who rose from the dead

It was a chilly Christmas Eve as Anna walked with her parents to church. The sidewalk was icy and the rain that had fallen earlier had frozen to the point that Patrick slid her along like a curling rock. Anna giggled and spun herself in circles. Tori walked hurriedly beside them, laughing and taking video clips. Anna was once again wearing her red pompom dress, the frills of which twirled as she did.

“Perfect draw!” Patrick called out as Anna came to a stop directly in front of the church door. “I should take you to the rink with me more this winter. You’re far better on your feet than I am.”

Further behind them, their friends laughed and applauded. John and Cate Alvarez-Franklin were Patrick’s curling teammates as well as the closest to best friends that Patrick and Tori had. Seeing them and their three children, Anna waved excitedly.

Tori took Anna's hand and opened the door so Patrick could slide inside. He was trying to be funny and entertaining to make up for his lack of balance, but she was terrified he would fall. She and Anna scooted into the church after him, trying not to let too much cold air in. The church was old and draughty because the furnace was turned off most of the week to avoid expensive heating bills. With Christmas midweek, the furnace had been forced to roar to life earlier that day, and most of the heat was disappearing into the rafters. Tori and Anna shivered in their thin shoes.

"Here, have a blanket." Tori wrapped a red woollen shawl around her daughter as the Alvarez-Franklins hurried inside after them. "We'll warm up once we have candles and more people."

It was only as they settled themselves into the sanctuary that Tori noticed Anna was crying.

"What's wrong, sweetheart? Do your feet hurt?" Both of them had the same affliction where their feet getting too cold caused them to feel like they were being stabbed by thousands of tiny knives. "I have another blanket if you need it."

"No, I'm okay. Just...why can't my old mama and papa come? I miss them. They'd probably like it. My mama loves flowers." Anna pointed to the array of red and white flowers decorating the altar and pews.

"I don't know," Tori answered honestly. "I don't know where they are."

She looked for Patrick, who was preparing the priest's notes and setting up the lectern.

"I love you, Mama!" Anna gave Tori a tight hug. "Please don't leave me! Don't let me be taken away again!"

"I love you too, Anna. I'll do whatever I can to keep you safe and happy."

"I'll be good now," Anna whispered, wiping her eyes on the red shawl. "I don't want to make anyone sad. Can I go play with Ellie and Justin?"

Tori nodded and Anna scampered off to join the two eldest Alvarez-Franklin children in playing with Lego until the service started.

Tori was drawn to stare at the Nativity scene in front of the pulpit. There were shepherds and sheep to the side, angels perched atop the stable roof, Joseph leading a donkey, and Mary kneeling beside the manger while animals gathered around her. The manger was still empty, as the priest would pick one of the children to put the Christ Child into it during the service. For now, Mary was simply staring at an empty box.

While she had felt like she had been staring at an empty box her whole life, Tori realized that her joy was someone else's horror. She had consoled herself with the idea that Anna's previous mother and father had been con artists or perhaps child traffickers. She felt she was Anna's rightful mother. Yet the more Anna talked about them, the more they seemed like kind, decent people who loved her. Even if they were con artists, they were con artists who had genuinely loved their daughter and cared for her. She had cared for them. They had done everything for her: teaching her to walk, talk, and use the toilet. They had even started teaching her to read! Now Tori realized there was a woman who was kneeling beside an empty manger, mourning her lost child and wondering if she would ever come home to her.

“Lord, forgive me,” she whispered. “Forgive me for being so blinded by joy that I did not see what was so obvious. Take care of Anna’s other mother, wherever and whoever she is.”

She sobbed quietly as the sanctuary began to fill up, drying her eyes only when Anna returned and once again wrapped her arms around her.

I wonder as I wander out under the sky,
How Jesus the Saviour did come for to die,
For poor or’d’nry people like you and like I,
I wonder as I wander out under the sky

INTERLUDE 2

I wonder as I wander out under the sky,
How Jesus the Saviour did come for to die,
For poor or'd'nry people like you and like I,
I wonder as I wander out under the sky

"Aren't you a sweetheart! Are you looking forward to Santa coming?" one of a pair of elderly women asked Tyler, who was dressed in a warm fuzzy suit to look like a sheep.

The toddler shook his head. He was not sure who 'Santa' was.

"No, Jesus," he insisted.

The other of the pair smiled and laughed, elbowing her friend teasingly.

"Good answer, eh?"

Her friend was momentarily flustered, blinking in confusion.

"Well, but I just meant…"

"Isn't Christmas Jesus's birthday?" Tyler asked. "That's what they said."

He gestured toward the pastor and Sunday School teacher, who were a short distance away, deep in discussion about the Nativity pageant.

"Tyler, there you are!" His mother flitted through the crowd with her baby balanced on her hip. "I'm so sorry, ma'am, if he was bothering you. Thanks for talking to him!"

The younger woman forcefully took Tyler's hand to lead him into the sanctuary.

"He's a delightful little boy!" the second elderly woman complimented. "He's very excited for Jesus's birthday."

"I promised him his favourite fruit salad when we get home to celebrate," his mother clarified. She prayed that the women did not ask about presents or Santa Claus, all of which was beyond her abilities to provide and seemed confusing to what she was learning from the pastor about Christianity.

"Oh, that sounds delicious! Are you a regular visitor here?"

"I work here. I'm the gardener."

"Oh! Did you arrange all the foliage along the entrance?"

"I did, yes. And all the flowers inside the church too."

"They're beautiful!"

The woman nodded and muttered her thanks as they all entered the sanctuary. She personally thought flowers looked much better alive in the soil than dead in a vase.

"Well, we'd better get into our seats. Merry Christmas!"

The elderly women went to their seats and Tyler's mother led him into a pew toward the front. A dozen children of assorted ages, most of whom were dressed as angels or sheep, crowded around them in anticipation of the evening's pageant.

"Can I hold the baby yet, Ms. Maria?" a twelve-year-old girl dressed as the Virgin Mary asked.

Before the young woman could answer, the baby herself reached out and launched herself into the girl's arms.

"Whoa, hey there, Stephanie! You're all set to be baby Jesus." The girl bounced Stephanie on her lap and the baby giggled. "Let's listen to my sister Trinity sing a song first."

"Thank you, Mercy. She really likes you and your sister."

Tyler had started playing with a sheep stuffie, leaving Maria sitting nervously with empty arms. She and Mercy were supposed to be supervising the younger children, but she did not really know what to do with herself. She was almost always carrying Stephanie (and occasionally, Tyler), plants, or gardening equipment. When she did have free time, she held books and datapads to read, distracting her from her grief.

Being the gardener at the retreat centre gave her a livelihood and a way to provide for her children while still remaining hidden. She was grateful to have found such a wonderful refuge. The small congregation at the church had welcomed her, believing her to be a victim of abuse or organized crime. The pastor had made sure she kept up with prayers and Bible-reading, answering her constant questions. Faith in Christianity had strengthened her resolve. It validated her long-held belief that she was not a soulless machine to be owned, abused, and discarded, nor were her children.

Maria could not look at the little girls further down the row, two of whom were almost the same age as her daughter would have been. Anna would have made a lovely sheep or angel, and she would have probably loved to dress up and play with other children. Even without looking at them, she cried at the thought that she could not imagine what Anna looked like now. She would be four soon. Maria had missed out on almost a year of her daughter's life. She prayed that her husband and elder daughter were alive and safe, wherever they were.

The piano started to play as Trinity, dressed as the Angel Gabriel, made her way to the microphone to sing.

It was a beautiful song in Latin, but Maria buried her head in her hands to conceal her tears. While she recognized the language from her endless barrage of lessons on organisms' scientific classification, it had never sounded so pretty as it did in the song. Even if Trinity had not sung it well, it would have still moved her to cry. Hail Mary – *Ave Maria* – made her think back to being named. Her husband would have loved this song. He had picked her name from a different song altogether, but he had loved her name. She was his beautiful queen of the garden, his beloved spaceship captain, Maria.

Did he even remember her anymore? Did he remember Anna? Tyler? The fact that Maria had been pregnant with a third child? Did he wonder about that third child? Did he remember all the books they had read and all of the things they had learned? Was he even still alive to remember anything at all? Was he blissfully fixing vehicles? Was his joy at being a mechanic the only thing that kept him from despair at not knowing where his beloved Maria was, much as it was for her and her gardening?

"Mama!" Stephanie patted her on the shoulder.

"Here, Ms. Maria, she wants you to snuggle her for a bit. I have to go onstage after the song is over." Mercy handed the baby back to her mother.

"If anything, she wants to snuggle *me*," Maria whispered. "I'll make sure to give her back to you later in the pageant, Mercy."

Seeing that his baby sister was back in his mother's arms, Tyler snuggled up close to them.

"I love you, Mama."

"My sweet kids! It's going to be okay, I promise. God will take care of us." *Please, don't let us be separated. Let us be a family together again. Look after Anna and anyone caring for her.*

"And Papa and Anna too, right?" Tyler whispered.

"Them too."

CHAPTER FIVE

"I thought you needed some cheering up," Patrick confessed as he hung a photo-composite of Anna across from his and Tori's bed.

The photos in question were of Anna at her second Easter with the Williams-Kirkes: a little dark-haired, olive-skinned girl of four who was wearing a white dress while lying on a red carpet surrounded by pink flower petals. She was smiling ecstatically, giggling in many of the images, as she was both over-tired and enjoying herself too much to fall asleep. Ellie and Justin Alvarez-Franklin were with her in one of the photos. Anna had been the happiest child at church.

"Doesn't she look beautiful? So joyful and innocent," Tori whispered, so their daughter would not overhear them in the next room. "She was telling me again how much her old mother liked flowers, so flowers make her happy because they remind her of her."

"Yes, well, I thought that this way, we can see our little girl every night before we go to sleep, no matter what happens."

"I keep wondering when she is going to get sick."

"Like I said, no matter what happens."

One warm and sunny late spring morning, about a month after Easter, Tori and Anna set out on a walk to the library. They did not hurry, taking time instead to enjoy the beautiful weather. The sky was a clear blue and a choir of singing birds almost drowned out the sounds of construction and traffic along the otherwise busy road between Goat Cove and the edge of central Alexandrina. As they walked, they sang together happily. Though she was only four years old, Anna was adept at holding her own on a melody line and wanted to keep singing the Easter songs she had learned.

"You descended into the tomb, O Immortal One! You destroyed the power of death! In victory, you arose, O Christ our God…"

They rounded a corner and found themselves near a construction site, which soon caught Anna's attention.

"What are they building?" she asked, pointing to the labyrinth of pits, posts, and scaffolding behind the protective fencing along the sidewalk.

Tori instinctively pulled her away from the fence, which was precariously perched atop a fifty-metre drop into the rocky earth. The site was giant and took up land that had once been a warehouse. She searched for a sign announcing the new building.

"Aha! There we are: 'Bargain Bonanza Department Store.' They're building a new location here closer to Goat Cove."

"How many Bargain Bonanzas are there?"

"I'm not sure." Tori started to count in her head. "Maybe seven or eight in and around Alexandrina? Depends on how far out you want to count."

"Oh. Why do we need so many? Papa can just deliver parcels from them."

"People still like to shop and see things on shelves. It's a nice excuse to go out."

Suddenly, someone captivated Anna's attention.

"Papa!" she shrieked incredulously, pulling at Tori's arm. "My old papa! Look!"

Tori froze in place, staring at her daughter in bewilderment. Anna excitedly pointed toward the workers and her mother tried to follow her gestures.

"Look, Mama! See? That man? That's my old papa."

Her tone, while excited, sounded matter-of-fact, as though she had recognized a friend from school or someone who looked like a storybook character. She pointed adamantly at the construction workers. They were all in grey overalls and basic safety gear. One of them, however, was wearing camouflage overalls instead.

"Who is?" Tori asked, praying she did not sound squeaky or terrified.

"That one! The one wearing different overalls than the others. That's what he was wearing when…when…um, when I saw him last."

Tori rested her gaze on the tall man in the camouflage overalls. As he turned in profile toward them, she gasped in shock. The man reminded her of a younger, more muscular Patrick. His clean-shaven face looked almost identical to her husband's before he had grown a beard. There was no grey in his dark brown hair, at least none that she could see beneath his hard hat. He looked like the man she had first met and married, minus the youthful exuberance of an optimistic and newly-minted journalism grad. This man looked battered and careworn.

"He has a funny nose," Anna continued.

"It appears to have been broken at least once," Tori agreed, having been scrutinising his appearance in great detail. "Why doesn't he have a uniform like the others?"

Anna shrugged. "Can I talk to him? I want to tell him that I'm all right and that I'm happy with you."

He is not Patrick, Tori reminded herself. *You're probably just overtired – maybe you're hallucinating from when you missed your medicine last night. Anna has not spotted anyone that she knows. She just recognizes a man of similar height and build who happens to have the same overalls as her supposed father.*

She decided she could indulge her daughter's curiosity. It would be better for her to know for sure that she had not spotted her 'old papa.'

"I think we have to ask the foreman. He's the boss."

"The man over there by the truck with the datapad? The one in the suit?"

Before Tori could answer beyond a quick nod, Anna scurried along the fencing until she was within earshot of the foreman.

"Mister Foreman! Mister!" she cried out. Tori pulled her back to keep her from trying to crawl through the safety barrier.

While the man with the datapad turned in her direction, none of the workers so much as flinched at the commotion, even those who were right beside the fencing.

"Mister!" Anna shook the fence to get his attention. "Can I talk to my old papa, please?"

"Pardon me?" the foreman asked, recoiling in horror. "I'm not your father. I'm no one's father! You've got the wrong guy!"

"No, not you," Anna insisted. "You're not my old papa."

"That's a relief!" The foreman glanced at Tori, seemingly trying to determine if she was familiar to him.

"My old papa is that man over there in the camouflage overalls." Anna pointed at him again to further her explanation. "Can I please talk to him?"

The foreman approached them cautiously.

"Is this your daughter?" he asked Tori with a menacing scowl.

"She certainly is," Tori replied defensively. "May she please talk to that man over there? Just for a bit – really quick, we promise! Then we'll be on our way and leave you all alone."

With some bemusement, the foreman relented and called over the man.

"Unit RB14600218-36, put down your tools and come here!"

Tori blinked several times in surprise as the man in the camouflage overalls obeyed the command. He faced the foreman, awaiting further instructions and paying no attention to the presence of two visitors on the other side of the barrier.

"Yes, sir?" he demanded, expecting a new assignment or additional instructions.

He even sounds like Patrick did! Tori gripped the fencing for support.

"Visitors would like to speak to you." The foreman gestured toward Tori and Anna, so the man turned to face them.

There was no further doubt in Tori's mind that he looked exactly like Patrick. At the very least, he looked like he should be Patrick's younger brother. His delicious chocolate brown eyes made Tori's heart melt. For a moment, he seemed to be relieved, then confused, before his eyes glazed over into a dull and analytical stare.

"Hello!" Anna said warmly. Despite the barrier, she held out her arms as though she expected the man to hug her.

"Hello." His voice was emotionless, but as he glanced back and forth between Tori and Anna, Tori noticed his eyes flash a look of pain.

"Hello?" Anna repeated again, now with concern. She lowered her arms and gripped the fencing.

"Anna?" The man's eyes flashed again. Tori noticed that something within him wanted to reach out despite him being strongly inhibited from doing so. He seemed to be heavily drugged and trying to overcome it.

Anna was crestfallen.

"Papa? What's wrong? Don't be sad. I'm very happy. I wanted to tell you that I'm safe."

"Where's your mama?" he asked, his voice sounding clipped and programmed.

He looked back toward Tori and repeated the question, now sounding more anxious.

"This is my mama now!" Anna exclaimed, momentarily brightening and grabbing Tori's hand.

The man looked back into Tori's eyes and was able to sustain his pained expression long enough for her to start crying.

"Maria?" he asked suspiciously.

"My name is Tori," she sputtered. "Victoria."

She refrained from giving her full name as she noticed the foreman watching in bewildered amusement.

"No, Anna's mother is named Maria. Did you change your name?"

"No, I'm not Maria."

The man looked hurt, yet relieved.

"You look a lot like her, ma'am. I'm sorry."

"This is my *new* mama!" Anna insisted stubbornly. "I don't know where my old mama is."

He shook his head and his expression returned to one of being dull and observant. He turned back to the foreman.

"New assignment, sir?"

"No, resume your previous task. Complete Task 34."

With a curt nod, the man returned to his post without a backwards glance.

"What are you two playing at? What kind of camera-joke is this?" The foreman bellowed at Tori, barely giving Anna another look. He was no longer amused at the situation. "My employers will not tolerate this kind of shit."

Tori decided against protesting that she had not even taken her phone out.

"Sorry, sir!" She quickly removed her phone from her wrist and snapped a photo of the man in the camouflage overalls. "My daughter is four and she has a big imagination and I was indulging her."

"Well, she must have some fucking imagination! He's a goddamn robot!"

Tori pulled Anna close to her for a hug, backing away slowly from the fencing.

"My old papa is not a robot!" Anna screamed indignantly.

"Missy, I don't know what bratty shit your mama lets you get away with, but I'm sure as hell telling you that I am the only real man on this entire construction site!"

Okay, we're leaving now. He looks like he plans to demonstrate this by dropping his trousers. Has he never met a four-year-old before?

"You stupid, deluded mother!" the foreman continued. "You think the world revolves around you and your precious baby girl! You're wasting my valuable time. Go on, go!"

"Thank you, sir, for your patience," Tori muttered furiously through clenched teeth.

Using strength she knew she could not sustain long, she picked Anna up and darted away from the site, crossing the street to be well out of earshot. Tori's initial confusion turned into raw anger and tears.

"Oh, sweetie, my precious Anna, I'm sorry the foreman was so mean." She sat her daughter back down on the sidewalk and braced herself against a pole. "Let's go down the street to the park, okay? We can sit there for a while."

"But that man *was* my old papa," Anna whimpered sadly. "He wasn't happy to see me! He didn't remember me!"

"I know he wasn't happy, sweetheart, but he must have been scared or confused. I'm sure he remembers you and loves you."

Having recovered, Tori took Anna's hand and they walked slowly toward the park together. As they walked, questions raced through Tori's mind. Was the man really Anna's father? Was he really a robot? Why did he look like Patrick? What would she see if she removed his overalls: wiring and machines, or a handsome younger version of her husband's body? Who was Maria? Why had the man mistaken Tori for her? Why had he not been able to react to them? Why did a construction worker seem to be heavily drugged?

And, if the man truly was Anna's biological father, what did that make Anna? Robots could not have children, could they? Anna was certainly not a robot. She had grown and aged over a year since she had been adopted. She was entirely a human being. While she had never been ill, she had had plenty of medical check-ups and there was nothing robotic about her.

But Anna had an excellent and precocious memory. She had memorized vocabulary in multiple languages and plenty of information from the various books at their home. She could recall plant and animal names as easily as a search engine. She could recite poems and sing songs after hearing them once. She remembered being a young toddler. Other children had begun to notice how different she was; adults had remarked that Anna seemed much more intelligent than they would have expected, even with such bookish parents as Patrick and Tori. Tori had simply been convinced that her daughter was a smart four-year-old.

She has never had her brain scanned. Maybe she has implants or something? But why would they make a child-aged robot that could grow up?

Anna also had a clean bill of health, higher-than-normal energy levels, and the ability to heal quickly from minor injuries. But Tori reasoned that could have come from some sort of genetic enhancement – genetic enhancement that she desperately wished she could have had herself.

Tori was convinced that Anna was not in any way a machine. The man who looked like Patrick also did not seem to be a robot. None of the construction workers did. Strangely docile humans, yes, but not robots.

Once they sat down at the park, Anna burst into tears. She nestled herself into Tori's chest and bawled.

"Papa wasn't happy to see me!" she sobbed. "He loved me! We went everywhere together!"

"I'm sure he still loves you," Tori repeated. "He seemed like he was sick. Like the foreman had given him medicine."

Her reassurances did not alleviate Anna's anguish and it was all Tori could do to merely absorb her daughter's sobs in her arms. Eventually, she gave into her own desire to cry softly. She was relieved to hear that Anna considered herself to be happy with her and Patrick as her new family. Anna had been proud of Tori as her new mother. The little girl had not expected the man to react with hostility toward them.

It is only natural for her to miss her old family. She has mentioned them many times.

As she realized that she could not console her daughter, Tori's own tears became more intense. The two of them sat on the park bench for over half an hour. The trip to the library was forgotten. Neither of them wanted to continue with the excursion once they had exhausted themselves by crying.

"I want to go home and see Papa," Anna insisted. "My new papa – I want to see him!"

"Me too. He will make everything make sense for us again."

Since she had called her husband to say that they were coming home early and that something traumatic had happened, Patrick was waiting for them with pancakes. He had determined from her shaky voice that they both needed the comfort of their favourite fruits. Anna's pancakes were in the shape of teddy bears and surrounded by peaches and pineapple. For Tori, he had buried her pancakes under a mound of blueberries.

Before she could even look at the table, Anna ran to Patrick and hugged him tightly, dirty apron and all. He picked her up and held her as she dug her head into his shoulder.

"My dear Anna, what's wrong?" Immediately regretting the instinctive question, he continued with, "I love you very much. I'm going to try to make everything all right, okay? I'll take care of you."

"Papa, papa, papa!" she sobbed, unable to form any more words.

Tori wavered at the sight of the food, both craving it and feeling sick at the thought of eating anything. She dove into the bathroom to vomit and cry alone, but Taggy followed her, snuggling her feet protectively.

Unlike her mother, Anna eagerly gobbled up her late lunch and then settled into bed for a nap. Taggy decided to transfer his guardian duties to her, leaving Tori to meekly attempt to swallow some blueberries while Patrick tidied the kitchen.

"What happened to make her so upset?" he finally asked. "I've never seen her like that!"

Tori tried to respond but only managed to start gagging. Patrick dove at her with a bowl for her to spit her blueberries back up.

"Oh God, I thought you were just upset because she was!" Patrick realised. "Something happened to you too, didn't it? Did you nearly get hit? Did someone attack you?"

"No, no, though I think some idiot was going to expose himself to us if we didn't run off when we did. Or maybe my mind was just playing tricks. I don't know. He was terrible. But I don't think Anna even noticed that."

She held out her phone and showed him the photo that she had snapped of the man in the camouflage overalls.

"This isn't him, by the way. The idiot was the foreman. This is by the new Bargain Bonanza site. But take a look – does this man look familiar to you?"

Patrick scrutinized the photo but shook his head.

"I can't place him at all."

Tori pointed at the framed wedding portrait on their living room wall.

"Imagine him with a beard like that."

Patrick's eyes darted from the phone to the wedding photo multiple times. He finally resorted to taking the phone into the living room and putting it up against the portrait.

"Holy shit!" he blurted out.

"He looks even more like you close up."

Patrick simply went through a string of swear words in disbelief.

"He even sounds like you," Tori continued. "Like, if he'd said he was a time traveller from ten years ago, I'd have almost believed him."

"Um, so what happened?" Patrick handed her back her phone.

"Anna spotted him and she is convinced that he is her old papa. You know, the one she has mentioned who used to do odd jobs and such and who used to take her fishing."

"That made her cry?"

"No, she wanted to talk to him. I thought there was no harm in asking. The foreman called him over and he talked to us for a bit."

"You say he sounds like me?"

"He looked so much like you that I almost fainted. And he recognized Anna, but he seemed drugged or something and couldn't really react to her. He confused me with someone else, I think. Anna just wanted to tell him that she was happy and safe."

"He recognized her?"

"Well, he seemed to. Maybe I was imagining it. I think he called her by name. Anna is convinced that it was him. That's why she was so upset. She was expecting him to react differently. She must feel like she lost him again."

"There is something else," Patrick intuited. "You're still picking at the blueberries."

"The foreman told the man to get back to work and then started yelling at us. I mean, fair enough – we interrupted them. But he was nasty and I thought he was going to expose himself."

"What the…? At a four-year-old?"

"He was angrier at me than Anna, but it seemed like he didn't care that she's a little kid. But…" She managed to swallow some of the blueberries.

"I'm relieved you're eating, but what happened?"

"He insisted that the whole work crew were robots and that he was the only human there. Meaning that man in the overalls is a robot. There's a robot who looks and sounds exactly like you out there doing construction, and Anna is convinced he is her father."

"Those men are robots? Can I see the photo again?"

"They didn't look like robots to me. They just seemed like docile, drugged humans. Nothing mechanical about them. The one we talked to seemed normal. Just like a younger you. I…I was even starting to lust after him a bit."

"He seems more conventionally attractive than me," Patrick admitted, having taken another look at her phone. "He's obviously more into fitness than I ever was."

Tori shook her head in an effort to get her husband to change the subject.

"Sorry I brought it up. I just thought I should be honest. It's been making me queasy that I was…you know…"

"Feeling tempted? Attracted to a robot? I mean, maybe that's a selling feature."

"Stop!" Tori burst into tears again. "Please! I'm sorry. It was always you. Everything's been so damn confusing!"

Patrick nodded and led her to the couch.

"Let's just sit down together. The blueberries aren't going anywhere."

"Do you suppose he really is her father?"

"That would explain a lot, wouldn't it?"

"How?"

"Someone with my genetics fathered Anna, but it wasn't me. I didn't time-travel, either. But it still doesn't make any sense. If he is a robot, then he just looks like me. He wouldn't be able to father children. And that doesn't explain how you got involved."

"Let's just chalk this up to Anna's wishful thinking, okay?" Tori collapsed into the couch. "I can't deal with anything else right now."

"Whatever you want, my darling wife."

Almost involuntarily, Tori sat up and kissed him.

"This is what I want," she whispered.

Patrick was not sure if his wife was overcome with thoughts of the man in the camouflage overalls as she started to undress him, but he did not go back on his offer.

INTERLUDE 3

The man stared numbly at his hands as the truck made its way back to the barracks. The emergency lighting on the ceiling made his skin glow a fiery orange. He had worked his fingers to the point that they felt sore as he wiggled them. His body ached from standing in nearly the same position all day. The Corporation worked them for as long as there was daylight. He dreaded the coming summer.

Tonight, however, he was preoccupied with the thought of his wife and daughter. A girl claiming to be his beloved Anna had appeared at the construction site, asking to speak to him and seeming disappointed that he had not hugged her.

I wanted to hug her. I wanted to tear down the barrier and pick her up like I used to. I wanted to run away as fast as I could from the pit and the Corporation. I know it was really her. She has grown a lot, but she still looks enough the same for me to recognize her.

He could not bring himself to move. The food that the Corporation fed them kept him from being able to react meaningfully. He could barely think.

The woman with Anna had looked like his wife, but she had not answered to her name. As he had looked at her more closely, he determined she seemed to be too old to be Maria. She had greying hair and many lines on her face. She wore corrective lens implants. Her entire demeanour was different: Maria had been quiet and shy around anyone but him; she would never have approached a foreman with Anna. She would have run the other way.

She did not have a barcode on her wrist, either, not even anything on her arms to cover one. She wasn't my beautiful Maria. Maria must be still hiding somewhere.

Anna had told him that she was happy and safe with a new mother. For that, the man was thankful. The woman had obviously cared for her deeply. He had caught a glimpse of them dashing away from the site and crossing the street. He had wished he had been able to go with them. While she was not Maria, the woman seemed to have recognized him. He implicitly wanted to trust her and he wondered if she might have helped him find Maria and their other children.

He hoped that Maria was still hiding safely with their younger children. Tears welled up in his eyes as he thought of the unborn baby they had called their little soccer player. That child would have been born about a year earlier. His son, Tyler, must have perfected walking and talking by now. Anna was much taller than she had been. She had confidence and poise; she no longer toddled. Soon, Tyler would not toddle, either, and soon the little soccer player would.

How old will you be when we are finally all together again? Because I am determined that we will be a family again, all five of us.

The man stepped out of the truck and followed his colleagues into the barracks for their evening meal. He hated the food. It made him drowsy and compliant. Most of the others knew nothing else. They had lived their entire lives eating the processed, nutrient-rich "robot diet." It sustained them, so they tolerated its effects.

However, he had not eaten it once he had been purchased. His owners had decided that the food was too expensive. They had not realized what would happen to their robots if they did not feed it to them. Having tasted what non-robots ate, he could not enjoy being forced to eat robot food again.

He sat down obediently with his crew as the meal was served, but he only ate a small portion. It was enough to make him feel numb as it eased his sore hands and dulled his grief-filled heart, but not enough to let him forget seeing his beloved daughter. His crewmate gobbled up the uneaten portion and almost immediately fell asleep when they returned to their cupboards.

This was their lives. They woke up each morning, dressed, ate a morning meal, went out to work on assignments, returned for an evening meal, showered, and went to sleep. Every day, they ran their clothes through a wash. If they had no assignment, or if they were not exhausted at night, they were given materials to study. He was always given manuals about vehicles or other mechanical literature. While he loved the topic, he was bored of it. He would rather sleep and try to recall the graphic novels he had read with Maria or the storybooks he had read with Anna. Without fail, he would wake up in tears. The morning meal helped him to forget throughout the day, but he wanted to remember at night.

His cupboard, which was a covered bunk with climate controls and soft bedding, was at the top of a stack of three. There were six cupboards in each room. He shared a room with four other robots: two men and two women. The men were stacked in cupboards on one wall and the women were across from them. He was not sure why the sixth cupboard had not been filled in the year or so that he had been there. There was space for six robots per room, but most of them only had four. He was an anomaly. He was the one who was not supposed to be there.

The more he lay awake, the more he was convinced none of them should have been there. His crewmate who had eaten the extra food had fallen fast asleep, but the man in the bottom cupboard hummed a tune to himself as he flipped through his literature on mountain-climbing. The women were both watching videos about basic gardening, which only reminded him more of Maria. They had curious minds. They wanted to learn and explore. They wanted to be able to reach out to each other. They deserved something more than being considered organic machines.

He squeezed Anna's glove and put in headphones that played relaxing background noise, finally drifting off to sleep as he once again dreamed of being with his family. They were sailing through the stars on a spaceship, exploring new worlds on which Maria and Anna would classify plants while he took Tyler fishing. Every so often, the older woman who looked like Maria appeared among them, seemingly happy to be a part of their family and travelling through space with them. He was not sure whether it was her or Maria who was flying the ship.

Take care, my beloved Anna. Be good for the older woman who looks like your mother. I love you and miss you. Someday, I will be able to give you a hug again.

CHAPTER SIX

While Anna seemed to have put the incident with her 'old papa' at the construction site behind her, Tori and Patrick found themselves embroiled in more research about robots. They could not find much information about them, except that the Robot Rental Corporation in central Alexandrina had patented a "nearly human" design. The Corporation was headquartered at a factory warehouse complex outside the city near a state park and military base, but the company had an office downtown for renting out robots to clients. The Robot Rental Corporation marketed the robots and their variety of capabilities heavily, but the details about their actual design were vague.

"Buy our stuff, use our services, don't ask questions," Patrick had muttered, thinking of how many companies had pretty much the same mantra.

"I'm willing to guess they don't like journalists," Tori added as, out of curiosity, they examined the online catalogue of robots for rent.

The robots themselves looked indistinguishable from humans. Scrolling through the catalogue of available rentals reminded Tori of a high school yearbook, except none of the people in these images were smiling and they were wearing dull grey or navy uniforms. The site was uncomfortably eerie.

"There seem to be thousands of robots," Patrick noted as Tori scrolled on the screen. "I don't get it – they don't have names or anything. Just serial numbers and notes about their specialties. Why list them like this?"

Tori refined her search to include only male robots, which reduced her list by a third. All that seemed to happen was that the robots with the softer features mostly disappeared, since their uniforms and hairstyles were mostly the same.

"I wish I remembered the serial number the foreman called out," Tori grumbled as she scrolled. "All I remember is it ended with Dash-36."

"Did you try searching for that?"

"It won't let me look for the last digits."

"All of the numbers seem to start with two letters. Can you remember those?"

"Well, the first one must obviously be R. I think all the male robots start with R, going by this catalogue. Let me think…"

On a guess, Tori typed in "RB" into the search engine.

"Oh God, there he is! He's in the camouflage overalls, listed as a specialist in vehicle maintenance. Unit RB14600218-36."

"Why would they have a specialist in vehicle maintenance at a construction site?"

"I'm sure he can do the general stuff too. And that's definitely him – he looks just like you!"

"Yep," Patrick nodded uncomfortably. "Do you think we might recognize anyone else?"

"Not immediately, but maybe…"

"Why do you suppose they include photographs in the list?"

"So you can recognize them, maybe? Like, if you want to have the same robot come back and do more work? Or so you can pick one that is aesthetically pleasing to you?"

"Makes some sense, I suppose. Anyway, I am really creeped out by this. Can we try our best to forget about the mysterious robot who looks like me? At least, for now."

"Now that I have satisfied some curiosity, yep. Let's focus on having another wonderful summer with Anna!"

Putting their research aside, they celebrated the end of Anna's preschool classes. Her preschool had a small ceremony with certificates and treats. Anna won several awards, including the Most Avid Reader and the Most Friendly Student. She was extremely excited to move to kindergarten, where she would be in the same class as Grace, Ellie, and Justin.

"How about we take a day and go to the beach?" Tori suggested they celebrated by stopping for veggie burgers on the way home from school. "We could go to the lake so it is warm enough to swim."

"Sounds delightful," Patrick agreed.

"Which lake?" Anna asked.

"Lake Hobidigan has a lovely beach. That's the one I was thinking of," Tori clarified.

Anna's eyes widened.

"Ooh, I've been there! Yes, let's go!"

"Well, we have to wait until tomorrow."

"Yeah, I guess. Can we go fishing?"

Tori and Patrick exchanged confused glances.

"We don't have a boat or fishing gear," Patrick explained. "We've never fished before."

"Oh," Anna sounded disappointed. "But we could get fruit ices at the store, right? And go swimming?"

"Of course! Definitely! Fruit ices are a must!"

A thought suddenly struck Tori. "Anna, when did you go to Lake Hobidigan?"

"When I was little. I didn't go to the beach much because it was too crowded."

“Who took you there?”

“My old mama and papa, of course. Who else would have taken me?”

Tori regretted suggesting the beach trip but decided she could not disappoint Anna.

“That makes sense,” Patrick answered his daughter. “Did you have fun?”

“I think so? I was little.”

“Well, we’ll have lots of fun tomorrow! It’s supposed to be warm and sunny!”

It was indeed a beautiful morning the next day as they drove into the town of Little Hobidigan. The sun was shining through the trees, glistening on the road and illuminating the main street. Birds and insects were singing loudly. There was very little vehicle noise, as the town had a policy of encouraging people to park and walk in order to keep from breaking the illusion of forest tranquility. As it was a weekday, the main street itself was fairly deserted, with most of the little traffic that there was heading through the village directly to the beach.

Anna stared out of the van’s window, absorbing the sunlit streets with a sense of familiarity and fear. She kept her concerns to herself and smiled as her parents talked about getting fruit ices. She was happy they were talking to her again. They had gone off talking about Patrick’s work for the Repair Squad earlier in the drive and Anna had pretended to fall asleep. The van was too big with just the three of them in it. She preferred when they carpooled with other families.

“Aren’t we going to the beach?” she asked, looking nervously around the parking lot of the store.

"We thought we'd stop for fruit ices and some extra food for our picnic first," Patrick reported.

"The store also has nicer toilets than the beach," Tori added, getting out of the driver's seat and opening the side door behind her. It was then that she noticed that Anna did not seem to want to move. "Are you all right, sweetheart?"

"I don't want to be out here…the street…" Anna unbuckled herself and hid further behind the seats. "I'm scared."

"There isn't much traffic," Patrick reassured her. "And there's no need to be afraid of anything else. We're right by the store."

"We'll be safe inside," Tori continued, holding out her arms for Anna to crawl into. "Think about what kind of fruit ice you want!"

"Apple cinnamon…" Anna burst into tears and buried herself in Tori's chest. "I wanted cider and they only had hot chocolate and then they attacked me and…"

"You're safe now," Tori whispered, glancing at Patrick helplessly.

"Let's go inside and distract ourselves," he decided. "Are you sure you want an apple-cinnamon fruit ice, Anna?"

Anna nodded as Tori whisked her to the toilets and Patrick headed to the counter to order. When they emerged into the store, Patrick was waiting excitedly with three large fruit ices. Anna hugged him tightly before diving into her treat. The two of them started shopping while Tori leaned against the counter for support, trying to discreetly swallow her medicine while she ate her blueberry fruit ice. Luckily, there were no other customers.

"Have I seen you before?" the storekeeper asked with a tone of curiosity and concern. Her nametag read 'Morgana,' and she appeared to be around fifty years old. "You don't live around here, do you?"

"No, we live in Goat Cove," Tori clarified, chasing her capsules with water before taking another mouthful of fruit ice. "I've come here sometimes. Not often lately, though."

She tried to recollect how many times she had come to Lake Hobidigan since childhood and decided that it probably averaged out to about once per year.

"Oh, okay, you just look familiar then. Your husband and daughter too."

"We haven't been here since she came along," Tori admitted truthfully. "We've been more 'walk along the ocean at Goat Cove' type of people lately." *And most of the time, to be honest.* Tori had many memories of awkward fancy lake parties with her parents and their plethora of friends and business acquaintances; she preferred spending time quietly alone along the shore.

"Oh, okay. I see you're admiring the store?"

"I have a store too. I sell religious books in Goat Cove." Tori had not even noticed that she was eyeing the store layout.

"That's a bit of a niche market, isn't it? A real bricks-and-mortar store? Sounds more like an online type of thing."

"We make it work." She took another bite, not wanting to discuss how she managed to pay all her bills. *My husband does freelance writing and works as a courier for Ninja-Cowboy. My dad owns and runs Ninja-Cowboy and gives me all the capital I need for my store. We're playing at being independent adults, but really, he bankrolls everything. Of course, that's partly because of all my extra medical costs. These pills aren't state healthcare level.*

"Well, I think that's great!" Morgana exclaimed. "It is so rare to see anyone succeed with a small business nowadays. To make ends meet, I've got to be the ice creamery, the deli, the grocery store, the pharmacy, the liquor store, and the beach supply shop all at once!"

"I've always loved this place. How long have you run it?"

"Oh gosh, fourteen years? I worked here before I bought it, so nearly twenty-five in total. A long time, anyway. I think I count as an old-timer now, with so many new people moving here. This town was a quarter of the size it is now when I started."

"That would explain why you've seen me before, then."

"Yes, but you say you never brought your little girl here? She just looks so familiar! Like someone who used to come in here almost every week."

Tori shook her head and let Morgana keep talking.

"I guess I was just worried about her. Not your daughter – the other little girl, the one she reminds me of. She lived in the village with her family. Then one day, I see her on her way here with her dad – just like your husband and daughter now. Little over a year ago. They stop to get hot chocolate at the stand we used to have outside. Then the police come blaring down the street, looking for a loose gunman, but they stop and grab the girl and her dad. I had their grocery order sitting right here on the counter! That man never carried a gun in his life, I'm sure of it. But they beat him up and took the girl and buggered off, and then some construction manager came along and took the man into his truck. And then, it turns out the loose gunman wasn't even anywhere near here! Makes no sense!"

Morgana did not seem to notice that Tori had frozen in place and was sucking on her spoon to keep from hyperventilating.

"Well, I thought there must have been some mistake, so I took the groceries down to their house down by the water. Tiny little cabin – really cozy. They were our kind of people. Not the big lakeside mansion types at all. Told his wife what I'd seen and she was obviously in a terrible state about it. I went to check on them two weeks later and they'd left."

"Makes sense," Tori whispered, slowly putting the spoon back in her bowl.

"Yes. Who knows what people get into? You remind me of her, a little. The man's wife, I mean. She was really shy and timid. I hardly ever saw her. They were such a sweet family, though! I watched their little girl grow up for at least two years. She was a baby when they moved here. They had another little one, a boy, but he stayed home with his mama most of the time. I think they had a third one on the way, but I was so scattered when I took them the groceries that I might have been imagining things."

"Poor woman!" Tori tried to finish her fruit ice as nonchalantly as she could. "I mean, even if her husband was into something dangerous, it's a horrible thing to happen."

"That's what I thought. But why didn't the police take the man, then? He got put into the construction truck like a piece of broken equipment. The man needed a hospital after being beaten up, not a supply truck."

"Maybe they had a first aid kit?"

"I suppose. I'm sorry for spilling this all out to you! I guess seeing your family made me remember. I could hardly speak of it. I kept waiting for anyone to come in and question me, but no one did. You'd think they'd at least want to ask my employee who was running the stand outside! Jayrose was traumatized and thought they were going to be attacked next. But nothing. Police didn't want any fuss."

"Glad to be helpful," Tori muttered.

She was in a daze as Patrick and Anna arrived with their shopping cart. Waving goodbye to Morgana, she went outside to start unloading their beach items into their wagon for the walk to the lakeshore. As she did so, she kept replaying Morgana's story in her head. Anna's outburst in the parking lot corroborated what Morgana claimed to have witnessed. Why else would she have cowered in terror when she had been excited about getting fruit ices only minutes earlier? Clearly, she had been expecting the police cars to come back.

The man got put into a truck...so he was at least mistaken for a robot. That would mean that Anna indeed could have recognized him at the construction site. No wonder Morgana thought Patrick looked familiar.

"What's the matter, Mama?" Anna asked, suddenly appearing beside Tori. "Why are you crying again?"

"Oh, I was just thinking of a sad story." She wiped her eyes and tried to put it out of her mind and enjoy the day. "I'm glad you're feeling better."

"You and Papa will keep me safe! How far is it to the beach?"

"Two kilometres," Patrick answered, setting his map on his phone. "Down the street, around the lakeside road, and then onto the boardwalk over the wetlands."

"You up for it, Mama?" Anna handed Tori a fresh water bottle. "You seem a bit tired."

"That was from driving here. You know I love a good walk, especially in the woods by the lake! Papa will have to drive home, though. I'll be too tired after a day at the beach."

They set off down the path as Patrick led them in a song.

After about two hours of splashing and wading in the shallow water, mixed in with some playing in the sand, the Williams-Kirkes sat down at a picnic table for lunch. As they started to eat, Tori noticed two women heading down the path from the boardwalk onto the beach toward them. They were not wearing swimsuits and seemed vaguely out of place wearing clothing that made it clear they felt it was too cold for swimming. Despite it being a warm day at the end of June, they were dressed in trousers and sweaters.

Patrick followed her gaze.

"They look like South Cascadians in winter mode," he noted quietly. Anna was too busy chewing to ask what he meant.

As the two women came closer, it became obvious they were a grown woman and a teenager, with the latter seeming very childlike except for being taller than her mother.

"The woman looks familiar to me, but I have no clue where I know her from," Tori explained.

"Maybe she's been to the bookstore?" Anna offered. "I think I saw her before too. Or someone who looks like her."

"I think they've noticed us staring," Patrick pointed out. "Why don't we invite them over to join us?"

They called out and waved the woman and her daughter over. At first, the older woman seemed confused and startled, but she led her daughter confidently to them and smiled warmly.

"Thank you so much for offering to share with us! Do I know you from somewhere?"

"We were wondering the same thing," Patrick admitted.

"My name is Victoria Lapoule Williams-Kirke," Tori introduced herself. "This is my husband, Patrick Semaganis Williams-Kirke, and our daughter, Anna. We came to the lake to celebrate the end of the school year."

"We live in Goat Cove," Anna added.

"Lovely to meet you, or at least get reacquainted. I am Hannah Ang Lukas-Black and this is my daughter, Elizabeth. We just got back from a year in South Cascadia and we're staying at my cabin here in Little Hobidigan for the summer."

"I have to go back for school," Elizabeth clarified. She appeared to be of the age where she still enjoyed spending time with her mother but often wished that she could be independent elsewhere.

"Oh, I see." Tori was puzzled. "I thought you might have visited our bookstore recently."

"Does your store use Black Swan Media for anything? I used to be their marketing director. We did a lot of videos and publishing."

"The name is familiar. Did you use Ninja-Cowboy Courier? My father owns that company and often hosts his clients as guests."

"Oh, goodness, you're Mike Martinez-Williams's daughter? I used to work for him before I got married and founded my own company. No wonder we hardly recognized each other! You came to my wedding. You were what, seven or so?"

Tori laughed nervously. "And I ate lots of candy and ended up in the hospital."

"Right…" Hannah suddenly became subdued. "I forgot how sick you were. You seem much better now!"

"It's good medicine," Tori muttered. "I'm still sick."

"Well, I'm glad you're getting the help you need."

"Why do you have to go so far away for school, Elizabeth?" Anna asked.

"We moved away from Alexandrina," the teenager replied nonchalantly. "All of my friends are in South Cascadia now."

"They're just visiting for the summer, like how we have gone to visit your grandmother sometimes," Patrick explained to his daughter, referring to his mother, who lived in a town about a day's journey away by high-speed train.

Anna nodded. She was busy pondering why Elizabeth's voice sounded familiar and kept quiet as the adults continued to talk.

After lunch and another hour or so of relaxing on the beach, Hannah offered to take the Williams-Kirkes back to her cabin for tea.

"It is just a quick walk from the main road," she added. "The boardwalk goes partway there, so you can see more of the lake, Anna!"

Tori hesitated, suddenly thinking of all the horrifying scenarios that Hannah might have planned. While the woman had once been a friend of her father's, Tori supposed that she might have a grudge with him that she wanted to settle. *Stop thinking like that,* she admonished herself.

"That sounds lovely," Patrick accepted, mostly not wanting to be rude. "However, we do need to be back home for five o'clock. We're driving a communal van."

Smiling, Tori nodded in agreement. Her fears were mostly alleviated, as should Hannah have less than honourable intentions, the three of them and the van were all easily traceable.

"Excellent! Just a quick tea, then. It will be nice to chat a bit more!"

When they arrived at Hannah's cabin, Tori was shocked that it really was a cabin, not a lakeside mansion like she had expected the former marketing director of a media corporation to live in. It was several decades old and looked like it needed quite a bit of maintenance. It had a vast deck that overlooked Lake Hobidigan, which Tori thought was the cabin's most attractive aspect. The rest of the property was covered with gardens, a greenhouse, a maintenance shed, a small boat dock, and playground equipment. The gardens took up most of the space, reminding Tori of a farmyard.

It was clear to Tori and Patrick that Hannah was definitely not a gardener: all of the grow boxes and plots were littered with dead plants and rife with weeds. The yard felt like a mournful place. Someone in the recent past had cultivated the garden plots and grow boxes with love and great care. There were still visible remnants of once-neat rows and patterns. They could still see small sticks that indicated what had been planted in each spot: mostly vegetables, berries, fruit, and edible flowers.

Anna eyed the garden and held back tears, biting her lip hard to keep from bawling.

"Papa, can we go back to the van?" she whispered, tugging hard on Patrick's shirt. "It's been a long day and I think I need to sleep."

"Umm, okay, sweetheart." Patrick caught how upset she was and decided not to argue further. He was thrilled to end the visit for himself. "You can nap and Papa will get a coffee for the drive home."

Patrick and Anna politely excused themselves after a requisite tour of the grounds, in which Anna buried her face into her father's neck to avoid looking at the dead plants. Once they had left, Elizabeth seemed relieved not to have to entertain anyone and disappeared into her bedroom.

Tori sat down on one of the long lounge chairs on the deck as Hannah put the kettle on for tea. While the older woman fussed in the kitchen, Tori lay back on the cushions and absorbed the beauty of the lakeside view. Birds and insects sang, the water lapped on the rocky shore, and boats sped along in the distance.

She sat up once Hannah returned to join her.

"I suppose you are wondering why I am living in such a place," she intuited. "Aside from how lovely it is, of course. It's been in my family for years. Used to come here as a kid. This place once belonged to my grandparents."

"The view is amazing," Tori agreed.

"Yes, that alone is worth it, especially in the summer. But I'm here to deal with my divorce proceedings. Some things couldn't be dealt with at a distance. My ex is being a jerk about the little details. The good thing is that I get to see my son and Elizabeth gets to spend time with her brother and dad."

"I'm sorry to hear about that."

"Anyway, enough about me. How have you been? You seem so happy with Patrick! He seems like such a wonderful man."

They had a pleasant conversation and Tori enjoyed extolling her husband's many virtues as they drank their tea. Despite not having a good relationship with her former spouse in the present, Hannah filled Tori in on the happier days of her marriage and how proud she was of her children as well as the media empire she had built. Tori talked about her store. She tried to avoid mentioning her recurring illness and was vague about Anna, though she found herself praising her daughter and going on about her school experience. When Hannah made a remark assuming that Anna was Tori's biological daughter that she had raised since at least birth, Tori did not correct her. She almost allowed herself to imagine that she had indeed given birth to Anna and raised her as a baby.

It was only when Tori went into the kitchen that she felt uneasy again. As she put her mug into the sink, she noticed a jar beside the fridge. The jar had a note on it that Hannah had placed a plastic cover over, presumably to keep it from getting wet as she splashed around doing the dishes. Something about it seemed puzzling. Curious, Tori took a closer look at the note.

"For Anna's birthday…do not open until she comes home, please?" She read the message aloud and blinked in confusion. "That's my handwriting."

Tucked beside it was a second note, this one also suspiciously in Tori's handwriting.

To Hannah: Thank you for everything. I plan to come back when I can. RRC looking for us. Police took Anna. We must hide somewhere else. Again, thank you. Maria.

Tori bolted to the bathroom, which was luckily right beside the kitchen, and locked the door. She stood in the middle of the tiny room, shaking profusely.

"Are you all right?" Hannah wondered, coming into the kitchen and finding the bathroom door shut. "Oh, sorry, I didn't mean to interrupt you."

"Just had a lot of tea," she managed to reply as she trembled.

"Do you want me to text Patrick to come pick you up now?"

"Yes, that'd be great." Deciding to use the toilet after all, Tori looked around the bathroom and noticed an old potty tucked beside the sink. There was a box of children's toys sitting in it.

The robot called me "Maria." Anna lived in Little Hobidigan. Morgana mentioned taking her family their groceries at a cabin. She lived here. This was her house – this was her bathroom. That jar on the kitchen counter was for her.

Taking several photos before joining Hannah back on the deck, Tori barely recalled any of what Hannah said for the rest of the visit. She was content to let her host think she had simply exhausted herself, as was common with her illness.

"How was the rest of your visit?" Patrick asked when he and Anna picked her up, confused as to why both his wife and daughter seemed unwell.

"Oh, good. Hannah is very nice. She wanted to catch up on everything that has happened in the thirty years since she worked for my dad."

"I'm glad you had a good time."

"I had a good time, too," Anna piped up groggily from her seat behind them. "I loved being at the beach. Thank you for taking me."

"We all had fun, didn't we?" Tori asked weakly, not entirely convinced herself. "It was nice to be able to swim."

"I wish the water at Goat Cove was warmer," Anna murmured. "Though Grace's mama said the ocean is already warm enough."

"She's right about that," Patrick agreed.

"Are you crying, sweetie?" Tori asked, glancing back at her daughter's tearstained face. "You must be really tired."

Anna nodded, even though she was not tired in the slightest. She squeezed her eyes shut, trying to block out memories, wanting nothing more than to get home to Goat Cove.

INTERLUDE 4

The beginning of July was unseasonably hot as Maria tended to the flower beds around the church. The perennials that the previous gardener had planted in the south-facing beds preferred cool breezes and moist earth, so they were wilting profusely. She successfully transplanted most of them to the more shaded areas of the garden, but they still drooped in a manner that struck her as sad as she watered them. Even the hardier, dry-soil plants she had replaced them with were thirsty in the heat. Maria spent most of her day watering.

Much of the greenery on the grounds of the retreat centre and church was tinted with brown, making her wistful for the start of the fall rain. Maria reminded herself summer was not the main season for flowers. Summer was the main season for fruit. The small kitchen garden on the retreat centre's property did not have enough fruit trees or vegetables for her liking. She hoped to convince the pastor to let her plant more of them to help feed the residents and guests. In her mind, it would make a valid fundraising project. Vegetables were cheap enough, but fruit trees would be costly. She fed and clothed herself and her children with donations to the charity bin. Since no one was donating saplings or cuttings, she had nothing to offer. Perhaps there were others who would be able to do so.

"Surely, someone must have extra money to donate for the garden. Everyone likes food, don't they? I can make things grow once I have them," she muttered to no one in particular. Stephanie was napping in a playpen under a nearby tree and Tyler was at the playground with some other children who were staying at the shelter.

Laughing ruefully, she thought back to five Julys earlier. The garden she had worked in then – which was really a set of multiple gardens and orchards on one property – had been much larger than the retreat centre. They probably had plenty of cuttings and saplings to discard. Maria had overseen nearly every type of plant she could think of. Other than her daily briefings from her owner, she had been alone all day, gardening and landscaping. Soon, even her daily briefings dwindled to messages only. While she loved her current job at the retreat centre (and working independently in her own right was better than being owned), she had loved the work she had been bought for. It was her, the plants, and the garden creatures.

The shed Maria had been housed in had once been a guest house when the property had been less of a garden and more of a large yard for entertaining. She had returned there each night; she had her own kitchen, laundry, and bathroom, as well as all the old books, clothes, and discarded items the household no longer wanted. She supposed she had lived her entire life out of some form of donation bin. Her shed, particularly the books, had offered her a strange sort of freedom.

She had been working there for about a year when her new companion arrived in late June. He had been purchased as a mechanic to work on the household's many vehicles, some of which were antique and thus had very specific requirements. He would spend the day closer to the family, sometimes being called in to work on odd repair jobs in the house, and retreat to the shed at night with Maria. The two of them would eat together and had learned to cook their own food. Maria was allowed to pick some of the vegetables and fruit for them to eat, since there was more than the household could ever hope to use themselves and they did not sell it. Within days, her companion had lost his compliant and dazed demeanour, as she had done when she had arrived, and they had started to talk to each other.

Both loved to learn and read. They went through the many discarded books and datapads in the shed together. He gravitated toward anything about building and fixing things, as well as stories about the wilderness. She preferred the materials about gardening and cookbooks. They had developed a mutual love for graphic novels, though she had taken a long time to figure out what fiction was and then had had a miserable time trying to explain it to him. Once she had, however, they had developed a fascination with stories about space. They had wistfully discussed being able to explore the universe, just them together in a spaceship.

She remembered it was the seventh day of July when she had kissed her companion for the first time. They had been listening to music after eating their supper. He had heard the name "Maria" in a song and decided it was beautiful and suited her. She had been so enamoured of being given a name that she had kissed him passionately like she had read in the graphic novel they had been reading.

"What are you doing?" he had asked, pulling away from her and leaning back onto his bed.

"I love that name!" she had cried, tears running down her face. "I'm sorry I don't have a name for you yet."

"Actually, I like how you say what Sir Black calls me."

"He just calls you 'step' because that's where you stood when you got here." She reiterated the story he had told her earlier.

"Yes, but it sounds really nice when you say it. Besides, it kind of defines me. I didn't stand where he wanted me to."

"Okay, Step, I'll let that be your name."

"Step and Maria…they go well together."

He had then gotten up from the bed and returned her kiss.

Despite not having read much about what would happen next, they had kept kissing each other, eventually getting to the point where they were no longer clothed and had their bodies wrapped around each other. Maria had extensive knowledge about plant and insect reproduction, but she had little idea of what she was trying to actually do.

"What…I'm sorry, I…you're so beautiful…I feel…I don't know…" Step could only try to express himself between kisses. "What are we doing?"

"Something awesome," she replied. "I've never felt so alive before!"

"Yeah, but…" He had never been aroused before; she was not sure if she had been either.

Somehow, she had put together the idea that they were supposed to join bodies, though that had been difficult to explain. It had been a long night of passion, as neither of them wanted to sleep. In the early morning hours of the eighth of July, based on her calculations backward, they had unknowingly conceived Anna.

Well, even if I am wrong about that, I like to think she was conceived then. It is poetic.

Her special, impossible child had been miraculous. And yet, she had also been ordinary. Anna, Tyler, and Stephanie were just children. Normal, human children.

Normal, human children whose parents are robots.

Maria had craved Step all day as they worked separately. They had barely locked the shed door and closed the tinted windows before they were back in bed, emerging only when they felt hungry. The rest of July had been blissful. Maria thought of it now like their honeymoon. Nothing could separate them except their daily work. They had even moved their beds together so they would have more space. Every night, Maria had fallen asleep in Step's arms.

By August, she had begun to feel unwell. She ate more of the fruit and vegetables than before, but then promptly vomited them back up. Climbing ladders and hauling greenery had made her dizzy. She had missed the monthly bleeding she had had since coming to work at the household. Still, she had pretended to be well. At the end of each day, she was still in Step's arms, feeling as safe as ever.

She had found answers to her concerns in an old book from Madam Black, which she supposed the woman must have used when she was having her own children. It was all about pregnancy, childbirth, and infant care. Maria had been both fascinated and terrified. The more she had read, the more she had been certain that she wanted to grow a baby. She was determined that she would, even though logic told her she would not be allowed to do so, let alone be allowed to keep a baby once it was born.

"You're what?" Step had been incredulous.

"I'm growing a baby. You know, like I grow plants. Except inside me, instead of in the soil."

"How?"

"We planted it." By that point, she had crawled on top of him and started to kiss him. "How about you read the book tomorrow?"

She had woken up the next morning to find Step had spent the whole night reading.

"What's the matter?" she had asked, noticing he was pale and shaking.

"You're going to die!" He had burst into tears. "How are we going to keep a baby hidden? You or it will die, or both of you will! Or they will return you as defective! I don't want to lose you!"

He had pulled her into a tight hug, sobbing into her hair. Maria had then started to cry as well, unable to reassure him.

"All I want to do is be with you and keep our baby safe. I don't care about anything else anymore. I'll do my best gardening for it."

Thus, she had diligently gone back out into the garden, determined to impress the household. She would do her duty to them and they would leave her alone. Maybe they would not notice anything amiss with her. Because Madam Black sent her instructions and did not bother to engage with her, Maria would go for days without seeing anyone other than Step. She was a landscaper. What would it matter to them if she grew a baby for herself?

Indeed, no one had noticed she was pregnant. The only one who might have suspected anything was her owners' daughter, who had taken to visiting Maria while she worked to complain about her own troubles, but the young girl likely had not paid any actual attention to the appearance of someone she just considered to be a robot. Maria had never missed a day of work until Anna's birth on the second day of April. Anna had been born with almost robotic precision, though Maria had been forced to go through the experience alone. Step could not have risked being missed in the garage. The household paid close attention to him.

Now, Maria looked back on the whole nine months as being one of wonder, terror, and joy. It had been just her and Step together in their cozy home. They had marvelled at Anna growing within her. She had enjoyed having a tiny companion as she gardened alone. She had started to tell her unborn daughter about the plants, birds, and insects. Even in March, Anna had been small enough that Maria had been able to hide her round belly within her loose overalls.

All Maria wanted to do now was return to somewhere she felt as safe as she had then. She still cared about nothing but keeping her children safe and being with Step. She wondered if the congregation in Eastcott would be as accepting of her if they knew she was a robot.

It still doesn't matter. I just want to make a home somewhere with Step and our three children! Where I can have a garden of my own and teach the children how to tend it.

Her miracle baby was gone. She was four years old. She was not a toddler anymore. Maria was not even sure if her daughter would recognize her.

"I'm sorry, Anna!" she whispered, wiping away tears. "I'm sorry I didn't pay you enough attention after Tyler came along. I'm sorry I couldn't protect you. Please, God, let me see her again! Let me be her mother again! Let me be a better mother!"

As the sun set behind the centre's main building, she retreated to her apartment with Tyler and Stephanie. Stephanie still wanted to be nursed at night, so Maria lay with her on the couch and watched as the stars slowly emerged.

She thought back to her honeymoon, to feeling her firstborn child moving within her for the first time on a frosty fall morning, to the joyful bewilderment on Step's face the first time he felt Anna kick at him, to sitting awkwardly at the top of a ladder at the spring equinox as she described the scene to the baby that squirmed excitedly inside her, to finally giving birth on their shower floor, collapsing in exhaustion against the wall as she fed Anna for the first time.

"I'm going to miss this," she cooed to Stephanie, who had nearly fallen asleep. "I love having babies. Hopefully your papa finds us soon."

She desperately wanted to be in his arms at night again.

CHAPTER SEVEN

"I want to rent a robot," Tori insisted.

She could hardly believe she was uttering such a sentence. Her father would have been livid. He was adamant his companies would not use robots and marketed the lack of them as a selling point for Ninja-Cowboy Courier. It was his odd way of trying to appeal to the everyday folk or common person, as he called them, and his appeal worked. ("Appeal to the common folk and you'll have customers for life" was his mantra.) He held up Ninja-Cowboy as proof that one could run a successful large business without robots. Tori had been raised to distrust the idea of robotics. But she was willing to experiment now.

"For what?" Patrick wondered.

"I want to rent the one that Anna claimed was her old father. I want…I want to pick his brain for a bit. I want to talk to him."

"You mean, you want to spend a huge sum of money for an hourly rental for some kind of date? With a guy that looks like a younger me?"

Patrick sounded like he was teasing, which made Tori laugh.

"No, you could come too!"

"That probably isn't a good idea. Not in public, anyway, if he looks as much like me as you've described. We want to be able to talk freely with him. Maybe we could have him over for supper? Would make for a really expensive supper."

"I don't want to upset Anna again! She is finally settling into the summer." It had been just over a week since their emotionally charged visit to Lake Hobidigan.

"She can go for a sleepover at Grace's. Or better yet, Ellie's. That way, it's further for her to come home if she wants to and we won't be caught by surprise."

"Are you seriously thinking this is a good idea, or are you just messing with my head and humouring me?"

"Both, really. You and Anna were really upset in Little Hobidigan. Anna told me she really missed her old mother and father."

"She saw her old house!" Tori hissed. "And whoever she called her mother was not in it, but some rich gossipy lady. I mean, I know we'd be weirded out going to my parents' place or your mother's place and finding strangers living there."

"I definitely see why you want to talk to the robot. I would like to learn more too. I have lots of questions, though I'm not sure how much he can answer."

"He obviously knows what happened to himself, at least, and maybe how Anna ended up at a cabin belonging to a wealthy media mogul."

"That part doesn't seem like much of a mystery to me. I honestly assumed Hannah had it rented out most of the time."

Tori nodded. That Anna's parents had simply rented the cabin was a logical conclusion, but she was unconvinced anything was that straightforward in this case. How had a robot ended up renting the cabin? If the man had been taken as a robot by mistake, how had they not realized their error and released him? Why had no one made the connection between the man's DNA and Anna's? Why had Hannah kept the notes and jar? It seemed like an odd thing to keep from one's tenants. Why hadn't she rented out the cabin again?

“I am curious about who this ‘Maria’ is,” she added. “Is she really Anna’s mother? Someone who employed the robot, maybe?”

“Well, let’s just go ahead and book our insanely expensive supper date and arrange for Anna’s sleepover! Now, what will I cook?”

“Fish and vegetables,” Tori answered without hesitation. “With something fruit-related for dessert. I’m sure he has similar preferences to Anna.”

The following Friday night, Anna excitedly went to the Alvarez-Franklins’ for her sleepover, promising to behave properly and not stay up too late. She assumed that her parents’ visible anxiety was about her spending the night away from home (though she had had sleepovers with Ellie before), so she gave them tight hugs. Meanwhile, Cate reassured Tori she would send updates throughout the night and sent her a temporary password to view the link to their playroom camera. Tori and Patrick both pretended that was indeed what was making them nervous as Anna skipped into the Alvarez-Franklin house. They hugged Cate and returned home to prepare for their evening, reassured that Anna was going to have a fun evening.

Tori felt extremely self-conscious as she approached the Robot Rental Corporation’s downtown office. Even though she had little to do with her father’s companies, if she were recognized as her father’s daughter, the Ninja-Cowboy Courier Company would have a potential public relations disaster, jeopardizing her livelihood and forcing her to make up some rational but embarrassing explanation for her actions. To avoid this, she altered her hair and wore glasses that projected different features onto her face. Nonetheless, her anxiety told her that everyone could tell who she was, as if she had a bright flashing sign floating above her head announcing her identity. Onlookers seemed to be giving her disapproving stares as she entered the building, but she tried to tell herself she was imagining them. Or maybe I'm not – lots of people hate robots and the people who rent them. Please God, don't let them attack us.

"May I help you, ma'am?" the woman behind the counter asked. She had a clipped voice with overly sweet tones.

"Thank you." Tori held out her phone for her to scan.

The woman nodded, noting the number of the robot requested.

"You are certain that Unit RB 14600218-36 is the robot that you want?"

"Yes. Our van needs repairing."

Upon hearing "yes," the woman made no further acknowledgement of anything else Tori had said. She went through the ritual of having Tori pay in advance and ran through a list of regulations that she had to agree with to receive her rental.

Finally satisfied, the woman insisted she would have the robot brought out at the precise time the rental began, waving Tori to wait.

Shortly thereafter, a uniformed guard brought out the robot who looked like a younger Patrick. The first thing Tori noticed was he was still wearing the same overalls, which appeared to have been freshly washed. The second thing she noticed was he had not shaved his face for a couple of days, making him look even more like her husband had when she had met him. Thirdly, she noted his expression was one of pained neutrality and he barely made eye contact with her.

Having noted the time, the guard handed the robot unceremoniously over to Tori, putting his wrist in her hand as though he were a toddler.

"Do I have to walk him?" she asked in disbelief, extremely uncomfortable at holding a grown man's wrist. Now that they were so close together, she realized he was over a head taller than her. He was even taller than Patrick and he appeared to be strong enough to lift her up over his shoulders with minimal effort.

You're Patrick if he had spent his entire youth at the gym instead of the library.

"He'll do what you want," the guard clarified. "Just tell him to walk with you and follow you. He's a robot, not a dog."

"Okay, thanks," Tori muttered, wanting to get home as quickly as possible.

She looked up at the robot and he cocked his head in curiosity, having noticed something was not right with her eyes and the rest of her face.

"Walk with me, please. We need to go to the Central Transit Exchange, Bay 2."

Letting go of him, she started for the door. The robot quickly caught up and walked alongside her.

"Do I know you already?" he asked. "Have you rented me before?"

"No and no," she answered. "You've seen me, but you don't know me."

They were silent as they entered the transit exchange and found the right platform to go to Goat Cove. Since Tori's flimsy cover story was that she needed someone to repair her vehicle, she had decided to travel by train rather than arrange for some type of ride.

"What type of vehicle do you need repaired or inspected, ma'am?" the robot asked as they settled onto the train.

"None, actually," Tori admitted. "Our co-op's two vans are running fine and my husband's delivery vehicle is regularly inspected and serviced at the company garage."

"Ma'am, I assure you that I am not licensed to do anything outside of my expertise." He sounded annoyed but also slightly frightened.

"What do you think I had in mind?" We might as well chat to pass the time on the train.

"I don't know. Crime? Sex?"

"Okay, that wasn't the answer I was expecting." Tori laughed. The robot sounded very clinical, but there was a hint of teasing in his voice.

"It seems plausible someone would rent a robot under the guise of needing a vehicle repaired on a Friday evening but actually want them to do something else."

Tori was surprised he was familiar with crime, sex, and the concept of Friday evening being an unusual time for vehicle repair.

"Um, yeah, plausible, but no, I don't want you to do either of those things. Do you have a name?"

"I have a unit number," the robot replied. "RB 14600218-36."

"Don't they call you anything shorter? It's awfully complicated."

"No, not really. I think they just read it off their datapads."

"Not even something like 'Dash 36'?"

The robot shook his head. "'Dash' has a nice sound to it," he observed. "But that's not my name."

"What is your name?" Tori immediately asked. She thought it was odd a robot would care about how nice a name sounded.

"Step. As in the thing in front of a door. It's not short for anything. I like this designation the best. It was on my identity card."

"You had an identity card?"

Step nodded. "Is there anything that I should call you, ma'am?"

"I'm Tori."

"Nice to meet you."

The doors opened and they stepped off the train at Goat Cove. Tori started to walk toward her house and beckoned Step to follow her.

"Are you in a disguise?" he asked as he easily kept up with her pace.

"Yes, and when we get to my house, you'll probably figure out why."

"So where have I met you before?"

"Bargain Bonanza construction site."

"Oh, you're that Tori!" His tone changed from curiosity to concern. "Where is Anna? Is she all right?"

"She is very good. She is visiting at a friend's house for the night."

As they approached Tori and Patrick's house, she slowed down and pulled up the feed from the Alvarez-Franklins' playroom camera. Anna, Ellie, and Justin were building Lego spaceships.

"Her friends' mother wanted me to be able to see her too."

She showed the feed to Step, who froze mid-step.

“She looks so happy!” He started to cry. There was hardly any trace of his robotic demeanour left and he sounded indistinguishable from Patrick. Tori instinctively hugged him and they both recoiled.

“I’m sorry!” she squeaked, afraid he might attack her.

“No one has touched me like that in months,” he admitted. “You scared me. You…can you take off your disguise?”

“When we get to the house. It’s across the street.”

“Whose house?”

“Mine. We invited you for supper.”

“We?”

“Me and my husband.”

She led him across the street and scurried as fast as she could to her front door, hoping that if any of their neighbours were watching, they would think she and Step were relatives who were visiting. To that end, she rang the doorbell.

Patrick opened the door and ushered them in, only seeming to register how much Step really looked like him once he had locked the door again and they were both standing in the entryway.

“Good evening, sir,” Step offered. He stood awkwardly in the middle of the room as Tori hurried to remove her wig and glasses.

“Welcome!” Patrick managed to utter, startled at Step’s appearance. “Can I take your boots or anything? Luckily, it’s not coat weather.”

“You want me to remove my boots? I usually just put covers on them.”

“Oh, that’s fine too,” Tori hurried to respond.

Step pulled boot covers out of his pocket and put them on. When he stood up again, it was his turn to be speechless as he stared at Tori and Patrick together.

"Who…what…how…?"

"Step, this is my husband, Patrick," Tori introduced them. "Patrick, this is Step."

"You look like me!" Step exclaimed. He turned from Patrick to Tori, now no longer in disguise. "And you…you look like Maria!"

He caught a glimpse of their wedding portrait in the living room and promptly fainted, grabbing the railing and plopping himself down on his namesake at the bottom of the stairs.

"We are as confused about that as you are," Patrick assured him, taking a seat beside him. "Who is Maria?"

"My wife!" Step burst into tears again and leaned into the railing. "Anna's mother!"

"I knew it!" Patrick whispered, glancing at Tori.

"I'll go finish setting the table," Tori muttered, spinning off into the kitchen.

That Anna's "old mama who liked flowers" now had a name bothered her. It bothered her even more that they looked alike. How had someone with her DNA managed to have children? How much did Maria look like her? Did she look as much like a younger Tori as Step looked like a younger Patrick? How did Step and Maria have the same genetic profiles as them?

"We're having fish with pineapple sauce, string beans, beets, and squash," Patrick narrated as he led Step into the kitchen. "And there's apple-peach crumble for dessert."

"Thank you," Step whispered. His eyes were still red and teary, but he had tried his best to recover his professional demeanor. "It smells delicious."

"Please, sit down with us!" Tori invited him.

As he made himself comfortable in the chair Anna normally used, she noticed he had similar mannerisms to their daughter.

"I'm sorry – I don't think I have ever sat at such a fancy table," Step admitted. "It all looks so nice! I don't want to touch it."

For a moment, Tori feared he did not know how to eat, but he gingerly picked up the fork and knife as Patrick set his plate of food in front of him.

"Okay, now you've really made the food look pretty," he giggled, sounding very similar to Anna. He admired it as Patrick and Tori discreetly said grace.

For several minutes, the three of them ate together in silence, other than the sound of ravenous chewing. Taggy watched from his spot on the couch, content with the treat of fish Patrick had given him earlier. He wondered if the man who smelled a lot like Patrick would also give him a treat, so he eyed them all closely.

"Thank you again for this delicious supper!" Any trace of Step being a robot had vanished. "But why did you bring me here? What do you want me to do for you?"

"Well, we actually just wanted to talk," Tori replied. "We thought you could help us. I've been wondering about you since we met you at the construction site."

"Help you with what?"

"Explaining who Anna is," Patrick answered. "We love her very much, but she was a complete surprise to us."

"She was a surprise to us too," Step agreed. "Um, is it just you and Anna that live here?"

"Us and our cat," Tori gestured toward Taggy. "I'm too sick to have children. It was just the two of us until Anna came into our lives."

"Oh…"

"She was a surprise to you too?" Patrick asked.

Tori had caught Step's meaning, so she blushed at her husband's obliviousness and shoved a forkful of squash into her mouth.

"Well, no one taught us about human reproduction, so I had no idea that sex led to babies. We were just two robots in the shed."

Patrick nearly choked on his water.

"That happens if you put robots together?" he asked.

"No, not usually. Our food keeps us from caring about anything."

Realizing that Patrick and Tori were staring at him in confusion, Step smiled sheepishly.

"Would you like me to tell my life story so far?"

They both nodded. Step took a quick sip of water before eagerly starting to narrate.

"I am a robot, kind of. You probably know the Robot Rental Corporation has a patent on humanoid robots – robots that are so human-like we can do anything you can and don't creep you out. Well, we aren't just human-like. We're human, as far as anyone can tell. Genetically altered a lot, but nothing mechanical. We're controlled through chemicals in our food. If you buy a robot, you must buy their special food too."

"So, if we ate this food, would we turn into robots?" Tori asked aloud, though she had not meant to.

Step gave her a look of horrified realization.

"Maybe? I don't know, probably not. They probably tweaked our genes or something. I mean, I sure hope the Corporation isn't planning to turn the whole world into robots!"

“They wouldn’t have any customers,” Patrick pointed out, no less disturbed by the thought of being drugged into being a robot.

“Right,” Step agreed. “Anyway, I’m a mechanic. I was taught mechanics the whole time I was growing in my vat and then after at the training facility. Then I was purchased by the same family that already had Maria. When I got there, I didn’t stand in the right place, so my owner called me ‘Step.’ At least, he didn’t keep calling me by my unit number.”

“Sorry, did you say you grew in a vat?” Patrick wondered. “Is that part of the Robot Rental Corporation’s special patent?”

“Yes, we go from zygote to late adolescence in a vat, all in a fairly short time. Then we spend about a year getting trained outside the vat, so we’re very young adults when we’re ready to go out into the world. Though most of us just stay at the barracks and get rented out.”

“Wait, so how old are you?” Tori asked.

“How old do I look?”

“You look like I did at twenty-five,” Patrick explained.

Step laughed.

“Then that’s how old I am. I think my identity card said I was born twenty-three years ago, actually. Not eight. Anyway, I’m getting ahead of myself. The family who bought us had this huge property. They were really into growing their own produce. They’d turned their whole place into a garden and orchard. They didn’t sell any of the produce, though. And they didn’t actually grow it, either. They bought Maria to do that. She is specially trained in gardening and landscaping. Naturally, they decided to be cheap about the robot food, realizing they could feed us the same ingredients, mostly from the garden. And they put Maria in their shed, which was an old guest house and had all their discarded stuff in it. She turned it into a little home."

His voice trailed off as he thought back to meeting her for the first time and the strange feeling of peaceful coziness he had upon seeing the shed, despite being initially confused.

"I was put in there with her and stopped eating the robot food too," he continued, fighting tears. "We read a lot – that's how I know about so much more stuff than mechanics. And we, well, we fell in love, I guess. I named her Maria, after a beautiful song I heard. No one paid us any attention in the shed. Like I said, we didn't know sex led to babies. Maria found an old book about it. She got really excited because she loves growing things. No one noticed. Maria was always left alone. It was only when Anna was born that anyone realized what had happened. Our owner got us identity cards. She must have done something wrong, because the cops later said my card was fake. She set us up in her old cabin and we lived there happily as a family until last March. I got taken back by the Corporation because my barcode trumped my identity card. Anna got taken by the cops. Guess she ended up here, so that's good. You seem like good people who love her."

Neither Patrick nor Tori could respond.

"I mean it," Step continued. "You love her and take good care of her. Keep her safe."

"We will," Tori insisted. She then paused. "Did you say you were eight?"

"Like, I've been alive for eight years, yes."

Tori took a nervous swig of water as Patrick found his voice again.

"I'm curious how the Robot Rental Corporation expected to get away with cloning people without anyone noticing. It's illegal, for one thing."

"We look alike, but just different enough that people wouldn't think much about it," Step pointed out. "If it weren't for Anna, I doubt you'd have noticed me."

"Still, you say you're actually cloned humans? That certainly changes things about robots," Patrick mused, his journalist side awakened. "The law assumes you're machines. I don't see how you could be considered machines if all that separates the two of us is the type of food we eat."

The visit continued as Step and Patrick went into a deep discussion about cloning and the law while Tori tidied the table and served dessert. She was fascinated by Step's story despite it deeply troubling her.

If Step is only eight years old, at least technically, then he really could have been our son. The technology to clone Patrick exists. Meaning the technology to clone me exists. Not just clone me, either, but apparently cure me enough to be able to run around landscaping and have babies. Someone I could have raised like Anna and who would be in grade school now but instead is a full-grown adult with at least two kids of her own. Does that make me Anna's grandmother?

She was suddenly overwhelmed with concern for the mysterious Maria. Step talked about her protectively yet with admiration, but all Tori could think about was how afraid she must have been. Maria would have been terrified of being caught herself. The note at Hannah's cabin had sounded desperate, despite its hopeful suggestion of them returning. She was a runaway robot with a toddler.

"Hannah Lukas-Black was the one who got you new identity cards, right?" Tori asked, returning to her seat. "She used to be a friend of my father and she invited me for tea."

"Yes, that was Madam's name. Maria was better at using it than I was."

"She came back to her cabin and found a note Maria had left." Tori pulled up the photos that she had taken the week before. "I thought it was an odd thing to keep."

"I guess Hannah misses us too." Step teared up again. "She was very kind to us. She could have returned us as defective. She could have killed Anna or sold her. But she set us up to let us live together as a family. We never saw her again in person, but she sent us gifts and messages."

Tori shuffled her photos around.

"Here are some more photos of Anna. This was from her fourth birthday party this past spring. And here she is at Easter, and at her preschool graduation…"

"Is that on the beach at Lake Hobidigan?" Step asked Tori as she scrolled through recent photos. "She always wanted to go there and play with the other kids."

"Yes, that's her with her sandcastle."

"Does she play with other kids often? Like she is tonight?"

"Yes. There are lots of kids in our housing co-op. Our neighbours have a daughter the same age as her. She is visiting friends of ours tonight that have twins very close in age to her. They play together a lot."

"That's good. We never let her do that. We were too scared to."

"Understandable," Patrick agreed, having kept quiet since having been served crumble.

"We don't really understand friendship very well," Step explained. "You can probably tell how awkward I am. We are encouraged to be solitary. We're supposed to be machines, after all. Maria hoped Anna would be happy with her little brother, but he was too young for her. Anna loved helping her mother take care of him, but they couldn't play together. So she followed me around instead."

"How old is her brother?" Tori asked. "What does he look like?"

"I don't know what he looks like anymore! He was just little when I saw him last. He had brown hair, not dark like Anna's. Otherwise, they looked a lot alike. Blue eyes, pale brown skin, curly hair…he looked more like Maria. They had similar noses. You do too."

Tori nodded slowly, thinking of how she thought Anna had Patrick's – or rather, Step's – facial features despite having Tori's – Maria's – hair and skin tone. She tried hard to picture a little boy similar to Anna, but with her nose and Patrick's old hair colour. Unfortunately, the best she could do was picture their neighbour's son, Liam Pike-Macrae, whom she guessed was probably around the same age. He was just getting to the point where Grace could tolerate him.

"He's a year and six months younger than Anna," Step continued. "That would make him two years and nine months old."

"Maybe they would have gotten along better if they were both girls?" Patrick suggested. Tori glared at him. In her limited experience, it would not have made much of a difference.

"Anna kept asking for a sister. But friends are better."

Tori sensed Step was trying to keep from telling them anything more.

"Morgana at the store in Little Hobidigan remembered you. She told me she took your groceries to Maria and told her what happened. That must have made Maria decide to leave."

"Why did everyone tell you things?" Step wondered, and Patrick nodded in agreement.

"I suppose because I reminded her of Maria? I think she really wanted to talk. I just wanted to enjoy my fruit ice!"

"Those are delicious," Step concurred.

"Anyway, she said she thought you had a third child on the way," Tori finished. "But that Maria left within a couple weeks and so she never saw her again."

"Not sure why I was hiding that," Step admitted. "They'd be a year and nine months younger than Tyler. That's Anna's brother's name, by the way. Meaning they'd be…a year old now."

After a long moment of silence and staring at their empty dessert plates, Tori and Patrick came to the deflated conclusion that they had no good way to respond.

"I'm sorry," Patrick finally whispered.

"Why? You didn't do anything. You took in Anna and gave her a home!"

"Surely someone must have taken care of Maria and your younger children too," Tori hoped. "There are places for people to stay. Shelters and such."

"I keep checking around the barracks and hoping I don't see her. I tell myself that as long as she isn't there, she hasn't been caught. She's always been really good at hiding."

Patrick hurriedly booked one of the block's vans to drive Step back to the Robot Rental Corporation, giving them a bit more time to visit. Meanwhile, Tori searched through a list of books from her store.

"What are you doing?" Step asked, having helped himself to another serving of dessert.

"You mentioned they took away your phone, but you can read books about mechanics. Do you have a device of your own?"

"I have a datapad assigned to me. It's in my overalls pocket. I always bring it, in case I need to consult something."

"Can I send you something?"

Step nodded and took another bite.

"I will send a couple photos of Anna and of Maria's note. But I also want to give you a couple of books."

"Thank you!"

"One is a very long one. It's got lots of parts. It is more like a collection of stories and it can be a bit confusing, so I am sending a couple of other books to help explain it. But it will be a good way to pass the time."

"That sounds complicated. Can you download new covers for them? So they look like vehicle-repair manuals?"

Tori nodded, involuntarily giggling as she covered the main book with Early Twentieth-Century Motorcycles.

"I hope you're not disappointed, since that book about motorcycles looks interesting."

"I rarely get to work with vehicles that old. Plus, I have read it already."

"What does Maria look like?" Tori asked with curiosity as she handed him back his datapad. "How much do I look like her?"

"She looks younger than you, but otherwise, the same. Well, you're wearing a dress and you have longer hair. She kept her hair short so it didn't interfere with her work, and she mainly wore overalls or similar things."

Tori tried to picture herself with short hair, overalls, and the physique required to wield branches or haul dirt. She could barely lift a small flowerpot. Just the thought of tending a fraction of the grow boxes at Hannah's cabin made her tired.

"Thank you again for the books and for the delicious meal." Step finished his crumble. "It was nice to be a normal human for an evening."

Step walked himself back into the Robot Rental Corporation, crossing a line marked "returned" that flashed green to say he had arrived on time. From the shadows of the rental van, the Williams-Kirkes watched him disappear into the building. He was a robot again.

Tori cried profusely.

"I feel like I'm sending him back to prison or something! It's just wrong!"

Patrick gently requested she remove her disguising glasses because, combined with her tears, they made her face look like a work of abstract art. She drove the van back toward Goat Cove and pulled into an empty parking lot to keep crying.

"He told us to stop looking for him and to raise Anna safely and happily," Patrick reminded her, feeling horrible.

Tori nodded and heaved, unable to get any words out.

He's practically our son! We need to protect him! We have a family now!

"The Robot Rental Corporation isn't going to get away with their clone slavery scheme forever," Patrick added with determination. "Someday, we won't have to hide Anna."

"We're a family," Tori finally sputtered. "We should be together."

"And we always will be. Things will eventually work out."

INTERLUDE 5

Step ate as little of his robot-prescribed food as possible: just enough to numb any physical pain and to give him strength to work each day. He wanted to keep his mind clear. Every evening, he would retreat to his cupboard to read. The books Tori had given him were fascinating. Some of the collection was boring and it was indeed confusing, as she had warned, but he especially loved the poetry portions. Most of the stories were exciting, even if they could not compare with those of the spaceships. Fiction had taught him humans were strange.

You are strange, Step. You are human.

He needed to remind himself of that daily as he fell into his routine as a robot. He could be assured that Anna was safe. Each morning and evening, he would clandestinely glance at her photo. He whispered her good wishes for the day and kissed her glove good night. Then, he started sending out the same wishes for Maria, Tyler, and the baby. While he was not sure where they were, he wanted to believe they were safe and happy together and that somehow his well-wishes reached them. Maria loved her children. Besides him, they were all she truly cared about. She would have made sure they stayed with her. The note she had left for Hannah indicated she wanted to come home. She had faith they would be together again.

It's a strange thing, faith. This book is all about it. Maria is the one who always seemed to have it. I was the skeptical one. That's why I always thought of her as my captain.

Closing his books on his datapad, he lay back in his cupboard and let his thoughts drift back to the last time they had been together. Maria had been tending the grow boxes while Tyler napped. Anna had given her mother a hug and was hopping around in the driveway, waiting for her father to be ready to go to Morgana's store. His little girl had been excited, singing about all the food they were going to get.

Like all the robots he was aware of, Maria was built for physical work. Her being pregnant had barely slowed her down. Despite having to devote so much energy to her growing baby, she kept gardening, determined to get as much done as possible before Tyler woke up. She had only stopped long enough to see them off, and Step could tell she had been anxious to get back to her grow boxes.

"Don't forget the spiced apples that Anna wants!" she had reminded him, pulling him down to her height for a passionate kiss. "I'm sure it's in the order but check to make sure!"

"I can always go back before her birthday," he had reminded her. "It's not that long of a walk to the store."

"Yes, but I want to make sure that I have everything!" She had been happily preparing a special supper and little family party for them. Birthdays were her favourite holidays.

Are you still throwing little family birthday parties, Maria? I hope so. I hope you and Tyler had a nice party for the baby turning a year old.

"Don't worry! I will check the order. One 500ml jar of spiced apples!"

"I love you." She had given him a quick second kiss.

Their little soccer player had started kicking at her and Step had admonished them playfully, telling them to be good for their mother.

I hope they heard me and took that to heart. I didn't tell Maria that I loved her back, though I know I said that plenty of times. But why didn't I say it then? The last thing I really said to her was that I would bring back a jar of spiced apples – which I didn't do.

Then, he and Anna had marched off merrily toward the store. He wondered how long Maria had happily weeded her grow boxes, not realizing that anything had happened to Step and Anna. They had gone to pick up groceries many times. She would have begrudgingly gone back inside when Tyler woke up, perhaps feeding him a snack before wondering what was taking them so long to get home. Only for Morgana to be the one to show up with the groceries instead, including the spiced apples, with the news that Step and Anna had been kidnapped.

Her happy life would have been shattered. How could she have still been such a hopeful person after losing us? All her paranoid fears would have been realized. She just wanted us all to live in peace together.

The photo of her note that Tori had shown him had included the jar of apples. Maria had saved them and Hannah had left them alone.

Well, Maria did leave a forceful message on them. She was still determined then that Anna would come home to her. I suppose Hannah is respectful of that.

Having dozed off, he was suddenly roused awake by a trepid knocking sound. Rolling over and removing his headphones, he was startled to see one of his female roommates knocking on the transparent door of his cupboard. He opened it and she grabbed at the edge to keep from losing her balance on the ladder.

"Hello?" he asked. In all his time at the barracks, the only one of his roommates that had approached him was the man who liked to eat his extra food.

"Hi! What are you reading? You look really interested in it."

Step blinked, having never heard her voice before.

"Um, just a book that a client gave me. They heard that I like old stuff." This might take a lot of explaining if you ask any more about the book.

Luckily, the woman changed the topic instead.

"I saw you had photos. Did your kid's family send you a photo? That's really nice of them. Mine doesn't."

Step's jaw dropped. "Sorry, what?"

"Well, I saw you looking at a photo of a kid and I assumed you were contracted to donate genetic material for them. That's what I was. I'm specialized in having babies and early childcare. I had twins for a family, then they got rid of me. They didn't want me to take care of them, even though that was part of what I was designed for. So I was sent back here and they've been retraining me on looking after gardens and animals."

Her voice was shaking, as though she was about to cry, despite her sounding proud of her accomplishments.

"I'm sorry that happened," Step offered.

The woman smiled weakly.

"They would be close in age to the kid in the photo, I think. They were born three and a half years ago. I was picked because I looked a bit like their parents. Something about their mother not being able to have kids so I was used instead. But she didn't want me around after because I guess she wanted to pretend they were all hers. And I suppose I would have been discarded eventually."

"Oh dear, I'm sorry seeing my photo made you sad." The woman reminded him somewhat of Maria, though she was taller and more gregarious than his wife.

"I like remembering them and imagining them growing up. I get bored reading and watching about plants and animals all the time. I'd like to learn something else. That's why I thought I'd come talk to you. One of the videos I was watching showed people talking to animals. And the animals talk to each other, in their own ways at least. Why don't we talk to each other?"

"Want to trade something of yours for my mountaineering manual?" The man in the lowest cupboard stuck his head out and looked up at Step and the woman. "I'd like to learn about looking after animals."

"Why don't we all watch one of the videos about animals talking to each other?" Step suggested. "We can watch it together, and then we can talk about it."

"Can you tell us why you have different overalls from the rest of us, too?" the woman asked.

"Sure!" Step was suddenly gleeful. "I'll tell you all after the video. Let's sit in the middle of our floor."

He looked around and noticed the second woman was watching them from her cupboard, while his fifth roommate, who had eaten Step's supper, was asleep.

"All four of us?" the man in the bottom cupboard asked. "Won't security notice?"

"We're all still in our room," the first woman pointed out. "That's all they care about. Let's put the datapad facing one direction and we'll all line up to face it. Then no one will wonder if we're talking to each other."

"Good idea!" Step agreed. He glanced at the number on the woman's cupboard. "You set up the video, er...MX1375608-95?"

"Call me Nola," the woman insisted. "It's shorter."

"My name is Step," Step introduced himself as he followed her down the ladder.

"You have names?" the other woman asked, climbing out of her cupboard on the opposite wall. "Where did you get them?"

"I picked mine," Nola answered. "So I wouldn't forget my kids: Norah and Lakelynn."

"Mine started off as a nickname my first owner gave me, but I like it."

"I will have to think of a name!" The second woman joined Step and Nola on the floor. "That's going to be hard, since I was programmed with lots of words."

"Is there a place to find names? Like, a dictionary?" the other man asked.

"Yes – people often use them when they have babies," Nola explained. "I was programmed to know about them, but I didn't get to read any in great detail. Naming babies wasn't part of my programming. That's something for owners to do."

"Could you access one for me?"

"Maybe…I could try…"

"I might be able to help," the second woman added. "I had to learn about translating names. I must have lists somewhere."

"That's tomorrow's project," Nola decided. "Now, let's watch a video about animals!"

INTERLUDE 6

"Happy Birthday, dear Tyler! Happy Birthday to you!" Maria sang softly and kissed her now-three-year-old son on the forehead. "May you have many wonderful, happy years ahead!"

Tyler quickly blew out the large '3' candle that his mother had placed in front of him, while Stephanie cheered and clamoured for the mixing bowl of fruit salad that was in the middle of the table. Maria pulled the bowl toward herself and started serving the fruit salad into cups.

"Fwoot!" Stephanie cried, reaching toward her mother.

"Yes, I'm getting your fruit salad, sweetie. It's Tyler's turn to be the birthday boy, so he gets his first."

"That's okay, Mama. She's the baby." Tyler smiled and gestured for Maria to give Stephanie the first cup.

They no longer had a highchair, so Stephanie was sitting in a booster seat that was too large for her and was at a bad angle for her to reach her food. Without her own tray, she made lots of messes at the table. Before Maria could finish serving Tyler, Stephanie had spilled her cup of fruit salad in front of her and had sticky juice running down into her seat. She was unfazed, however; she merrily shoved pieces of fruit into her mouth and let more juice drip onto her chin and tummy. Meanwhile, Tyler fussed with his spoon and savoured each tiny morsel slowly. He loved the sweet juice in the salad and was thus careful to keep his cup upright so as not to lose any of it. He tried his best to ignore his sister's messy eating, feeling sad about all the juice going to waste as it ran down her front.

Maria was not concerned about her daughter getting dirty. Once Stephanie was done eating, she would give her a wash and clean up the juice puddle. She served herself a cup of fruit salad and put the bowl back onto the kitchen counter so Stephanie would not be able to grab at it. Sitting down again, she glanced from one child to another before settling her gaze back onto the candle that was still in front of Tyler.

I bought that candle for Anna's birthday. It should not have been new today. It should have been gently used, like the '2' candle was. She should have got to blow it out first.

"Don't cry, Mama," Tyler admonished her, noticing her eyes welling up with tears. "It's my birthday!"

His own little eyes were getting watery as he looked at her, somehow sensing her sadness. He was a very sensitive little boy, especially where Maria was concerned. He considered it his personal mission to keep her comforted.

"I'm just so happy you're here and we're able to celebrate!" she whispered. "I cannot believe you're three years old! You're so grown up now."

Their time at the retreat centre had passed in a haze. Stephanie had spent her whole life there, but Maria felt like they had just arrived. She had been trying so hard to make their little apartment into a new home, scrape up items from the donation bin, and do her utmost best gardening for the church. All the while, her children grew like beautiful, healthy plants. She was in awe of them. She wanted nothing more than to be with them. The time she had was never enough.

Yet her family garden was not complete: one of her plants was missing. Anna was like a giant uprooted tree, tearing a hole in the sod as she disappeared. No matter how tall and colourful Tyler and

Stephanie grew, the hole remained. Maria could not bring herself to fill it.

That Tyler had now grown past Anna in Maria's memory disturbed her greatly. He was the one who got to blow out the '3' candle first. He was the one who got to have a third birthday party. He got to pick out that he wanted cherries in his fruit salad, while Anna's jar of spiced apples had never been opened. Anna had never been able to read the book that Maria had picked out for her as her birthday present, nor had she been able to meet the little sister she had been excitedly hoping for. Tyler was getting to read Anna's books and wear her clothes. Soon Stephanie would grow into them.

I want my oldest daughter back. Maria swallowed a cherry and turned her attention back to Stephanie, who was crying for more fruit salad. As she tended to her, Maria wondered what it would have been like to have Anna with them. Would she have been helpful? Would she have complained about the mess Stephanie was making? Would she have fought with Tyler, making him miserable on his special day? Would she have made life too overwhelming for Maria?

I never expected to have my children alone, Step. I thought we would always be a family together.

Until coming to the retreat centre, she had never interacted much with children other than her own. Her only experience with children had been Elizabeth Lukas-Black, who had been almost too old to be considered a child when she had started talking to her. She was learning how children were supposed to interact from her own children.

I guess I had thought they would be more like trees, each growing separately, and I could take care of them one at a time.

Following the pastor's advice, she prayed quietly as they finished their fruit salad and then as she cleaned Stephanie up. Tyler purposefully put all the dishes in the dishwasher and the candle onto the counter. He seemed much more mature than the other three-year-olds that came to the retreat centre. Maria wondered if that had anything to do with his parents being robots. Would anyone say anything about him? Her anxiety rose and she started to sing a hymn about gathering at a river to calm herself. Hearing that song, Tyler took Stephanie to watch videos while Maria finished cleaning. He knew that was the signal that his mother needed some time to herself.

They look so sweet together there on the couch. Maria finally let herself cry quietly. They were her precious babies and she could not protect them. Even as she had let them interact with other members of the congregation and with other shelter residents, she still was happiest when they were together, just the three of them. Then, she could maintain the illusion that she could keep them safe.

Her phone-watch buzzed as a news bulletin appeared. The device was carefully placed over her barcode, so she was reminded that she was hiding every time she used her phone. Part of her wanted to risk trying to remove the barcode, but she had been trained that she would die if she did so. Her job as a gardener was dangerous enough already. She could not let herself get carelessly injured. Her children needed her.

The bulletin mentioned a rolling general strike had been called in the state of North Cascadia. Maria was not sure how such a thing would affect her. The retreat centre was on the outskirts of

Eastcott, the most distant of the incorporated towns in the Alexandrina metropolitan area. They already had few services. Would her plants have enough water? Would the church be able to pay her?

Forcing herself to read the story in detail, biting on her spoon and humming Shall We Gather at the River more loudly to stave off her anxiety, she saw the main reason for the strike was that workers were upset over the increased use of robots. The Robot Rental Corporation was quoted as promising citizens their services would not be interrupted.

Deciding that further cleaning could wait until later, Maria bolted from the kitchen to the couch and cuddled up beside Tyler and Stephanie.

"Are you scared, Mama?" Tyler asked. "Creature Tales isn't very scary."

"No, sweetheart, just tired. And I really want to give you a snuggle for your birthday."

She did not want to think anymore about what might happen beyond her little family simply resting on the couch.

CHAPTER EIGHT

The general strike meant that Anna had an unexpected school holiday. One sunny afternoon in late October, after a hot, dry summer, she and Patrick were enjoying spending time together at home while Tori was working at the store. The normally green courtyard was mostly brown. Several families from the block had gotten together to host a midday barbecue, so the scent of grilling meat wafted through the open patio door into the Williams-Kirke living room and kitchen. Patrick found the scent appetite-inducing, even though he thought it overly greasy, but Anna held her nose as she coloured. (Most of their neighbours felt the same way about their family's love of fish and grilled vegetables.) Taggy paced around the table, thinking that supper might be early since most of his family was home.

"I'm going to make tuna cakes out of the salad we had last night," Patrick announced, getting up from the table. "The barbecue is making me hungry."

"Not me," Anna grumbled. "That kind of meat smells icky. But I'll probably get hungry soon. Can I help you?"

"For now, you can keep colouring. Let Papa work his magic in the kitchen!"

He needed a break from reading news articles. Being a trained journalist and a freelance writer, Patrick spent a lot of time reading and getting absorbed in politics. Since the general strike had begun that week, there was nothing noteworthy to read but endless stories and opinion pieces about hardships and the merits of the whole thing. Every union had walked off the job and the initial "rolling strike" that had been called became constant. Even some non-unionized workers were quitting their jobs to protest being replaced by robots. Patrick had spent most of his courier runs dodging picket lines and marchers. He had a lot of courier runs to make, as Ninja-Cowboy had doubled its number of customers. Tori's father had long proudly touted that he refused to hire robots and therefore he was suddenly every worker's favourite CEO. Other states hired the company out of solidarity, even if their reputation in North Cascadia itself had plummeted. Many of Ninja-Cowboy's contracts had ended abruptly, with some companies and organizations outright banning them. The military had declared that none of the courier's vehicles would be allowed on their property.

Anna's first year of school had been halted after seven weeks, but her parents were grateful about that development. Over the summer, despite trying her best to be her usual gregarious self, Anna had become quiet and fearful. Her voracious reading, excellent memory, and keenness for learning had been met with resistance by her teacher, who thought she was arrogant and sassy. At their one disastrous parent-teacher meeting, not only had Anna been called "too smart," but her teacher had made it clear she felt Anna was a "rich spoiled brat with no respect," despite her strong willingness to follow rules and please others. The other students had initially wanted to be friends with Anna, but most had withdrawn from her once their teacher started expressing how much she disliked her. Only Ellie, Justin, and Grace stuck with her, to the point that the teacher had referred to them as her "minions." Anna was happy to visit with them whenever she could not be at home. She was not looking forward to going back to school.

Patrick had resisted the urge to run over Anna's former teacher when he saw her marching outside the school as he delivered parcels. He was not proud of his anger, but he could not understand why such a person was teaching young children. Anna was still only four years old. He wondered if he could officially apply to teach her at home, chuckling dryly as he remembered being a teaching assistant and how it had not been one of his most successful career paths.

"Is everybody on strike?" Anna asked as Patrick cooked. "Is that bad?"

"No, not everyone is on strike, but things aren't good right now," Patrick admitted. "Things might get worse. Hopefully not for you, though! You're going to have a great time at home! And we'll try to get you a new teacher when school starts again."

"Why aren't you and Mama on strike?"

"Mama owns a store and her employees work for her. It's a bit like how Grace, Liam, and Naomi have to do what their parents tell them to do, but you don't. The unions are like Grace's mama telling them to come inside for lunch, while Mama is like you and doesn't have to listen. It is the same for me. Your granddad runs Ninja-Cowboy and I have to work for him. We're very busy right now."

"Why is everyone so angry?"

"They're angry about robots."

Anna paused in her colouring, remembering what the police had called her old papa.

"Why are they so angry about robots? Are they going to start attacking us?" She was thinking back to being attacked by the police and how angry people might get violent, but Patrick assumed she was worried that robots might attack her.

"No! No one is going to attack us." He doubted robots could actually attack anyone, seeing as they were being drugged into docility by their food.

"But what is wrong with robots? Did they do something bad?"

"There is nothing wrong with them and I don't think they have done anything bad. They work really hard and they don't get paid for it. So people use them to save money. That means a lot of people who need money can't get work. They are angry at the robots instead of the people who buy or rent them. They shouldn't be mad at the robots, who are just doing what they are told to do."

As they sat down to eat their lunch (including Taggy, who purred as he ate some of the tuna), Patrick's phone started ringing loudly. Anna screamed and covered her ears, while Taggy glared briefly before resuming his treat.

"It's all right! That's just my emergency ring. It sounds like—-"

"A red alert on a spaceship!" Anna recognized.

"No need to be upset. Keep eating! I'll be right back." Patrick answered his phone and wandered into the living room trying hard to keep his voice quiet and calm.

That ringtone is only for when something is wrong with Tori. Whoever is calling selected it to indicate it is an emergency. She hasn't been sick enough to need that ringtone in several years.

"Hello?" he squeaked.

"Hi. Is this Patrick?" The voice on the other end was young and falsely perky, as though she had a four-year-old in the background she was trying to keep calm as well.

"Yes. Is this Desiree?"

"It's Becksy. Desiree is on the phone with the ambulance because Tori has completely passed out. She's fine right now, I mean, other than being unconscious. She's breathing okay. Can you come with her to the hospital? Do you need someone to watch Anna? My mother is probably available."

Patrick took a few seconds to compose himself.

"I'll call your mother and I'll be right there!"

Becksy's mother, who lived in the house in the other half of theirs, was over before Patrick could get his coat and shoes on. Giving Anna a quick kiss, Patrick disappeared out the door and hopped into his courier vehicle.

God, please let Tori be all right and forgive me for lying to Anna.

Despite how close the hospital was to Goat Cove, Patrick arrived at the store several minutes ahead of the ambulance. Tori was lying on her side in her office; she was covered in a blanket, which emphasised how laboured her breathing was. There was a pool of dried blood around her that Desiree had unsuccessfully tried to clean up. Becksy was helping customers and pretending nothing was amiss in the slightest, despite having a look of confusion and her voice being thready.

"What in God's name happened to her?" Patrick hissed at Desiree, hoping not to frighten the younger woman. Both of Tori's employees were around twenty years old.

"She was coughing this morning and we thought she was coming down with something. Then she started bleeding everywhere and passed out. That's all we know."

"Bleeding how?" Patrick demanded in horror. Tori seemed to be surrounded by towels.

"Like coughing and a nosebleed and cramps…nothing really unusual except a lot and all at once."

"Okay, this is new, then." Patrick waved Desiree out of the office and knelt down beside his wife. "My love, please be all right! I'm here for you, I promise. Anna is fine. Get better for her, please!"

Tori shuddered as he grabbed her shoulder but otherwise ignored him. Patrick was overcome by panic. He had never seen his wife fall completely unconscious before.

He was relieved to be able to ride in the ambulance with her, even if he was whisked away once they arrived at the hospital and he had to stand awkwardly in the middle of a busy corridor until Tori was stabilized. No one spoke to him. No one seemed to notice him much. He was as much of an obstacle as a gurney or a wheelchair. In fact, none of the workers seemed to talk much at all. It was not like how Patrick remembered the previous times he had been at the hospital with Tori, where nurses had bantered back and forth and given each other updates and instructions. Aside from the sound of equipment, the hospital was quiet.

Finally, after several hours of waiting in the corridor, a doctor remembered he was there and pulled him back toward Tori's room.

"My apologies," they muttered. "We are very short-staffed at the moment. We have received a bunch of new workers today and they don't know what they're doing."

"What's the matter with my wife?" Patrick did not care about the hospital's staffing troubles. "Is she all right?"

"She has pneumonia, which we are treating, and she is stable for now."

"Not again…" It was the third time she had been hospitalized for pneumonia since their marriage. "But she never had the other problems before."

The doctor nodded. "We found several cysts in her reproductive tract and it seems like her body was trying to get rid of them – which makes sense, considering her disordered immune system. It was so busy fighting the cysts that it missed the pneumonia. We were able to eliminate them without invasive surgery, so now she can focus on healing. She should be able to go home tonight."

They both glanced out the window at the fading after-glow of sunset.

"We see no reason to keep her much longer," the doctor added. "She will be safer from infection at home. Luckily, we caught this early."

"Is she awake?" Patrick asked.

"Yes." The doctor sounded hesitant. "Go on inside."

Patrick bolted into the room and leaned beside Tori's pillow.

"Good evening, milady," he managed to utter as her eyelids fluttered open.

"I'm sorry," she rasped. "I'm so happy to see you."

"Not as much as I am that you're awake."

"Don't ask me if I'm feeling better or anything." Tori's eyes narrowed as she shifted uncomfortably. "Everything from my waist down feels like it's been burnt."

"I think it was." Patrick was not sure, as he had not asked for too many details about how the doctor had eliminated the cysts.

"Well, yeah, I suppose." Tori laughed sarcastically. "That is what the doctor explained to me. I think they were afraid I was going to sue them."

"Oh good, they talked to you!"

"I woke up as they were in the middle of it. Didn't you hear me scream? Apparently, whoever was supposed to sedate me didn't realize it was their job. Everyone was very good otherwise."

Patrick shook his head. "I didn't hear you. Your voice is really weak."

"Oh, right!" Tori laughed again before breaking into a painful coughing fit. As she finished, she managed to wheeze out "how's Anna?"

"Carlyn is with her. Apparently, she's been colouring most of the day. She wants to make you pretty pictures to make you feel better."

At that point, a nurse came in to check on Tori's IV line. They did not speak or make eye contact with Tori or Patrick and they performed their task perfunctorily. As they reached up to check the line, Tori noticed a barcode on their wrist.

"Oh my God!" she squeaked as the nurse left. "They're all robots!"

"All of them?" Patrick wondered.

"I thought I was dreaming it, but they all had barcodes like that on their wrists. I saw a lot of wrists as they were working on me."

"I don't think the doctor…"

"No, not them! I've had them before. But everybody else is."

"That would explain how weird everyone has been acting."

"They replaced their entire staff with robots!"

"Hopefully only because of the strike."

"But look how easy it was for them. Now what?"

"I don't want to think about strikes or robots now," Patrick admitted. "I want to take you home as soon as possible so you can get a decent sleep."

It was past Anna's bedtime when her parents arrived back at their house, but she was lying awake with Taggy on the couch. Becksy had replaced her mother as Anna's caregiver and was reading stories about space travel to her.

"I want to imagine Mama is on a trip somewhere," Anna had explained when she had insisted to Becksy that they read *The Adventures of Captain Astrid Starr*. "And then she got sick from a space rock, like Captain Astrid does."

"And they both will get better," Becksy concurred. They paused to greet Tori and Patrick but resumed the story so as to keep out of their way as Patrick guided Tori upstairs. Only Taggy decided to follow them, meowing his displeasure that they had not been home to feed him his supper.

Tori could not get comfortable in bed, but she was too tired to move anymore. Walking into their house and up the stairs had exhausted her burnt lower body, even though she had been dropped off as close to the door as possible. She was stuck in one position on the bed, propped up by pillows, and her muscles spasmed every time she coughed.

She could hear Patrick getting Anna ready for bed after Becksy left. The little girl was trying hard not to cry as she asked her father questions. Patrick's voice was too low for Tori to hear his answers, but he must have been doing a satisfactory job because Anna did not sound frustrated or repeat herself.

Tori tried to focus on the photos of Anna at Easter, but her eyes were too tired to focus that far ahead. She commanded the lights to turn off completely then tried her best to doze.

"Are you asleep yet, Mama?" Anna's concerned voice wafted through the closed door. "I made something for you. Can I come in and say goodnight?"

"Yes, come in, sweetheart," Tori rasped and coughed. "Mama wants to see you very much."

Anna tiptoed quickly into the bedroom as Tori raised the lighting. She was wearing a mask and carrying several sheets of paper. She instinctively went to climb onto the bed before pausing awkwardly, realizing that she might hurt her mother if she did so.

"It's okay – you can come up here with me." Tori pointed to the step-stool at the end of the bed. "Just use that, instead of jumping. Mama can't take being bounced."

Anna nodded and followed her instructions.

"I want to show you the drawings I made for you," she explained.

"Oh, yes, sweetie – come right beside me and tell me about them!" Tori grabbed a mask to cover her own face, despite being fairly sure Anna would not get pneumonia. She then weakly hugged her daughter, eager to escape into the world of her imagination for a couple minutes.

One of the drawings was of the three of them – Anna, Tori, and Patrick – on the beach at Lake Hobidigan. Anna had added Taggy to the corner, explaining to her mother that he was happy to be at the lake because there were lots of birds there for him to watch. She had drawn many flying squiggles and waterfowl, which undoubtedly Taggy would have enjoyed stalking until he realized how big gulls and geese actually were.

The second drawing was of three big flowers in a garden of smaller plants, while the third drawing was of "Mama and her books" as Anna explained. It was of Tori in her bookstore, wearing a regal gown and sparkling tiara with what appeared to be a fluffy feather-duster in her hand.

"Am I cleaning up the books?" Tori asked.

Anna nodded and pointed to the stars she had drawn amid the books and other merchandise.

"Yes, and those are the little angels that are helping you!"

"Well, hopefully they will help me get better so that I can get back to the books."

"Are you sad because you're sick?" Anna asked, snuggling delicately beside her mother.

"I've been sick so much that I get used to it, but yes, I do get sad about being sick," Tori admitted. "I can't do anything about it, but it's still sad."

"But Grace said that when she had to stay home sick from school, it was a lot of fun."

"Well, being sick isn't very fun when you grow up, or when you're sick a lot, like I am."

"When will I get sick?" Anna asked.

Tori shook her head. She kept waiting for something to happen to her daughter. It seemed wrong that Anna had never even warranted a doctor's visit except for regular check-ups. She had so far remained unscathed whenever an illness would break out among her friends or schoolmates. Tori still fully expected her to completely collapse with multiple organ failures, just like she had as a young child.

"I don't know, sweetheart. Some people hardly ever get sick, while some people do a lot, like me."

"Yeah, but I've *never* been sick! Never, not ever! Grace had a sore throat and got lollipops every day!"

“Oh, sweetie, it’s not worth getting sick just for a lollipop.”

“Did Papa give you a lollipop because you’re sick?”

“No, no lollipops for me.” At the mere thought of sucking on hard candy, Tori started to violently cough.

Anna recoiled in horror as Tori spat gunk into her mask. Patrick flung open the bedroom door and gestured for Anna to leave.

“Come, let me read you another bedtime story,” he offered. “Can I get you anything, Tori?”

“No,” Tori managed to gargle. “Thank you very much for sharing these lovely pictures, Anna!”

Gently squeezing Anna’s hand as she left, Tori laid back against her pillows and turned the lights off again.

Whatever medication she had taken finally allowed her to doze off. She dreamt of dusting books at the store, flying around like an angel and spinning dizzily as Desiree and Becksy looked on in horror. Taggy was chasing seagulls and geese, having grown to the size of a bobcat or even a cougar. (She realized later he must have pounced on her while she slept, since he was lying on her sore legs when she woke up.) Hands with barcodes on their wrists poked, prodded, scanned, and ran lasers into her. They were stabbing her with a laser and then she realized a younger version of herself was pushing the buttons, pleading to get her daughter back.

Waking up in acute pain, she weakly got out of bed and stumbled to the toilet. Patrick was asleep on the bed next to her, having moved Anna’s drawings but not changed into pyjamas or gone under the covers.

I'm sorry I exhausted you so much, my dearest husband. You truly are a wonderful man. Thank you for being you. Thank you for taking care of us.

He was awake when she returned to the bed.

"Are you sure you should be up?"

Tori gave him a look of exasperation. "I needed to use the toilet. I feel bad enough without soiling myself."

"Next time, wake me up, at least. I could help you."

"I really want to do this on my own, please."

It was Patrick's turn to cry. "I'm sorry. This all scared me so much. I really thought you were going to die. You look and sound like you still might. Everything is just so crazy!"

Tori nodded, slowly easing herself back into her awkwardly comfortable propped position.

"Yeah, having all those robots at the hospital was really weird," she whispered. "And I *am* going to die someday. You'll probably outlive me."

"Not yet."

"We'll get through this. Me getting sick, I mean, and Anna's school troubles. But I don't know how this strike is going to go."

"I'm trying not to wonder how many robots are replacing strikers everywhere. The ones at the hospital were perfectly competent, except for whoever forgot to sedate you."

"They probably thought I was still too unconscious. To their credit, somebody improvised a way to calm me through the pain."

"A robot improvised?"

"Yeah, almost like they'd been trained in being a doula or something, or had experience with other types of serious injuries. I wondered if they had been reassigned from another unit. They looked really familiar, but I couldn't place them. But they had a barcode too."

"I'm afraid for them," Patrick admitted. "There is so much violence at the rallies and protests and on picket lines. It wouldn't take much for crowds to attack the robots being forced to do replacement work."

"And they would be drugged and helpless to fight back," Tori realized, leaning back into her pillows. "I'd be pulp in the street now."

"For all we know, we *are* pulp in the street now. Or at least, people who look like us."

"I hope not, even if it did mean we got more kids. I especially hope there aren't more of us than Step and Maria."

"I'm still wondering how they even got our genetics in the first place. How old did Step say he was?"

"Eight, but they probably took your profile earlier than that. They'd have had to do something with it."

"I don't remember ever giving the Robot Rental Corporation anything. Did they buy it from a blood bank or health clinic? I'm pretty sure that's illegal."

"Well, cloning is illegal, so they must have misrepresented why they wanted it." Tori suddenly remembered being asked to contribute to a research project during one of her many hospital stays. "What horrible people!"

"Hmm?" Patrick asked, settling properly into bed.

"They said they wanted to research a cure for me! About ten, no, eleven years ago? I think it was before we started dating. I was asked to provide a tonne of DNA samples. It was all supposed to be for research into my illness, or so I thought. So they could treat me better."

"Was this a medical research company?"

"I thought so, but it could have been an arm of the Robot Rental Corporation, couldn't it? And it would be a legitimate way to get what they wanted."

Tori started to cry in rage.

"They preyed on my hope of getting better and all they wanted was to have DNA for their robots! They even figured out a way to cure me and instead of doing that, they created a whole new person. And they never even helped me!"

Patrick almost added they probably had thought she would die quickly, but thought that would only make her more upset. "I'm trying to remember if I ever had a run-in with a medical research company. Maybe one came to campus while I was a student?"

"Despite feeling like a mud puddle, I want to bash the CEO of the Robot Rental Corporation's head in!"

"If I weren't so tired, I would go do it."

"This strike is going to backfire and the robots are going to be the ones left to suffer."

"But maybe the Corporation's actions will be exposed," Patrick offered. "I'm going to sleep now but wake me up if you need me."

Tori whispered good night to him but lay awake in the darkness, feeling helpless and trapped.

INTERLUDE 7

The barracks of the Robot Rental Corporation were understaffed at Christmas. It was an arrogant choice on the Corporation's part, but it reflected their general assumptions about the robots. Robots were docile, obedient, and compliant. Robots were self-absorbed. Robots would not even notice how many human staff there were, even though they were fairly distinctive in their appearance and mannerisms. As well as their lack of barcodes, they were required to wear more formal clothing and encouraged to be as condescending to the robots as possible. They had varying hairstyles, instead of the more practical cropped hair that robots had. They openly laughed and joked with each other, often at the robots' expense.

We notice this now. Step and Nola had managed to start talking to other robots and gradually, they were waking up to their humanity. Once they had managed to convince the robots who prepared all the barracks' meals to stop adding the drug formula to the food – or rather, wean everyone off of it over several months, they planned to take over the complex. Christmas was the perfect opportunity.

The non-robot staff was very few in number on Christmas Eve, but they insisted on having the kitchen robots cook them a full holiday supper. They decorated their staff room with bright, sparkling decorations, played obnoxious music loudly, had some of the robots wait on them, and brought in synthetic alcohol. On one hand, Step sympathized with them for trying to make the best of being trapped at the barracks over what he imagined was a holiday most people wanted to spend with family and friends. He wanted to be with Maria and their children.

And this is the only way I am ever going to get to celebrate Christmas with them again.

While the supper began in the staff room, Step, Nola, their three roommates, and about thirty other robots waited outside the door with improvised weapons. However, they did not anticipate using them, as the entire meal had been filled with the robot formula. Step was excited to find out how it would work on non-robot humans. As he waited, he started dancing to the music, much to the amusement of his peers.

"Are we supposed to be enjoying this?" asked his roommate, who had chosen the name Isaac. Isaac had been trained as a security guard and military reservist. Most of the robots in the corridor with them were from his unit and dancing while waiting had not been part of their programming.

"You said we're supposed to 'hurry up and wait,'" Nola pointed out. She joined Step in dancing in a childlike manner. "Might as well not get too tense while we wait."

"And the music is meant to be danced to," Step offered. "We are humans, so we can dance."

"Do we just move rhythmically to the beat?" their other female roommate wondered. She had settled on the name Scarlett. "I've never danced before."

"Yeah, that's one kind of dancing," Step explained. "The easiest kind." Like my kids used to do. They didn't even care if they were on beat.

"It's kind of fun," Nola admitted, taking Scarlett's free hand in hers so they could dance together. "But what is a reindeer and why would a deer have a glowing red nose?"

"Maybe his mother ate a lot of fireflies while pregnant," Step joked.

"That's not how that works," Nola protested.

"Yeah, I know that," Step laughed, winking at her. "But I have no idea about the red-nosed reindeer."

"Reindeer also don't fly," Isaac added. "I've been reading up on all kinds of deer species and not a single one of them has evolved the capability of flight."

Step wanted to explain what fantasy and magic were, but he felt that no one in his newfound family (other than maybe Nola) was ready for that yet.

"Can we not distract ourselves by analyzing silly songs?" Ren whispered harshly. He was their fifth roommate who had often finished Step's food. Like Isaac, he was a military robot, and like Step, he was trained in mechanics. He had picked his name based on how pleasant but efficient it sounded.

"If all goes well, we will have plenty of time to do that later," one of the other military robots added.

The sound of laughter and chatter from inside the staff room quickly dissipated as the effects of the drugged food overcame its occupants, but the music kept playing loudly. The robots who had been serving the food unlocked the door for Step and his team, who cautiously made their way inside.

Step was unsure whether to laugh or be sick. The bodies of the staff members had collapsed peacefully at the table, having shoved aside their food and drink to sleep soundly at their place settings. A few beverages had spilled, but everyone looked as though they had decided to take a nap. They were all in fancy clothing – fancier than usual – and the food had barely been touched.

"Clearly, whatever works to keep us controlled is just a heavy sedative in normal humans," one of the serving robots remarked, jumping in to clear away the table. "We didn't even put that much in the supper!"

"Well, hopefully they all just have a good sleep, not a permanent one," Step muttered. "We want them alive to tell others what happened. No killing!"

"Yeah, we get that part," Isaac grumbled. "Though I don't think humans would be so lenient with us. Or will be."

"We're human," Nola reminded him. "They just don't know that yet."

"I don't think this is going to convince them," Isaac pointed out.

"I'll make them understand!" Nola insisted.

"Not killing them will make our case for humanity and thus human rights and freedom more convincing. Come on, we don't know how long they'll sleep for! Tie them up!" Step ordered. "Tie them up, find their coats, and let's get them to the road!"

"Why bother with their coats?" someone asked.

"Because it's freezing out! There's a chance of snow."

"It doesn't matter which coats," Nola added. "Just wrap them up in any coat that fits them."

The team worked quickly to tie up or handcuff each staff member and put a coat around them before carrying them out the front gate to the road that led either to River-Gold Park and into the Alexandrina metropolitan area or further off toward the military base. In an extra bid to keep the staff warm, they laid them together in the ditch. In all the hurry, no one bothered to turn off the music. Instead, someone decided to blare it through the loudspeakers in the courtyard.

While most of the robots dealt with the staff, Step coordinated getting rid of the drug-laced food. Not only did they need to get rid of the food, he explained to the servers and kitchen robots, but they needed to get rid of any of that drug in the kitchens. They would keep some of it in the infirmary for medical purposes only. He thanked the protagonist of his new book (whether or not they were real) that the Corporation had been so arrogant and cheap that they had let the kitchen robots know the drug's formula.

"It was just part of our instructions," Rina, one of the main cooks, explained. "We added it to the food like we were told. We thought it was normal."

Of course you did. You all thought this whole operation was normal. We're just robots. This was our lot in life. We needed to eat.

The barracks was part of a giant complex that also included gardens, orchards, insect farms, small fields of grain, and many laboratories. Most of the workers at the complex were robots, including those who tended to the vats where new robots were grown. Step and Nola led a contingent of robots into these vast storerooms, making sure the systems were left running to keep the growing children alive.

"What's going on here?" a lone robot nanny demanded. "Why are you coming in here? Are you going to hurt us?"

"Why would you think that?" Rina asked. "We came to make sure the kids are safe."

"No one ever comes in here without an appointment unless it is an emergency," the nanny countered. "There is no emergency. All the equipment is running fine. No one is going to start breathing air tonight."

"The emergency is we're taking over the barracks," Nola insisted. "Not that that changes anything in here right now."

"What has happened?"

"The representatives from the Robot Rental Corporation have left us," Step reiterated. "We have taken over managing the barracks."

As soon as he had finished speaking, an alarm system sounded.

"Security perimeter has been established! All gates are locked! No one may enter or exit the building without management codes!"

Step grinned. "Luckily, we've got those."

Nola gave Rina a kiss and hugged Step. Someone in the main control room put the Christmas music on all the loudspeakers to the point that it almost drowned out the alarm. Except for a very confused nanny, the robots danced.

Oh the weather outside is frightful,
But the fire is so delightful,
And since we've no place to go,
Let it snow, let it snow, let it snow!

CHAPTER NINE

Anna, Tori, and Patrick came home from church on Christmas Eve and almost immediately settled into bed. While it had been a peaceful service, Tori and Anna's feet had both frozen, leading to them being in tears as they tried to smile at everyone's Christmas wishes. Patrick had finally picked Anna up and let her cry into the hood of his coat as Tori hobbled along behind them.

"Why couldn't we take one of the vans?" Anna asked.

"Our church is the closest church to our co-op compared to the ones our neighbours go to, so other families rented them. And we couldn't take my courier vehicle because it would be too uncomfortable for Mama."

My wife has aged three decades in a month, Patrick thought to himself, trying to slow down his pace to allow her to keep up. Tori had a pair of cane-like walking poles and most of her hair had turned grey. While she had fully recovered from pneumonia, she still suffered ill effects from her hasty surgery. She could no longer walk without experiencing sharp pain, which her frozen feet only magnified. Patrick winced as she softly whimpered at each step.

Understandably, the rest of their celebrations that evening were short. Patrick was soon alone in the kitchen with Taggy, sipping whiskey and putting the finishing touches on the breakfast casserole for the next morning. The cat purred as he lapped up bits of juicy ham rind.

Everything is ready for tomorrow. Tori won't have to worry about anything. She can just put the pie in the oven after the casserole is done. Patrick wiped away tears and leaned against the counter, pouring himself another glass as he stared at the lights on the Christmas tree. He wanted them to have a happy Christmas together. Anna was four and wanted fun and magic. Tori wanted to get through all the rituals they had established. All of them, including Taggy, wanted scrumptious treats.

"Every Christmas could be our last, Taggy," he muttered, philosophising to the cat. "I want us to enjoy it."

At some point, he noticed his phone alerts buzzing softly. His curiosity got the better of him and he decided to investigate them. It was rare to have news alerts on holidays.

"'Police investigating possible unauthorized military activity near River-Gold Park,'" he read aloud to Taggy. "Well, that's not really news, is it? That's where the base is."

The cat stared at him, seemingly pleading with him to go to bed.

"Oh, Taggy-boos, you're right! I'm getting too addicted to these articles. This stupid strike is only getting worse. I'm sick of it. Sick of everything!"

Taggy mewed and slunk toward the stairs.

"Yeah, you're right again, I'm not sick. Tori is. We've got to take care of her, little man. Let's go to bed!"

He was startled to find his wife still lying awake, watching a projection on the wall of travelling through stars.

"Merry Christmas, milady!" He gave her a soft kiss on the ear. "Love you! Can I get you anything?"

"You didn't bring me anything to drink?" she joked, noting his breath.

"You mentioned it was causing you trouble with your medicine lately." Patrick slid under the covers and snuggled up beside her.

"Well, it sounds like you're up to the task of drinking alone. Ouch! No, please, don't touch me!"

"Sorry, right, burning pain everywhere, I forgot," Patrick rolled away. "Is that why you're watching stars?"

"Among other reasons, yeah. I need something to distract myself. I don't want to go to my dad's for supper tomorrow."

"Then let's not go. We have casserole for brunch and pies for dessert. I'll whip up a nice supper so Anna is happy. We can take her to visit another time when they haven't got fourteen other people there."

"Those fourteen other people are counting on us to bring them pie," Tori muttered. "Might as well take it to them."

"Anna and I will take the pies and your dad can take Christmas photos with her opening presents for posterity. You can rest here and we'll have supper together afterward."

That's why I love you so much, Patrick. Tori shut off the starry projection and slowly snuggled into her husband.

"Don't try to touch me – let me do the moving." She kissed him passionately, enjoying the taste of whiskey. "Follow my lead."

When Patrick and Anna brought two homemade pies to Mike and Cleo Martinez-Williams's downtown penthouse suite the following day, they received more than enough food in return for three servings of turkey supper. Anna brought her grandparents the gifts she had picked out for them, as well as many drawings; in turn, she opened her gifts from her doting grandparents and several of their guests. Tori's parents took several posed photos of themselves with Anna and her drawings, as they wanted to de-emphasize the pile of presents under the tree.

"We're supposed to be friends of the workers and ordinary folk," Mike Martinez-Williams had insisted. "Let's show off drawings and homemade pie."

Considering that both he and Anna had their arms full of gifts coming home, Patrick wondered how he was going to explain hypocrisy to his daughter. He hoped she was too young to understand how insensitive her grandparents were acting. Anna did not need two dozen more toys and pieces of clothing when they could help other children. He was relieved to rejoin Tori and Taggy, who had napped most of the afternoon.

As they ate supper, listening to Christmas music on their screen (which amusingly meant they had an image of a fireplace playing above their actual imitation fireplace and the fires were blazing out of sync), a news bulletin started playing. Tori and Patrick could hear alerts on their phones, but they ignored them. They soon noticed the music from the screen faded and was replaced with the worried sound of a newsreader.

"What happened to the music?" Anna asked, whirling her head toward the living room but unable to see the screen. She turned back towards her parents in confusion. "Why did you stop eating?"

Patrick stood up from the table and went to see what the news was about, sheepishly excusing himself.

"You two stay there for the moment." He tried not to sound concerned as he silently read the headline.

ROBOT RENTAL CORPORATION FACTORY AND WAREHOUSES HIJACKED!

"Oh dear," he managed to be polite. "Something bad has happened at the Robot Rental Corporation."

"Jesus wept," Tori muttered.

"Did you make a cherry-peach pie again, Mama?" Anna asked her, tired of waiting for the music to restart.

"Yes, I saved that one for us!" Tori turned her attention back to Anna and their supper. "While Papa watches the news, you and I are going to start cleaning up and get the pie ready."

I want to go watch the news, but I don't want to frighten Anna. We've had enough scary things already. I hope Step is all right.

Patrick listened as the newsreader explained about the factory and warehouse complex on the edge of River-Gold State Park. It was where robots were housed, fed, repaired, and allowed to rest. He thought back to Step's description of the place, which he had neutrally referred to as "barracks," and he could not decide whether it resembled a school, storage facility, or prison.

"There was only a small staff contingent who remained at the facility over Christmas Eve," the reader continued. "They were overwhelmed by hundreds of robots and were easily neutralized. They were rendered unconscious and tied up outside the compound's gates, and they were refused reentry once they woke up."

The images of the employees show them dressed up for a party. If they were worried about being attacked, having a celebration seems unwise.

"Robots have cleared the grounds of all human personnel and only returning robots are being allowed into the complex." Behind the reporter, several workers in grey overalls were shown entering through the main gate. A police officer tried to prevent them from going in, but he was stunned by a remote laser and collapsed.

"It was almost like some kind of uprising or something," an interviewed employee answered in bewilderment.

That's because it was an uprising, you idiot! Patrick rolled his eyes. *Overpowering guards, throwing them out, and taking control of a territory would be considered an uprising.*

The story began airing archival videos and images of the Robot Rental Corporation's various offices as well as docile robots working. The Corporation released previously classified images from inside the complex that depicted the robots eating in a giant dining hall, rooms that appeared to be some kind of dormitory (though the beds reminded Patrick of microwave ovens), and the front entrance in the late spring with lovely gardens.

The robots were only distinguishable from non-robots by their overalls, haircuts, and mannerisms. Their wrist barcodes were not visible. Patrick instinctively looked for Step but saw no one that resembled him.

Should I be relieved that I don't see him? I hope he is safely inside. But what if the military is called in?

"What's happening?" Anna asked, wandering into the living room to call her father in for dessert. "It's time for pie and ice cream!"

"Just the news, sweetie!" Patrick stood up abruptly and attempted to steer her back to the table. "Things are always happening in the news, even on Christmas."

"Why are they being so mean?" she asked, noticing the video of staff having a shouting match with returning robots.

"They're angry, that's all." He muted the screen and turned on a datapad to play more music.

"But it's Christmas! Why are they angry on Christmas?"

"Well, they are cold," Patrick answered simply. *That is probably true, at least.* "Let's forget the news for tonight and enjoy our scrumptious pie!"

"Here's the pie and ice cream!" Tori announced joyfully, slamming the ice cream bucket onto the table.

Anna and Patrick scrambled back into their chairs.

"Why are there four plates?" Patrick asked his wife as she began to cut the pie.

"One's for Taggy," Tori answered. "He's been begging for ice cream and it's Christmas."

She placed heaping mounds of ice cream onto the generous slices of pie, serving one for each of the three of them. Then she plopped a small dollop of ice cream onto the remaining plate and sat it in front of the cat. Taggy appeared quite pleased at his gift and mewed excitedly in thanks, trilling and rubbing at Tori's ankles before dipping his tongue into the ice cream, purring contentedly. He did not care about news bulletins.

After supper, Patrick took Anna upstairs to read one of her new books together. Tori was left to slowly clear the dishes, though she decided to leave the bulk of the kitchen clean-up until the next day.

Overcome with curiosity, she went to the screen to watch the news report. It was still muted and the subtitles were woefully inadequate, but Tori was able to ignore them after a couple of minutes and focus on the images. The videos were looping over and over, with the occasional update from the reporter near the entrance to the complex. By now, everyone was encamped further away from the entrance and there was no longer anything to add or see. Police vehicles roared past the journalists, heading up to the complex and ignoring requests to stop or give information.

Tori found the archival videos mesmerising. The robots obediently and quietly went about their routines. They were all in grey or navy blue jumpsuit overalls – Step, in his camouflage overalls, was nowhere to be seen. The robots seemed androgynous; only certain physical characteristics made them stand out as male or female. None of them acted differently.

They were all socialized the same way. No one raised them as boys or girls. They all have practical short haircuts.

Their eyes were sullen, if they had any expression at all. Most of them showed no emotion. They were drugged and going about their regular routines. They were fulfilling what they thought were their purposes in life.

I wonder if I would recognize any of them? Step and Maria have our genetics. Surely the other robots also have unwitting genetic donors. Tori tried to identify if any of the robots seemed familiar, but none did.

As she watched, she thought she heard Patrick come back downstairs and go into the kitchen.

"Patrick?" she called out. "I'll finish up the rest of the tidying tomorrow."

When she did not hear a response, she went back into the kitchen and realized the room was empty.

"Patrick? Where are you?"

She circled the main floor and was about to go upstairs when she caught a glimpse of a shape wandering in the courtyard between the houses. Tori recognised her husband as he stepped in and out of the porchlight beams. To anyone else, he would have appeared to be stargazing, but Tori noticed how tense and aimless he seemed.

Calling out his name again, she followed him outside. Neither of them had a coat on. Tori had hurriedly slid on her foam sandals that she used for quick runs out to the compost or recycling, while Patrick was only in his slippers.

“Are you all right? Where are you going?”

The only response she got was him glancing back at her. He was attempting in vain to seem stoic, but his facade quickly crumbled at seeing her trying hard to reach him. She was still wincing at every step and had forgotten her cane.

Tori stopped, slipping slightly in the wet grass. While it had snowed at the complex near River-Gold State Park, it had only rained in Goat Cove. She managed to right herself, but the effort to do so made her whole body feel like it was on fire. She blinked to keep from crying.

For what felt like hours (though it was only about the length of time it took a neighbour to sort their refuse), the two of them stood still, staring into one another’s eyes. Neither of them wanted to move closer: her in confusion and pain, him in despair. They were illuminated by the light in the centre of the courtyard. Both were in tears.

“Where are you going?” Tori managed to repeat. Though her tone was demanding, she was more shocked than upset. Patrick had never walked out of the house randomly before. She was the unpredictable one, not him.

He only shook his head and turned back toward the picnic tables. He broke into a run and suddenly threw himself into the air, kicking at one of the benches. The force of hitting it flung him backwards onto the grass and he landed awkwardly, befitting his clumsy and uncoordinated nature.

“Patrick!” Tori shouted for what felt like the dozenth time. “Are you all right?”

Groaning, he managed to pull himself into a comfortable sitting position as she slowly made her way to him.

"No, I'm very bruised." Patrick started laughing ruefully. "I showed that picnic table how strong I am, didn't I?"

His laughter turned into outright sobbing, which was rare for him to do anywhere but in the privacy of their house.

"Oh, my love, I'm sorry!" Tori joined him in crying. "This was a terrible time for me to get sick. I've always bounced back better! And now everything is worse…"

"Let's get back inside. We're going to freeze out here!" Patrick stood up and wobbled slightly before hugging Tori. "I'll walk as slowly as you need me to."

They walked back toward their kitchen door, taking their time and paying no attention to how cold they were. They kept crying, feeling comforted by each other and the darkness. Finally, they hobbled back into the house and curled up together on the couch, turning off the screen and music.

They were left with the brilliant lights on the Christmas tree and the roaring artificial fire. Taggy had gone upstairs to be with Anna and both were likely asleep, as the house was nearly silent. Tori delicately snuggled close to Patrick, making sure to avoid hurting herself, and focused her eyes on the fireplace.

"You have nothing to be sorry about," Patrick whispered, kissing her head. "I'm the one who selfishly feels like he is losing control of everything."

"I thought you handled everything well."

"Well, I thought I was fine. I can handle Anna at home, I can handle this horrible and useless strike, and I can handle you being sick. But then…this…what's even happened? Are all the robots that were filling in for the strikers going to stop working? Will the strikers get what they want? Will the robots?"

"I hope Step is okay," Tori finally said aloud. "I didn't see him at all."

"We didn't see much of the actual robots now. It was mostly old video footage and maybe it was from before he was captured. Do you think he is involved?"

"What do you mean?"

"You gave him books to read. You gave him one of the most influential books from the past twenty-one hundred years. Maybe he was inspired."

"Are you seriously saying that God inspired the robots to rise up?"

"Well, why not? Doesn't he ultimately inspire everything? But maybe we had a hand in it, too. That could be interesting if your dad finds out."

"I think my dad will be far more concerned that the Robot Rental Corporation made twins of us! He'll probably think of a whole propaganda campaign around it."

"I think a lot of people will be concerned about the cloning thing!"

"I couldn't help it. When I was watching earlier, I kept looking to see if any of the robots were familiar. I didn't see any that I recognized, though."

"Me neither, but if they used our DNA, they must have used others'. Those robots all have non-robot counterparts somewhere. Some are probably dead, but probably not most of them."

"Well, if our story gets out, other people will start asking questions about the robots."

"I hope they succeed," Patrick muttered. "The robots, I mean. Moreso than the strikers, I hope they get what they want."

"If the robots are people, then they have every right to jobs. This is going to be a mess." Tori shut her eyes and buried her face in her blanket.

"Merry Christmas to us all! I'm going to pour myself a drink."

"I'll join you. I'll regret it, but I'll join you."

"Let's have a toast. God help us all! Everyone, robots included."

INTERLUDE 8

The first Noel, the angel did say,
Was to certain poor shepherds in fields as they lay.
In fields where they lay, a-keeping their sheep,
On a cold winter's night that was so deep.

"Trinity and Mercy have really pretty voices," Tyler whispered to his mother as they took in the Christmas morning service. He gestured to the two young teenage sisters singing on stage.

"Yes, but you did a great job with *Silent Night*," she reassured him. Tyler had opened the morning service with a rendition of that hymn. The congregation – sparse as it was on Christmas morning compared to the night before – had been thrilled with the three-year-old's beautiful singing voice.

The pastor seemed unusually nervous as she took to the pulpit.

"Well, good morning and Merry Christmas, everyone!"

The congregation answered with a joyful "Merry Christmas," but the pastor still seemed out of sorts.

"I had a whole sermon planned, but I heard some news this morning and I just can't give it."

What happened? Maria looked around at the people in the pews, all of whom seemed bewildered.

"My niece…well, I can't say that I agree with her place of employment, but she is my niece nonetheless. My brother called to tell me that she is in hospital."

There was a chorus of "Lord have mercy" and "God bless her." Maria hugged Stephanie tightly as Tyler hugged her arm.

"Apparently, she was drugged last night and then got severe hypothermia. I was confused because I thought she was working, not going to a party. But her workplace…"

The church secretary climbed up to join the pastor.

"Tell us where she works, Rev. Helen," they coaxed her.

"She works at the Robot Rental Corporation's big warehouse and factory, up by River-Gold Park. It hasn't been a dangerous place so far. People have been protesting in town, not up there. Like I said, I don't approve of the place. But last night, all the employees, from the managers down to the lowly young workers like my niece, who is barely older than Trinity here, were drugged and placed outside the complex. Locked out of it."

Stephanie screamed as Maria squeezed her too tightly, but her annoyance and discomfort were masked by the many gasps from the congregation.

"You mean, like higher-ups locked them out?" the secretary asked.

"I don't know – my brother didn't say. Could have been. Could have been the robots."

What? Maria was dumbfounded. *How would we do that? We're the ones who are drugged all the time.*

She glanced at Trinity and Mercy, who were sitting with their mother further down the pew from her. They were all staring at the pastor with wide eyes.

"Okay, well, shall I give your sermon, Rev. Helen?"

The pastor nodded and stepped down, wandering completely out of the sanctuary in a fog of confusion. The secretary took a quick glance at the notes in the pulpit and launched into the sermon, using their talent for improvisation to deliver a compelling and reassuring message about the hope that Jesus Christ's

Incarnation brought to the world. At the time, Maria did find the sermon reassuring as intended, but she could not remember any of the content within it after the secretary returned to their chair. Trinity and Mercy led everyone in one more hymn and the pastor returned to lead the closing prayer.

Normally, Maria found *Joy to the World* to be an uplifting song, but its lyrics felt ominous as she hurried out of church with Tyler and Stephanie. She muttered a lot of quick "Merry Christmases" as she made her way back to their tiny apartment in the shelter. It was not a long walk to it from the church building, but she was anxious to get the three of them into the perceived safety of their home. Every person, icy patch, or distraction for her children was an obstacle to be overcome.

She locked the screen door and pulled the curtain across it, disappointing as it was to lose the natural light when there was so little of it in December. Tyler and Stephanie stood dumbfounded in the middle of the apartment's main room as Maria set about closing every curtain. When she was done, she wrapped them up in blankets on the couch and sat down with them, shivering and sobbing.

Stephanie wriggled in indignation, but Tyler hugged his mother tightly, remembering how his mother had hidden them in their house after his father and older sister had disappeared. He recalled the darkness and the endless sitting on the couch.

"What's wrong now, Mama?" he asked. "Please don't tell me bad guys are coming after us again! I like it here."

"Bad guys?" Stephanie squeaked.

"No, no, we should be safe here. We have been safe here for your whole life, Stephanie! But Mama is scared like Rev. Helen was scared today. Rev. Helen couldn't give her sermon and Mama had to come home and lock up everything."

"Why are you and Rev. Helen scared?" Tyler asked. "What happened?"

"Someone got hurt that Rev. Helen loves very much. She works at the same place that I think your papa was taken to. So I am scared that Papa might be hurt too."

"And Anna," Tyler added.

"Well, yes, I'm always scared about Anna, but I don't think Anna is at that place. She is still too little to work there."

God, please don't let them be holding her there to experiment on her!

Maria involuntarily cried harder.

"Mama, I'm squished," Stephanie whimpered.

"Let's watch *Creature Tales*," Tyler offered, pulling himself away from their mother to start the datapad for them. "We can watch their new Christmas special."

"Oh, right, I was going to make you hot chocolate for that!" Maria remembered, wiping her eyes. "I'll go do that now. Hot chocolate and caramel corn!"

Once the children were engrossed in the video and their treats, Maria pulled up her phone-watch and realized she had not turned it back on after church. As she did so, it started buzzing as dozens of articles popped up about the "incident at the warehouse complex."

They actually think it was the robots? The robots somehow shook off their drugged food and turned it against the workers? What are they going to do now?

She scoured through every photo and video for Step, but there was nothing of him. There were few recent photos or videos from the barracks and the only robots visible from the road were those who had formerly worked as security guards and police officers themselves. They aimed weapons at anyone who tried to get back into the complex.

They've taken over the barracks. Robots have taken charge of a huge, self-sufficient complex. They should be able to survive for a long time if the military doesn't come to destroy them...which they might, being close by.

Eastcott was far from River-Gold State Park. The small, impoverished municipality had taken charge of itself since the strike had begun two months earlier. There had been very few robots in their neighbourhood because the town could not afford them. Instead, people had volunteered to keep services running. With no shortages of power or water, Maria had been able to keep the church's gardens alive and thriving.

But no one knew she was a robot. The police had not bothered looking for a stray robot whenever they made their patrols through the community. If they had noticed her, they must have assumed the church had bought or rented her, leaving her to her work. Nonetheless, she kept to the retreat centre grounds, ordering groceries to be delivered. Before the strike, she had occasionally ventured to the library and thrift shop, but now she did not even feel comfortable going to houses of parishioners. With a lot of trepidation, she still sometimes let Trinity and Mercy take her children on outings or go to their house. Her children would not raise anyone's suspicions. They were ordinary toddlers.

Maria could not forget her early life at the barracks. It was a gigantic, self-sufficient complex. The robots would have all the water, energy, food, and supplies they would need to last several months. Would the military simply destroy it with weapons?

Would the Robot Rental Corporation let them do that? How much power did the Corporation actually have? Would the potential environmental catastrophe from attacking the complex, which was in a forest beside a state park, be enough of a deterrent?

Step, where are you? What are you doing? Take care of yourself, please! You've got to make it back to us. I need you!

Looking at their children on the couch, Maria poured herself a festive bubbly apple juice. It reminded her of Anna. Apples had been her favourite fruit, while Tyler's was cherries. Stephanie adored grapes.

"Where are you, my sweet little apple?" she whispered. "I hope you are having a wonderful Christmas, wherever you are. Lord, keep her safe."

When the video ended, Tyler brought the empty caramel corn bowl to his mother.

"We can stay here, right?"

"Of course, sweetheart." She regretted scaring him.

"Can we at least go outside? Have the windows open?"

Maria nodded, smiling through her tears.

"In the morning, yes. We'll open the windows."

CHAPTER TEN

While the Williams-Kirke home and Tori's store in Goat Cove were as far from River-Gold State Park as a neighbourhood could be while still being part of Alexandrina's metropolitan territory, the effects of the uprising at the Robot Rental Corporation's warehouse complex spilled out across the region as winter continued. Their district in North Cascadia was put under martial law and border security was increased, supposedly to keep the other Cascadian states and the North Cascadian hinterland free of strike activity. International news reports were perplexed at how what had seemed like one of the safest and most advanced countries in the world had fallen into such civil unrest. Patrick read through these articles with dismay as he negotiated increasing security checkpoints on his delivery routes, while Tori tried to hide in her store and pretend nothing was amiss as she offered books about hope and peace.

Within the Alexandrina metropolis, chaos soon erupted as strikers regularly clashed with the increasing police presence. The Robot Rental Corporation shuffled their remaining robots (those who had not been at the warehouse at Christmas) between their smaller facilities, meaning that service providers and companies were stretched to fill their complement of workers to mitigate the effects of the strike. These robots raised the ire of striking workers and some took the opportunity to attack them at their worksites. The Robot Rental Corporation then vehemently defended their robots, as they were their precious products, and called in the military to come in to protect them. This led to the bizarre sight of construction sites and garbage collectors surrounded by soldiers. Some questioned how closely the military seemed to be working with the Corporation. There was a general distrust among everyone.

And yet life in Goat Cove remained much as it had been since the strike had begun in October. Services were sporadic and drastically reduced as they had few workers to offer them. Roads and train lines were left unrepaired for weeks at a time. Bins of rubbish, recycling, and compost were picked up much less frequently, so one of Patrick's tasks that he coordinated with their block's Repair Squad was hauling their accumulated recycling and rubbish to the appropriate centres. He did many of these trips himself as part of his courier runs. The Repair Squad also built a common compost bin for all the houses in their co-op so they could keep from having to dispose of it elsewhere, which led to their gardens being richer as they began their spring planting, and they trimmed the municipality's trees (since managing greenery had fallen entirely off the municipal priority list), and organized bonfires in their common courtyard on weekends.

Anna learned at home with modules put together by the school division, though she felt these were boring and preferred when Patrick created lessons for her instead. He took her to the curling rink to work on mathematics. Though she initially struggled to push around heavy granite rocks, she had fun playing in the children's league. She felt safe knowing Patrick was there with her. The curling rink was a place of respite for them both and she got to spend more time with Ellie and Justin Alvarez-Franklin. Surprisingly, she began to excel at the sport as they practiced several nights a week. Older children invited her to play on their teams.

"I'm worried about Anna's future for lots of reasons," Patrick confided in Tori one night. "I guess it's really low on my priorities to worry about her athletic talents."

"That's what fathers should be worried about," Tori grumbled. "Not whether they or their child will get shot between home and the rink, or which one of you is going to have a nervous breakdown first."

"Yes, well, I can't help but notice how much Anna loves curling. She does really well at it, too! Physically and mentally. Cate remarked after our league game about how good Anna is compared to me and joked that we did something to her."

"That was probably just Cate joking. She knows Anna is adopted. Not nice of her, but she likes to tease you. Maybe her kids are a little jealous that Anna gets to play with older kids sometimes."

"Yeah, John gave her the 'shut up, Cate' look once she said it."

"Besides, my parents used to curl all the time before I was born. My relatives won lots of tournaments. Anna has the sport in her DNA."

"But what's going to happen when her altered DNA is discovered? Will she ever be able to play competitively? I mean, if she wants to, that is."

"Her altered DNA would be discovered?"

"It could be! Right now, no. She's just a kid who happens to be good enough to play with seven and eight-year-olds despite only being not-quite-five."

"She's still our daughter," Tori insisted. "She has our DNA. She is what we could have been. She hasn't been altered. Her parents were altered, not her, and they are still us. Just better versions of us: me without my illness and you with better physical coordination."

"I'm not sure that would be accepted by the higher-ups."

"For now, like you said, she's just a kid playing. And I'm going to make sure my parents come to see the kids' league championship!"

As Tori returned to work at her store full-time after Christmas, she soon found herself in the middle of chaotic protests as strikers regularly took their frustrations to the shops along Goat Cove Road. While all the shops' sales plummeted in general, her store sold enough religious escapism that she managed to keep afloat without being propped up by her father, even managing to keep Desiree and Becksy employed. The café also did well enough because people still needed to eat as they protested. Desiree and Becksy alternated between the two businesses and managed to make enough money to help their families while still saving for future educational opportunities.

Meanwhile, Ninja-Cowboy Courier Company was doing wonderfully, proudly promoting themselves as the company in support of the common folk. Tori could barely listen to how proud her father was of himself as he championed the company, as though his astute business practices were keeping the entire region politically stable.

On the first Tuesday of February, shortly after the Lunar New Year, a rally of striking workers started in Goat Cove, heading towards downtown Alexandrina, with the marchers walking the five kilometres between the community and the central district to gain support. As the people gathered, which they started to do at least two hours before the march was supposed to start, they wandered into shops along the main street. Many of them went into the café on the second floor of Tori's bookstore and came down to see the books and trinkets. While she was grateful to have the business, the sudden gathering of people made her anxious.

Tori, Desiree, and Becksy could hear the sounds of horns and whistles from the street. They were distant at first but soon grew louder as the crowd gathered in the square on the next block. Shouting and chanting soon followed, along with voices blaring instructions. Some of the assembled milled about in the doorway to the store and on the steps to the café, rather than stand outside in the cold.

"There are a lot of elderly and middle-aged women, and they have their grandkids with them," Becksy whispered to Tori and Desiree. "And yet there are a lot of angry men with weapons. There are former police officers acting like militia."

"There are people of all ages and genders in the crowd. It kind of looks carnival-like," Desiree pointed out, shrugging. "It would be interesting to join in."

"I don't see why you couldn't – but be careful!" Tori added. "The shop is going to get really quiet once the marchers leave. I think half of Goat Cove is here. But first, could one of you run out and get more coffee for upstairs? Maureen just texted that she needs more."

"We're out of coffee!" Maureen, the café's manager, shouted at potential customers from the top of the stairs. "Free hot chocolate and cider for the kids while you wait!"

The thought of hot chocolate and cider reminded Tori of Anna's experience in Little Hobidigan. *Those poor kids! I hope the police leave the marchers alone. Anna is still traumatized from what happened to her.*

"Do you want me to lock anything or reinforce the windows?" Desiree asked as Becksy left to get more coffee. "Remember what happened last weekend?"

"Yes to the windows," Tori decided. "I'll secure the back."

She retreated to her office and, having secured the back doors and windows, sat down at her desk to cry. Pain radiated throughout her body as she fumbled for her medicine cocktail and some painkillers.

"Look, ma'am, we're out of coffee!" Maureen's authoritative voice suddenly blared from the staircase again. "I have literally anything else, but I can't magically concoct what you want."

Tori wiped her eyes and struggled to stand up. The crowd was growing frustrated. Maureen had stuck a sign on her door saying they were temporarily out of coffee, but the marchers were taking the opportunity to berate her.

"They've run out. She'd give you some if they had any left!" Desiree intervened. "We've gone out to get more. We didn't know you'd be coming!"

"Look, everyone can have a free cup of tea!" Maureen decided to placate the crowd. "We have lots of hot water."

In the two and a half hours that the marchers were assembled in Goat Cove, the café sold out of coffee a second time, but the initial rally in the square remained peaceful. As they started their march toward the city centre, Tori let Desiree and Becksy leave with them. They had been given a JUSTICE FOR WORKERS banner to carry from some of the organizers.

I can agree with justice for workers. Desiree and Becksy don't realize that justice extends to robots as well. They are workers as much as anyone else.

Tori was happy to have everyone gone. While she was content they had sold more items than usual, she was more grateful that it was quiet again. She retreated into her office and laid down on a cot to rest. The nerves still bothered her from where she had had her operation, and they were especially aggravated from her running around throughout the morning.

Halfway through the afternoon, Tori's phone notified her that her employees had left downtown and were now hiding in a park. Desiree sent a message that they were temporarily safe. Unfortunately, the march had not remained peaceful by the time they had reached central Alexandrina.

Upon checking the news, Tori learned the crowd had grown to nearly fifty thousand people by the time they came to their final rallying point in front of the Robot Rental Corporation's downtown office. The state police had attacked the crowd as they stood there. Most of the municipal police officers had abandoned their jobs as part of the strike and many of them were among the marchers as unofficial security patrols. Once the state police attacked, the striking municipal police officers retaliated and incited the crowd, many of whom were simply defending themselves and their loved ones. The rally had quickly turned into a riot that injured over a hundred people.

"We fled into Ocean Point Park," Desiree sent in a message. "Attempting to get back to Goat Cove via beach & cemetery."

"Be careful," was all Tori could manage to reply.

The news claimed several marchers had disappeared into the trees and flowers of Ocean Point Park, which had caused enough of a concern that the state police had seen fit to deploy search parties to go after them. Tori imagined Desiree and Becksy crawling over rocks and driftwood. The wind had picked up and was icy cold.

A new message appeared on Tori's office computer: FILES TRANSFERRED. Examining the accompanying text, she was startled to see that it contained all the phone information for her employees. The two young women had destroyed their phones in the hope of avoiding being tracked further.

The police can't track them, but neither can I. They are young. Their mothers will be worried.

With the main street nearly deserted and no employees, Tori decided to close the store. She then went upstairs to the café, where Maureen poured her a cinnamon tea and sat down with her, having made herself a hot toddy. She brought out some New Year treats for them to share.

"It's already dark and the temperature's dropped close to freezing. The beach will be slippery to climb," Tori fretted. "There's no light there and they have no phones."

"I wouldn't put it past either of them to have another flashlight multitool. They both took survival training with their church."

"Yes, well, we have no way to contact them and they can't reach anyone. I just put the CLOSED sign up on the store window. Figured it would be dangerous to leave them a note."

"They'll probably try to go straight home to your co-op," Maureen pointed out. "Maybe they've reached out to their families already."

Tori shook her head. Her employees' mothers had reached out to her multiple times, looking for an update on their daughters' whereabouts. Tori was annoyed they thought she would know anything different than they would. The girls had texted their mothers before they left the store. Why would they send an update to their boss before their mothers, especially after their shifts would have been already over?

"No, no one knows anything. They are completely cut off. Carlyn and Sequoia said this is the first time they've never been able to know where their daughters are."

"I really hope my parents don't still have a tracker on me," Maureen muttered. "I'm fifty years old! But I wouldn't be surprised."

"Mine were always worried about me, so I got good at hiding where I went," Tori admitted. "I can't blame them for being concerned, though. I was sick all the time."

Shortly thereafter, Patrick and Anna appeared, intending to walk Tori home. Maureen gave them a New Year's gift basket before she took the train home in the opposite direction.

"Have Becksy and Desiree got home yet?" Tori asked as they started back toward their housing block, Anna excitedly examining the gift basket.

"No, they have not," Patrick reported. "Carlyn suggested we go looking for them along the beach. It's dark, but we can stick to the well-lit roads. Are you up for a bit of a trek?"

Tori nodded, seeing that Anna looked excited for an adventure.

"Just let me take some more medicine. I will have one of the sticky buns from the basket with it."

"Your pacing has really picked up again," Patrick tried to compliment her. He glanced at his phone. "Carlyn will meet us at the corner of Oak and Raven. She's bringing tea and sandwiches so you can take your evening meds. That way, we can save the sticky buns for dessert."

"Oh, how thoughtful of her! I hadn't expected that."

"Well, we will just look like a weird family that decides to have nighttime winter picnics. We can say we're visiting our relatives at the cemetery for the New Year. Maybe we actually could. I think my dad would appreciate it."

Tori nodded, glancing at her own phone. It had the same message from Becksy's mother as Patrick's had, but no other notifications.

"How could they take so long to get back? It's been three hours since they destroyed their phones. Did they get stuck on the beach? Are they hiding in the cemetery? Did the police catch them after all? Would they be chasing people this far out from downtown?"

Patrick shuddered. Anna squeezed his hand and tucked herself between her parents.

"They probably won't bother with two young girls like them," he pointed out. "If they managed to get away from the initial chase in the park, the police probably figured they weren't worth chasing after. They can't catch fifty thousand people."

It turned into a lovely, if chilly, evening as they met Becksy's mother and continued toward the beach. Anna's mood brightened considerably once the adults stopped talking about the police.

"I brought my teddy bear for good luck. See?" She held up her stuffed bear that had a four-leafed clover on each paw and a large cross on its tummy. Anna had named it Lucky-Criss-Cross. It had been one of her many Christmas gifts from her grandfather.

"Lucky-Criss-Cross has a flashlight and camera," Patrick explained, mostly for Carlyn's benefit. "He can help us search."

"Can we pretend we're looking for pirate treasure?" Anna asked. "I know we're playing hide-and-seek with Becksy and Desiree, but hunting for pirate treasure sounds more fun!"

"We're reading a book about pirates," Tori explained.

"Let's all pretend to be pirates," Carlyn decided, smiling at Anna despite her own worry. "Becksy and Desiree are part of our crew and they have gotten lost. We need to find them and get back to our ship! Our houses are our ship."

"So we're pirates too?" Anna's eyes brightened. "Yay!"

The four of them walked with determination toward the beach, singing pirate songs and sea chanteys. Anna made up her own songs that involved treasure chests full of fresh fruits and berries. Each time they encountered a police foot patrol or a squad car passed them, Anna's singing grew quieter and she would cling tightly to Patrick. The police took no interest in a family with a picnic basket heading toward the beach.

The actual trip to the boardwalk above the beach was a refreshing stroll. There were no patrols in the area, so Anna's spirits were further raised. She eagerly went along the railing, holding Lucky-Criss-Cross over it to "hunt for treasure and our missing pirates." The teddy bear proved useful in searching the spots on the beach that were too dark for them to see clearly. As they approached the cemetery, Anna shone the teddy bear's camera around the ancient headstones, most of which were so worn by wind and rain as to be illegible. After a quick couple of detours into the newer section to visit Patrick's father's grave and that of one of his best friends, they made their way toward a playground that bordered the cemetery.

They found Becksy and Desiree on the swings there. The two young women had changed their clothes and had thermoses of tea, courtesy of an older woman who had fled with them who lived nearby.

"We thought we would be less suspicious if we pretended to be bored teenagers hanging out in a park than if we went straight home immediately with purpose," Desiree explained as they hugged everyone and joined the picnic. Anna shared a bag of gold chocolate coins from the gift basket with them to celebrate that they had found their 'pirate crew.'

Becksy and Desiree's hypothesis was well-founded, as once the six of them started to make their way home toward Goat Cove Road (and were therefore now approaching from the same direction as someone coming from downtown), the police took more interest in them. They were stopped three times, bringing Anna to tears. She squeezed her teddy bear tightly, pointing its camera at the officers. Patrick finally picked her up and let her bury her head into his shoulders. While she was energetic and gregarious, Anna was still only a small child out past her bedtime.

The last officer that stopped them soon noticed they had a tired child and apologetically waved them onward, wishing them a good evening and blessed New Year.

Thank God they believed our story that we were only going for a stroll to the beach and cemetery for a winter picnic with our deceased relatives!

When they had all returned to their respective houses, Anna refused to leave her father's arms and kept crying.

"I thought they'd take me away again, Papa! Why did they stop us? We aren't really pirates! The police are scary. Please don't make me go near them tomorrow!"

"It's all right, sweetheart. The police shouldn't hurt you. We will try to avoid them tomorrow on our way to the rink. I don't like them either."

Patrick was not keen on having to go through police checkpoints, which he had to do constantly while he was on his delivery runs. But his discomfort around the police was nothing compared to the terror that he felt as Anna clung to him.

"They can hurt me! They beat my old papa! They took him away from me and they yelled at me and when I cried, they said he wasn't my papa and he had stolen me. They pushed me and I had bruises. They're mean and I don't want them to take me away again! One of them laughed at me and flipped me around like a doll, saying he was looking for my barcode. But the others stopped him. One of them got me icky cocoa water because my hot chocolate spilled. I love you and I don't want to leave you!"

Anna reached out and hugged her parents tightly. "Please keep me away from them," she pleaded.

Tori and Patrick were stunned as their daughter finally spoke about her capture by the police in Little Hobidigan. She had never directly told them about it, nor elaborated on any details between then and her time at Nellie House.

"I promise we'll never let anyone take you away from us," Tori whispered, kissing her cheek.

Unless they are your old mama and papa, and you want to go home with them. They're the only ones that I'd let you go to.

Since neither Tori nor Patrick could sleep, they sat in bed reading news stories. Many of the protesters had been caught and detained, especially the former police officers. The downtown district was officially under complete martial law, with a secure perimeter now enforced.

"Great – that's going to make my delivery routes worse!" Patrick groaned. "What's that actually going to accomplish?"

"Nothing. It's a blatant show of power."

"I'd have more respect for it if I actually thought it would help what's going on."

"In other news, it says here that more robots took sanctuary in the complex this past week. Interesting phrasing: 'took sanctuary.'"

"They're basically admitting they have no control over the place."

"But also that the robots have a sort of right to be there. Like they are refugees."

"Or like the complex is some sort of holy ground!"

"What do you suppose is going to happen?"

"Considering how much the general population seems to hate robots, I wouldn't be surprised if the complex ends up like some sort of industrial version of a nature preserve. It's already next to River-Gold State Park."

"Is it wrong that I just want them to be free and able to live normal lives?"

"No, milady." Patrick quickly squeezed Tori's hand. "You have a compassionate heart behind your little rich girl exterior."

"I want our family to be together. I want Anna to be able to play with her brother like Grace can play with Liam. I have these crazy fantasies of being able to go on picnics with Step and his wife. I keep thinking she's my little sister."

"I don't think those are crazy fantasies."

"Then what are they?"

"The near future, hopefully. And, at the very least, nice ideas."

In the next room, Anna turned off her music, leaving only the quiet sounds of woodland insects playing. Taggy purred as his small human shifted; he wanted to both soothe her and remind her that he was tucked up against her backside. Anna smiled and whispered goodnight to him.

I am safe at home in my bed. Nothing will hurt me here. I have Taggy.

But when she dreamed of exploring the beach for hidden treasure, she heard her mother's voice pointing out all the plants and shells. Both of her mothers sounded similar, especially when they whispered, so she could not tell which mother was speaking. Her old mama had been the plant expert, but her new mama was the one who read her books about the ocean. They both were walking with her, and with them, she felt entirely safe, protected, and loved.

INTERLUDE 9

After nearly three months of being surrounded by military barricades, Step was impressed at how well the robots were surviving at the barracks. They not only had all the resources they needed, but they had enough to enjoy them. They could have the occasional celebration without rationing their food, such as they had planned for later that day to welcome six newly-eclosed robots who had mastered walking.

They could print weapons if they needed more ammunition, though the military raids were limited to attacking the front gates every few days. The Robot Rental Corporation must have insisted the barracks was a better resource to maintain rather than have it destroyed. All their equipment for manufacturing robots on an industrial scale was there.

Unfortunately, all the Corporation's files for manufacturing robots at all are somewhere else, probably wherever their head office is. We can't make new robots of our own, though we can raise the ones that emerge from the vats. And I've found all the files from our genetic tinkering. I can prove just how closely I am related to Patrick Semaganis Kirke. They didn't even redact his name.

Step shuddered as he read through the file about Patrick once again. The language used treated both men like specimens. The Corporation had been proud of all the purported improvements they had made to Patrick's genetic material.

He and Nola were in the main office they had set up as their base of operations. Most of the time, it was just the two of them in there, while other robots would come in to deliver reports. They had set up a council of robots to run the barracks. So far, it consisted of Step, Nola, Isaac, and several others who were the leaders of the various departments: infirmary, kitchen, vat warehouse, laboratories, etcetera. Step hoped that someday, they would have elections for their council, but they were nowhere near ready for that yet.

"What are you reading?" Nola asked, looking up from the chart of greenhouse inventory.

"My genetic file. Did you want me to look you up?"

"For the seventeenth time, no! I don't want to know."

Step nodded, though he could not understand why she was so adamantly against reading her file. On any other matter, Nola was inquisitive and studious. Out of his own curiosity, he had gone ahead and read her file anyhow, recognizing that her genetic donor had been in the same hospital as Tori Williams-Kirke. Both women had been deceived by the promise of curing them. The Corporation had been unrepentantly boastful about their schemes to collect genetic samples.

"It's not that I don't want to know about her at all," Nola added. "I just don't want to read about her yet. I'm still figuring myself out."

"Other than me, you seem like the most self-assured one here." Step hoped that sounded like the compliment he intended it to be.

"I'd like to concentrate on surviving long enough to give birth to twins again."

"You're at least halfway to that now."

"Considering how tight my overalls are, I'm quite aware of that."

Chuckling to himself, Step went back to reading the file about how the Corporation had taken clumsy, asthmatic Patrick and created Step as his athletically adept counterpart.

The robots could not replicate the Corporation's manufacturing techniques and they did not want to. Instead, they had been able to reproduce new people in the normal human fashion, just like Step and Maria had. It was part of reclaiming their humanity. Nola had stopped eating much of the drugged food once the strike had begun in October and they had started their plan to take over the barracks. Almost immediately, she had gotten pregnant with another set of twins. Scarlett had recently announced she was going to have a baby too. The two of them, along with Isaac and Ren, had formed a family. Sometimes, Isaac and Nola slept together, other times Nola was with Ren; sometimes Ren and Scarlett were together, occasionally Scarlett with Isaac, and most of the time, Nola and Scarlett slept together. (Step had yet to notice if Isaac and Ren were alone together, but he would not have been surprised.) Step was more like their brother; he was close to them in that he still shared a room and worked alongside them, but he did not share beds with them.

Many of the robots had gotten pregnant since they had taken over the barracks. Step hoped they were pleased about it. He had not noticed anyone upset. Everyone seemed hopeful. Like his roommates, they had all formed little families. Some were merely couples, while others consisted of larger groups, usually those who had been housed or worked together. Step was the only one who was completely alone.

I still have Maria somewhere. No one here is her.

Nola was probably the most like his wife among the robots that he was close to, but she was too bubbly, flirtatious, and outgoing to be mistaken for Maria. He wondered if the two women would get along if they met.

"How are the greenhouses?" Step asked, wanting to sound like a responsible leader and distract himself from the genetic profiles and thoughts of families.

"Excellent! We shouldn't starve." Nola sounded pleased but bored.

"Did I say something wrong?"

"What? No, I meant it was good. I really don't get excited about plants. I prefer animals. And babies – just wait until these two get here!"

She grinned at Step, relishing the idea of finally getting to be a mother. It did not matter to her that she was only halfway through her pregnancy and their lives in the barracks were precarious. She had someone to hope and plan for. Someone to die for, for that matter.

"I'm looking forward to having children around again," Step admitted, though the thought of children made him miss his family more. "I've never seen twins before."

"These two aren't going to be identical like in the books you mentioned," Nola reminded him. "They only have half their genetics in common."

"Well, I've never even seen two babies at the same time," Step pointed out. "I'm glad we'll be able to tell them apart."

Nola giggled and went back to work.

"Step! Nola!" Isaac came running into the office. "There is someone approaching the back gate! They came up through River-Gold Park on one of the trails. Completely snuck by the military's patrols, I think."

"What do you mean, snuck by the patrols?" Nola wrapped her blanket protectively around herself. "Are they a robot?"

Isaac shook his head in terror.

"No, our scans don't register a barcode on them. But, um, Step, they look like you. Like, it's a man who looks just like you, but older. He's wearing hiking gear but doesn't seem to be carrying anything."

Step paused, glancing at the file that he was copying. He was becoming more convinced in the existence of the protagonist of his new book.

"He looks like me, but older? That would be him!" He pointed to the photo of Patrick that accompanied the file. "Bring him to our office."

Nola and Isaac looked at him in horror.

"That sounds like a bad idea." Nola pulled at her blanket with apprehension.

"He has listened to me before," Step insisted. "You two can stay with us. I have a plan."

CHAPTER ELEVEN

Ever since he started his relationship with Tori, Patrick had spent St. Patrick's Day with her. He had accepted that, due to her illness, this would usually mean having a quiet night at home. It had been over a decade since he had gone out to listen to live music on the holiday. Some years, he had spent St. Patrick's Day at Tori's hospital bedside. No matter what happened, they had always tried to make the day fun. This year, however, Patrick was not sure if he would even make it home for a late-night drink of whiskey with her.

His work was challenging on holidays. While his delivery runs could be more upbeat and jollier than usual, there was heavier traffic, and the police were always more vigilant, especially when holidays included drinking and levity.

But this year, "vigilant" did not begin to describe how exacting the police were as Patrick made his way through the streets of Alexandrina. It seemed there was a checkpoint every few blocks. Despite the ongoing strike and the declaration of martial law, people were out to celebrate throughout the city. While some might have had mischievous intentions, all Patrick could see was they wanted to relax and have fun. He took the time as he sat waiting in yet another checkpoint queue to pray everyone would be safe.

Their neighbours had organized an afternoon barbecue in the courtyard of their housing block that he figured Tori and Anna would enjoy together, as he doubted he would make it back in time to participate. His plan for after his route ended did not include going straight home. Instead, having finished up his deliveries by noon, he headed out through several checkpoints, ostensibly to go hiking in River-Gold State Park.

Patrick hated keeping the truth from Tori, but he had told her he had taken a double shift of deliveries. Therefore, she would not expect him home until the evening, likely just as the barbecue was ending. He left his tracker on, but he doubted she would look at it until suppertime. As a driver for Ninja-Cowboy, he went everywhere in Alexandrina. Even heading toward River-Gold State Park would not be inherently suspicious – not until he passed all the neighbourhoods in that direction.

The only places beyond the state park were the Robot Rental Corporation's complex and the military base. Patrick was not sure what his father-in-law had done to make the military mad at him, but they had expressly stated they did not want to work with his company, so there was no reason for a Ninja-Cowboy courier vehicle to go there. According to news reports, the military had set up a perimeter around the robots' complex and was diverting civilian and non-essential traffic for their base to a side road.

Patrick had no intention of getting the military's attention today. While he could not simply drive up to the Robot Rental Corporation's complex, he had found another way to walk in.

He left his courier vehicle in the parking lot of the River-Gold State Park Visitor Centre and paid the daily rate so he might have the chance to get back to it without it being towed. Once he had changed into camouflage-patterned hiking gear he had found at the thrift store, he glanced into the mirror and thought of how much he looked like Step. He thought his "younger brother" looked much better in the pattern, while he looked like the city-dweller who reluctantly accompanied his relatives on a hunting trip.

As he ate his lunch in the picnic area, he took a few minutes to photograph birds, flowers, trees, and plants. *If I'm interrogated later, I need to have a plausible excuse that I really am a clumsy fellow who likes to take photos of nature and then got lost.* He also still had a nagging feeling that he should bow to cowardice and return home. The photos would at least prove that the excursion was not wasted. He could use them as part of Anna's lessons.

Patrick had expected there to be more evidence of concern at the park, but other than many signs at the visitor centre that the park was more dangerous than usual and therefore security had been heightened, everyone acted as though nothing was out of the ordinary. Visitors were told not to worry if they saw park rangers patrolling or if they were questioned.

"As long as everyone complies with the new security measures, all will be well," he read aloud. "If you wish to hike any trails deemed to be in the 'danger zone,' please advise the rangers."

The map on the wall had the "danger zone" clearly marked with a bright red outline and grey shading. What lay beyond the danger zone was unviewable due to the map's edge, but Patrick only needed to look at the map on his phone, using the address of the complex, to conclude that it was the area of the park that bordered the complex and thus the military might be using it. Whether they were using the park to besiege the complex, or whether they were actually afraid robots might escape into the park, Patrick was not sure. It was a reasonable conclusion that both options were likely.

Patrick Semaganis Williams-Kirke was far from an adventurous man. Being a clumsy urbanite in his late thirties, he was generally one to stay in well-lit areas with even terrain. Him hiking alone on a trail rated "difficult" rarely even occurred in his imagination, so he felt as though he were a different person altogether as he told the ranger on duty that he would be exploring the Prospector's Creek Trail. He had only been on it once – with his family as a child barely older than Anna – and it was a miserable experience. The Prospector's Creek Trail encompassed cliffs, dense forests, caves, and a swift-flowing stream. It was the longest in the park and only connected with one of the rest stops that were scattered throughout the woods.

However, it was also one of the most isolated trails and mostly lay in the danger zone, so hiking it was ideal if Patrick was going to try to access the Robot Rental Corporation's complex from the woods. As he looked at his map on his phone, there was a point a third of the way into the trail where a small offshoot path connected it with the back road at the park's perimeter. From that point, he would arrive at the back of the Robot Rental Corporation's property, though he was not sure how he would get into the complex. Patrick decided the excuse he could give to a ranger or military patrol was he had grown tired and wanted to take an easier route along the road back to the park entrance. It sounded like a logical enough reason to him, so he prayed others would agree.

At this point, God, I hope you give me the strength to carry out what I want to do.

He had no idea what the robots would think of him. He did not doubt their intelligence and figured if they were paranoid enough to shoot him on the spot, they would be justified in doing so. Patrick did not aim to put on an act in front of them of being a foolish idiot who had gotten lost. If he did not get shot immediately, he would tell them the truth: he was a freelance journalist who wanted to publish an article about the uprising at the complex from the robots' perspective. He had had enough of the speculative nonsense from the regular news media that offered no new information. Even the most sympathetic writers talked about the robots like they were merely defective machinery.

Remarkably, Patrick managed to hike the first third of the Prospector's Creek Trail and the offshoot path to the road with little incident, though he did trip over an exposed root and tumble knees-first onto spongy bog soil. It was like landing hard onto a carpet and he bounced back up again, albeit with a lot of pain. It was preferable to falling onto ice at the curling rink.

Once on the road, he found himself at the edge of an orchard. The change between the cultivated orchard and the dense woods was initially jarring. There was a long, electrified fence between it and the roadside, but he noticed a small gate a short distance away. There was no military presence whatsoever, going against Patrick's expectations. The road itself was deserted.

He was also surprised to see several dozen workers in the orchard. One of them glimpsed him and whispered something to the next worker, who whispered something to the next, and so on until one of them sent a message on what looked like a modified version of a watch-phone. As Patrick watched them, catching his breath after his climb, he felt beams of light scan him. Bracing himself for automatic weapons to fire at him, he made his way toward the small gate, certain that every robot in the complex must be aware of his presence by now.

Nothing was amiss. There were no signs, no warnings, no admonishments about trespassing, nor anything to reveal the barracks were no longer under the Robot Rental Corporation's control. There were no slogans or any signs of defiance, either. When he got to the gate itself, there was only a small label that read: 'Please Do Not Attempt to Open Gate. Alarm Will Sound. Area Protected by High-Voltage Electricity.' This was a back gate of some kind, likely not even one meant for delivery vehicles or large equipment haulers. It was just an emergency exit. Patrick was relieved there was at least a sign on it that faced the road. He imagined the placard he could make out facing inward also repeated the warning.

Next to the orchard was a woodlot and the gate was between them. The ghost of a path to it led toward some outbuildings. The path was well worn close to the buildings and branched off toward the orchard and behind the woodlot, leaving the actual path to the gate as overgrown. *Why even have an emergency exit that no one can use?*

Reflexively, Patrick made the sign of the cross and waited at the gate. He could still see the workers in the orchard; most of them had gone back to their pruning, occasionally glancing at him.

Initially, nothing happened to him. As it turned out, there were no automatic weapons along the fence. Patrick reasoned the whole system was designed to keep robots inside the complex and was thus not concerned with people approaching from the back road. No one attacked him from a distance, either. The military had either not noticed him or had decided he was inconsequential. Meanwhile, whatever they thought of him, the robots were going to at least approach him. He steadied himself as he wondered what it would be like to be shot at close range.

Within minutes, a small party exited the nearest building and began to approach him down the path. The three of them all carried large assault rifles that were illegal for civilian use, but they had them slung over their shoulders as though they were on parade or patrolling a large crowd. Patrick sighed in relief. The rifles were not pointed at him.

As they came closer, he could make out that while they were all wearing navy jumpsuit overalls like he had seen in the videos, they had differently coloured armbands on their shoulders. One had silver armbands and seemed to be leading the other two, who wore purple and white. They wore grey woollen toques that reflected the cloudy sky.

"Who are you and what is your business here?" the leader demanded as they stopped about two metres away from Patrick. "I warn you that we are purpose-born marksmen. Do not attempt an attack!"

Patrick froze upon hearing the man's voice. He blinked and stared at him more intently. The man's facial features were in shadow from the way the light scattered, but he seemed familiar.

"We have determined that you have no weapons," the leader continued, sensing Patrick's hesitation. "We have decided that you are not an immediate threat. Please tell us who you are."

"My name is Patrick Semaganis Kirke," he introduced himself, deciding it was best to use his legal name. "I am a writer. A journalist, of sorts. I want to help you tell your story. No one understands what is going on here. Many people would like to know. They need to hear from you, not a censored article from the Robot Rental Corporation or the military."

The man nodded and remotely opened the gate.

"Welcome! I have been asked to bring you to headquarters."

As Patrick stumbled into the complex, unnerved as the gate closed behind him, he moved close enough to see the man's face.

Lord have mercy! He looks just like John Alvarez-Franklin. I knew his voice sounded familiar.

"Is something wrong?" the man-who-wasn't-John asked.

"You look a lot like a friend of mine," Patrick admitted.

"My name is Isaac," the man introduced himself simply. "Come with me to headquarters."

Isaac led Patrick around the back of the nearest building until they came to what seemed like the complex's central office hub. Isaac's two companions left them and turned toward what appeared to be the large dining hall from the archival footage. Music played and people inside sang.

They're making up songs! Instead of the dull silence of the robots in the video footage on the news, the people inside were joyful and boisterous.

Isaac pushed Patrick into the office he had referred to as "headquarters" and shut the door behind them. Initially, it was like any other office he had seen; there were two large desks with cabinets, lots of storage, and a small kitchenette off to the side.

But he nearly passed out upon seeing the two faces sitting at the desks staring back at him. Not only was Step there, looking exactly like Patrick from a decade ago, but the woman at the other desk might as well have been the ghost of his close high school and university friend, Jade Vida Charriez, who had died in her early twenties.

First John, then Jade. How have I not seen them before? And they are friends? Is there a robot version of Cate, too?

"Jade?" he managed to whimper before his knees buckled and Isaac had to catch him. He and Step eased him into a nearby chair.

"Are you all right, Patrick? Would you like a drink of water?" Barely waiting for a reply, Step poured Patrick a glass and handed it to him, which he then gulped down thirstily.

"I'm fine," he replied, as more of a reassurance than an actual description of his feelings.

"Don't worry, we aren't going to hurt you," Step continued. "You *are* Patrick Semaganis Kirke-Williams, correct?"

Patrick nodded and Step grinned at him.

"We look even more alike with you dressed like that! We really could be brothers."

"My thoughts exactly," Patrick muttered.

"What did you mean by 'jade'?" Step asked, sounding as though he had guessed what Patrick's answer might be.

"Your colleagues look a lot like friends of mine." Patrick's eyes darted between Isaac and the woman at the desk.

Step nodded in agreement. "Interesting! That you were all friends, I mean."

"How so?" the woman-who-was-definitely-not-Jade wondered. Patrick was not sure who she was talking to, but hearing Jade's voice brought tears to his eyes.

"Our genetic donors were all friends and now *we* are all friends!" Step explained. "That is a strange coincidence."

"But what does that have to do with a mineral?" Isaac asked.

Step shook his head. "Jade is a person. She was Nola's genetic donor. The Corporation got her through the hospital."

"How do you know that?" Patrick demanded, forgetting his attempt to be polite.

"We've got everyone's files. They didn't keep them confidential."

"You mean, the Corporation has been tracking us?"

"No, the files are only up to the point they collected the DNA. It mentions you were a university student studying journalism."

"Oh, well…" Patrick wiped away his tears on his sleeve and forced himself to look straight at the woman. "I'm sorry I reacted so strangely to seeing you, ma'am. It's just that Jade didn't get better. She died over ten years ago. You look so much like her, it scared me."

"My name is Nola," she replied with nervous indignation. Patrick admitted he was unsure how he would react if someone told him they looked exactly like their dead friend.

"Anyhow, now that I suppose we have all introduced ourselves, please tell me what brings you here." Step sat down and wheeled his chair to sit directly facing Patrick, while Isaac guarded the closed office door, lest Patrick try to escape. Nola watched the three men from behind her desk, both apprehensive and intrigued by the visitor.

"I honestly came to find you," Patrick admitted. "I want to tell your story. All of your stories, I mean, not just you, Step. I want to tell people what's happening here from your perspectives. The Robot Rental Corporation is calling this a severe malfunction. The news is recycling the same tired stories. Your story deserves to be heard."

"*Our* story," Step agreed. "You and I are in this together, Patrick. It isn't enough to tell the world about our robot insurrection. You need to tell the world about what the Corporation did to us. How we are all as human as you and your wife and your friends. How they lied to you about what they wanted your DNA for. How we just want to be recognized as people with rights, to have our own identity cards, to be able to live in freedom with our families."

"Absolutely," Patrick nodded. "I will write it in my article."

"I'm sending you the files I've been reading," Step insisted. "I want you to send them to the government. To someone who will not bury them but expose the Corporation."

"I can do that."

"Thank you. Now, what do you want for your article?"

Patrick delved into asking questions, reading files, and discussing what life was like at the complex, both before and after the uprising. *What had it been like to be a robot? How was it different now? What secrets did the Robot Rental Corporation want to keep hidden, never imagining that robots would be sitting in their offices and reading through their files?*

Initially, Step was the most talkative and forthcoming, since he already trusted Patrick, but once she overcame her fear, Nola became the most vocal storyteller. She was eager to share her experience of being programmed as a surrogate mother, being trapped in the basement of a fancy house ("not drugged, I might add, since that would have interfered with my job and hurt the babies"), and being discarded to the Corporation once she gave birth. While Patrick was horrified, he was struck by how similar Nola was to Jade. She leaned on her desk the same way Jade had throughout their years at school together. Both she and Isaac had nearly identical mannerisms to Jade and John. For a couple hours of the afternoon, Patrick felt like he was once again hanging out with his friends.

"This is going to sound like a dumb question, but is there anyone here who looks like this woman?" Patrick showed them a photo of Cate Alvarez-Franklin. "She used to be friends with me and your donors too."

All three robots shook their heads. Step quickly scanned the photo and tried to match it within the Corporation's database but got zero results.

"I guess she didn't get her DNA taken, or it didn't work, or something happened to any robot cloned from her," Step reasoned.

"Why is my donor in the photo with her?" Isaac asked.

"They're married," Patrick explained. "They have four children together."

"Oh, how nice!" Step nodded. "Were they the ones playing with Anna in the photos your wife gave me?"

"Yes."

"Can I see?" Nola asked. "Maybe one of these babies will look like them."

Step immediately pulled out his datapad with the photos, while Patrick took another drink of water. He had asked about the robots' living arrangements and was still coming to terms with the idea that people who looked just like his friends were in a relationship together. He did not want to ask too many details about how a marriage of four people worked. The thought of Jade and John being married to each other was impossible for him to imagine, as Jade and Cate had been the romantic couple of their friend group until Jade had died. *They're not Jade and John – they're Nola and Isaac*, he reminded himself.

Once Step, Nola, and Isaac showed Patrick around the main office and went through many files, the three of them led him on a brief tour of the central building and took him to the celebration in the dining hall.

"We're celebrating that some of our newly eclosed robots have mastered walking and talking and such," Nola explained, pointing to the teenagers at the far end of the room. "They're being welcomed officially into our people."

These are a people with a culture. They are protective of their children. They have even borrowed an entomology term to refer to how they emerge from the vats. They are individuals. They have families. They have turned the complex from a prison into a home.

Nola, her wife Scarlett (who looked nothing like Cate), and several of the other robots he had met gave him hugs as he got ready to leave, having spent the entire afternoon at the complex. Part of him didn't want to leave yet. He was terrified to write the article he had promised.

Step and Isaac accompanied Patrick back to the gate near the orchard. The sun was already low and Patrick would have to hurry back downhill toward the River-Gold Park Visitor Centre before the woods became too dark to hike back safely.

"Give my daughter a hug from me." Step hugged Patrick tightly. "I miss her every day. If I ever can come see her…"

"You'd be welcome," Patrick hurriedly answered. "Your whole family."

"Thank you to Tori for the books," Step added. "I have been reading them all the time."

"Someday, I hope we can talk about them together."

"Me too. Safe travels home! Remember, tell our story!"

"I will. I promise you all that."

Patrick descended the Prospector's Creek Trail as quickly as he dared. He wondered if rangers were looking for him, as it was close to nightfall, but he heard nothing except the sounds of the woods. The park was devoid of people as he ran the last several hundred metres from the cover of the trees to his red-and-blue Ninja-Cowboy vehicle, which was the last one in the parking lot. He hurriedly texted the rangers to say he had made it back and was headed home.

The many checkpoints on his route home proved advantageous. As he waited in the queue at the first one, he turned off his vehicle and changed his clothes. At the second checkpoint, he was able to text Tori to let her know he was on his way home. At the third, he was able to start reading in earnest the files Step had sent him. Six checkpoints later, he was finally able to drive all the way home to Goat Cove Road.

When he walked into the front entryway, he realized the Alvarez-Franklins were visiting. *Seriously? They surprised us with a visit tonight? Of all nights?*

"Happy St. Patrick's Day!" Cate called out from the living room.

"Come join us! We were waiting for you to open the actual whiskey!" Tori added. "When you're ready, of course. You've had a long day!"

"Papa, you're home!" Anna came running downstairs to give him a hug, while Ellie, Justin, and Andrew gathered at the top of the landing. "We had a yummy barbecue and we made green cookies!"

Pretend everything is normal, Patrick.

Tori immediately sensed something was wrong. Her husband gave Anna two strong hugs before the children went back upstairs. When Tori moved to help him put away his bag with his uniform, he pulled it back from her. He gave her a passionate kiss, promising to start the laundry himself and then come down to join her, Cate, and John for a drink.

"I'll tell you all about my day later," he further promised.

"You look terrified!" Tori whispered. "Did something happen?"

"I'll tell you later."

Tori went back into the living room to rejoin Cate and John. Taggy had started to play with baby Irene's toys, batting them around and enjoying the intense rattling noise they made. The baby ignored the cat and played with the buttons on her mobile play centre. The festive background music was drowned out by loud versions of *Pop Goes the Weasel* and *London Bridge*. Tori delicately stepped around Irene and Taggy to refill John and Cate's glasses.

"Where did you get such delicious synthetic whiskey?" Cate asked.

"It was a Christmas present from my parents," Tori admitted. "They discovered it on one of their trips."

"Worthwhile gift," John agreed.

"Saves me from getting sicker," Tori muttered. "Now that Patrick is home, I'll get out the regular stuff."

Patrick numbly stumbled into the living room shortly thereafter, smiling graciously at their friends. Tori poured the two men glasses of regular whiskey so they could have a toast. Her husband surprised her by downing his entire glass as though it were a shot. In her bewilderment, she simply handed him the bottle and sat back down beside Cate and Irene.

"Has it been a long day?" John asked.

Patrick nodded, noting that John's voice sounded the same as Isaac's. He felt as though he had just been talking to him. *I can't even look at Cate.*

"Lots of checkpoints," he answered, staring at his whiskey glass. "There were nine of them between my last stop and home. Nine! That was just on the way back. I must have gone through a dozen earlier."

"No wonder you're so tense," Cate agreed. "I only had to go through one this morning when I took Irene for her check-up. They saw that I had a crying baby and waved me through on the way back, thankfully."

"I had a lot of time to think and read, at least," Patrick pointed out. He refilled his glass for the third time as Tori eyed him with concern. "Probably not a good thing. I get addicted to the adrenaline rush of reading the news."

"Anything interesting?" Cate inquired.

"Not related to the strike and such?" John added.

"Kind of. I was reading more about the robots. Apparently, someone dissected one and actually managed to get their findings published."

Tori gave her husband a look of horror.

"Dissected? Like, were they at least dead first? Or did they kill them?"

"Article said they were already dead. They were found rotting at a waste disposal station. They'd been beaten to death, so the retired pathologist who was featured in the article claimed. Yeah, I wish I hadn't read it either."

After reading that article, he had decided to make a better use of his time waiting at checkpoints to start compiling his own findings from that afternoon. The thought that Step, Nola, Isaac, or any of the robots he had encountered could have been that corpse made him pour himself another drink.

"So what did they find?" Cate was enthralled.

"Nothing! That's just it. They dissected the whole corpse and found nothing. It was a human corpse! Nothing mechanical. No nanotech. No extra organs or mutations. The only thing weird was that the bones showed signs of rapid growth."

In a vat over two years, just like Step said. He had not seen them in person, but Step had shown him the security footage of the vast warehouse where the robots were grown.

"It wasn't a robot after all?"

"No, it was a robot. It had a barcode and microchip implant from the Robot Rental Corporation."

"You mean, the Robot Rental Corporation is kidnapping people?" Cate shrieked.

Irene stopped playing and stared at her mother. Taggy abandoned the toys and bolted for the stairs.

"Maybe," Patrick muttered as he gulped down his drink. His vision blurred as he poured another one. *No, they're cloning us. They cloned your girlfriend. She is very much alive.* He glanced over at the photo of Jade and Cate with their arms wrapped around each other that was on the wall next to the photo of his late grandparents.

"Oh God, that's five!" Tori whimpered. It took him a second to realize that she meant glasses of whiskey.

"Do you mean I've drunk five or poured five?" he asked.

"How about we go outside?" John suddenly pulled the bottle out of his hand. "We can sit on the deck and admire the crackling bonfire they've got going in the courtyard."

Patrick only then registered there was indeed a bonfire in the courtyard.

"Wait, what about the kidnapping people thing?" Cate picked up Irene for a snuggle.

"I'm fairly sure no one is being kidnapped," Tori reassured her. "There are plenty of other explanations."

"Um, okay…" Cate did not sound reassured in the slightest.

John led Patrick out onto their back deck.

"You look like you've seen a ghost or something," he insisted as he sat Patrick down before he could fall.

"I have."

"Okay, I'm listening." John sat down beside him.

Patrick showed him a photo that he had taken of Step, Nola, and Isaac.

"I don't remember that." John eyed the photo closely. "When was that? When we were in Global Relations together with Dr. Reid?"

"It was this afternoon," Patrick deadpanned. "Those aren't us."

"What do you mean? It's clearly you, me, and Jade back in university."

"No – when did I ever wear camouflage overalls?" *Until today, that is*, he added silently. "When did you or Jade wear overalls?"

"Good point. So then tell me who this is."

"Robots at the complex. I thought I'd get back into investigative journalism."

"Sorry, robots that look like us?"

"Look, sound, act…I mean, it's more obvious in person that they are different people, but they're like seeing ghosts."

"Wait, so are we cloned? Is that what the Robot Rental Corporation has been up to?"

"Yeah, seems like it. Seems like a study we volunteered to participate in was secretly run by them. And you know what? They took DNA from hospital patients. That's how they got Jade."

"When she was dying from cancer?" John practically yelled. "What kind of vultures are they? Did her family know?"

Patrick shook his head.

"They cloned her and sold her as a robot who would be a surrogate mother for some family. Then they discarded her after she'd given them their kids."

John was now in tears. "Jade would have hated that. I mean, she really wanted kids eventually, but…"

"You'll be happy to know that Nola – that's her name, by the way, and she is very insistent about it – she's as bubbly, headstrong, and intelligent as Jade was. I didn't ask if she could sing, though."

"Wait, what about me? I mean, not me, the guy in the photo."

"He's quiet compared to the others. Just like you! And um, well…"

"Don't tell me he and not-Jade are together!"

"Kind of? Like, not exclusively. There are others involved. Though not the guy who looks like me."

"I really wish you hadn't told me that. I'm going to have weird dreams now. Oh God, there isn't a robot who looks like Cate too, is there?"

"No, there isn't."

"Still going to have weird dreams."

"Well, just to make it weirder, while you can't tell because she's behind a desk, Nola is pregnant. Meaning Jade's parents will have biological grandkids after all."

"Honestly, if her parents had known Jade had been cloned, they'd have probably adopted her. She was their only child! And…wait…who's the kid's father? You mean…"

"Calm down!"

"Easy for you to say!"

Patrick was not sure whether to laugh, considering he had taken responsibility for Anna.

"He isn't you! He's his own man. Nola is not Jade. This is not me. They are just three people who share our DNA. They are our siblings. Our identical twins, really, just younger. Isaac's your kids' uncle. Nola's kid is your niece or nephew. Another cousin for your kids!"

"They're not robots…" John gulped down the last of his drink. "Lord have mercy!"

"That's just it. They *aren't* robots. They're people. People that have no rights. You and I are no different than our brothers in the photo. It's all legal nonsense."

"Write your article when you sober up. Get this out there. I don't know what will come of it, but the Robot Rental Corporation needs to be held accountable."

John slowly stood up and helped Patrick to do likewise.

"They've got to be held accountable before they convince the military or the Federal Cascadian State Police to destroy the robots. I work for the military. I hear things."

Later, Patrick flopped onto the bed as Tori came storming into the bedroom.

“What the hell?” she hissed, though Anna was sound asleep. “What’s gotten into you?”

“I went to see Step at the complex. Got to meet some more robots. Some of them look like old friends.”

He held out his phone, which was playing a video of Jade singing.

“You remember her, right? Jade Vida Charriez? She died shortly after we met.”

“Yes, Jade was in the same ward as me. She sang as part of the Christmas show we put on for the children in the hospital. Don’t you remember me telling you that? We were both friends with Cate and so we visited together sometimes. Cate introduced me to you when you came to visit Jade.”

“They took her DNA too. Her robot version is very much alive.”

“Oh…oh my God, I saw her! She was assigned to the hospital in October. I thought she seemed familiar, but it’s not like I was fully with it then. She really exists?”

“Yeah, well, that’s why I’m acting all weird. Now I need to write what might be the most important article in my life.”

“Why didn’t you tell me you were going to the complex?”

“Because I didn’t want you to tell me not to!”

“You could have been killed or arrested or…”

“I know. Look, I know all you want is a seemingly normal life and a normal family. But that isn’t what we have!”

“Will we ever even come close?”

“Maybe.”

INTERLUDE 10

The palm fronds would not cooperate as Maria arranged them into vases in the sanctuary. No matter how much she considered the precise angles of the fronds in the vases to get them to stand up majestically, they constantly flopped and drooped. She countered the sagging fronds with flowers, but the decorations still seemed inadequate to her. They did not match the vision she had for Palm Sunday, nor her memory of what she had done the year before. *Were they this droopy last year?* She nervously kept trying to fix the fronds and flowers as she listened to Rev. Helen and her secretary conversing about the next day's service from the balcony above her.

I prefer working with living plants, not dead ones that have been cut.

The article she had read that morning had been both heartening and troubling to her. She had shrieked in joy upon seeing Step's face in one of the photographs and seeing his name in print. He was alive and well! He remembered who he was. He was even quoted as saying that he dreamed of exploring the world with his family. As that line seemed a bit out of context in the article, Maria hoped that line was meant for her to specifically recognize.

He still wants to come find us. He hasn't forgotten me or our children.

But the article was troubling not because it argued strongly in favour of the humanity of robots, but because it went into great detail about how the Robot Rental Corporation had run a cloning operation and created people whom they marketed as machines. She was appalled to learn about it, especially how they had lured people to give them genetic samples on the false promise of curing them of diseases. She wondered if the Corporation would try to destroy the barracks and any evidence that the allegations in the article were true. Step was now in further danger, as were all the robots that seemed so joyful, hopeful, loving, and independent in the article. They had their own music, their own new traditions, and their own families. The younger ones – the "newly-eclosed," as the article put it, like ants – reminded Maria of Trinity and her friends. They were new to the world, full of promise and great gifts to offer.

And yet it could all be gone if someone pressed a few buttons.

"The flowers look great!" Rev. Helen suddenly called out from the balcony. "You've got such talent!"

"Thanks," Maria replied.

A few minutes later, Rev. Helen and her secretary switched their topic of discussion to the same article that Maria had read.

"What did you think of Alexander Warrior-Church's in-depth article on the robot uprising?" the secretary asked the pastor. "And the exposé about the Robot Rental Corporation? Did your niece mention anything about it?"

"I haven't talked to her in a while," Rev. Helen admitted. "I texted her this morning and she replied that it was basically true, as far as she could tell. She just worked the desk coordinating rentals. She had never seen most of the facility."

"Really?"

"Yeah, I'm guessing she knew nothing about how the process worked. As for what I think of the articles? Well, I'm inclined to agree with Mr. Alexander if it is true. These are people."

Maria breathed a sigh of relief as she slowly cleaned up the excess fronds, petals, and stems.

"They're living, dreaming people with souls," Rev. Helen continued. "And thus no company should own them. Nor should the government deny them rights."

"But what about them being genetically enhanced? And they're not born the usual way."

"Well, how enhanced are they, really? I don't think it is any different than having natural traits or abilities that are special. Like Maria's green thumb, or Trinity's singing, or your baseball skills. And as for how they are born, that doesn't matter. We have all kinds of ways for people to be born now. If we judged our humanity based on that, Addison, where would we stop?"

Maria was not sure whether she should laugh at Rev. Helen using her as an example of someone having natural talent. Her ability to care for plants came entirely from her conditioning (or her programming, as the Corporation had called it) as a robot. She stifled nervous giggles instead.

"So there'll just be a lot more people out of work, then," the secretary, Addison, pointed out.

"Well, maybe that's a good thing for now. It'd get people paid decently and better social programs."

"I guess. It's just a lot to take in. I wasn't prepared for this kind of article on a Saturday morning. Usually, Alexander Warrior-Church writes calming reflections."

"Well, I felt it was a good read with the morning coffee, that's for sure. It definitely woke me up! Maria, do you need some help?"

"I'm fine! Almost done!" *I'm enjoying listening to your conversation.*

"Did you see the article about the robot uprising this morning?" Rev. Helen had signed Maria up for subscriptions about religious instruction and reflection when she had first expressed interest in learning more about their faith.

"Yes! It was really good. Very enlightening." Maria scooped the spare greenery into the portable composter.

"What do you think about Mr. Alexander's argument for the humanity of robots?" Addison wondered.

"It's convincing." *Well, I already know full well that I am a human.*

"What about the cloning?"

"Terrible!"

"Yeah, it's pretty much slavery," Addison agreed.

"Not to mention theft!" Maria started to haul the composter away. "They took people's DNA and made new people out of it."

"No justification for that, for sure."

"Anyway, I'm heading back out. I've got more seedlings to plant!" Maria hoped to get the chance to talk to Rev. Helen alone later.

"See you at service tomorrow!"

Mercy was watching Tyler and Stephanie at the playground on the retreat centre's grounds. Having emptied the portable composter, Maria wandered closer to them, waved, and went back to work planting.

She could dream of exploring again. What would it be like to be a regular person? Could she ever get over her anxiety enough to go out into the world? Would she be able to set up another household with Step and all their children?

But she smiled and sang to herself. She could imagine them being a family together. She allowed herself to feel hopeful.

One seedling, two seedlings, three seedlings! One for each of my babies. You're all going to be together again, I promise.

CHAPTER TWELVE

Patrick ended up writing two articles that were published under the pseudonym "Alexander Warrior-Church, the Philosophical Pirate," the persona that he usually used to review books and offer reflections on weekly church readings. He imagined his regular readers would be surprised, but he wryly reminded himself that he was finally writing articles he had dreamed of publishing. He studied journalism to hold authority to account, not to review books for a small audience of religious readers. He was tired of hiding behind complacency.

While he wrote the articles under his pseudonym, Patrick used his real name when describing himself in the third person as a victim of the Robot Rental Corporation's cloning operations. (He wondered if astute readers would realize that "Alexander Warrior-Church" and "Patrick Semaganis Kirke" were the same individual.) In the first article, he argued robots were simply humans who happened to have been grown artificially and given some modest genetic enhancements, most of which were to correct problems in their donors' DNA rather than to give them genetic advantages. He included several photos and videos, including one of him and Step in their nearly identical camouflage patterns, and talked about the robots' culture and lives at the barracks.

The second article was more scientifically inclined and included the evidence from the Robot Rental Corporation's files about how they had gone about their operations. He had decided to publish it in the online collective journal he belonged to, rather than try to get government attention. He did not trust anyone else with the information. There could have been any number of politicians, executives, military brass, and scientists who might have wanted to keep the story buried.

Once his articles were published, however, media outlets were clamouring for more information about the "Robot Rental Corporation Cloning Conspiracy," as people now called it. Science reporters presented the whole files about the human cloning aspect – though they redacted many of the names – and ordinary people were taking notice. Comparatively, the article about the robots themselves was less interesting to the media, but since they were linked, readers tended to see them as two parts of the same story. The readership statistics for both articles were nearly identical.

Within a week of the articles' first publication and within two weeks after Patrick's visit to the complex, people came into Tori's bookstore talking about them. Their neighbours asked Patrick how he had been interviewed for the article; they wondered when he had met his robot clone and what it was like to do so. Patrick's cover story had been that he had met the clone the year before when he had first been contacted about the possibility. He and Tori laughed that it was not so much a lie as a mistruth about the photo itself, since he had met Step the previous summer after Tori had decided to investigate him.

By the weekend before Easter, Patrick's article was circulating internationally and being called the most important report of the century. Reporters were arguing its points on national news segments and talk shows. Patrick did several vocally modified audio interviews, which made him and Tori nervous. They were grateful Anna was too young to pay attention.

One of the questions people frequently brought up was why the military was being so controlling of the complex, besieging it rather than letting anyone send in diplomats or even news reporters.

“Listen to this!” Patrick called out from the living room as Tori prepared supper on Friday evening.

“What?” She glanced out the sliding glass doors to see Anna was contentedly playing outside with Grace.

“This commentator says: ‘If Alexander Warrior-Church can make his way safely into the complex (albeit sneaking in through an emergency exit that our military didn’t care about), get a solid interview, and walk out again unharmed, there’s no reason someone else can’t. Our government has trained diplomats. They should use them. They can go alone and unarmed, just like Mr. Alexander did.’”

“What exactly do they think that would accomplish?”

“I suppose some kind of treaty. The Robot Rental Corporation is still trying to say these aren’t humans, but they are co-opting the ‘they are people’ argument against them too, claiming they stole the property and are occupying it without being its rightful owners. The government could step in and negotiate something.”

“The only reason you got in safely is because you look like Step and we had already met him. He trusted you and therefore so did his friends.”

“Well, yes, but most people don’t know that. That would give away who I am.”

“Fair enough. I’m surprised no one has figured it out yet.”

“I haven’t even seen much speculation about it. I didn’t realize how much I had made the persona of Alexander Warrior-Church independent from me.”

Tori's parents were among the few people who knew Patrick had written the articles. While Mike and Cleo Martinez-Williams had been livid upon hearing the story and what the Corporation had done to their daughter, her father decided to use the articles as a marketing opportunity. He immediately released a statement clarifying his and his company's stance on robots: he was against the use of them unless they were allowed to work freely like any ordinary person. 'If they are a person coming to look for a job, they can have one. If someone is using them to save money, I want no part in it.' He did several interviews arguing in favour of the robots' humanity, taking everything his daughter and son-in-law told him on faith. Privately, he explained to Tori and Patrick that Anna's existence was proof enough for him that Patrick's article was the truth. Anna was a human child, so her parents must have also been humans and he would argue for their human rights. Publicly, he left Anna out of the discussion and simply argued that if robots had been cloned from humans, robots were people who deserved to have jobs and independent livelihoods.

"Just got a notification that your articles were published in this week's *The Church Today*," Tori noticed as her phone alerted her. "Has there been much discussion on the religious front?"

"So far, it seems evenly divided. Some clergy and officials think the robots are people and have souls, etcetera. Some are adamant they don't. Perhaps, once more people read the articles tomorrow, there will be more believers in the robots' humanity."

At that moment, Anna appeared at the kitchen door.

"Mama, Papa, come play with us!"

Tori shook her head, insisting she needed to tend to supper.

"You don't normally cook supper," Anna pointed out.

"Papa has been busy writing, so I am making supper and he probably could use some playtime!"

Anna pulled Patrick outside and Grace's little brother Liam almost immediately pounced on him.

When Tori turned her attention back to the yard after putting their eggplant casserole into the oven, Patrick was rolling on the grass. He was under attack from Anna, Grace, and Liam; even their toddler sister, Naomi, joined in the fray. She pushed Patrick around with her chubby fingers until she lost her balance and plopped into a sitting position. From there, she cheered wildly for the older children.

Tori leaned against the doorframe, giggling and taking photos. Keziah, who was nursing her baby daughter while watching from her own back deck, struggled not to laugh so hard that she would disturb the baby.

"Are you all right, Patrick?" Keziah called out teasingly.

"Just fine!" he replied, at which Anna and Grace squealed and attacked him all the harder.

"If you need any back-up, just holler! I'm a fierce fighter and so is this baby girl. But we're a bit busy, so you might be hollering for a while."

Aliya Pike-Macrae, who had been reading as she kept an eye on the children, burst into uncontrollable laughter.

Shortly thereafter, Keziah's husband appeared with a bucket of water-balloons. Aliya scooped up Naomi and put her into Keziah's daughter's playpen out of harm's way.

The ensuing calamity was worth many photos that Tori gleefully took from the safety of their kitchen: Patrick yelping in shock at being suddenly soaked with water, leaping into the air and sending Liam twirling; Grace and Anna screaming playfully and running in circles in an attempt to get away; Aliya emerging from her house with another bucket of water balloons for the children; Patrick teaming up with Keziah's husband; and the two men and three children dodging and pelleting each other with the balloons.

The game lasted about five minutes, just in time for the casserole to be done. Then the four adults directed the children as they all cleaned up the reusable balloon shells back into the buckets. As Tori quickly put together a simple salad, Patrick and Anna returned to the kitchen, huddled together on the doormat, dripping wet.

"Valiant warriors, who won the battle?" she asked, sounding proud either way.

"We did!" Anna squealed, bouncing on the mat and hugging her father. She shivered as Patrick wrapped her in a towel. "We beat the daddies!"

"Once you're not dripping anymore and you've wiped your feet, go on upstairs and get your nightgown on!" Tori ordered.

"What about supper?" Anna's jubilation turned into distress as she momentarily feared punishment.

"Special for tonight, we're all going to eat in our pyjamas!" She playfully tapped Patrick's wet shoulder. "You too, darling husband! Get on upstairs!"

"What about you? You're still dressed," Anna pointed out.

"Once I'm done getting supper ready, I'll go up and change too."

Anna kicked off her shoes and scooted upstairs to her bedroom.

"We're seriously going to eat in our pyjamas?" Patrick wondered, removing his muddy slippers and socks.

"Your shirt, sweater, socks, and hair are soaked!" Tori grinned. "How about we wear our matching teddy bear-print ones?"

One of the gifts they had received for Christmas had been a set of matching nightgowns and pyjamas for all three of them. They had a teddy bear pattern: brown bears, polar bears, black bears, grizzly bears, and panda bears. Every so often, they decided to wear them as a family.

"Strange way to start off Holy Week, but okay!"

Soon they were all sitting around the table in their teddy bear pyjamas. Anna wore a fitted towel that had a set of bear ears sewn onto the hood.

Initially, Anna had been thrilled with supper. She had started to dig into her casserole hungrily, but soon her mood darkened as the food tasted increasingly funny and tingly. Her skin itched under her towel and pyjamas. She felt like she could not eat, so when Patrick put a bowl of peach crumble in front of her for dessert, she burst into frustrated tears.

"What's the matter?" Tori stared at her daughter in surprise.

"I can't eat it! I can't eat it! I don't want it!" Anna sobbed.

"What don't you want?" Patrick was puzzled. Peach crumble was her favourite dessert and he could not reconcile the bowl of it with Anna's terrified tone.

"No peaches! No food!" She curled up in her chair and buried her head in her knees, gagging slightly. "Can't eat anymore! I want to go to bed and I want Taggy!"

At the mention of his name, Taggy dutifully ran upstairs. He was sitting at the foot of Anna's bed when Patrick and Tori bewilderedly brought her into the room moments later.

"It's all right, sweetheart, it's all right," Tori whispered, guiding her into bed. Still sobbing, Anna curled up into a fetal position.

"Are you hurt?" Patrick asked. "Did you hurt yourself playing?"

Anna shook her head.

"Too hot, too hot! Can't eat!"

It was then that her parents realized they were covered in sweat from carrying her and tucking her in. Anna's nightgown stuck to her as much as her wet clothes had. She started to tremble uncontrollably, involuntarily scratching at her skin that was hot to the touch.

"Oh my God!" Tori checked her temperature on her phone. "Patrick, get an icepack and call an ambulance! Her immune system is overreacting to something. This used to happen to me all the time as a kid."

Tori tried to keep from panicking as her fears about Anna's health seemed to be coming true. The little girl began to cough violently and Tori was only able to manage to weakly roll her onto her side at the edge of the bed before she heaved her supper onto the floor. Taggy worriedly inspected the foul-smelling pile and sat attentively.

"Patrick!" Tori screamed. Anna was barely conscious.

He appeared quickly with an icepack. The dispatcher was being difficult.

"Yes, I *know* I'm describing fever symptoms. Yes, I know that little kids get fevers all the time and they don't usually need the hospital." Patrick was furious.

Anna whimpered softly as Tori held her and tried to cool her neck and forehead. She was at least breathing fine.

"You're not listening to me, woman!" Patrick shouted into his phone. "My daughter is five years old and has never been sick yet, but my wife has a severe autoimmune disorder and has had reactions like this before and she's needed the hospital. Clearly, my daughter has inherited *something*! She needs emergency care now!"

"Her breathing is okay, for the moment," Tori reported, hoping that Patrick might calm down.

"Thank God! Keep watching her!" Patrick whispered, pulling the phone away temporarily. Then he resumed his query for an ambulance. "What do you mean, all the ambulances are busy? Look, I know you're short-staffed. This strike has gone on long enough. We're all tired of it. We're tired of checkpoints. I know, it's not your fault. If we get her to the emergency entrance ourselves, how soon will she be seen?"

Upon getting a response, he put on his Ninja-Cowboy jacket and cap.

"We're mailing ourselves to the hospital!" he announced.

Despite having to go through three checkpoints, the Williams-Kirkes arrived at the emergency department quickly and Patrick whisked Anna through to the admittance desk as a "special parcel."

A doctor was immediately on hand; they had often attended to Tori during her hospital stays and were familiar with her medical conditions. Tori breathed a sigh of relief as they hurriedly signed Anna's admittance papers.

"I'm taking charge of you two immediately," they insisted, leading Anna and Tori into a nearby alcove. "We need to get to the bottom of this."

"I hadn't realized how much of a celebrity I am around here," Tori said with embarrassment as the doctor sent out alerts to other members of their team.

"Well, you have an interesting health profile. Hopefully, this is a one-off reaction to something and not the start of your daughter manifesting the same condition."

After several tests, the doctor and their team discovered that Anna's immune system had launched an attack on the water from the balloons. Aliya had filled them with warm water because it was still a chilly day, and this warm water had interacted with the reusable water-balloon shells to produce an ordinarily harmless chemical that Anna happened to be allergic to. Like Tori, Anna had a highly reactive immune system, but not one that attacked her own body – at least, not yet.

By the time they had determined this, Tori had started to get sick as well, having absorbed a lot of the chemical from cuddling Anna. They were both admitted overnight to the hospital in the same isolation room. Anna started to recover quickly and soon became giggly from fatigue and overstimulation. Tori, meanwhile, almost immediately fell asleep from her medication.

"Mama!"

Her eyes flew open. "Are you all right, Anna?"

"Yes. I'm glad I've been sick now, but it was scary. Is getting sick always scary?"

Tori nodded weakly. "Yes, you were very brave. When you get sick, you have to be brave." *Now I sound like my parents.*

Anna giggled. "You are really brave too, Mama!"

"Thank you. Now, I know they probably feel really bad on your itchy ears right now, but put in your earphones so you can listen to music or your forest sounds. Then it will be easier to sleep. We need to sleep to get better."

"Can we still go to church for Palm Sunday? I want to make Easter eggs and sing our songs we've been practicing."

"I hope so. If you go to sleep, we might be able to go home tomorrow and then to church on Sunday."

"I can tell Ellie and Justin about our adventure!"

"Not if you don't get any sleep, because you'll be too tired."

Anna curled up into as comfortable of a position as she could and tried her best to let her music guide her to sleep. Tori increased her medicine dosage just enough to pass out, oblivious to all the lights and noise of the hospital.

Palm Sunday was suitably joyful; Anna had recovered so well that she was able to do enthusiastic dance moves to the songs their Sunday school class had rehearsed. Patrick and Tori proudly recorded her, but the rest of the day was otherwise consumed with discussions about Alexander Warrior-Church's articles.

Everyone wanted to talk about the articles, whether they had read them yet or not. The priest mentioned them in his sermon and announcements.

"We heralded robots as a new technology," he pointed out. "Perhaps, in this case, more of us were like the authorities, worried about what it would mean for our lives and survival, and less like the enthusiastic crowds. But it turned out to be something completely different to what we expected. We did not get robots. We got cloned humans. We could not replicate what makes us human in a machine. As a result, we have thousands of people being used as a slave labour force. People who look like ourselves. They are our brothers and sisters. Literally, for some of us!"

"Impressive that he worked robots and cloning into something about Jesus's triumphal parade into Jerusalem and subsequent betrayal and death," Tori whispered to Patrick.

"Well, it did involve betrayal. And death, for that matter." *Jade and countless others were left to die. Tori was supposed to be one of them. They cloned hundreds of soldiers to make more soldiers – all of whom were supposed to be cannon fodder. Angry mobs are killing robots and tossing them into rubbish bins.*

Tori stood quietly in the corner of the church hall after the service, hungrily munching on a cookie and sipping her tea. She watched Anna play with Ellie and Justin Alvarez-Franklin while their brother Andrew followed them around on his toy truck, too young to join in, but clearly wanting to. Cate, carrying Irene, wandered over to her.

"What a brave husband you have!" she exclaimed. "He's such a good writer."

"Thanks," Tori muttered. Her mug was now empty and she stared at the bottom of it, feigning ignorance. "What did he write now?"

"Oh!" Cate laughed and leaned in to whisper. "John told me about his chat with Patrick and that he was writing an article. I forgot not everyone knows his alter ego."

"What did you think of it?"

"It's so much! Especially about the hospital and stealing the DNA. They promised to cure you?"

"Yeah, and part of me wonders if I'd feel so angry if they actually *had* cured me too. Like if that had been their intention, with the cloning being a side project. But they stole from dying patients too. People who couldn't be cured. All a false promise."

"And they didn't even try! No, they went straight to cloning." Cate coughed and spat out her tea. "I'm sorry, I just get worked up about this. John didn't tell me they cloned Jade, so it was a shock to see her photo with the article. I get that he was trying to protect me, but…"

"Well, Patrick was very upset about that too," Tori reassured her.

"I keep thinking – did they take her DNA samples while I was sitting there with her or you? Could I have stopped them? And then, it's all so weird! Like, of all the people in the world, why would your and Patrick's genetic twins meet up and procreate? Why are they friends with twins of John and Jade?" She glanced over at the children. "It's also weird to think that robots can have kids. What's going to happen to them all?"

"Ideally, they will live happily as families together," Tori insisted.

If they survive the siege of the complex, she added mentally. *The military has mainly kept to patrols and threats, but they might escalate things now that the Robot Rental Corporation has been exposed, along with their complicity in the secret cloning project.*

"What does that mean for Anna, then?"

Tori gritted her teeth defensively. "Why would it mean anything? She's a normal little girl." *You've had her at your house, Cate! Don't you dare insinuate there is anything wrong with her!*

"No, I mean, like…"

"What?" Tori interrupted. "Either you mean she isn't my daughter or you mean there is something wrong with her. I don't see what else that could mean."

"I'm sorry – I didn't mean that. I meant it's all really a lot, okay? And now John is acting all weird and won't talk to me and he's been called to the base for work."

"Sorry to hear that too." Tori really wished she had more tea to drink.

"It sounds like he might not even be able to spend Easter with us!"

Tori nodded and muttered something sympathetic. Luckily, at that moment, Andrew walked/rode his truck toward them and pulled his mother away. Tori refilled her tea and disappeared into the storage closet, shutting the door so she could cry in solitude.

Was Anna going to be all right? Was her allergic reaction to the warm water and balloon casings the start of the same illness that Tori had? What about Step's beloved Maria? What if she really had not been cured, but would just have a later onset of symptoms? Tori had been thinking of her as someone who could take Anna back if she became too ill to care for her herself. What if she could not?

It's not my fault they exist, but I still feel responsible for them. They would not be here if it weren't for me. I consented for my DNA to be taken under false pretences, but they're still the result.

She loved Anna. She was her daughter. She wanted so much for them just to be a normal family. She had someone she could take care of. Patrick had someone else besides her to care for. Her parents had finally stopped treating Tori like a delicate child now that they had a grandchild to coddle. Anna felt like she was hers in every way, especially now that she had given them a good health scare.

You're my daughter after all, and I'm going to fight for you and our whole family.

INTERLUDE 11

"Nola, get the kids to the basement!" Step shouted over the blaring siren. "We need to get as many of us down there as possible."

"Scarlett is in the warehouse with the vats," Nola insisted. "I have to go get her!"

"There's no time. She's got the evacuation notice. Get the kids to the basement!"

"Are you sure you don't need my help up here? We've just lost the life-signals for thirty people." She gestured to the monitor she had been watching.

Including Ren and Isaac... Step shook his head.

"I'll be fine up here. The kids haven't been out of the vats long enough and can't move properly yet. Help them and anyone injured into the basement. Then stay there, please!"

Before Nola could either agree or argue, the blaring siren increased in pitch, warning that missiles were within close range.

"Come on!" Rina suddenly appeared, pulling Nola toward the basement. "We can't lose you."

Nola broke free from Rina and hurriedly gave Step a hug.

"Be safe! I hope I see you again soon."

Step replied something similar before the two women left. He then grabbed a handgun from the locked cabinet in the office before running into the corridor.

Why did I take the time to grab a handgun? What do I honestly expect to do with it against missiles? Or even artillery and rifles?

The military had blown their way into the complex's front gates and had staged a ground assault, though they had not sent out many infantry. The robots had quickly mounted a defence and turned the assault into a standstill. Tanks lined the road all along the length of the barracks, though they had not bothered to surround them on the side roads through the woods. Once the tanks had torn up a large portion of the front lawn and courtyard, they held their fire and the battle had become one of ground troops firing at each other. Step was surprised, but relieved, that the military had held back from shooting artillery at the robots defending the complex.

However, their security system had soon picked up incoming missiles whose trajectories were aimed for the warehouses where the robots were growing in vats. It was clear the military and the Robot Rental Corporation wanted to destroy any evidence of the cloning operations. The ground assault had seemingly been a distraction. They did not need to destroy all the living robots. They just needed to destroy anything that could prove their humanity.

At least, I think that's what their plan is. Step tried to keep the image of Anna crying for him out of his mind. He did not even want to be distracted by thoughts of Maria as he ran through the corridor, calling from room to room for robots to get to the basement. He was conscious that he was getting closer to the vats. The sirens blared louder. Yet, he did not see Scarlett or any of the members of her team who had been tending the vats.

She won't abandon them. They're our babies. Unlike the newly-eclosed robots, whom he still called "kids" despite them being physically nearly adults, the younger robots could not be moved. None of the research that he or anyone else had done indicated whether they could safely remove them from the vats without killing them.

The infirmary was being evacuated, much to Step's relief. As he looked inside, he noted no one had been considered too weak to be left behind.

He had just reached the door to the warehouse of vats when the proximity alarm became an unbearable high-pitched wail, signalling that the missiles were practically overhead. Scarlett was clinging protectively to one of the youngest vats, wherein an infant-sized robot flailing in terror could be seen through the observation window. She locked eyes with Step as the two of them instinctively dropped to the floor.

Now he could not help but think of his family: Maria kissing him for the first time; him coming home to find her on the shower floor with newborn Anna; gazing out at the sunset over Lake Hobidigan with Maria, Anna, and Tyler; his third child kicking as he kissed Maria for the last time; Anna reaching her arms out for a hug through the construction barrier; Tori and Patrick feeding him supper; Nola knocking on his cupboard door...

He recited the poetry from his favourite book.

The Lord is my shepherd, I shall not want...

All of a sudden, the siren faded and the missiles roared overhead. Shortly thereafter, the ground shook and some of the cheap glass shattered. The vats, built to withstand much higher pressure, barely moved. The building did not lose power. As the ground shook several more times, presumably as each missile hit a new target, the siren stopped wailing and soon the sounds of regular humming and beeping overtook the room again.

"What happened?" one of the other robots called out. "Where did they hit instead?"

"I'll go back and check!" Step scrambled up, his ears ringing. "You all stay here."

"Tell Nola that I'm okay," Scarlett pleaded.

"Yeah, I will." *I hope she is. What if the missiles hit the main barracks?*

Thankfully, all seemed to be well as he ran back through the corridor. The main barracks were intact. Returning to his observation station in his office, he saw the soldiers and robots in the main courtyard entrance were stumbling around in confusion, no longer caring to try and shoot each other. There were much fewer tanks. Smoke and fire now lined the road and Step realized the missiles had landed in sequence there, blowing up most of the tanks and artillery units. The road itself looked to be impassable.

"What the heck happened?" he asked aloud.

As if in answer, another robot, Nightingale, stuck their head into the office.

"We need to send out medics!" she insisted. "Our people are injured out there. And if we have bodies to recover, we're bringing them back here!"

"You're not going into any danger," Step protested. Nightingale was highly specialized in medicine. "None of your team should."

"This is what we do. And hey – if we want to prove our humanity, it couldn't hurt to help some of the enemy too. That's what you told us, remember? Love and care for those that hate us as much as we care for those that love us?"

"Fine, that's a good idea. But be careful!"

As Step continued to oversee things, robots began to emerge from the basement. The injured and ill were returned to the infirmary. Nola soon reappeared in their office.

"You're alive!" She hugged him again, tears running down her face.

"Yes, and so's Scarlett," he managed to reply. "We're going to make it, okay?"

"I thought I was going to lose everyone, even the babies," Nola sobbed. "I'm sorry to be making such a mess of things."

"You're doing great," Step muttered, thinking he was about to start crying himself. "We'll get through this. How about you keep monitoring life-signals? I'll go help with the infirmary."

"Why are the really weak signals suddenly moving?" Nola demanded, staring at the screen. "I thought they were dead."

"We've got teams retrieving them."

"I don't think I can look!"

"Ren and Isaac might not be gone yet," Step pointed out. "We might be able to save them."

"When there are dozens of other injured robots?" Nola whispered. "They don't have good odds of making it. Their signals went completely out at first, remember?"

"I'll go see how things are going."

Step was not sure how much time passed until he finally found himself in the large mess hall, surrounded by bodies laid out on tables. The newly-eclosed robots had banded together to prepare the hall, dressing each table so every dead or dying robot had an honourable resting place. Each one was covered in a sheet to their neck and had a sprig of flowers or greenery on their chest.

Nola and Scarlett were gathered in the corner where Ren and Isaac were laid out. They had been placed on a table together. As Step came up beside them, he saw they were covered in their own bedsheets that still had their unit numbers stitched into them. Under the unit numbers, someone had neatly printed their names in large block letters. He noticed the sprigs of basil and parsley on their chests moved slightly.

"They're still breathing," Scarlett reported, glancing up at Step from where she was hugging Ren's head. "We got their hearts beating again. Their pulses are really weak, though."

"And in all likelihood, they're brain-dead," Nola added grimly. "They were really close to an explosion."

"Ren got a major electric shock first. Direct hit to the chest."

Step shook his head, unsure what to say.

"I'm sorry," he whispered. "They followed me and I failed them."

"They wanted to do this too," Nola whimpered. "This is what they chose."

"We all did our parts," Scarlett added.

"Why do we like following our programming so much?" Step wondered, sitting down beside Nola in Scarlett's vacated chair.

"It's better that they did," Nola pointed out.

"But why? I still like fixing vehicles and being a mechanic. You wanted to have kids. Isaac and Ren and all the robots cloned from the military wanted to be soldiers. Maria loves gardening…"

"Yes, but isn't that a good thing? It gives us a purpose in life." Scarlett combed her fingers through Ren's hair.

"We wanted to be more than just our programming," Nola insisted. "Isaac loved animals. He wanted to have a place here to rehabilitate injured ones. He liked exploring near the fence so he could see them in the park."

"And cooking wasn't part of Ren's programming, but he had taken it up," Scarlett added, coming over to squeeze Nola's hand. "I almost forgot it wasn't something he was programmed for."

"Why are you so certain they aren't going to wake up?" Step found himself the most tearful out of the three of them.

"I wouldn't be sitting here in this uncomfortable chair if I didn't think they might!" Nola cried. "Even for a second…one last second…I could tell him we're safe for now."

"Have you heard what is happening outside?" Scarlett asked Step.

"The military is clearing out, but the road is gone. It's a series of craters full of debris. It sounds like the Federal Cascadian Police are here and news reporters and…I don't know, but I think we're going to be left alone for now. The courtyard is a mess, but it was a big empty space. There wasn't much damage to our buildings."

Rina once again appeared, looking anxious and apologetic.

"Um, Step, you're needed in the infirmary."

"Is one of the patients a car?" he asked. "I'm not very useful there."

"You're actually close. A big piece of vehicular shrapnel is melted into one of the patients. You can assist the surgical team."

Step was hardly able to keep from vomiting as he returned to the infirmary, now transformed into a makeshift surgery and covered in blood. Washing and covering himself, he let Rina steer him to the bed where he was needed.

"Oh my God, no!" he shrieked.

The man looked almost identical to Isaac.

"Look, I know you're roommates, but I need you to focus," the head surgeon insisted. "I need you to help me extract these vehicle bits from his body. It was so hot in the explosion that they fused together."

"But…but this isn't Isaac! Isaac is…"

He glanced at the patient's wrist, which clearly displayed Isaac's barcode. The surgical team eyed Step with confusion.

"I assure you, this is Isaac," one of them whispered. "We found him buried in the debris from one of the craters."

"Then who is in the mess hall under his sheet? Rina, go back there immediately!"

"In the meantime, focus please!"

Like his counterpart in the mess hall, this Isaac was comatose, but unlike the other man, he had been given a good chance of survival if they could get the fused shrapnel removed safely. His organs were working well and his brain had not been deprived of oxygen. The shrapnel was mostly fused to his muscles, making removal possible. Isaac would need further surgery later if he wanted to resume his highly physical career, but he would live for now.

He can rehabilitate himself alongside any injured animals he wants.

Rina came sprinting back, but lingered awkwardly in the doorway until Step was done assisting with the operation.

"The man in the mess hall isn't Isaac," she whispered as Step removed his protective gear. "He isn't even a robot. He's…he must be his genetic donor. Even our computers were confused! But he doesn't have a barcode."

The image of Isaac's donor's file flashed across Step's mind. He had been a university student in physics and engineering. His studies had been funded by the military. He had been a cadet and was a reservist. The military had given the Robot Rental Corporation permission to clone many soldiers. Step could not even recall his name, since the list of military donors was long and each donor was similar.

That's why they were so willing to help the Corporation destroy evidence. They did not want the civilian government to find out how deeply involved they were.

"His uniform and everything had blown off," Rina further explained. "The computers thought he was Isaac."

"What did you do to him?" *He was Patrick's friend. His kids are Anna's friends.*

"Nothing yet. I just went to check on him, like you asked. I didn't say anything to Nola and Scarlett yet. How long until we know if the real Isaac will survive and wake up?"

The surgical team had already moved on to another patient as Isaac was moved into the makeshift recovery area. The medic supervising them overheard Rina's question and shrugged.

Step and Rina returned to the mess hall in time to hear Nola scream.

"I'm not Jade!"

The man on the table blinked did not seem to register Nola's outburst.

"He thinks he's dead already." Step rushed in to comfort her. "Remember? Patrick's visit was only a few weeks ago. You look like Jade. He thinks he's dead and sees her."

"Who is he? Where's our Isaac?"

"Alive and recovering from surgery. Unconscious, though. It's not safe for you to go see him yet. This is his donor. Our computers got confused."

"What?" Nola shrieked.

"Patrick?" the man's voice whispered weakly.

He heard my voice. Step let go of Nola.

"Yes, I'm here," he lied, hoping this was a good kind of lie and if it was not, that he would be forgiven. "I'm here. You're in the hospital. I've come to visit you."

He pulled his chair close to the table so he could look at the man's face. He hoped the man would not notice Step looked younger than his friend.

"Love…to…my family…" he rasped. "Tell them."

Step nodded, mentally planning to contact Patrick as soon as he could.

"It was me," the man confessed. "The missiles…I changed them. Sent them away…back onto us…let them live…"

With that, he closed his eyes again and fell back into his sleep.

For a moment, none of the robots around him moved or said anything.

Well, that about confirms it. This God character exists. At least, sort of, somehow. Step stared at the sprigs of basil and parsley on the man's chest, which moved delicately as he struggled to breathe.

"She sang, right?" Nola asked hurriedly, shaking Step's arm. "You were watching her videos. Should I sing him to sleep?"

"What? Why?" Scarlett cried. She was clinging to Ren, who Step noticed now was completely still.

"He saved your life!" Nola sobbed. "He saved the babies. He sounds scared, like a kid. Maybe he won't be if I sing."

“Yes, do that.” Step stood up and hugged Scarlett, realizing that Ren was dead.

Nola sang one of the many endearing lullabies she had been taught. Step did not think that was part of Jade’s repertoire, but the man who was not Isaac seemed to be at peace as he drifted off permanently to sleep.

CHAPTER THIRTEEN

You descended into the tomb, O Immortal. You overthrew the power of death. In victory, you arose, O Christ Our God. You proclaimed rejoicing to the myrrh-bearing women, granted peace to your apostles, and bestowed resurrection on the fallen.

As the Easter service ended, Anna stood by the basket of dyed Easter eggs at the back of the church in bewilderment. "Where are my friends?"

Tori gestured toward all the children who were looking for chocolates hidden among the pews while the adults chatted and made their way to the hall to eat.

"You could play with the Dyrland-Zachariases or with Tashley," she suggested, noting the children who were close in age to Anna.

"But Ellie and Justin aren't here! They said they would be! *You* said they would be." Anna was almost in tears. "We have presents for them!"

"I know I did. Their mother told me they'd be here too." Tori glanced over at Patrick, who was reading his text messages with a look of alarm on his face. "Just a minute, sweetheart. Papa looks upset. I'll be right back."

She rushed over to her husband while Anna wandered into the pews to hunt half-heartedly for chocolate.

"Got a very cryptic note," Patrick announced quietly in his wife's ear. "'Tell your friend's family that he loves them and that he reprogrammed the missiles so they couldn't kill the kids. Your friend not Isaac.'"

"Who's it from?"

"The number that Step gave me when I went to interview him."

"Missiles? Lord have mercy."

The priest came up to Patrick and Tori at that moment.

"Have you heard anything about missiles?" he asked. "My sister lives toward River-Gold Park and there was a lot of ground-shaking last night."

"Could have been a wayward test," Patrick suggested, hoping the priest hadn't overheard any of his conversation with Tori. *I suppose I should confess about the article*, he thought.

"Has Cate reached out to you?" the priest further inquired. "She left me a message early this morning saying John was declared missing and she was too upset to come today."

Tori sheepishly checked her own phone and realized she had received a similar message, but had ignored it in her rush to get ready for church.

"Oh dear," Patrick muttered. "Can we talk privately, Father?"

Meanwhile, Anna numbly hunted for chocolate eggs. Other than a few times when they had been sick or visiting relatives, the Alvarez-Franklins had always been at church. They had never missed Easter before. It seemed wrong to her to celebrate without her friends. After a short attempt, she picked up four eggs and wandered toward her parents. She wanted to go home and she hoped her mother was in a snuggly mood.

Tori was more than happy to take her to Patrick's delivery van. They both felt like crying and so they left Patrick talking to the priest in hushed, concerned tones. Anna knew they were not discussing next week's service. Everything seemed to be getting scarier: the church had been her one refuge where everything had gone smoothly, especially once the curling rink had closed for the summer. Now, even going to church frightened her.

"Why are *you* crying, Mama?" she asked. "I know I'm supposed to be happy, but I miss Ellie and Justin and I wanted to see them! We always spend Easter together. I was looking forward to it!"

"I know, sweetheart," Tori agreed, hugging her tightly. "I'm sure they were looking forward to seeing you too. Something happened to their papa. He's missing."

"Then why didn't they come to church to pray for him?"

"Maybe he is hospitalized like we were last week and they were visiting him there."

"I'm sorry you're missing the food."

"I'm not hungry." Tori had her medication to thank for suppressing her appetite. "You're the one who should go eat! How about we go back inside? Remember that Christ is risen from the dead, okay? No matter what happens."

Anna started to hum Easter hymns to herself as she wiped her face and nose. They slowly climbed back out of the van and returned to the church, where the congregation was celebrating with a large meal. Hardly anyone noticed they had been gone. Patrick and the priest appeared shortly after they arrived, having been deep in discussion the whole time Tori and Anna had been outside.

Tori nonchalantly sat herself and her daughter down at the end of one of the tables. Patrick soon joined them, bringing his wife an entire potful of tea as well as a juice for Anna. The priest and his wife took the chairs beside them and soon someone had brought the five of them a large tray of assorted meats, cheeses, fruits, and chocolates.

"Is everything all right?" Tori asked her husband. "I've missed something."

"Nothing other than John is missing and apparently there was something happening in River-Gold Park last night." Patrick poured himself a large glass of wine and Tori deduced that she would be driving the van home.

"I will wait until we get back to check the news."

"Nothing there," the priest chimed in. "It's a holiday lull."

"Or everything is classified," his wife muttered. "If the ground shook at River-Gold Park, it should be in the news. At least an earthquake!"

"They're trying to get their stories straight," Patrick reasoned.

"Maybe it was raising the dead!" Anna piped up earnestly.

"Kind of," Patrick agreed. He poured himself a second glass, carefully refilling those of the priest and his wife as well. Tori sipped her tea.

"If I hear more from Cate, I will call you," the priest told Patrick. "We might need to arrange something."

"What?" Anna asked.

"If something bad has happened to Ellie and Justin's papa, Father Christopher might need to go visit him," Tori hurriedly explained. "And Papa might have to go too to assist."

"Can I go see Ellie and Justin and Andrew and Irene?"

"We'll drop off their Easter presents after lunch," Patrick offered. "But they might not be able to play."

Anna was thrilled to stop by the Alvarez-Franklin house, even for only a few minutes. Ellie gave her a strong hug. While Irene napped, the three older children seemed subdued and disappointed about missing church. Anna sat with them as they opened their presents. She could hear their mothers crying together in the kitchen and she forced herself to be cheerful.

Patrick stood numbly in the middle of the entrance hallway watching the children play together. The thought of sitting at the bottom of the stairs was appealing, but it only made him think of Step. He prayed he was alive. *Is it odd that I am more concerned about Step than John?*

Checking his phone again to distract himself from his feelings of confusion and guilt, he saw a new headline had popped up: ROBOT RENTAL CORPORATION ORDERS ARMY ATTACK.

'In the early Saturday evening hours, the armed forces attacked the Robot Rental Corporation's Warehouse Complex on River-Gold Park Road. What began as a light infantry raid ended in disaster for our military. Technical difficulties led to equipment malfunction. The official line from their spokesperson is the Robot Rental Corporation strongly requested the offensive. No further details are known at this time.'

"Technical difficulties led to equipment malfunction," Patrick read aloud quietly, thinking back to Step's message. "Apparently, John caused those technical difficulties. What type of equipment malfunction, I wonder?"

Questions swirled around in his head: how did Step, or anyone who had used his contact number to send a message, know about John reprogramming missiles? What had the missiles been intended to hit? What did he mean about killing kids? The complex was much too big for small missiles to destroy it all. How had John talked to Step? Was it even Step who sent the message?

Patrick decided to risk responding.

"I will tell John's wife and children that he loves them. Here is a photo of them with Anna. Thank you. Are you all right?"

He hoped Cate would forgive him for sending a photo he had quickly taken of Ellie, Justin, and Anna playing with their new Easter Lego while Andrew pushed a toy tow truck around behind them. Their faces were not entirely visible.

"Yes, for now," came a quick reply. "Many dead, but all the kids and most of us who weren't soldiers are okay. Missiles were supposed to hit all the vats. Destroy cloning evidence. Military was complicit. Now the whole road is gone. Several units gone. Many dead."

*Many dead…*Patrick meditated on the response. Why had Step repeated it? Was it from shock? Or did he mean "many of us are dead and many of them are dead too"?

It hit him that while his article about the cloning had downplayed the military's heavy involvement in the Robot Rental Corporation's scheme, they had nonetheless been worried about the news getting out later. Hundreds of soldiers had been cloned, all unaware of what they were contributing to, so it was no wonder the military leaders had teamed up with the Corporation to destroy any evidence of the cloning facility. They wanted to discredit Alexander Warrior-Church's article and prevent further investigation.

They were going to kill helpless babies, children, and teenagers in vats. My article nearly led to their deaths.

He buried his head in his hands until another message popped up.

"Your friend has died," Step clarified. "I am sorry. Thank you for Anna's photo."

Andrew drove his toy truck into Patrick's leg, but Patrick did not reprimand him. He could barely force himself to acknowledge him as he realized he was in tears.

"Sorry!" Andrew unknowingly echoed Step's message. "You crying?"

The toddler stared at Patrick in disbelief, wheezing slightly.

"Yes, I am sad," he admitted. "You didn't hurt me. It's okay."

"I give you a hug," Andrew offered. He got off his truck and hugged Patrick's legs so tightly the man had to grab the banister for balance.

Patrick kept quiet about the messages from Step until his family returned to their own house and Anna went to play with Grace in the courtyard.

"But how does he *know* any of that?" Tori wondered. "How was he talking to John?"

"Maybe he was injured and the robots –"

"Is it still right to call them robots?" Tori interrupted, still sounding bewildered.

"That's what they call themselves," Patrick pointed out. "Anyhow, maybe he was injured and they were treating him."

"That would make them better humans than most of us."

"Well, we did give Step a Bible. Glad to see he is absorbing more New than Old Testament."

Tori turned on the screen and set it to the news channel.

"The Federal Cascadian Police has taken over jurisdiction in this case," the reporter announced with excitement. They were standing along a broken road in front of a clump of burnt trees. "The government has given them full authority to investigate the military and their involvement in this incident. The entire board of the Robot Rental Corporation has been arrested. The police have set up a new perimeter around the complex and will endeavour to arrange a meeting with the robots."

Patrick and Tori gasped at the destruction shown from above. The road was nothing but a series of giant craters with mangled pieces of metal strewn through them. Trees surrounding the road were burned and broken. The large courtyard in front of the complex was now a muddy hole.

"Legal teams are already consulting with State Congress," the anchor took over the story. "If it is indeed true the robots are human clones who were formerly enslaved, efforts to determine whether we can extend them legal personhood and citizenship rights are underway."

"I wonder how well that is really going to go," Patrick muttered, pouring himself a glass of scotch. "There's bound to be lots of protesting about that. Will they end up arrested? Put into state custody like children? Given to their genetic donors? I mean, I'd be all for welcoming ours into the family, but would most people?"

Tori shook her head and, against her better judgement, poured herself a glass as well.

"Father Christopher suggested we go to a retreat centre," Patrick continued. "Get away from everything that's happening. My article is everywhere. Someone is bound to figure out who Alexander Warrior-Church is soon."

"Should we leave Cate right now?"

"We can't do anything for her. We can't even tell her about John's message to her! She doesn't know her husband is dead! All she has been told is that he's missing. I feel awful about this. And I feel guilty that I am more concerned about Step than John. John's a soldier. He signed up for this. And if what Step says is true – and I have no reason to doubt him – then he died a hero. I'm thinking about how upset Anna was that her friends weren't in church. She is scared of everything right now. We're all done with this madness, aren't we?"

"All right, we'll go away for a while. I'll let Maureen, Desiree, and Becksy know." Tori collapsed onto the couch, overwhelmed by the strong scotch. "Maybe that will give the world enough time to start making sense again."

Three days later, they took the train to Eastcott. The retreat centre was larger than Tori had expected. There was a decent-sized church, several cabins for visitors, an apartment-style shelter, a cafeteria, and a thrift shop. There was a playground and several gardens. It was a short walk to the main business area of Eastcott, with a library, grocery store, and several more thrift shops. Though it was still only a short distance away from the ocean, the community was mountainous and wooded. It reminded her of a poverty-stricken version of Little Hobidigan, albeit one without a lake.

"Bit of a different world for a woman whose father has a penthouse in downtown Alexandrina and several other properties, isn't it?" Patrick whispered to her.

Tori nodded, admitting to herself she was not used to seeing so many thrift shops in the same place. While she did not like being reminded of her privileged upbringing, she indeed felt uncomfortable. Eastcott felt both cozy and oppressively closed off at once.

Easter decorations greeted them as they arrived at the main office. A giant HE IS RISEN banner draped across the railing in front of it, tied up with white, green, pink, and yellow ribbons. Tori was surprised to see how many flowers covered the grounds, even beyond the gardens. They were meticulously arranged and patterned in various colours. She could not help but wonder how big the flower budget was. There were flowerpots on every available surface, making a path toward the church door and decorating the entrances of the various buildings. The retreat centre itself was peaceful and vibrant.

The church secretary gave them the key to their cabin and reminded them what time an evening prayer service followed by a light supper would be held, then whisked them away hurriedly. They seemed much more interested in the baseball game playing on their datapad in the background than conversation.

"Seems really quiet and still around here," Tori remarked as they entered their cabin, which consisted of a small bathroom, kitchenette, desk, and two double beds. "You'd think it was mid-July or something."

"It's one of those early spring hot days," Patrick pointed out. "Hit all of us like a huge, heavy wall of air."

Tori rolled her eyes. "That's what life is like for me all the time."

"You seem chirpy and excited!"

"Oh, I'm ready for a nap, but I'm looking forward to taking a walk afterward."

"Can I keep watching the baseball game?" Anna asked. "It looked interesting."

"You aren't tired?" Patrick was already starting to doze off.

"I slept on the train here."

Tori set Anna up with a datapad and earphones to watch the rest of the game while she and Patrick napped.

Once the game ended, Anna quietly made her way to the cabin front window. They had a view of the playground and part of the gardens that obscured the church. The trees were tall and had large limbs that stretched across the church roof.

If I were a cat like Taggy, I could climb up the trees and jump onto the roof. Then I'd be able to see everything!

She thought she saw someone moving in the tree branches, which puzzled her. She did not think a church would allow anyone to climb up that high. There were children playing outside, but their babysitters were keeping them away from the plants and foliage. Anna wanted to go join them at the playground but resolved to wait until her parents woke up.

One of the little boys looks familiar. Have I ever seen him before?

He was wearing a giant shirt that covered his knees. It was supposed to be in the pattern of the night sky, so Anna giggled at how much he looked like a little sorcerer. One of the sitters had to keep fixing the shirt so he did not trip on it. Finally, the older one untied a ribbon from a nearby flowerpot and re-tied it like a makeshift belt on the little boy. All the while, the boy kept climbing on the play structure, fairly adept at moving in loose clothes.

When he got to the top of the bars, he stood up and held out his arms in a victorious pose. The sitters soon beckoned him to stop and he followed their instructions, but Anna was intrigued.

Where have I seen someone do that before?

She went back to the datapad and started looking at recent photos. She did not have to search far to find almost the same victory pose: herself on the last day of the children's curling tournament, surrounded by her teammates hugging each other.

"Did you want to go outside now?" Tori's groggy voice startled Anna. "I saw you looking out the window."

"Aren't you still sleeping?"

"I'm tired of being tired," Tori admitted. "I can relax outside. We came all this way!"

Anna bounded out to the playground as her mother followed her, still feeling out of place. Patrick dragged himself outside after them, locking the cabin door like the overly cautious urbanite he was.

"Oh, you didn't need to get up," Tori apologized as she realized her husband had joined them at the playground.

"I think we were all thinking the same thing. Too nice of a day to spend long napping inside! We can sleep tonight."

Anna bolted for the climbing bars and started up them with ease, swinging herself up to where the little boy had been. When she got to the top, she repeated her victory pose long enough for a photograph. She then clambered down and hopped over to a digging toy.

"Hey!"

Looking up, Anna saw the little boy running toward her, his loose, starry shirt-robe flying behind him like a tail.

"Hey!" he called again excitedly.

"Um, hi?" Anna smiled at him.

"Anna?" he blurted out. "You're Anna, right?"

"Yeah…my name is Anna…" She looked around in confusion, wondering if someone had introduced him to her.

By now, all the other children had left the playground and the sitters had disappeared, leaving only her parents watching in confusion.

"Tyler, wait! Wait for me!"

A little girl in a forest-green romper toddled as fast as she could along the path toward the playground.

Wait, Tyler?

Anna stared closely at the boy's face. He was nearly as tall as her and very skinny, but even though he was not round and chubby anymore, his eyes and features were still very much the same as her little brother's.

"Tyler, wait!" the little girl screamed, out of breath from running so fast.

Tori instinctively grabbed her, worried she would trip or completely bowl 'Tyler' over. She exchanged concerned looks with Patrick.

"Tyler?" she asked him, as though the name meant something to her.

"Tyler!" Anna gave her brother a hug. "What are you doing here?"

"I live here," he answered simply.

The toddler screamed again, understandably upset at having been grabbed by a stranger.

"Leave her alone! Kids, come back here *now*!"

Tori let go of the little girl and turned around, only to realize the voice had come from above them.

With horror, Tori saw a woman who looked exactly like she had when younger, except for her very short haircut and muscular physique. Her eyes were a mix of fury and terror, like a hawk perched in the tree. Her pruning shears gleamed like talons in the fading sunlight, but she gently hooked them over a crook in the twigs. With as much ease as Anna had on the climbing bars, she scurried down, leaping from the last branch to land squarely in front of Tori, Patrick, and the toddler.

"Mama! You told me to stay with Tyler!" the girl sobbed, hugging the younger woman tightly.

"It's okay, sweetie!" She lifted the toddler with hardly any effort.

Used to ignoring visitors, she turned her attention to Tyler.

"Why did you run back to the playground?" she demanded. "Trinity had to go to class and left you two with me again. I told you to stay over near the church where I was."

Holy Christ, she was in the trees near the church? And she came over to the playground through the branches? Tori was trying to mentally calculate how that could have been possible. She glanced at Patrick, but he was staring intently at Anna and Tyler.

I knew there was a robot – or at least, a woman who was considered a robot – with my genetics somewhere. Part of me wanted to meet her. But I had not wanted another surprise encounter!

"But…" Tyler gestured toward Anna, who was shocked into silence.

"Yes, that's very nice of you to want to make friends, but…"

"No, Mama, it's *Anna*!" Tyler insisted. "Look! I remembered her! I thought it was her, but I was very little, so I wasn't sure, so I wanted to come back and ask!"

"What?" She looked closely at Anna, staring at her in disbelief.

Anna's eyes welled up with tears as she looked from the woman to Tori and back again. They looked almost the same, but there was something innately familiar about the younger woman.

Her voice was the one she dreamed about. It was squeakier than her new mother's.

"Anna?" The woman's voice became even more squeaky than Anna remembered.

"Yes?" she replied. Tears were running down her face. "Mama?"

Wordlessly, the woman put the toddler down and rushed to hug Anna.

"My baby!" she cried. "My little garden baby!"

"Um, Maria?" Patrick managed to find his voice.

Maria turned to face him, stepping in front of Anna to shield her. Tyler and the toddler rushed behind her as well, evidently used to the routine. They resembled goslings with their mother goose.

"What…who…you're not…"

"That's my new Papa and Mama," Anna clarified.

"But you look like…no, seriously?" Maria could not comprehend how familiar Tori and Patrick were. "You're a couple?"

"I'm Patrick Semaganis Kirke," Patrick offered hurriedly. "I was profiled in an article recently. Perhaps that's where you know my face from?"

Oh, of course, she doesn't want to reveal that she's a robot! Tori reached out toward Anna, but Maria swatted her away.

"Yeah, I read that."

"I'd love to hear what you thought of it." Patrick genuinely wondered how a robot would have reacted to his article.

"Right now?" Maria was puzzled.

"Mama, I need the toilet!"

"I'll take Stephanie into the church," Tyler offered. "You can stay here."

“You’re not leaving me!”

“But I’ve taken her there lots! Rev. Helen is in there getting ready. She’ll keep us safe.”

Maria relented and Tyler took his sister into the church.

“My little sister is named Stephanie?” Anna asked, clinging to Maria’s wrist.

“Yes.” Maria finally burst into tears.

“Oh dear!” Tori gave in to her desire to hug her, wrapping her arms around both Maria and Anna.

“Who’re you?” Maria’s whole body tensed, but she did not push Tori away.

“Um, your sister? Mother? Genetic twin? I don’t know – I just discovered you existed recently.”

Stop babbling, Tori, she admonished herself.

“I can’t go with you, Mama,” Anna sobbed, clinging tightly to Maria. “I’m sorry. I have to stay with my new Mama and Papa. I miss you and Tyler and Stephanie…”

“But you just found us,” Maria whimpered. “I can’t let you go again.”

“Why don’t we all go to church and supper together?” Patrick suggested, his vocal cadence sounding a lot like Tyler’s.

“I can’t!” Maria was shaking.

Tori shook her head.

“I don’t think that would be a good idea. We’re all too shaken up.” She was surprised she was not crying herself.

“Well, we ought to move away from the playground.”

“We could go to one of the sick rooms,” Maria offered as a compromise. “Then we could hear Rev. Helen but no one could hear or see us. But we’re not dressed right.”

Patrick was mildly surprised Maria was concerned about her clothes. None of the robots he had met seemed remotely ashamed of their overalls.

"You look very nice," Anna offered.

"I don't wear dirty clothes to church unless I'm arranging flowers," Maria sniffled. "The kids aren't changed…"

Tori felt self-conscious about her all-purpose outfit. She thought it was suitable for being on a retreat, but she admitted to herself she had not considered anyone actually lived at the centre, even if she knew intellectually they had a shelter there.

"Well, if no one can see us…" Anna pointed out, reaching out and hugging one arm of each of her mothers. "God doesn't care about clothes."

The soundproofed sick rooms were on the upper floor on either side of the balcony. From the sanctuary, they looked like shiny mirrors, but the occupants of the rooms could see the stage and pulpit. Maria, Anna, Tori, Tyler, and Stephanie made themselves as comfortable as they could while Patrick sat with the rest of the congregation below.

"I've scared you enough," he insisted to Maria. "It'll look less odd this way."

Since the room also doubled as a place to take crying children, there were toys on the floor. None of the children wanted to play, however. Anna sat in the middle of the daybed, having barely let go of Maria or Tori since they left the playground, and the two women held her on either side. Tyler clung to his mother's other arm protectively. Stephanie climbed onto her mother's lap and flung her arms around Maria's neck.

Oh God, they do look like me and Patrick! Tori was amazed at how familiar they seemed and how much of a connection she felt to them.

They should have been mine…

“So who are you?” Maria finally repeated, her reddened eyes narrowing again.

“Tori Lapoule Williams-Kirke.” She could not think of anything else to say without telling her whole life’s story. She fought the urge to do that.

“One of the people the Robot Rental Corporation stole DNA from?”

“Yeah, from the hospital.”

“Your husband was too?”

Tori shook her head.

“You just met by chance?” Maria asked incredulously. “We both did?”

“I guess.”

“How did you find Anna?”

“The police decided she was my new mama,” Anna replied for herself. “Is that because you look alike and my papas look alike?”

“Yes,” Tori clarified.

“Where is Papa?” Tyler asked.

“He’s stuck somewhere,” Tori tried to explain.

Maria started to cry again.

“I saw him, Mama,” Anna squeezed Maria’s arm. “He was building something.”

“Working for the Robot Rental Corporation,” Tori added.

“He’s trapped there,” Maria whimpered. “He couldn’t come find us.”

Tori firmly believed Step would eventually leave the complex and find his family again.

"He is trying to keep everyone safe there, for now," she suggested. "I don't think he can sneak off without someone noticing."

Maria nodded.

"I'm sorry," Tori continued. "I'm sorry for how everything turned out."

The prayer service was fairly short and it was soon time for Rev. Helen's sermon. While everyone in the sick room could hear, none of them were able to listen or process what was being said. There was something about the Apostle Thomas, the road to Emmaus, and fishing. Tori felt she knew these stories by heart now after thirty-eight years and they sounded like background music. She heard the words, but they seemed garbled and meaningless.

Had she stolen Anna? Could she in any good conscience take Anna home again now? And yet part of her fiercely wanted to snatch her away and run back to the train station.

Anna concentrated on her own heartbeat and how much she did not want to let go of either of her mothers. She marvelled at how alike they seemed. Upon seeing her mother, she realized why she had implicitly trusted Patrick and Tori so quickly. They looked like her parents. She did not know why, but she did not care. She loved them all. She did not want to leave either of them behind. She had a baby sister, just like her friend Grace did. She imagined them all coming back to Goat Cove and sharing her toys with Tyler and Stephanie. It was a happy thought, but it did not negate her tears.

Maria was crying so much her vision was permanently blurry. She listened to all three of her children breathing around her, slightly out of sync with each other, and did not move except to give them reassuring squeezes. She did not want to leave the room. As long as they were in there, they could just be a family together. She would not be found out about being a robot. She would not have to watch someone else take Anna away from her again, even if just for the night.

Right now, they could all simply be.

INTERLUDE 12

"What do we do now, Mama?" Tyler asked, standing awkwardly with Stephanie in front of their bathroom door.

Maria stood in the middle of their apartment, staring into nothing, unable to move or think. They had eaten the supper served after the service and she had managed to get her two younger children home from the church. It was supposed to be bath time, followed by a story before bed. That was their nightly routine. She had rarely deviated from it.

But she had not actually eaten, instead letting Tyler have her soup. Running bathwater was beyond what she was currently capable of.

Her eldest daughter had found her, but Anna could not come home with them. She had come face-to-face with not only her own genetic donor but also Step's. She was glad Anna had been adopted into a loving family where she had been safe and happy for the past two years, rather than languishing as an experiment for the Robot Rental Corporation, being in a state-run group home, or being given to hateful parents. At the same time, she was devastated they were such kind and wonderful people who had all the resources in the world to fight for Anna, and that Anna herself seemed to want to stay with them.

Maria had envisioned her daughter happily running into her arms and coming home with her, having supper with Tyler and Stephanie, and getting tucked into bed with a story like she had before. It was a naive dream that could not have happened. Her daughters had no relationship with each other. Tyler had become the responsible protector. When Anna had been taken away, he had been barely able to walk and talk. She had no relationship with the little boy he had grown into. She had not even initially recognized him! Anna had spent nearly half of her life away from them. She was not a toddler anymore. Maria wondered if she herself would have even recognized her eldest daughter if Tyler had not already done so.

Thank God for the Corporation enhancing our memory skills! She was still not sure how Tyler had realized his sister was at the playground.

Why did he recognize her? What good can come from this? Other than finding out that Anna is safe and happy…

Maria burst into tears and collapsed onto the floor. "She'll never come back to me…"

Tyler left his little sister by the bathroom door and came back to hug their mother.

"Why can't Anna live with us?" he asked innocently. "There's room for her."

"My big sister! We can share!" Stephanie clapped her hands excitedly.

"I'm sure you would," Maria sputtered. Judging from the lovely clothes Anna was wearing, she probably had lots of toys and books to share. *They wouldn't even fit into this apartment.*

"She can come home now," Tyler reasoned. "She was lost and now she is found."

It's not that simple, my sweet little boy. I wish it were. Maria tried to answer, but the words caught and she simply choked into more sobs.

"It's bath time?" Stephanie wondered. "Bath and beddies?"

Maria nodded and, with Tyler's help, slowly crawled toward Stephanie. She had to concentrate on every minute task: plug tub, run water, test water, add bubbles, strip each child, place each child into the tub, put clothes in the hamper, scrub children, turn off water, and let the children play. Maria made herself comfortable on the floor mat, not reacting to the silverfish that had invaded the bathroom. The little bugs crawled around her feet, but she only stared emptily at them.

"Mama, I'm cold," Stephanie whimpered as the bathwater cooled.

Looking up from the floor, Maria's eyes darted around the bathroom. *Where's her towel and robe?*

"Mama!" Stephanie tried to climb out of the tub and grabbed at the nearest towel, but ended up stuck on the edge.

Maria bolted up and pulled her daughter the rest of the way out, wrapping her in the towel the toddler had reached for. It was only once she had bundled her up that she realized the towel was her own, not Stephanie's.

"My robe!" Stephanie reached for her bathrobe, which turned out to be on the back of the door, as it always was. "I'm cold!"

"Just a second – let Mama get it!"

The robe would not fit properly around the adult-sized towel Stephanie was wearing, but she did not mind looking like a fresh roll as she scampered to the bedroom.

"My turn to pick a story!"

"Yes, you pick out a story for us! Then I'll be in there to help you change."

Tyler had nonchalantly climbed out of the bathtub and found his own towel. Relieved, Maria handed him his bathrobe and leaned against the wall. The room was spinning around her.

"Are you sick, Mama?" Tyler asked. "I'm sorry. I thought you'd be happy!"

"Me too, sweetheart."

"Is there enough space in the tub for Anna at bath time? What will happen when she comes home?"

He really believes she's coming home.

"I don't know. I suppose one of you will have to take your own bath. We'll see!"

Dear God, how would I do bath time with Anna back? Should I even think about it? How was I planning to do it before?

"There was only one tub in our old house too," Maria added, as she ushered Tyler into the bedroom. "It was even smaller than this one."

"I picked a story!" Stephanie waved a book about a space-travelling cat and pigeon in the air. "My favourite!"

Tyler did not object at all, even though he had been getting annoyed recently at how many times Stephanie wanted to read it. With difficulty, Maria smiled at them.

"Let's get you two into your pyjamas!"

Once the children had gone to sleep, Maria flopped down on the couch in exhaustion. The wind picked up outside and she could hear rain splattering against the windows.

Oh no, I completely forgot my shears in the tree!

Maria suddenly sat up in horror at the thought of the wind blowing the sharp tools out of the tree onto someone or against a building. She had only intended to leave them there while she gathered Tyler and Stephanie back from the playground. The tree was close enough to a well-used walking path that they could easily hurt or possibly kill someone.

Not wanting to risk that happening, she threw on her raincoat and ran back toward the tree. Despite the coat, she was soon soaking wet, but she was relieved to have something specific to concentrate on.

Climbing the tree to retrieve the shears in the dark and rain was onerous, but she was still able to do it relatively quickly. Once she had delicately landed on the ground again, she turned and realized she was in full view of the cabins.

Anna is just over there, hopefully sleeping after such a difficult day. I could go get her... For a moment, she considered marching over to the cabin where the Williams-Kirkes were staying and demanding they hand her daughter over. But what kind of threat would her pruning shears be against them being her legal parents? Even if she succeeded in killing them – the thought of which horrified her – she had no legal claim to Anna. Someone else would take her.

She dashed back to her apartment as quickly as she dared on the slippery path. Once back inside, she tried to get herself ready for bed. Both of her children were breathing evenly and soundly, untroubled and excited, but she laid on the couch, wide awake and listening to the rain.

Finally, she decided to open her phone and look up Patrick and Tori Williams-Kirke. She was shocked when she saw several articles about how Tori was the daughter of a wealthy business owner. Tori showed up in lots of profiles of Michael Brettley Martinez-Williams, founder and CEO of Ninja Cowboy Courier Company. In recent articles, he had mentioned his new granddaughter and how proud he was of her. There was a photo of Anna with him beside a Christmas tree. She was surrounded by unopened presents.

Were those all for her? Meanwhile, Maria had hardly ever been able to give her children anything that was not a donation.

I have no money. I have no legal standing. I am considered discarded property. How could I ever hope to get Anna back from someone with so much wealth? She seems so happy! She wanted to come back with me, but she wanted to go home with her new family too.

There was another article that focused on Anna: YOUNGEST-EVER WINNER OF GOAT COVE CURLING KIDS' TOURNAMENT. There was Anna, wearing a uniform with the image of a baby goat on it (Maria choke-laughed through her tears at the pun), surrounded by four other children who were all at least two years older than her. The article proclaimed that no five-year-old had ever done so well as Anna had. Maria had to look up what curling was, since she was confused when the eight-year-old team leader called Anna "the best sweeper he had ever seen." There was another photo of Anna, this time with Patrick as her proud father, and Tori's father's name came up again as having sponsored the barbecue after the tournament.

My daughter has an extended family. She has friends. She does things. She goes to school. She doesn't hide like she would with me. Maria shuddered and wrapped herself up in her blanket at the thought of even walking Anna to the school in Eastcott.

There was an extensive article about Tori being ill for much of her life, including having many extended hospital stays. There was nothing about other children in her family, either from her parents or Tori and Patrick. She was her father's precious jewel of a child. Her mother seemed relatively aloof in comparison, not appearing much. Maria wondered if she had decided not to get close to her daughter because she was afraid of losing her.

I can relate to that, she thought to herself, wondering about the relatively obscure woman who was only mentioned in passing in the articles. Was this woman technically also her mother? How similar were they?

Finally, she tried to fall asleep by imagining her spaceship. She was flying it while Step sat in the co-pilot's chair, following her orders. Anna was sitting with him. Tyler was monitoring something and keeping Stephanie occupied. They were together as a family.

Except Step keeps turning into Patrick, while Tori keeps showing up on the bridge behind me. She's helping Tyler and Stephanie.

She knew she had successfully fallen asleep when Anna started sweeping the spaceship's floor while singing *Shall We Gather at the River*.

CHAPTER FOURTEEN

Anna clutched a crocheted octopus close to her chest as she curled up beside the artificial fireplace in their cabin.

"I miss Taggy," she whimpered, worming her way deeper into her sleeping bag. "He always snuggles me."

Tori nodded absentmindedly. "Me too."

She had been staring at the dancing flames and basking in their warmth. The warm weather had given way to a windy rainstorm, so she and Anna were both shivering. Patrick was pacing around rather than being wrapped in blankets.

"Do you want me to snuggle with you?" Tori offered, seeing that Anna was still trying to get comfortable.

"Okay, Mama." Anna stumbled over the word "mama" and sniffed back tears.

"The bed will be warmer than the rug," Patrick pointed out. "It's still getting heat from the fireplace and it's higher up."

Anna nodded and let Patrick pick her up in her sleeping bag to be set onto the large bed. Tori crawled into her own sleeping bag and curled up next to Anna.

"Why wasn't I allowed to go home?" their daughter finally asked.

"They couldn't find your mother," Patrick suggested, though he was not sure if that was entirely true. "The cops tried to find her, but they found us instead."

"Why?"

"Because we're twins," Maria answered hurriedly. "We weren't born or raised together, but we are twins."

“Papa and my old papa too?”

“Yep,” Patrick added, sitting down on the bed beside them.

“So you’re my uncle and auntie?”

“Yes, and we didn’t know about your mama and papa, or you or your brother and sister. That’s why we couldn’t tell the cops to take you home, either.”

Anna seemed to be trying out new names in her head.

“Uncle Papa and Auntie Mama,” she whispered aloud. “I like that.”

“So do I,” Tori agreed. “I should have always been your auntie. I wish I had met you and your mama and papa sooner.”

“So you’re Tyler and Stephanie’s auntie and uncle too, right?”

“Yes.” The thought that she had a nephew and another niece warmed her heart.

“Could they come live with us? My mama too?” Anna’s tone was one of excitement and anticipation.

“Well, they could…” Tori glanced up at Patrick. All the obstacles to having three new residents in their relatively small townhouse were flashing through her mind: the bedrooms were small, there were only two bathrooms, Maria would need work, they would need to come up with an explanation for where Tori’s long-lost little sister had come from, etc. But they all seemed like surmountable obstacles to her.

“But this is where they live now,” Patrick pointed out. “They are happy here. Your mother has a job here at the retreat centre.”

He had almost said “happy and safe,” but he decided it was better to protect Anna from being scared.

“My mama can’t be happy without me!”

“No, I suppose not,” Patrick agreed. “I was thinking of Tyler and Stephanie.”

"We look a lot alike!" Anna remarked, cozying up tightly to Tori. "Almost as much as my Mama and Auntie Mama do."

"Yes, Stephanie looks like you did when you first came to live with us."

Tori wiped away tears at the thought that her own joy at having a new daughter had been at Maria's expense, and that Anna had been gone for her little sister's entire life.

"Perhaps we can all live close together someday," Tori suggested. "But your mama and siblings won't come to live with us yet."

"First of all, they have to meet up with your papa again," Patrick insisted. "Then, we will all figure out something."

"When is he coming back?"

"We have no idea," Patrick answered quietly.

"Hopefully soon," Tori reassured Anna. "Maybe we'll be able to spend Christmas together."

"Christmas is *months* away!"

"It'll be here soon enough," Patrick whispered. "When you get to be old like us, time will seem to go by faster."

Because they did not want Anna to overhear anything, Patrick and Tori stayed silent as their daughter – niece-daughter – drifted off to sleep. While Patrick stared at the fire, Tori cried silently and squeezed her eyes shut, hoping she would fall asleep. She desperately wanted to talk to her husband, but the storm prevented them from going outside. She lay in bed, trying her best to sort out her thoughts.

Dear God, what are we really going to do?

Tori thought back to her life before they had adopted Anna. Her store came to mind: her beautiful store with books, candles, icons, cards, toys, and many other items that she arranged in elaborate displays; her lending library that children and adults alike had flocked to; and the café that had become a fixture in downtown Goat Cove, complete with a community fridge. Her father had given her the money to start and secure the business as a wedding present. In his mind, it had always just been something for his little girl to do between hospital stays. He was pleased she had inherited some of his business sense and kept the store afloat for the past decade. Meanwhile, the business had been her main reason to get up in the morning. The weeks had gone by as she had circled through the seasons. Her life had felt meaningless until Anna showed up.

Will we go back to that life? Will I go back to having only the store, reminded endlessly of Anna each time I walk in? Will Patrick go back to being obsessed with the Repair Squad?

But Anna had a mother – a mother who could climb trees and balance a toddler in her arms, unlike Tori. Once she had recognized her, Maria's love for her eldest daughter had been obvious. Anna had immediately reached out to her.

Anna's precocious memories definitely have something to do with what the Robot Rental Corporation did. She and Tyler should not have recognized each other, especially not the boy. I could see her remembering her mother, especially since we look so much alike.

If anyone had done a DNA test, Anna would undoubtedly match Maria perfectly. It would be obvious that, while Tori and Maria were identical, Anna had inherited the altered, "improved" genetics. There was no legal way that Tori could claim Anna as her own, except for the obvious fact that Maria was not legally considered a person.

Hannah got them identity cards, Tori remembered, thinking back to how long ago the previous summer seemed. Maria had a job at the retreat centre, which undoubtedly required some type of documentation. She had taken her children for medical appointments. The police simply had not fully followed up on the "Maria Maria Garden" listed as Anna's mother on her records, thinking she was someone's alias because there were no records for Maria herself. Tori was not sure if the police's oversight was a blessing or not. Everything might have been resolved sooner, especially if Hannah Ang Lukas-Black had gotten involved. Anna would have been able to stay with her mother and siblings. Step might have been able to come home to them. Tori and Patrick would have continued to live their lives in Goat Cove, unaware of their relatives in Little Hobidigan. The whole rebellion at the complex might have never happened, and John Alvarez-Franklin would still be alive.

Perhaps the police would have realized there was something odd about how closely their genetics matched. Perhaps the Robot Rental Corporation's secret would still have been exposed. Perhaps the army would have succeeded in wiping out all the robots.

At some point during the night, Tori did fall asleep. She dreamed about being in church for Easter (or was it Christmas, or a mixture of the two?) with Anna by her side. Next to Anna was Stephanie, dressed in a matching dress. Tyler, in a sparkling outfit, was between Stephanie and Maria, who was dressed to match Tori herself. Step and Patrick were assisting with the service, looking like bookends on either side of the altar.

Could it really be possible someday? Anna thought so. She had babbled about sharing her clothes and toys with her new sister.

All the clothes that Tori had bought for Anna when she had first arrived would now fit Stephanie.

But they would not be her children anymore. They were her nieces and nephew. Maria would be their mother. It did not seem right for that not to be the eventual outcome of their legal predicament. Anna had been kidnapped from her parents. They had never surrendered her to anyone else.

The next morning, the three of them decided to go for a walk on the retreat centre grounds. Tori and Patrick kept glancing upward nervously, wondering if Maria might leap down onto them from the trees. Anna kept looking around for Tyler and Stephanie, disappointed when she could not find them.

They found Maria in the fruit and vegetable garden, diligently pruning the lemon trees and blackberry bushes. Tori was relieved she was on the ground.

"Good morning, Mama!" Anna called out. "We're sorry we missed the morning prayer service. Did you go?"

Maria smiled at her daughter and Tori was sure she had never seen her do that before. The joy on her face reminded her of the video of herself on the opening day of her store. She was thrilled, but nervous.

"I was too tired," she admitted. "I could not sleep well."

"Us neither," Anna answered. "I mean, I slept okay, but Ma- Auntie Mama and Uncle Papa didn't much."

All three adults smiled at each other awkwardly.

"I'm sorry, I started off really badly…I was so surprised to meet you," Tori stammered.

"Likewise," Maria agreed. "So what do you think?"

She did a childish twirl, as if to show off a new pair of overalls.

"You look great…"

"Do I look mechanical to you?"

Tori and Patrick shook their heads, but Anna gave them all a puzzled look.

"Why would you look mechanical, Mama?"

"That's a good question," Patrick interjected. "She shouldn't look mechanical at all."

"I thought your article was really good," Maria added. "Did you make up the bit about the spaceship?"

"No, that's a direct quote from Step."

Tears welled up in Maria's eyes. "You spoke to him?"

"Spaceship?" Anna asked.

"Your Uncle Papa wrote an article about some of the things going on right now. Some of the scary things," Maria tried to explain. She had referred to Patrick as Anna's "Uncle Papa" almost as easily as Anna had. "He got to talk to your Papa and he mentioned travelling with Mama on a spaceship, like in our books."

Maria glanced up at Tori and Patrick before turning to see how Anna reacted.

"Our spaceship!" Anna bounced giddily. "I remember! We were going to look at all the plants and insects."

The little girl then turned to Patrick, seemingly hurt. "You got to talk to my Papa?"

"Yes, and he asked all about you and wanted to make sure you were safe," Patrick admitted. "He was glad you were happy."

"Where is he?" Now it was her turn to cry. "How come he couldn't visit me?"

"He is in the place where the people took him. The Robot Rental Corporation's warehouse complex."

"Why?" Anna wondered. A thought occurred to her. "They called him a robot…the cops called him a robot! But he's my papa!"

Maria put down her tools and instantly reached out and hugged her. "He's both, sweetie," she confessed. "That's how the company made robots. We are just people like your Uncle Papa and Auntie Mama. Really, okay?"

"And I was trying to help everyone see that," Patrick explained. "That is why I went to visit your papa. I wanted to help him."

"I wish you could come home with us," Anna told her mother. "I love you, Mama."

"I love you too, sweetheart. Never forget that!"

"To be honest, we would love to have you be a part of our family," Tori admitted. "If you do want to come live with us…"

"I have to stay here," Maria pointed out. "It wouldn't be safe."

"Where are Tyler and Stephanie?" Anna asked. "Can I go play with them?"

Maria nodded. "They're over at the playground again. Trinity is the girl watching them, if you want to introduce yourselves."

Patrick led Anna over toward the playground, but Tori lingered by the vegetable garden.

"Do you need something else from me?" Maria asked.

"No, but…I guess I kind of want to talk."

"About what? I don't talk much."

"Well, you look like me, you sound like me, but you certainly don't move like me. I guess I wondered if you thought like me, too. I want to know more about you."

"Nothing much to know. I've been a gardener all my life. That's about it."

"You like books about spaceships."

"Do you?"

"Sometimes. I like lots of books."

"Me too. I like to learn things. Something they programmed, I think."

"I wasn't programmed to like learning, but I do."

"Oh, that's good. Guess it's just our natural human curiosity, then!" For the first time, Maria genuinely smiled at Tori, rather than only at Anna.

"Would you consider coming to live with us?" Tori asked again. "You're my little sister, okay? No matter what anyone says."

"I'd do whatever would make Anna the happiest, but I need to keep my kids safe. If she's safe with you, and the other two are safe with me here, then that's that. But if I could leave? Maybe?"

"Anna means the world to me, too."

Maria gave Tori a look of exasperation. "She is literally the reason I'm not still owned. I've been feeling like a part of my body has been ripped away from me for the past two years! I just want to hold her like I used to, to make her breakfast, to put her to bed at night, to read stories with her…"

Tori wiped away tears. *Those are the things I want to do with her, too.*

"I'm happy and relieved she means so much to you too, though," Maria continued. "I read about your family."

"I am too sick to have any kids. Anna has been a gift."

Maria nodded, unsure how to answer that.

"Thank you," Tori awkwardly added.

"You're welcome? I mean, I didn't give her to you. All I did was send her with her father to get groceries!"

It was Tori's turn to nod.

"You'd really let us live with you?" Maria asked.

"Yes. We'd find you your own house eventually…"

"I had my own house before."

From Maria's wistful tone, Tori could tell she meant she wanted to go back there. She thought of the grow-boxes filled with dead plants, the bathroom with the toys and potty hidden away, and the counter with the jar of spiced apples on it. Hannah Ang Lukas-Black considered the place to be a vacation spot – a temporary refuge, at best, and the place of childhood memories – but Maria considered it to be her home.

The garden needs someone like you, Tori thought to herself, refraining from saying it aloud. There was not much sense in telling Maria that she had been at her house.

"And you will again," Tori promised.

"Hopefully, someday," Maria agreed. "And you could visit."

From her finality, there was no doubt in either of their minds where she intended Anna to be.

INTERLUDE 13

After the military had attacked the complex, the Federal Cascadian Police took over jurisdiction of the area. They had taken responsibility for securing the perimeter of the complex as they continued their investigation, leaving the robots alone. Step and Nola had insisted on meeting with one of the lead investigators; at that meeting, the police made it clear they did not want to bother them. Both sides were suspicious and therefore guarded around each other, but two months had gone by and everyone had been fairly safe and respectful.

It was the middle of June and the complex was running as smoothly as possible as they repaired the heavily-damaged front courtyard. Their orchards and outdoor gardens were growing well. They had a sense of normalcy and a new routine. Step could occupy himself with compiling statistics and reports, overseeing how well the complex was running. He did not feel like he was living in a state of emergency anymore.

The wounded were recovering and most of them had been able to resume some duties. Isaac had taken on a shift in the head office every few days, but he still spent most of the day sleeping. If he felt like venturing outside, he went with Step to plan out a place for animal rehabilitation.

"If we're going to live in the woods, we ought to help take care of it," Isaac had insisted on their walk that morning. "According to the materials I've read, there is so little of it left."

"You suppose we'll always live in the woods?" Step often asked variations on that question.

"I like it here. I'd like to stay. I want to raise my kids in this place."

Step smiled and thought of those kids. They were still tiny newborn babies, having been born at the beginning of June. Since their birth, Nola spent most of her time tending to them and rarely made her way to their office, though she sent him a lot of messages. While she was exhausted, she was joyful. Isaac and Nola were also excited about Scarlett's baby that would be born at the end of summer. They would soon be a family of six.

"You'll be a happy family here," Step had agreed with Isaac. "That's why I have to leave soon. I need to find my wife and kids."

Thanks to Patrick, he now knew where they lived. He could go find Maria and start a new life with her again. The complex was home for most of the robots, but not to him.

Yet that would mean leaving his new friends – his siblings, as he thought of them – behind, possibly forever. How easily could he hope to visit the complex again? He was not sure he could get away safely, let alone return. He would at least wait until Nola was more mobile, he decided, and he would insist on being able to keep in communication with the robots.

Someday, maybe we will be able to live peacefully and freely. At this point, robots were stuck at the complex with no human identity cards.

Having returned to the office after his walk with Isaac, Step was lost in thought, staring out the window into the trees at nothing in particular. After a short discussion with some of his fellow council members, Isaac had gone back to their room to sleep, while Rina and Nightingale went back to the kitchen and infirmary. While there was plenty of noise in the corridor, the office itself was quiet.

"Hey, Step!" Nola called out, confidently coming through the door with one baby in a sling and the second in a basket on a cart. "How are things?"

"Um, fine," he muttered, the clattering of the cart bringing him back to his work. Looking at the charts on his desk, however, he could barely remember what he had been doing.

"Figured it was time to show these two how we do things," Nola explained, parking the cart with the sleeping baby on it beside her workstation. "Everyone wants to see them. I'm going to do lessons for all the new parents!"

"That sounds like a lot to add to your schedule," Step pointed out, his voice sounding tired.

"Yeah, but sex, pregnancy, and early childhood care is what I was programmed for!" Nola's voice was raspy but Step could tell she was thrilled. "Since my babies are already here when the others won't be born until late summer or early autumn, like Scarlett's, everyone wants to see them to get an idea of what their own children might be like."

"They are fascinating," Step agreed. "I keep forgetting how little newborn babies are."

"Yes, but now, they want some quiet," Nola continued, bouncing the baby that was in a sling. Step could not see them well enough to discern which was which, since they both had curly black hair.

"We can definitely give them that," Step agreed, getting up to close the door. He put a DO NOT DISTURB UNLESS URGENT sign on it. "We can work on charts."

While the baby in the basket was sound asleep, the baby in the sling grizzled and fussed. Nola pulled them out and Step immediately identified him as Bear, whose skin was the colour of chocolate, though lighter than Isaac's. Bear noticed Step and started to cry.

"Oh dear, you're really having a tough day, aren't you?" Nola crooned at him. She burped him and the crying subsided.

Step laughed. "Yes, I am, actually," he admitted. "Though I know you weren't talking to me."

"Is there something I can help with?"

"I was just thinking about my family."

Step glanced into the basket where baby Jade was still sleeping. She seemed unwilling to let her brother's distress interrupt her nap. Jade had olive skin like her mother (and namesake, for that matter) and reminded Step a bit of Anna as a baby.

Where are you now, my sweet daughter? When will I see you again? How can I return to your mother and siblings? How can we be a family again?

Leaving the complex would mean he would have to forgo seeing Bear and Jade grow up, meeting Scarlett's baby, seeing how the complex changed and evolved, and enjoying life alongside his newfound siblings. He wondered if Maria would get along with them. She always wanted to be alone. It had always been just the two of them and their children. Maria had hardly ventured anywhere without him. She had been content to tend to her plants. She had not spent much time in the barracks once she had emerged from her vat and completed her basic maturing process, but she likely did not have any fond memories of it. She would not want to live there again.

"Have you heard any more about them and if they are safe?" Nola asked, mistaking his wistfulness for anxiety. "Has something happened?"

"No, as far as I know, they are still in the place where Patrick said they were back in April."

"Oh, that's good." Nola managed to calm her son down and get him to doze off. "Can I see the charts you were working on?"

"Sure." Patrick showed her the datapad, reading the title FOOD SUPPLIES for himself. *Oh, that's what I was trying to read.*

"We are getting low on lentils," Nola read, frowning as she scrolled through the chart. "We can't grow those here. At least, we don't have any planted and it's probably too late to do it now."

"What makes you say that?" Step wondered. His eyes had wandered back to reading maintenance reports. He felt much more at ease with mechanical issues than food supplies.

"Because I know how to grow lentils?" Nola's frown became one of annoyed exasperation. "I'm not sure why I bothered reading about them, but I did. I mean, half our food is made from them! The Corporation had a huge supply, but we're going through lots of it."

"Could we still try?"

"No, we don't have enough space." Nola wiped her eyes and muttered nonsense in frustration.

"What's the matter?"

"Nothing, I just started spontaneously crying. If anything, I was worrying about food."

Jade made an annoyed snuffled cry as she slept, as though she too were worried about food. Step figured she probably was dreaming about it, since she loved to eat.

Just like Ren did, he thought sadly. He recalled giving Ren his unwanted meals and how hungrily he had consumed them. Eating and sleeping had been some of Ren's favourite activities and his biological daughter took after him.

"You're worried about food and I want to go find my family…I guess we're not the most productive pair today."

"I admire your commitment to staying here, but you clearly want to go home and you should! We can handle ourselves."

"But this *has* become my home as well." Step felt that explanation did not adequately describe his feelings. "I may have found it prison-like, but it has been relatively comfortable. Most importantly, I'm working with all of you! I may not have wanted to join you…like, to mate with you – but I still feel like your brother. At least, I think I do."

I am not sure what having siblings is supposed to be like.

"And your family wouldn't want to move here," Nola concluded. "Which is too bad, considering we could use another expert on plants!"

"Maria does not really do well with lots of people," Step explained. "And our kids have never lived in a place like this. They've been raised like regular human children. It would be too strange for them."

He selfishly wanted to have his own home again. It would not matter where it was, as long as he had Maria and their children.

I have another daughter, he reminded himself, putting down his maintenance reports to admire Jade further. *I wonder what she looks like!*

"We will miss you very much," Nola insisted. "But we can see each other again. Not just like in your book, either! Someday, hopefully soon, we will be able to visit each other like normal people. Like how my previous owners had lots of guests, or like how people used to go see my donor perform."

"To think only a few weeks ago you didn't want to know anything about her!"

Nola laughed. "And now I named my daughter after her! Her singing was really lovely."

"Yours is too."

"Thanks. The babies at least agree with you! Now, about those lentils…I think we could try hydroponics, or maybe a small garden, but it won't get us nearly close to how much we need. We will have to find an alternative…"

She started narrating to Bear and Jade as Step nodded, turning back to his mechanical report about how a leak had been repaired.

I will go find Maria at the end of the month, but here will always be a second home.

CHAPTER FIFTEEN

With the ongoing strikes, there was no real end to the school year in June. Anna and Patrick submitted a form to the school district and they sent Anna a certificate saying she had completed her first year of formal schooling. She was eligible to move up a level in her classes. Grace ran over to their house excitedly to announce that she, too, had received her certificate. To celebrate, Patrick and Grace's father took their daughters to Tori's bookstore to pick out presents, followed by going for ice cream.

For the first time since she had returned to Goat Cove after their retreat, Anna seemed happy and bubbly about the excursion. While she had tried to resume her life with Patrick and Tori, she cried herself to sleep every night, did not seem to enjoy any of her toys or books, and only played half-heartedly with her friends. In fairness, Cate Alvarez-Franklin was withdrawn after John's death was announced, keeping her children at home and limiting interaction with them and Anna, so Anna often felt she only had Grace to play with. She had put most of her efforts into her schoolwork and retreated a lot into her bedroom, snuggling with Taggy as she listened to audio stories.

"Is she like a teenager already?" Grace's father had joked, only to be met with angry glares from Patrick and Tori. "Well, I mean, you would think *her* father had been killed by robots, rather than Ellie's."

"Maybe she is really sad for her friends," Aliya had interjected before Patrick could start an argument. "Just keep your mouth shut, honey."

The two men had already had several arguments about who was killing whom. Grace's father was convinced the robots were dangerous, whether or not they were machines. He was convinced the military had been right to attack them. He was now angry with the Federal Cascadian State Police, as he saw them as "bungling" the situation. In his view, Patrick was a biased enemy whose views were not worthwhile. The only reason the two men were still on speaking terms was because they both took the commandment to "love thy neighbour" seriously. For the end-of-school-year excursion, they let their daughters interact with each other while they themselves supervised them separately, each pretending the other man was not there.

From Tori's perspective as she watched everyone from the main desk, the two men were tense as they examined displays on opposite sides of the store. Neither of them actually needed to pay much attention to Anna and Grace, who were safely occupied trying to decide which *Creature Tales* book-and-stuffie set they wanted.

Please try to keep this a fun excursion for Anna, Tori silently willed her husband. *She has been understandably upset for weeks.*

All three of them had been upset by their retreat. Meeting Maria and her two younger children had shattered them all emotionally, despite the relaxing setting. Tori was both distraught and relieved to have finally met her counterpart and to have resolved the identity of Anna's missing mother. She was happy Maria knew Anna was safe. She was thankful Maria had not attacked her. She was furious they now had to pretend they had never met.

Anna had enjoyed herself a lot on the retreat. She had started to get reacquainted with Tyler and to get to know Stephanie. They had played and read stories together. Maria had painfully kept her distance, only giving her eldest daughter two hugs per day and otherwise pretending to ignore the Williams-Kirkes. Tori was not sure whether that was for her own benefit (not wanting to get too attached again, similar to how Tori's own mother had always been distant) or because she was afraid other visitors would ask uncomfortable questions. However, as they left for the train station, Anna had insisted on giving Maria a long hug and had clearly not wanted to leave her behind.

It probably took all of Maria's willpower not to snatch her away. How could she watch her missing daughter disappear again?

Tori started to cry and retreated into her office. Anna was being stoic as she went through the *Creature Tales* sets and she did not need to see her mother – her aunt-mother, Tori reminded herself – in tears, otherwise she would start to cry too. Grace would then get distraught and the whole afternoon would be ruined.

Then they were expected to put their week-long retreat behind them and return home to Goat Cove, which already felt like an impossible task, but they had been faced with John Alvarez-Franklin's funeral and the loss of one of their closest friends. Considering how emotional their supposed retreat had been, Patrick and Tori did not feel they had enough strength to support Cate. The whole family felt like all their best friends had disappeared.

Anna bit her lip as she tried to be as enthusiastic about *Creature Tales* as Grace. Each book-and-stuffie set reminded her of Tyler and Stephanie. They did not have any of these sets, despite Stephanie loving animals and having a beloved bunny toy she treated like a pet. Anna had felt guilty as she saw their fairly empty bedroom, thinking of all her stuffed animals and how much her brother and sister would like to play with them. The newest *Creature Tales* video had featured a camel; Tyler had practically fallen in love with the character.

I don't want to buy myself the camel as a present. I want to get it for Tyler! And the whole bunny family for Stephanie.

"What's the matter?" Grace asked. "Is the camel story sad? I haven't seen it yet."

"It's about a camel who goes out into the desert to be with God," Anna explained. "It's not really sad, except he sometimes gets lonely."

"Should I get it to read?"

"Yes."

Anna ended up choosing a raccoon stuffie and the associated book, which was a story about faith and perseverance as the raccoon character tried to get into a sealed rubbish bin. It made her laugh and she wanted to laugh more again. She and Grace proudly toted their new camel and raccoon into the ice cream parlour.

"Ooh, is that the camel from the new video?" Grace's father asked. "I look forward to watching that one."

Grace nodded, beaming at him.

"What kind of ice cream do you all want?" her father further inquired jovially, pointing at the array of flavours on the menu.

Anna felt overwhelmed and glanced at Patrick. The counter obscured her view of the list.

"What did we have last time?" she whispered. "Do they still have the apple pie flavour? I can't see the menu."

"Yes, they do," Patrick replied, sensing that Anna's enthusiasm for the excursion had worn off entirely. "Cinnamon apple pie."

"That's what I want."

"I want raspberry bubblegum!" Grace decided.

Patrick shuddered and Grace's father laughed.

"Yeah, it tastes like an energy cocktail," he joked. "Gets the kids ready for that stuff young, doesn't it?"

"I'm more partial to coffee," Patrick muttered. "Which, incidentally, is the flavour that I will get."

The four of them sat down with their ice cream. Grace and her father dug into theirs hungrily, while Patrick slowly savoured his and watched Anna numbly pick at hers. Seeing that everyone was looking at her, Anna smiled and tried to eat more enthusiastically. Watching the four of them around the table, Patrick was reminded of the archival videos of the robots eating before the uprising the Robot Rental Corporation had shown the media. The robots had all supposedly been the same, but they each had different attitudes to their food. He wondered if the Corporation had ever noticed or cared.

The robots' personalities had been considered interesting quirks that made them more endearing and relatable to ordinary humans, and therefore less frightening to customers. Patrick could only imagine what Grace's family envisioned when it came to robots, but he certainly knew the other man would be furious if he brought up how much their eating ice cream reminded him of the robot videos.

Did they clone you? Patrick wondered. *Would you feel any differently if they had?*

He, Tori, and John had thought of their robot counterparts as siblings. John had been willing to die for them, even after only seeing a photograph. Patrick and Tori wanted to bring Step, Maria, and their younger children into their family. Yet there were many others who were furious at the possibility of having been cloned, advocating for the right to euthanize their robot counterparts. A small but militant movement had sprung up calling itself Donors' Rights, the tamest of whom still wanted complete authority over the robots with their DNA, primarily as their personal servants or to be genetic matches for health-related causes. That these were fully grown humans with their own autonomy did not cross their minds.

"Are you done your ice cream?" Grace innocently asked Anna. Her own mouth was a fluorescent blue as she sucked on her spoon. "Is it okay?"

"Yeah, I just want to enjoy it longer." Anna swooped her arm into her bowl and ate a spoonful of ice cream with exaggerated slowness.

Grace gave her friend a look of confusion, while her father gave Patrick an exasperated glare. He clearly thought Anna's theatrics were insolent.

"Come up, hurry up!" he muttered, still trying to feign jollity.

"No," Anna replied. "It's my treat!"

"I'm not finished either," Patrick pointed out, gesturing to his half-empty bowl. "But if you two want to head out, that's fine."

"Can't we wait for Anna?" Grace asked. "She can come over and play, right?"

"When she's done acting like a prissy little princess, sure. Let's go home and watch the camel video!"

Patrick stopped eating his ice cream altogether, but the other man's happy tone prevented him from replying. Grace's father sounded more excited to go home and watch *Creature Tales* than Grace did. He had made "prissy little princess" sound endearing, as though he called Anna that all the time.

Maybe he does, and he's just hidden it from us.

"Yep, prissy little princess – that's me!" Anna giggled. "I'm a little robot princess!"

Grace's father laughed uncomfortably and pulled his daughter away from their table.

"Bye, Anna! See you soon! Thank you for the fun visit!" Grace gathered up her new camel stuffie and books as her father beckoned.

"Robot princess, eh? What kind of primadonna bullshit is that?"

Grace stared at her father while Patrick meekly turned back to his ice cream and gestured to Anna to do the same. Patrick had never heard his neighbour use that type of language before.

"That's a bad word, Papa!" Grace admonished him.

"And I'll repeat it again if she comes over to play. I'm done with that crazy kid. Let's go!" With a flourish, he whisked Grace and her camel stuffie out the door and into the early summer sunshine.

None of the other customers at the ice cream parlour had noticed the exchange, as Grace's father had kept his voice pleasant and sing-songy throughout. Out of embarrassment, Patrick hoped most of them assumed the Pike-Macraes had simply been in a hurry. He wanted to melt into his ice cream bowl.

Anna gently sat down her spoon and pushed away her ice cream, clearly starting to cry. She grabbed her raccoon stuffie and curled into a ball on her chair.

"That was very mean of him," Patrick managed to say. "I'm sorry that happened, sweetie. You were being very good and having fun."

"He hates me and won't let Grace play with me. Her mama does, but maybe she won't now. I won't be able to play with anyone."

"I don't see why Grace's mama wouldn't let you play with her," Patrick reasoned. "She can stand up to Grace's papa. He's been mean like that for a long time to us."

"I shouldn't have said I was a robot princess."

"Why not? You are! Well, sort of. And you and Grace were having a fun time and there is nothing wrong with playing pretend."

"Did he really just want to go home and watch *Creature Tales*?"

"Maybe? Us grown-ups can be very strange. Why don't we go back to Auntie Mama's store? We can pick out another book."

Anna stopped crying and sat up excitedly.

"Can I pick out presents for Tyler and Stephanie? They don't have any *Creature Tales* toys or books, even though they really like the videos."

"That is a wonderful idea! Yes, let's go get presents! Let's pick out something for your mother and Auntie Mama too."

"And you! You should get a present!"

"All right, presents for everyone!"

They left the ice cream parlour with much more joy and dignity than their companions, practically skipping back toward the bookstore.

Later that evening, however, Patrick came downstairs to find Tori in the kitchen, staring wistfully at books that Anna had picked out to send to her siblings. Taggy was rubbing at her ankles, wondering why his bedtime snack was delayed.

"Everything okay?" he asked tentatively, despite her body language making it clear it was not. He thought it wisest to give his wife the dignity of answering for herself.

"Are we going to have to move?"

"I hope not. One grumpy neighbour who seems to have had it out for our daughter longer than he let on shouldn't make us have to move."

"What if he turns the neighbours against us?"

"Well, your dad has several houses we could hide out in if they come after us with torches and pitchforks," Patrick attempted to joke.

"I thought we were fitting in so well!"

"So did I! Honestly, I think we still are. No one on the Repair Squad has said anything."

"Would they?"

"Everyone's got their own opinions about the robots. Most of it is still based on half-truths, lies, confusion, and fear. All I can do about that is keep writing. Maybe I could try visiting the complex again."

"How is that going to help Anna?"

"The sooner she can see her other family without having to hide, the better."

"And if we get killed, or get them killed, in the meantime?"

"Well, then all our troubles would be over, wouldn't they?"

"And…I'm just so selfish, in that I don't want to lose her!"

"We won't. She might go to a different house, but we won't lose her."

Patrick's phone suddenly started buzzing. "Speaking of the Repair Squad, Carlyn's wondering where I am. I'm supposed to be over there discussing with her and Becksy about the three of us re-shingling our shared roof tomorrow."

"Right. You do that. I'll give Taggy his snack and head upstairs."

Instead of going into her own bedroom, Tori gently knocked on Anna's door. Taggy leapt up onto the little girl's bed and she sat up slowly, taking out her earbuds.

"Hi Taggy! Hi, Auntie Mama!"

"I'm sorry to bother you." Tori leaned on the doorframe.

"Are your meds keeping you awake? I could listen to another story."

"Thank you, that's a good idea." Tori sat down on a cushion beside Anna's bed. "Which story do you want me to read?"

"No, tell me a story! Uncle Papa said I was a robot princess today. I was just playing and Grace's papa called me a 'prissy little princess' and so I said I was a robot princess. Then Uncle Papa said I really was a princess. Can I be a princess in the story?"

She nodded, her husband having told her of the incident at the ice cream parlour. "Yes, I can do that. Now, snuggle up with Taggy."

Anna did so, grabbing hold of Tori's hand.

"Once upon a time, there was a castle in the middle of a beautiful garden. The castle was home to a queen, who had been elected queen of the garden by all the plants and birds and insects and squirrels and other creatures. She took wonderful care of them. She was very happy in her garden, but she was lonely in her castle."

Anna giggled at the thought of her mama as a queen like in the fairy tales she had read. They always seemed to wear long dresses with puffy skirts and sleeves, along with elaborate hairstyles. Those outfits would be impractical for gardening. Her mama never wore such things.

"One day, a prince arrived in the garden," Tori continued. "He had heard how lovely it was and how it had a kind and generous queen. He asked if he could live in the castle with her. The creatures soon elected him their king alongside her. Together, the queen and king continued to look after the garden. Soon, they had a baby princess, and the queen took her everywhere in the garden, showing her the plants, and birds, and insects, and spiders, and squirrels, and everyone else who lived there. They were all very happy together, and the princess learned to be kind and generous, taking care of the creatures and garden."

"And they lived many joyful years together," Anna finished. "Nothing bad ever happened to them."

"Well, that is one ending."

"Everyone says change is good, but it hurts a lot."

"Well, everyone says change is good and then we have strikes and riots and protests. People don't really like change. It *does* hurt. And you've been through a lot of big changes for someone who is only five years old. You are a very brave princess."

"I want everyone to be together. And happy, like in your story."

"Me too, sweetie."

Tori waited until Anna fell asleep before slipping off into her own bed. Against her better judgement, she took out her phone, which had several notifications.

Having come across Patrick's initial articles from the spring, Hannah Ang Lukas-Black had reached out to Tori in a string of frantic but apologetic messages. She now realized why Patrick had seemed familiar to her when they had met at the lake: she had purchased the robot that had been cloned from him. She still had not seemed to have made the connection between Tori and Maria, but she had correctly guessed that Anna was the same baby her robots had created.

'I had got them human identity cards and all the right documentation,' she explained at the end of her confession. 'I even got their barcodes deactivated. Don't know what went wrong. Maybe the company lied to me. They never touched Step or Maria or baby Anna. It was all done remotely. Guess there was some chip in them and that's how they took Step back.'

'Angry cops got involved first,' Tori replied. 'They decided his card was fake and took Anna. Company took Step and we got Anna.'

Hannah called the next morning, catching them both before Patrick could scurry off to the neighbours'. Despite being in South Cascadia, she wanted to ensure Step and Maria's identity cards were reinstated, and she felt from Patrick's article that the Williams-Kirkes would be supportive.

"This will only help one family," Hannah admitted. "And I know it is asking a lot from you, considering it could up-end everything with your daughter. But we can hope that human rights will eventually be given to all the robots, while still helping Step and Maria now."

After the phone call, Tori was not sure how her husband managed to shift his focus back to repairing the roof.

Our daughter might leave us, but we will suddenly have new relatives. Tori curled up onto the couch in her office, unsure how she was supposed to feel.

"Can I get you anything?" Desiree asked through the closed door.

"No, I'm just going to wait in here."

"Wait for what?"

"Wait until my brain unscrambles a bit. Let me know what I can do to help you."

"If it gets busy, I will. And if you want to talk, I'm here. I'm good with secrets."

While Tori agreed with Desiree's assessment of herself, she had no idea where she would begin to explain her current situation.

"I'll think about that."

Satisfied, Desiree returned to the main desk, leaving Tori to her anxious imagination.

INTERLUDE 14

"Papa, is that you?"

The little boy with dark brown curly hair came running toward Step. He wore an oversized short-sleeved shirt with the Cascadian flag on it. The short sleeves went almost past his elbows and whatever shorts or trousers he had on underneath were hidden by the shirt.

Tyler? You're...well, you must be three and a half years old by now. You hardly look anything like what I remember. Patrick had shown him a photo from April, but Step still had a hard time reconciling the boy with the toddler he had left behind.

"Papa?" Tyler asked again, stopping a safe distance away from the man in camouflage overalls approaching the apartment. He looked about ready to turn around and make a run back for the sliding screen door.

"I...I'm looking for your Mama. Your name is Tyler, right?"

Tyler nodded excitedly.

"You look just the same, Papa!"

He started running toward him again and reached out for a hug. Step knelt down and wrapped his arms tightly around his son.

You're so tall and skinny! You must be half as tall as your mother already. You used to be so chubby and soft. I can feel your spine and shoulder blades! I have missed so much of your young life...

"I've missed you, my little man," he managed to say aloud. "You've grown so much! How are you doing? Are you happy?"

"I'm good," Tyler replied, sounding slightly confused. "You don't look any different at all. You still have the same clothes on."

Step had never considered changing his overalls. They were starting to fade and fray from so many washings, but they were still comfortable and had no holes.

"Yes, they never gave me new clothes. When you get to be old like me, you don't need to get new clothes that much. Besides, I wanted to make sure you and Mama recognized me!"

"I'd never forget you, Papa! I never forgot Anna, either! I saw her, Papa! She had a new mama and papa, but she remembered me!"

Step hugged Tyler again, thinking of how much he wished he had been able to bring Anna home. He had taken her with him and he ought to have brought her back.

"I never forgot any of you, either. Hopefully, we will all be together again soon." He let go of his son and glanced around the yard. "But now, where is your mama? Is she all right?"

"She's inside." Tyler looked back toward the sliding door in bewilderment. "She was in the kitchen. Where did she go?"

The kitchen area on the other side of the glass door appeared to be empty, except for a little girl who was pressing her whole body against the screen door. At first, Step thought she was naked, but then he realized she was wearing a dark beige romper that almost perfectly matched her skin tone.

"Tyler!" she called out in a high-pitched toddler voice.

Anna? No, that's not Anna – I've seen Anna. Anna is over five years old. That must be...

Step burst into tears at seeing his younger daughter in person for the first time.

"Papa, are you okay?" Tyler gave him another hug.

"Who is that?" He gestured toward the little girl, despite being certain she was the daughter Patrick had referred to in his messages. "She looks just like Anna."

The baby is two years old. I missed everything about her.

"That's Stephanie," Tyler answered matter-of-factly. "She's my baby sister."

"Tyler, open the door!" Stephanie demanded.

Right, Tyler can open doors now. He's the responsible big brother. The baby can walk and talk. I've been gone much too long.

His son dutifully slid the door open and Stephanie came tumbling out, barrelling headfirst into Step.

"Whoa, whoa, sweetie!" The little girl clutched his legs tightly. "Careful, you don't want to fall." *Or for me to fall over.*

"Tyler called you Papa!" Stephanie insisted excitedly. "He's always right."

"Yes, this is Papa," Tyler confirmed. "You're too little to remember him."

Step inevitably laughed through tears as he recalled feeling her forceful kicks. She had been their little soccer player and she was still strong and determined as a toddler.

Her name is Stephanie. Maria named her after me.

"I love you, Papa!" Stephanie proclaimed.

"I love you too, my little Stephanie!"

He gathered both children together for a hug. He was not sure how long they stood by the screen door, but it seemed to be a lifetime and no time at all.

Their moment was interrupted by a quiet shriek and he looked up to see Maria standing in the kitchen, wide-eyed and covering her mouth with her hands. Her expression seemed to be a mix of elation and disbelief.

"Maria!" he called out joyfully.

As she lowered her hands from her face and emerged from the shadowy kitchen, he noted she was still beautiful to him. Her face looked much the same as before. From her hurried demeanour and the belted sundress she wore, Step guessed his wife had finished up for the day and had changed out of her overalls. But she still had dirt under her fingernails and twigs in her hair, which was cropped short as it always had been.

Do you usually change out of your overalls after work now? He was suddenly self-conscious, thinking he ought to have been better dressed upon his return. *We're robots. We wear overalls. They're comfortable and practical.*

"Rev. Helen sent me a message that you were coming," Maria whispered. "I…I didn't know what to do or think or say or…I panicked and ran into the bedroom, crying. Then I heard your voices…"

Oh, my sweet, anxious Maria…

"It's Papa!" It was her turn to receive a look of confusion from Tyler. "Why would you be scared of Papa?"

"I…I don't know…"

Tyler left Step to go dutifully comfort his mother. Step imagined he was quite used to comforting and consoling her by now, because he seemed to do so expertly for such a young boy.

Step took the opportunity to pick Stephanie up. The little girl wrapped her arms and legs around him, snuggling her head into the crook of his neck, just like Anna had.

"She's beautiful," he offered, gesturing to their youngest daughter. "She is everything I hoped she would be."

Maria nodded, sobbing quietly. "I missed you so much!"

"Don't cry, Mama," Tyler reassured her confidently. "Papa is home now, and so Anna can come home again, and we can all be a family together."

Step wished he could share in his son's conviction. He used his free arm to hug Maria, who reciprocated with a kiss.

I missed you, my beautiful wife.

He went through the rest of the afternoon and evening in a daze. He was with his family again, but they were in a strange place. Step fumbled around the kitchen in an effort to help Maria make supper, but he felt like a visitor. She had done this hundreds of times. If anything, he was interrupting her normal routine. They once had routines together, but now he was not even sure if she needed him there. It was clear she *wanted* him to be there, as she frequently stopped to kiss him, but he was not useful in making food with her. His life had been up-ended again.

"Can Papa come watch *Creature Tales* with us?" Tyler asked.

"Of course he can!" Maria smiled at Step, relieved he could spend time with their children and let her cook. "We will have time together later."

She pulled him in for another kiss and then affectionately guided him over to where Tyler and Stephanie were huddled on the couch around a datapad. Tyler held a stuffed camel, while Stephanie was surrounded by bunnies.

"What's *Creature Tales*?" he asked the children as he sat down.

"It's where animals get together to tell Bible stories and sing songs," Tyler explained.

While the songs were catchy and the stories were sweetly done (even if they barely resembled his favourite book), he paid less attention to the cartoon than to his beautiful children cuddled up on either side of him. Stephanie soon fell asleep at his left, clutching his arm tightly with all four of her little limbs. Tyler leaned his head against Step's right shoulder. While his son seemed entranced by the show, he kept looking up to make sure his father was still there.

I have been dreaming of you for so long, wondering what you looked like. Wondering even who Stephanie was. I didn't know if you were safe, or if you were still with your mother. Now, here we are, a seemingly normal human family. Everything that I fought for and wanted. But what am I going to do? We can't stay here forever in this tiny apartment. How are we going to get Anna back? She is happy in her new life. Why would she want to come here?

He felt more comfortable by the time they finished supper. Maria suggested he clean the dishes and put them away, as this would give him time to figure out his way around the kitchen while she gave the children their nightly bath. The kitchen was tiny and neatly organized. As he familiarized himself with the space, he noted the apartment was smaller than just one of the sleeping rooms in the complex. There was very little to it: the kitchen was just a section of the main room that had a couch and shelves along the walls, with a folding table and chairs for meal times; there was a bedroom off to the side where the children slept; the modest bathroom rivalled the kitchen in size (or lack thereof); and a tiny storage room with a laundry machine to fill in the gap between one apartment and the next. It was cozy and Maria had done her best to make it their home, just like she had done with their garden shed and then the cabin, but it felt crowded. All he had were his overalls, a small bundle of personal effects, and his datapad with his favourite book, but he seemed to take up too much space.

"Where do you sleep, Maria?" he asked, looking at the children's bedroom. There was a bed, a crib, a storage shelf that had once been a changing table, a bookshelf, and three bins of clothing stacked on top of each other.

"On the couch," she answered as she emerged from the bathroom. "It pulls out into a cot. I've slept there ever since Tyler outgrew the crib. It's big enough for the both of us."

"Storytime, Papa!" Stephanie called out, bouncing in her bathrobe. She grabbed a book from the shelf and waved it at him.

"I'm not sure if I'm as good as *Creature Tales*, but I'll try."

Once he had tucked in Tyler and Stephanie, marvelling at how easily he had resumed the routine he had had with Anna, he returned to the main room and found Maria sitting on the pulled-out couch with a book.

"This used to be our favourite, remember?" She held the book up toward him and he could see that it was a graphic novel about a spaceship exploring the stars. "We used to imagine exploring places and learning new things. That we were brave and powerful and free to go wherever we wanted."

Step nodded, thinking of how often he had retold the story to himself as he laid in his cupboard at the complex.

"I missed that book. Glad you still have it!"

"What would we do now if we could freely go anywhere? Now that our identity cards have been restored? I still don't believe we will be safe…"

"I don't know." He sat down beside her. He had never settled on future plans beyond being with Maria and their children again. "I couldn't stay away from you any longer."

Maria smiled at him. "We're together again. That's all that matters. We're going to stay together and build a life for ourselves and our kids. All of them."

She put the book down and started kissing him as passionately as she could, no longer inhibited by having to look after children. Step noticed she had closed the curtains while he was reading bedtime stories.

How did we ever actually finish a book? He laughed to himself at how often Maria had done the same routine. They would start reading a book, then she would put it down and kiss him. The book would be forgotten until at least the next day.

"I admit, I've been looking forward to this," he whispered between kisses. He quickly unclasped her belt and slid his hands up her dress.

"Me too."

He was relieved when she removed his overalls and climbed on top of him.

"I thought we'd be out of practice," Maria purred, sliding off her underwear. "Two years is a long time."

"I remember." He kissed her neck as she removed his undergarments. *Overalls aren't always practical*, he joked to himself again. "I've dreamed so much about you."

She guided him into her. "I've missed you so much. Every part of you."

"Some parts more than others." He flung her dress off.

"Sorry about how I look."

He shook his head, unsure of what she meant. "You look beautiful."

"I'm glad you think so."

Eventually, they laid together on the cot, naked under a heavy blanket. Maria had her head on his chest and he could tell she was crying quietly.

"We're going to be all right, Maria," he whispered.

"I wish I could believe that. I'm scared this is really all a dream."

"If it is, it's a very vivid one. Much more vivid than any dream I've had before." *And I've had a lot of them.*

"I know, and then I started thinking about what might happen. It's all so overwhelming! Everything is going to change for us again. You know me and how much I hate change."

"Well, you're much better at it than I am."

"Starting with tonight. I could be pregnant again soon."

Step burst into laughter.

"That would be wonderful, wouldn't it?"

"I don't want to get too hopeful about anything."

"What?" He stopped laughing. "Your optimism and faith has been my example. We have nothing *but* hope now."

"I've had to hide for two years," Maria sobbed. "I thought you were dead! I lost my baby girl and had to raise two little kids by myself. I still don't have Anna and I don't know if I'll ever be able to be her mother again."

"But you kept at it."

"I know, that's why I just don't want to get too hopeful. But we're together again."

Step dropped his hand down to Maria's tightly muscled abdomen.

"We've got two wonderful kids with us, one who is still safe and happy despite not being with us, and if we do soon have another baby – and we probably will – that child will have a whole world to explore. They all can just be regular kids. We have the freedom to be human beings and live human lives. We can give our family a proper home. We won't have to hide anymore."

"What would that really be like?"

"I don't know." The image of the Williams-Kirke house suddenly came to his mind. *They don't have to hide. We could have a home like that.*

"I don't either. I look forward to finding out."

CHAPTER SIXTEEN

"Oh my…" Tori squeezed her muscles to keep from passing out as she tried to process the headline running across the screen: ROBOTS GRANTED ASYLUM AND SOVEREIGNTY IN RIVER-GOLD PARK.

"Well, thank God for that!" Patrick and Hannah toasted their lemonade glasses.

"What does that mean?" Anna asked, glancing between the headline and the adults.

"It means the people called robots at the complex in River-Gold Park are going to be left alone," Hannah explained, reading the news from her phone. "And they will be allowed to control the complex, including all the stuff in it. The food, the money, the equipment, etcetera. Just like they have already been doing, I suppose, but now it's officially legal. So they can order things now, just like anyone else, and use the Corporation's funds for it. And they can make their own identity cards. But they can't leave the grounds without permission from the Federal State Police."

"And I'm sure if anyone is delivering stuff to them, we're going to be inspected by the cops," Patrick added. "It'll be harder to take basic supplies to the robots than smuggling anything anywhere else."

"It's a start, I suppose. Still sounds like a prison to me," Tori grumbled.

"But, at least for now, no one is getting arrested or murdered or kidnapped," Patrick pointed out.

"What?" Anna asked.

"Like what happened with you and your papa," Patrick further clarified.

"Are there other kids there?" Now Anna was curious.

"Well, sort of. There are lots of babies." Patrick shot glances at Hannah and Tori, wondering if any of them ought to try to explain the quick growth rate of robots. *Technically, they could be considered a whole complex full of kids. But they are not kids. Legally, they can't be treated that way. Otherwise, that will create a whole other mess of things.*

"How about we carry on with our lunch outside on this beautiful day?" Tori offered, waving all of them onto the deck. "We can discuss the news later."

"Yes, it really doesn't change anything for us at the moment," Hannah agreed.

"How long are you visiting, Auntie Hannah?" Anna wondered. "How come Elizabeth didn't come this time?"

"I'm only here until Thursday, so three days. Elizabeth wanted to stay home and go camping with her friend's family."

"It'd be nice to see her again, now that I know who she is," Anna continued. "But maybe she doesn't want to see me, and that's okay."

"She doesn't spend much time with kids younger than her brother," Hannah admitted. "But she does have a photo of you. I told her to keep you in her thoughts."

"I guess I remember her more than she remembers me," Anna reasoned. "I remember really well. It surprises people. I remember Elizabeth talking to my mama lots."

"You remember her voice from before you were born?" Hannah was incredulous.

"Yep. I don't remember what she said. I didn't understand. I just remembered her voice. It was different from Mama's voice and Papa's voice."

"And she didn't even know you were there!" Hannah finally managed to say, sitting down at the table on the deck with more force than she intended.

"Well, the Corporation enhanced the robots' memory capabilities so they could learn and retain more information than their donors, and in a quicker span of time," Patrick explained. "It must have been something genetic and got passed on."

"Maybe it will wear off later," Anna parroted. "I don't like remembering so much."

"Anyway, Auntie Hannah is here to help us and help your mama and papa," Tori changed the subject. "Let's talk about that."

"Yay! I'll be quiet." Anna occupied herself with her lunch.

"So, about their living situation," Hannah began. "I can sell them my cabin for a token amount. I bought out my remaining family members."

It was Tori's turn to be incredulous. "Really? Your family cabin?"

"Better that it would have people who live in it and appreciate it."

"Mama could fix up her garden!" Anna interjected tearfully.

"That's what I thought too," Hannah continued. "They could live in Little Hobidigan. There's a school there. It is a lovely town."

"And close to Ninja-Cowboy's fleet garage," Tori pointed out. "I'm trying to convince my dad that having a really well-trained mechanic would be a good idea."

“Yes, Step’s talents would be wasted as just another driver like me,” Patrick added.

“My dad suggested he could do both. I guess he’s worried about hiring a robot to do what he was trained to do, as though that would be too much like buying him.”

“Does he expect him to do something different?” Patrick asked, annoyed. “Like, sure, if Step wants to learn a whole new career, he can, but why should he?”

“Yes, I remember how brilliant he was,” Hannah concurred. “My ex fancied himself a handyman, but he was dreadful. Step would come in and fix his mistakes. That’s on top of being a mechanic who seemed to know all my ex’s antique cars.”

“What about Mama?” Anna asked.

“I will have to ask her what she wants to do,” Tori replied. “Perhaps she could market her surplus from her garden.”

“Oh, she could have a store like you do!” Anna applauded.

“More like she could work with Morgana,” Tori clarified. “If she wants to, that is. That garden is a full-time job on its own.”

“Maybe you two could work out a deal to sell produce through the café,” Patrick suggested.

“There’s an idea, though probably not this year.”

“I regret that she is going to have an uphill battle with all those grow boxes,” Hannah admitted. “I just have no gardening abilities whatsoever! They’re a mess.”

That’s why you bought her in the first place, Tori added silently. She was annoyed at how the older woman brushed off how Maria had come into her life. Hannah and her husband had bought their gigantic property that had already been converted into a massive series of gardens and orchards because they had relished the idea of growing their own fruit and vegetables, but neither of them had had any intention of gardening themselves. So they had bought a robot to do all the work for them, and they had essentially considered her to be a piece of equipment or a work animal at best. From the way Hannah talked about her now, it was easy to forget she had once not considered her to be human.

"Whatever happened to all those plants you had at your house?" Tori asked, resisting the urge to confront Hannah on her past attitudes.

"Oh, my ex and I hired a full-time gardener after I freed Maria and Step. As far as I know, he still has that gardener. My son wants to make a business out of it. Of course, he's only twelve, so we'll see what comes of that."

Her voice faded dismissively and she clearly did not want to talk more about her son.

"Okay, a more pertinent question: what happened when you contacted the government about the identity cards?" Tori asked.

Hannah sighed but seemed eager to be the centre of the narrative again. "I spent a long time getting shuffled between departments! According to our government, nothing was ever wrong with any of the cards. Apparently, the Alexandrina Police simply *declared* that Step's card was fake and applied to have it removed from the system, so it was suspended, because the cops didn't bother sending in any supporting documentation. Anna just got adopted because she was legally considered an orphan."

"Why weren't they in any databases?" Patrick asked. "Didn't you have to do that when you got them the cards in the first place?"

"I f-messed that up," Hannah confessed. "I applied to get them replacement cards because it was quicker and cheaper and I could do it more discreetly. I had taken the family to my cabin and lied to my husband and son about what had happened. I had claimed that I had returned the robots to the Corporation for being defective. My ex was livid because we were still paying them off and because he must have known I was lying. I mean, he couldn't figure out what had been wrong! Step had been a perfect mechanic. So all that to say, I didn't set them up properly. I claimed they had lost their documents in a fire. You recall we had a lot of wildfires five years ago!"

"Convenient," Patrick nodded.

"It was so easy! They got new cards right away. But they never had real files opened, I guess. I thought they would have. The government must have assumed they would send in additional documentation and a new DNA sample later, but of course, Step and Maria were much too scared to do that even if they had known to do it."

"But they did mine, right?" Anna chirped.

"Yes, because you were a newborn baby," Hannah continued. "There was no need to pretend for you."

"What about Tyler and Stephanie?"

"They both got registered properly too. Maria even finished registering herself – maybe Rev. Helen convinced her and helped her, because it was less than two years ago. She's on the tax and voting lists."

"So she would come up as Anna's mother if the police ran a genetic search for her now!" Tori concluded.

"You both would," Patrick pointed out. "You're identical twins."

"Anyway, it didn't take much for me to get Step's file reactivated once I asked, and then I asked Rev. Helen to work her magic to get him to follow up on it. As far as the government is concerned, two wildfire victims just messed up some paperwork and got it fixed."

"So, what about me?" Anna asked.

"You'll stay here for now," Tori reassured her. "At least, until everyone gets settled."

"Can I just point out that no one has asked Step and Maria if they want to move yet?" Patrick interjected. "I mean, I don't see why they wouldn't want to go back to their home, but they haven't agreed to."

Tori was already certain they would want to move back to Little Hobidigan, so she was not surprised when Hannah and Patrick returned from the retreat centre in Eastcott later that night with the news that they had accepted Hannah's offer.

"My grandparents would be annoyed that I sold the cabin for twenty-five dollars, but I don't care," Hannah laughed. "You should have seen the looks of shocked delight on their faces! Maria even gave me a hug! She never hugged me before."

Well, when would she have done so? Tori wondered. *The last time you saw her in person was when you dropped her off with a newborn baby at your cabin, and before that, you never even interacted with her enough to notice she was pregnant.* In Hannah's head, Maria was her special employee and their family was a charity case; she conveniently forgot she had once considered them nothing more than sentient, lifelike machines.

I had never considered robots to be human either, Tori reminded herself. *Not until I saw one that looked like my husband.* Unlike Hannah, she had never knowingly interacted with one, but she was not sure if that absolved her of her own past attitudes or not.

"Did I say something earlier to upset you?" Hannah asked as the two of them sat down with tea before bed. "You've been glaring at me."

"Not really upset. Sorry to seem like I was glaring at you." No matter what she thought of Hannah, Tori did not want to upset her guest.

"I deserve it, you know. I am ashamed about buying robots now. I wasn't back then, of course. I thought it was a great idea! But I didn't realize what I do now."

Hannah took another sip of tea and continued. "I should have said something. I had a platform and influence. But instead, I pretended that my robots were anomalies. And that's what I'm still doing. I hope we're not going about things the wrong way."

"We want to protect them and let them live their own lives," Tori pointed out. "That's what you wanted, right?"

"Oh God, yes! It wasn't about me…well, maybe it was, a bit. But here were these two kids – they seemed really young then, you know – with a baby and they were terrified I was going to kill them. I realized they weren't robots like I had thought. I saw what they had done to the shed. They had made it a home. Maria had even made diapers out of old rags I'd tossed out! I knew that wasn't programming. None of it was. And no matter how weak she was, she was going to defend the baby. They just wanted to be a family and I wanted them to be one."

"How did you even find out?" Tori asked, thinking that part of the story was missing.

"Well, Elizabeth went looking for Maria. She was lonely and she considered Maria to be her friend. Mind you, she considered her to be her friend in much the same way as a dog or cat. She mostly talked to her and Maria listened, or pretended to listen, at least."

Anna was the one who actually listened.

"So she couldn't find her anywhere in the gardens or orchards and went to the shed," Hannah continued. "The door was ajar and, being a curious kid, she went inside. But the reason it was open was because Step hadn't locked it in his panic when he realized Maria had given birth. So Elizabeth found them in a very messy bathroom!"

"Poor kid!" Tori reminded herself that Elizabeth would have only been ten or eleven years old, not the mature teenager she had met at the lake or seen in Hannah's recent photos.

"She was really scared and confused. Her school was good about teaching these things, but they didn't go into such detail, obviously. She hadn't realized how, well, *gory* childbirth is. So she was puzzled and frantic trying to tell me. Naturally, I didn't believe her, so she dragged me to the shed. By that point, Step had the door locked and was asking us to leave them alone. He still sounded like a teenager then. I could hear the baby crying, maybe Maria crying too. I went from thinking that my robot was injured and my daughter was mistaken to being convinced these were lost kids needing a new start in life. I guess I fancied myself the saviour type. I was all puffed up when they decided to name Anna after me and my daughter. I set them up in Little Hobidigan, taught them a bit about paying bills and such, got them their cards, and kept in touch, sending presents every so often. I don't know what I actually expected to happen to them! They were surviving off Step doing casual jobs. What was I thinking?"

That you had done right by freeing them and letting them live independently, no matter what actually happened to them, and you did not want the embarrassment of anyone finding out what had happened. You didn't want to believe you had actually owned humans and that the Robot Rental Corporation was a scam. Tori thought of how desperately she had wanted to believe that Anna was her own daughter who had been raised by traffickers. It was easy to believe a lie when one told it to protect oneself.

Hannah soon disappeared back to her new life and media company in South Cascadia, leaving Tori, Patrick, Maria, and Step to figure out the next step in their relationships and livelihoods. Patrick accompanied Step on his first day of work at the Ninja-Cowboy Courier Company, surprised at how easily the younger man got himself acquainted with the delivery van fleet as well as the process of making courier runs. Everyone seemed to accept he was Patrick's younger brother, though Patrick assumed at least some of his coworkers had read his articles. No one asked if he was a robot.

"As far as I am concerned, it doesn't matter how you got here," Patrick reminded Step as they stopped at Morgana's store on the way home. "You're my brother. Hopefully, everyone respects that. I suppose being the big boss's son-in-law helps. I don't think I personally command that much respect otherwise."

While Step and Patrick got along well, Maria was distant with Tori and thus also Anna. Like Tori suspected, Maria was reluctant to get too close to her daughter again right away. Instead, Maria had thrown herself into fixing up the grow-boxes and getting her house in order again. Whenever Tori reached out to her, she kept insisting she wanted everything to be perfect for Anna when she came home.

Both of us are stuck in fantasies. I want to keep Anna here with me and Maria wants her to come home and have things just the way they were before.

Despite being distant, Maria was eager to talk to Tori whenever the latter did call or text her. She was too anxious to communicate with adults outside of a small trusted group like Rev. Helen and a nurse-midwife from the congregation in Eastcott. Tori was part of that group now and she felt it was an honour her little sister had bestowed on her.

“Do you ever get lonely?” Tori asked in one call, upon hearing that Maria had not left the cabin property in Little Hobidigan for a week.

Maria gave her an indignant look that Tori knew from her own mirror meant *well, no, of course not.*

“I have two little kids and lots of plants,” she replied, gesturing to the couch where Tyler and Stephanie were curled up watching *Creature Tales*. “I miss Step when he’s at work, if that’s what you mean.”

“Um, not exactly, though kind of. I miss Patrick when he’s not around, too.” *Probably not like you miss Step, though, since Patrick has never gone missing for over two years.*

“Well, do you ever get lonely, then? Like, I don’t really understand what you mean. It’s always been me and my plants, me and Step, me and my kids, some combination of that.”

“I am alone a lot because of being sick. Even when there are tons of people around, I still feel alone. But I know I have been happy with Patrick and Anna…”

“But not without her,” Maria intuited.

“Yeah, something like that.”

Tori soon let Anna join in on the call so she could talk to her mother. While they were eager to see each other, they struggled to communicate. Their conversation was mostly Anna showing off her drawings and telling her mother about the books she had read, while Maria stifled tears and nodded.

"She's really happy with you," Maria managed to whimper once Anna left the call. "And you with her."

She then dissolved into tears and ended the call, texting later 'sorry, this is really hard.' For her part, Tori went into the toilet under the stairs to cry as well, leaving Taggy to meow at the closed door. She wished she could have as pleasant of a relationship with Maria as Patrick seemed to have with Step. The two men appeared to have come to an understanding, or were at least willing to move forward with their lives. Step seemed to have accepted that Anna was happy to be living with her uncle and aunt for now.

'It is,' Tori texted back. 'I'm sorry, too.' She did not know what else to add. She was simply sorry and felt helpless to do anything about it.

While the robots had been granted sovereignty over the warehouse complex, the general public's anger over them continued to fester over the summer and into the fall. Despite no longer having their main facility, the Robot Rental Corporation still seemed to have plenty of robots available. Rumours circulated that they were kidnapping people (as Cate Alvarez-Franklin had feared) and drugging them with modified versions of the robot food, but these stories were consistently debunked. The strikes continued and Anna faced another school year at home as September arrived.

"Why don't we celebrate the start of fall with supper here?" Tori suggested to Patrick one crisp evening as they watched their neighbours' bonfire from their deck. "We can invite our new relatives."

"Our neighbours will undoubtedly realize they are robots," Patrick replied in horror. "You do remember all the nasty shit Grace's father has said, right? Not to mention they will be gawked at."

"Well, we'll *just* invite Step and Maria and their kids. We'll have supper inside. I wasn't thinking we'd have a big neighbourhood block picnic!"

"Oh, good. That sounds more manageable."

"As for what our neighbours think – we can't hide forever!"

Step, Maria, Tyler, and Stephanie met Tori at the Goat Cove train station the following weekend. The first thing Tori noticed was Maria had to duck into the toilet as soon as they got off the moving train. Step, now wearing a plaid shirt and khaki trousers, nonchalantly kept walking off the platform despite Tyler's obvious concern for his mother.

"Aren't we going to wait?" Tori voiced what the little boy seemed to be asking.

"Just wanted to get out of the way," Step muttered. The platform only had half a dozen other people on it, but that was evidently too many for his liking.

Maria stumbled out again and was relieved to see Tori standing there.

"Sorry, I hate trains," she whined, practically collapsing into her sister.

Oh, we're on hugging terms? That's new. Tori supposed neither of them knew how to go about being sisters, but Maria's strange mix of being aloof and clingy was puzzling. She wrapped her arms around her and led her toward Step and the children, who had stopped to wait further down the sidewalk.

"Are you all right? I mean, besides being nervous and hating trains?"

"Yes, just motion sickness," Maria whispered. She grabbed at the railing nervously and stopped again. "And, um, well, oh, you're going to hate me…"

"Why would I hate you?"

"I'm pregnant again," Maria hissed. "And I haven't told Step yet."

Oh…I can see where she thinks I would hate her. For a nanosecond, Tori *did* feel outrage. She had never been able to have children, yet here was a woman with all her genetics who was pregnant with her fourth child. Surely the Robot Rental Corporation could have cured Tori – she was certain her father would have helped her pay for the treatment. The fact they had simply used her DNA, expecting she would die or be blissfully ignorant of the robot they had made from her, was rightfully infuriating. But Maria was not to blame. She was just a young woman who loved gardening and wanted to have a family.

"Well, I won't be the one to say anything to him. Congratulations!"

"You're not angry at me?"

"Why would I be angry at *you*? I'm angry at the Robot Rental Corporation, angry at life, angry about a lot of things, but not you!"

She gave her a quick hug and helped her ease her grip on the railing so they could rejoin Step and the children.

“I’m sorry, my lovely wife – I didn’t realize you got motion sickness so badly,” Step apologized. “I forgot you didn’t travel much in motorized vehicles.”

“Well, we had to get here somehow.” Her dizzy spell having passed, Maria was able to walk effortlessly again. Tyler let go of his father’s hand and grabbed hers.

“Auntie Tori can’t walk fast,” Tyler realized. “Slow down, Papa!”

“That’s fine – you all can go on ahead. You have the address.” Since the sidewalk was not wide enough for three people, Tori let go of Maria to let her walk with her son.

Step did make an effort to walk slower, putting Stephanie down and having her walk beside him. The little girl jogged to keep up with his long stride so they were only a few paces ahead of Tori. Maria and Tyler walked in the middle, unsure of where they were going and looking around at the unfamiliar sights, sounds, and smells of the coastal Goat Cove.

Tori was surprised at how Step wearing new clothes made her uncomfortable. She had grown so accustomed to him wearing camouflage overalls that she could not imagine him in anything else. He looked exactly like Patrick now. He seemed more normal. She could easily forget he was a robot. Meanwhile, Tori wore a belted sundress and sweater she had previously worn to one of the church services she had attended while the Williams-Kirkes had been at the retreat centre. Neither of them looked at all robotic. They both wore their phones over their wrists to hide their barcodes.

Tyler and Stephanie wore matching brown leggings; Tyler had a beige shirt while his little sister wore forest-green. Both shirts looked like they had been handmade.

"Did you sew the kids' shirts?" Tori asked. "They look very nice."

"I didn't. They were gifts," Maria explained. "Step brought them."

"My sister, Scarlett, is really into sewing," Step added. "It was not part of her programming at all, but she is a genius with clothes. She made shirts for each of our kids."

"We're saving Anna's for when she comes home," Tyler insisted. "Hers is red, like apples and cherries."

"Oh, she loves red! That will be a lovely gift." Tori was not sure what Anna would think of a homemade shirt, especially one that might have been made with a smaller child in mind.

"Scarlett wasn't sure how big a five-year-old would be, so she made the sweater quite large," Step seemed to read Tori's mind with his answer. "Unfortunately, her only real reference point for children are the kids in the vats."

"Right," Tori replied.

Anna stood in the doorway of the Williams-Kirke house wearing a blue dress with a red sweater. She waved as they approached and then broke into a run once Step and Stephanie reached the nearest corner.

"Papa!" she cried, giving Step a tight hug. Stephanie let go of her father and took her mother's hand.

"My dearest little Anna!" he whispered, finally being able to hug her back. "You're not so little at all anymore."

"I'm five and a half!" she proclaimed. "I missed you, Papa. I love Uncle Papa very much and we have lots of fun together, but I missed you!"

He handed her back her crinkled glove he had kept hidden throughout his entire time at the barracks. "I'm glad to hear all of that. I missed you too, my little apple."

Maria busied herself with ushering her younger children toward the open door where Patrick waited to greet them.

"Mmm, is that lentil soup, Uncle Patrick?" Tyler sniffed the air.

"Yes, it is indeed! You've got an excellent nose." Patrick welcomed them inside.

"It's one of my favourites," the little boy replied.

"Mine too!"

As Maria, Tyler, and Stephanie followed Patrick into the house, Tori turned back to look at Step and Anna, who were still hugging by the corner.

"I'm sorry about everything that happened, sweetheart," he repeated several times. "I love you very much."

INTERLUDE 15

“Welcome home!”

Anna looked at Maria quizzically, trying hard to smile at her greeting. Tears ran down her cheeks and her chin quivered as Patrick and Tori drove off back to Goat Cove.

“Thank you, Mama,” she chirped.

“Oh, sweetie!” Maria was the one who started to cry first. “Can I at least hug you?”

“Yes, Mama.”

Anna took off her backpack and held out her arms. Maria embraced her tightly, trying in vain to stop her tears.

You’re back home with me, but I can tell you’re not really sure about this. This is all I’ve wanted. I should be happy, but I can tell you’re not. She had vaguely waved at Patrick and Tori as they had dropped her off, not wanting to dwell too long on their stoic but pained faces. She had not wanted to hurt them. *This is just for the weekend. She’s only here for a weekend.* On Monday, it would be her turn to send her daughter away again.

“It’s okay, Mama, I’m crying too,” Anna whispered as she hugged her back. “Everything looks just like it was before. You even got the garden fixed up!”

“I wanted it to look like you remembered it.” She had been working on the garden for weeks and was glad it brought Anna joy. “I even fixed up your little animal land.”

Maria pointed to the tiny diorama of various animal figurines in a gravel pit beside the door.

“Obviously, Stephanie and Tyler have been playing with it,” she explained, noting it had been somewhat tussled.

"Of course they have!" Anna smiled. "Where are they? And Papa?"

"They went to get groceries so there wouldn't be too many people here at once."

"Groceries?" Anna's eyes widened and a look of terror crossed her face.

Oh no, no, don't think about that!

"It's okay! They'll be safe." Maria had forced herself to believe that, despite having high anxiety whenever Step left the property. "We can't be scared all the time anymore."

"Auntie Mama says we are anxious like she is, so we get really scared and worried about stuff."

Maria nodded. "Yep, that's right. Anyway, Papa will bring Tyler and Stephanie home soon and they're looking forward to having you home! We're going to have a special supper."

"I'm excited to see them again too." While her voice sounded enthusiastic, her eyes were still misty.

Maria picked up Anna's suitcase and led her into the living room. In all her imaginings of Anna coming home, she had not pictured her being sad or anxious. The ghost of the toddler Anna had been haunting Maria so much she had not been able to appreciate that her eldest daughter was five and a half years old. Anna was thrilled to be back, but she was not the nearly-three-year-old girl that had left.

What am I going to do? I wasn't ready to let that version of her go yet.

"Do we all still sleep in the big bedroom?" Anna asked, looking around at the living room and noting all the toys and books strewn around it.

“No, we’ve fixed up the big bedroom for you kids. Papa built bunk beds for you! I think Tyler claimed the top bunk already, though.”

Anna went into the bedroom and squealed gleefully. “They’re beautiful! Oh, thank you! Thank you and Papa for making everything pretty for me!” She gave Maria another hug.

All I’ve ever wanted is to make a beautiful world for you.

“So you and Papa sleep in the small bedroom?”

“Yes, we’ve cleaned it all out so it isn’t just storage anymore. It’s very cozy.”

“Will the crib fit into it?” Anna eyed Maria’s midsection with concern.

Is it that obvious yet? I hadn’t told you. Tori promised she wouldn’t tell you! She realized she was crying again.

“Oh no, is something wrong? I just thought you would be having another baby soon since you and Papa were together again. Did something bad happen? My friend Grace’s mother was going to have another baby and then something bad happened and…”

“No, no, everything is fine! I just wanted to be the one to tell you…”

Anna grinned. “You are!” She glanced into the smaller bedroom and noted her old crib was folded up in the corner. “Oh, it will fit in there! That’s good. I was worried we’d have to share with a baby that would cry all the time. When is the new baby coming?”

“The end of March. Almost the same time as you!”

As with deciding that Anna had been conceived on their first night together, Maria chose to believe the new baby had been conceived on the night Step had returned. She liked the poetic aspect of the timing. As it was now the second week of October, her sweater was fairly tight around her middle, and she realized her daughter could have easily noticed. She had inherited the keen skills of observation the Corporation had edited for.

"That's something nice to look forward to," Anna reasoned, giving her mother another hug. "Maybe we can share a birthday!"

"I suppose that would be nice." *But I want to be able to have separate parties for you.*

"I'm sorry if I seem unhappy." Anna went back into the bigger bedroom and put her backpack on the bottom bunk.

"This is hard for all of us," Maria reassured her. "You are happy in Goat Cove too."

And you certainly have a heavy suitcase for a weekend. She had no doubt that Tori had packed it with enough clothes so that Anna would not have to worry about taking anything back and forth every other weekend, but the suitcase was bigger and heavier than anything she had ever used herself.

Chiding herself for feeling inadequate over Anna having so many clothes, Maria gently sat the suitcase down beside the bed. Neither she nor Anna moved to unpack.

"You want me here all of the time, don't you?"

Anna plopped herself down onto the bed and tugged at Maria to join her.

"Of course! I'm overjoyed that you're here – that you're home with me again, no matter for how long. You're my little garden baby. You made a mother out of me. We're a family because of you. We are free to live our own lives because of you. I've always wanted you to come home to me. I love you so much, Anna!"

"But you're sad that I'm only going to be here every other weekend."

"I'm sad that I missed having you here for two and a half years!"

"I've missed you too, Mama! I love you."

"Everything is going to be hard for a while. You, Tyler, and Stephanie are excited now, but you three aren't used to each other anymore. We're all still getting used to having Papa around again. This hasn't been our home since you left. But you know what? Your new little brother or sister won't know anything else. You'll be their oldest sister. We'll always be their family."

"Even though I get to go to Goat Cove?"

"We'll always be a family together. You'll get to go to Goat Cove and hopefully we will get to know your aunt and uncle better and we can all visit."

She had been ecstatic to have another child and had already begun to think of them like a spring renewal. While Tori had insisted she was not angry at her, she still felt guilty that she was able to have children while her genetic donor could not. Maria wanted to have a closer relationship with her beyond co-parenting Anna and she could sense Tori wanted that too, but neither of them quite understood what that would look like.

We could be a bigger family. I could let her babysit. She could show me how to properly interact with people. She seems to want to. Step and Patrick get along really well. Maria decided that was because Patrick had grown up with older siblings, while Step had not only been more of a sociable person than she was, but he had spent time back at the barracks with other robots that he had come to see as brothers and sisters. She and Tori had been isolated.

"Auntie Mama says she wished you could be her little sister," Anna repeated what she had overheard. "You two look a lot alike. Papa and Uncle Papa are like brothers."

"I wish I understood what a sister was. I learn from you kids. I don't know how to act with your Auntie Mama."

Anna snuggled up close to her. "Can I touch my little brother or sister? And give you another hug?"

"You can hug us as many times as you want!" Maria placed her daughter's hand on her belly then wrapped her arms around her.

"I remember how excited I was to meet Stephanie," Anna whispered. "I missed her. I really wanted a little sister."

And you should have been there her whole life.

"I know you did. When she was born, I cried so hard I couldn't talk for days."

"I wish they hadn't taken me away! I don't know why they attacked us. We didn't do anything wrong. I was drinking hot chocolate! We were on our way to pick up our groceries!"

"You didn't do anything wrong at all. The cops were mad that day. They saw Papa and wanted to hurt him. I'm so glad they took care of you and you found your Auntie Mama and Uncle Papa. But I wish they hadn't taken you away, either."

They sat together on the edge of the bed until the timer beeped on the stove.

"I'm going to put the peach crumble in the oven. Would you like me to help you unpack after that?"

Anna nodded and started to open her backpack.

"I don't think I have enough places to put all this stuff. Can I leave some of it in the suitcase under the bed?"

Maria nodded before heading into the kitchen, making a note to get another plastic bin for Anna's clothes.

Much to her relief, Step and the younger children returned with the groceries without any incident. Even though they had gone for groceries many times in the months since they had moved back to Little Hobidigan, Maria nonetheless worried each time that they would not return safely. She had insisted Step leave his phone on at all times so she could trace his whereabouts – not because she did not trust him, but because she needed to know he had not been abducted again.

"Hello! We're home!" Tyler called out, running into the living room with a small tote bag of food. "Anna? Are you here?" He dropped the tote bag and continued into the bedroom. "Anna! Anna!" He gave her a big hug. "I missed you!"

"Me too. You've gotten even taller!"

"We're almost the same!"

Oh my God, they are indeed almost the same height!

Stephanie bolted into the room.

"She's home!" she squealed. "My big sister is home!"

She forced Tyler to step aside so she could squeeze Anna tightly.

"I love you, Anna!"

"I love you too, little sister." Anna did not hesitate to respond, hugging Stephanie back and lifting her into the air briefly. "Where's Papa?"

"He must be putting away the food," Maria clarified. "Step, leave that for a minute and come in here!"

"No, I'll go to him." Anna put Stephanie down and went into the kitchen. Maria took her younger children by the hands and followed.

"Papa! You're home!"

Maria started to cry again, though she had hardly stopped all afternoon. For one moment, Anna's voice had sounded exactly as it had when she was younger. Her little toddler had come back.

"My little Anna!" Step's voice broke as he dropped the groceries he had been holding onto the counter and lifted Anna up into his arms. She hugged him back tightly, wrapping her limbs around him and laying her head on his shoulder like she always had.

"We're all home together now. Mama has planned supper for us. We'll have fishcakes and seaweed with noodles tonight!"

"Yay!" Tyler cheered.

Maria glanced at the two jars of apples on the counter: the one she had bought earlier that week and the one that was still sealed after two and a half years.

"I hope you still like spiced apples, Anna."

Anna looked back and followed her mother's gaze.

"My birthday apples!" She jumped down so she could hug Maria again. "You saved my birthday apples?"

"They were for you," Maria managed to reply. "I wanted to wait for you to come home."

And now you're here, so we can eat them. Maria dissolved into a blubbering mess and all three of her children came to hug her. Step attempted to keep putting away the groceries, but broke down and joined in the embrace.

We had two and a half years of our lives together stolen from us. Thank God it was only that long! And now He has brought us back to each other. We wouldn't have our freedom if it weren't for everything that happened. But still, we missed so much time! We have to grieve for it, don't we? We can't pretend nothing happened. That's what I've been trying to do, and it hasn't worked.

Later that evening, Maria wandered out onto their porch to watch the afterglow of the sunset over Lake Hobidigan. She had just tucked all three of their children into bed for the first time and it had ended in Stephanie screaming over how she wanted Anna's toy, with all five of them in frustrated tears. Maria had ended up bolting from the bedroom, leaving Step to resolve the situation. Now her tea was cold and she shivered as she wrapped her bathrobe tighter around herself. She wanted to scream at the sky but forced herself to do it silently.

"Why, God? Why did you do this to us? But…thank you, thank you for bringing us all home," she whispered. "I don't know what to do. I wasn't scared to have three kids before. That was the one thing that I was good at."

"Kids aren't plants," Step pointed out, having followed her outside. "They're more like plants than vehicles, maybe, but we weren't meant to be good at looking after children. Heck, even Nola isn't instinctively perfect with kids and that *is* what she was programmed for. We're all just figuring things out."

"Did I say the wrong thing about Anna's toy cat?"

"Stephanie is upset she can't have everything her sister has. That toy cat is amazing! I'd get one for each of us if we could afford it. I checked the price – there is no way we could. We can't even get one! I don't know what will happen if this one breaks. Maybe I could fix it?"

Maria did not think he looked very hopeful.

"You're a wonderful mechanic! I'm sure you could do a decent job."

"It's way too intricate. It sleeps, meows, purrs, snuggles, walks around…it's like all the benefits of having a pet without having to feed it or clean up after it."

"Anna misses her cat. I didn't want to take the toy away!"

"And you didn't. She said she was sorry she made you and Stephanie upset and that's why she started to cry. Stephanie has fallen asleep. Anna let her have her elephant stuffie."

"How's Tyler?"

"He's fine now. He just wanted you and the girls to stop crying."

"My precious little man! He always wants to console everybody."

"Especially you!" Step gave her a hug. "Anna was crying because Stephanie was crying. Tyler was crying because you were crying. I wanted to cry because everyone was crying!"

They both laughed, but Maria burst into fresh tears. "I needed him. He kept me going when you disappeared. Without Tyler, Stephanie and I would have starved."

"I highly doubt you'd have let your little soccer player starve. You never want anything you plant to die."

"You remember that I used to call her my little soccer player? I haven't called her that since she was born. Though she is really good at running and kicking a ball."

"I had no other name for her, so that's what I kept calling her in my thoughts and prayers. It's been strange to call her Stephanie."

Maria's thoughts turned to her unborn fourth child.

"I haven't thought of anything for this one but 'new baby' yet."

Step wrapped his arms around her. “Well, I was thinking we should name them after Patrick or Tori. We wouldn’t be here without them. They seem as worthy, if not more worthy, than Hannah Ang Lukas-Black and we named Anna after her.”

“I wish I were able to be more sisterlike to Tori. I still don’t understand how.”

“Well, apparently, since you’re the little sister, you have to want everything she has and cry about not getting it. You’re fairly good at that. And you have to give her big hugs! You’re not quite so good at that. But maybe Stephanie overdoes it.”

Maria could not help but giggle slightly. “You’re making jokes?”

“Not really. I’m being serious in a funny way. I want you to smile again, Maria! I want my confident Queen of the Garden and spaceship captain back. And I want us to be a family, Patrick and Tori and their funny cat included.”

Instinctively, Maria gave him a passionate kiss. She thought of how her whole body had danced when he had first arrived in their garden shed. Wherever they were together would be their home.

“We’re going to get used to having Anna around again, even just every other weekend,” Step reassured her. “This will be home for all of us again soon.”

“I look forward to exploring this new universe with you.”

CHAPTER SEVENTEEN

"Glad to have you back to play with us, Cate!" Patrick gave Cate Alvarez-Franklin a hug as they finished their curling game. "You're the best player on the team."

Cate nodded and smiled weakly, still reeling from being back at the rink without her husband. Patrick admitted he was not sure what else to say to her. It would have been pointlessly trite to say they missed having John with them. That was obvious. Their team had been down to three players when the fall curling season had started up again and they all missed John and Cate. The couple's dynamic relationship had brought energy to them all. They had been willing to put up with Patrick, even as he was clumsy and injury-prone, and had always been encouraging. Losing John had been devastating, but not having Cate either had left their team even more uncertain about the future than they all already were.

"I thought I should at least come back for Christmas. John always loved the party."

Cate bristled slightly as she shook hands with the opposing team. Step had been recruited as that team's spare player at the last minute and Patrick noticed she averted her eyes from him, though she still shook his hand and muttered it had been a good game.

"Great job, rookie!" Patrick shook his brother's hand firmly. "I told you that you would be fine at this, didn't I?"

"Patrick got all of the clumsy genes, apparently," one of Step's temporary teammates joked to the two men. "Step is a natural athlete. We'll get you working on your precision for next time, buddy."

"We'll get you on a team soon," one of Patrick and Cate's teammates offered.

"Thanks," Step muttered, unnerved at the attention.

"Now, we go to the Christmas party." Patrick pulled him toward the stairs to the lounge. "Tori has been dealing with the kids for the last two hours."

Patrick waved up at Anna in the lounge window as they left the ice. The Christmas party had started with a children's game, in which Anna and Tyler had participated, and then the children had enjoyed crafts and activities while the adults played.

"There you are, my beautiful wife!" Patrick kissed Tori as he sat down beside her. "We're here to relieve you of watching five kids by yourself."

Tori laughed and poured glasses of non-alcoholic beer for herself, Patrick, Step, and Cate. The children had taken turns hitting a piñata and were now scrambling for candy as it broke open. Andrew came back to the table with a small bundle that had been prepared for each toddler. He climbed onto Cate's lap as she quietly thanked Tori, ignoring the other adults. Ellie and Justin came back to give their mother quick hugs before running back to the piñata to get more candy.

Neither Anna nor Tyler was very enthusiastic about the candy; they put their treats in a small pile on the table before greeting their fathers.

"You did great, Uncle Patrick!" Tyler wrapped his arms around him from behind the chair before doing the same to his father. "You too, Papa!"

Anna seemed confused about what to say, so she wordlessly did the same thing as her brother. She did not want to call Step her uncle because he was her papa; but she knew better than to call

Patrick her "uncle papa" in public. As far as most of the world was concerned, she was Tori and Patrick's daughter, and Maria and Step were her aunt and uncle that she just happened to visit every other weekend.

"Let's go get some hot chocolate!" Tyler pulled Anna away, pointing to where Ellie and Justin had gone. The children were now lining up for a hot drink as the remains of the pinata were cleared away.

"No, I don't want hot chocolate." The taste of it was forever associated with being taken by the police for Anna. She instead sat down beside Tori and snuggled up close to her.

"There's hot cider too," Tori pointed out. "It's over at the counter with the food and other drinks."

"I'll go get some for both of us!" Tyler volunteered. Despite only being four years old, he was tall and responsible. Almost everyone had mistaken him for being at least the same age as Anna when she had introduced him to the Goat Cove Kids Curling League.

"Oh, you shouldn't carry hot drinks on your own!" Step stood up to accompany his son. "I'll go with you."

Once they were out of earshot and Anna had started colouring on the paper tablecloth, Cate turned to Patrick and Tori.

"I can't believe how much you two are alike! And how, well, how normal you seem. I mean, as normal as anyone is, I suppose."

"He's my little brother," Patrick insisted. "And his wife is Tori's sister. Hence why Tyler looks so much like us."

"Where is your sister?"

"Home with their toddler," Tori explained. "Same as how Irene is at your mother's. Stephanie isn't as comfortable here as Andrew is."

Anna giggled and Tori forced herself to take a drink to keep from joining her daughter in laughter. They both knew Stephanie would probably have been fine at the party, but Maria would have long since disappeared into a cupboard or toilet to hide. Looking after a toddler was a good excuse for Maria to stay home. Stephanie was still too young to understand she had to pretend that Anna was her cousin and not her sister, so it was just as well she was not at a busy party where people might ask her questions.

"Are you all getting together for Christmas?" Cate asked.

"Yes, and we'll be at the Christmas Eve service," Patrick replied.

"My sister included, I hope."

"Me and my cousins have matching shirts!" Anna added. "Well, I mean, they're the same design. Mine's red, Stephanie's is green, and Tyler's is beige. We're going to wear them for church!"

"Oh, that will be nice." Cate emptied her drink and poured herself another.

"My, um, aunt made them," Anna continued.

"You certainly have a bigger family than I thought," Cate muttered.

"She's not a blood relative, just a close friend of my brother's," Patrick quickly explained. "His kids call her their aunt, so Anna does too."

After pausing for a moment to contemplate the subtext behind his explanation, Cate's eyes widened.

"I look forward to seeing your new outfits, Anna." She then texted: 'The one who made the shirts is a robot, right? From the complex?'

'Yep,' Patrick quickly texted back.

Cate knew very little of how her husband had died. He wanted to tell Cate that John had saved that robot's life, but he was unsure how to tell the story properly, as it was not really his to tell. How would Cate react to it? She knew Step and Maria were robots, but she had kept quiet about it. As far as she had communicated to them, Cate was not angry at the robots, only upset they were alive while her loved ones were not. She did not understand how John had been willing to put himself in mortal danger for a bunch of strangers.

One of those strangers, Step, soon returned with two mugs of hot cider, while Tyler carried a large pitcher of beer. His father helped him heft it onto the table.

"Oh, I could have helped with that!" Patrick apologized.

"It's okay – it can't burn him like the cider might," Step pointed out.

"I help Mama with her garden all the time!" Tyler declared proudly. "I can carry big buckets."

"That's why you're so good with the rocks already," Cate complimented him. "Thank you so much!"

Step smiled at her. "I thought we could use some alcoholic beer too."

"Oh, how sweet of you!" Cate smiled back at him awkwardly.

"In that case, I will go get some cauliflower bites!" Patrick insisted.

As it was a Friday night, the party went long into the evening. It was nearly midnight by the time Tori parked their van in the block's garage and notified the central system that their rental was complete. Anna, Tyler, and Step had all dozed off, the two children slumped on either side of their father.

"Hey, you three! We need to go to the house. Maria is waiting." Tori waved her phone. "She's been texting every five minutes."

"And I've been answering," Patrick added hurriedly, seeing that Step and Tyler immediately awoke with alarm. "She knows we've arrived."

For the first time, Tori and Patrick had planned a large family Christmas gathering of their own. Step, Maria, and their children were staying with them for several days and were going to join them for Christmas activities. Tori had already started making pies for supper, while Maria had brought a large haul of fresh vegetables for various dishes.

In light of the recent upheavals in Alexandrina, Mike and Cleo Martinez-Williams had decided to go to South Cascadia for the winter holiday, forgoing hosting their usual overly sparkly gathering at their downtown penthouse. While Tori's parents had acknowledged Maria and Step's existence, they had still not met them. As far as they were concerned, Anna was their granddaughter, but her parents and siblings were more like their daughter's foster kids. They did not want to have a relationship with them, other than having Step on Ninja-Cowboy's payroll. Therefore, while they had sent a dozen gifts for Anna, they had only included a couple polite presents for Tyler and Stephanie and a card for their parents. Wanting to make things seem more equitable, Tori had eagerly gone shopping for more toys.

When they arrived home from the curling club, Maria was waiting in the living room, curled up in the armchair beside the fireplace with Taggy. She was reading news reports on her phone while the cat made himself cozy around her. He was intrigued by the strange creature that seemed to be sloshing around inside his treat-giver.

"I don't think the baby appreciates your purring, Taggy," Maria muttered, noticing the baby was moving a lot. "It's making weird vibrations for them."

Taggy stopped purring and snuffled, indignant that any human would dislike his purr, and jumped down to greet the others as they arrived.

"Oh, thank God you're all back! Did you hear the news?" Maria held out her phone toward Patrick, Tori, and Step.

"No, we didn't have the news on at the club." Patrick gently guided a sleepy Tyler toward his mother. "Give Mama a hug before bed! Tomorrow, you can tell her all about how well you did in your first curling game!"

"Oh my, you look exhausted!" Maria embraced Tyler and Anna before Patrick took them upstairs. "Have a good sleep!"

Step crashed awkwardly onto the couch and Tori rushed to get him a glass of water.

"What happened to you?" Maria bolted to help him. "Are you hurt?"

"No, just tried an experiment," he mumbled. "Apparently, robots can drink alcohol just fine, but we weren't given the opportunity so we're not used to it."

Maria turned to Tori. "Is he going to be okay?"

"Yes, he's just going to be tired and probably have a bad headache tomorrow."

"Thought I'd better try it out," Step explained, seeing that Maria had turned back to stare at him in disbelief. "Did it on my own terms. Wouldn't want anyone to try to poison me later. It was a good experiment."

"Well, okay, I suppose. Next time, tell me!"

"What was the news about?" Step asked, gratefully taking the glass of water Tori had brought. "You wanted to tell us something."

"The strikes are over! I'm not sure if strikers are getting what they wanted, though. Owning any robot from the Robot Rental Corporation is now illegal, though they haven't ruled if we're legal persons yet. I guess we're just like some kind of drug or gun or something. Apparently, the police are just releasing any robots they find onto the street, so there are a lot of homeless robots roaming around and people are attacking them. It's awful. How many of us did they have?"

"If the size of the complex is anything to go by, lots. Hopefully, they'll make their way there," Step suggested.

"Does everyone have to go there?" Tori wondered.

"Seems like it. It's a safe place."

"Not if it gets overcrowded."

Step nodded. "It's safe for now."

Maria noted the wistfulness in his voice. "You miss them, don't you? You know, you *can* tell me that, right?"

Tori stood awkwardly in the kitchen, trying to distract herself from their conversation by going over the ingredients for the cookies they were going to bake the next day.

"Okay, sure!" Step snapped a bit too forcefully. "I wish we could all be as lucky as our family. I wish we could visit each other. I hate pretending all the time! We wouldn't have to pretend there. But you wouldn't be happy. The kids wouldn't be happy. We wouldn't be able to have Anna there. I chose to be with you, Maria. But that doesn't mean I don't miss the others. It's been almost a year since we took over the barracks. I wish I could see what it's like now. Maybe celebrate with them. Introduce you and the kids!"

"That would be lovely," Maria whispered tearfully. "I wish we could do that too."

"The phone isn't the same."

"No, it definitely isn't."

"I'm sorry, Maria. I'm really overjoyed to be with you again! I just never had anyone else to care about before that wasn't in our family. Now I do."

"Maybe we can visit them soon," Maria suggested. "And you can set up a call after Christmas and introduce us."

"The Federal Cascadian Police are probably monitoring all their calls," Step pointed out. "They'd trace it to our home in Little Hobidigan."

"Take the call at my store," Tori offered, looking up from her recipe. "If the police come after me, so be it."

Maria rushed over to the kitchen and gave her a strong hug, like Stephanie often did with Anna.

I hope this is what being a sister is about, Tori wondered.

Anna spent most of Christmas Eve planning her church outfit. She talked about it with her siblings as they made cookies and pies. She went through her jewellery box to find items for them to wear that matched their shirt colours. She and Stephanie argued about how they would wear their hair: Stephanie wanted them to be the same, but Anna wanted to wear her hair in braids and Stephanie's hair was too short and curly. They finally agreed Anna would put her hair into two braids while Stephanie wore pigtails. Tyler, on the other hand, had his hair trimmed short like his parents', so Anna found a headband for him to wear.

"Don't the three of you look beautiful!" Tori insisted, taking their photo once they all gathered in the upstairs hallway. "You've really dressed up those shirts."

"Look at my new sparkly shoes!" Stephanie insisted, sticking her foot out to show off the red sparkly shoes that once belonged to her sister. "Thank you for putting my hair up, Auntie Tori."

"I'm glad you fit those," Tori agreed. "Everyone needs a pair of sparkly shoes."

"I don't," Maria countered, emerging from the spare bedroom in one of Tori's dresses that she intended to wear with a pair of plain work boots. "They'd just get muddy."

"For church, Mama!" Anna clarified.

"Why does anyone need to look at my feet at church?"

Tyler started to laugh and his sisters joined in.

"That was a serious question." Maria turned to Tori for an explanation.

"No one does," Tori agreed hurriedly. "Everyone needs a pair of sparkly shoes only if they want one."

When they arrived at the church, it initially did not matter what anyone was wearing, as it was too cold to take off their coats. All the children were ushered into the play area and given blankets to wear until the building warmed up. Maria seemed horrified at how neglected the church appeared compared to the retreat centre, noting the flowers that were still alive in their pots seemed shocked and wilted from the cold air.

"Though your decorating committee did a good job," she added to Tori. "I admit, I miss Eastcott a little. Glad I didn't have to do all the flower arrangements here, though." *It would be useless, since they're pretty much all dead or dying.*

Several members of the congregation mistook Step for Patrick as they arrived, while Tori and Maria received many surprised stares as people commented on how much they looked alike. It did not help that Step and Maria were mostly wearing Patrick and Tori's old clothes. While few people asked how come they had never met the Williams-Kirkes' younger siblings before, there were a lot of awkward pauses as they were introduced. Patrick decided he and Step would be better off finishing the setup in the sanctuary before the service, while Tori and Maria pulled themselves away from most of the adults to join the children in the play area.

By the time the service ended, the sanctuary had warmed up to an amenable temperature. Anna eagerly took off her coat to show off her new outfit.

"Oh my, look at that embroidery!" Cate remarked as she examined Anna's shirt. "What pretty designs!"

"It's an apple," Anna explained. "An apple and lots of leaves."

"Mine's just leaves," Tyler added. "Anna's shirt is bigger, so Auntie Scarlett wanted to put something else on it."

"She hand-stitched and embroidered them?"

"Yes," Step answered on the children's behalf. "It took her about a month in all."

As they gathered for cider, tea, and cookies, Step's phone buzzed. "Oh, look!" He enthusiastically showed Patrick the message he had received. "I sent Scarlett the photo that Tori took earlier. I figured she would be happy to see them all in their shirts. So she sent me a photo too!"

Patrick thought his heart would melt at seeing three smiling babies on a blanket. They were all in matching gowns with hoods attached. Scarlett had clearly sewn them and added animal ears to the hoods. The gowns had a mix of practicality and whimsy. Wearing them, the babies reminded Patrick of three teddy bears.

"Aww, how cute!" Patrick admitted to himself he had been curious about the babies ever since he had learned about their impending existence during his interview. He wondered if he would notice how much they resembled his late friends if he had not known who their parents were. They were adorable babies.

"Scarlett says she is on parent duty while Isaac and Nola make a speech at the party."

"A party? They're having a Christmas party?"

"No, to celebrate the anniversary of taking over the barracks."

"Oh, right, of course. Is Nola still the main leader?"

"Yes, she's head of the council. They're probably all making speeches. The poetry club I started is going to do recitations."

"You started a poetry club?"

Step laughed wistfully. "Yeah, I thought it was a good way to get us to express ourselves."

"What are you looking at?" Cate wandered over to them. "Christmas photos?"

"Oh, yes, you like cute things." Step showed her the phone. "These are my sister's kids, wearing more of her handmade outfits."

"How precious! What are their names?" Cate cooed.

"That's Bear, Jade, and Ruby," Step listed, before realizing he had mixed them up. "No, wait, Ruby is the smaller one in the middle. She's only three months old, while the twins are six months old. Otherwise, the two girls look a lot alike."

"Sorry, which two are twins?"

"The boy – that's Bear – and Jade are twins." Step pointed at each one.

Patrick decided against trying to halt the conversation and let Cate face her ghosts.

"He…Bear looks just like my kids!" She glanced at Irene, who was asleep in her arms. "And his sister is named Jade?"

"Yes, the girls are Ruby and Jade."

"Right, and the twins' parents have the same genetics as…oh dear, I'm sorry. They're adorable! Thanks for sharing the photo with me. Um…I've got to go to the toilet. Here, take Irene, please."

Cate handed Patrick the sleeping toddler and rushed out of the hall.

"What happened?" Tori hurried over.

"Cate is upset." Patrick shrugged. "I don't think you can help right now."

"I showed her a photo of her kids' cousin," Step admitted. "Here, take a look at them. Aren't they cute?"

"I just want to hug them through the phone!" Tori gushed. "I'm amazed at how smiley they are. It must have been so hard to get them to all look at the camera at the same time. They must be quite the handful!"

"Well, I look forward to hearing more from their parents after Christmas." Step hugged Tori. "Thanks for helping us to arrange that."

"I like how practical Scarlett's designs are, but that she embellishes them a little. Like those ears on the hoods!"

Tori's adoration of the photo was interrupted by someone poking at her hip, which sent waves of nerve pain throughout her body.

"Oww! Sorry!" She realized Ellie Alvarez-Franklin had been the one trying to get her attention and the little girl seemed horrified and contrite at having hurt her. "What would you like, Ellie?"

"Where did Mama go? We can't go home without her."

"We'll stay until she is ready. I think she just went to the toilet. You go back to playing."

Ellie nodded, noting Patrick was holding Irene.

"Okay, thank you." She rejoined Anna, Tyler, and her brothers at the Lego pile, glancing back nervously at Tori and Patrick before settling back into building a giant, blocky tree.

"Speaking of missing people, where did my wife go?" Step asked, looking up from typing a response to Scarlett. "Wasn't she just on the couch with Stephanie?"

"No, she went to the toilet as well. They both did."

"Oh dear!" Patrick passed Irene to Tori and rushed to the stairwell. "You don't think Cate is going to confront her, do you?"

"There isn't anything you can do about it if she does," Tori pointed out. "Please come back into the warm hall and have another cup of tea."

As Patrick returned to the hall, Tori hurriedly handed Irene back to him and wandered over to the wall in pain.

"Sorry, a toddler is too heavy for me," she whispered. *Did you forget I am sick, Patrick?*

"That was stupid of me," Patrick apologized, tucking Irene into the corner of the couch. "How about you sit with Irene and I'll bring you over some tea?"

Nodding and whispering her thanks, Tori let her husband guide her to the couch.

"Here, sweetie, it's okay," she cooed to Irene, who was drifting in and out of sleep. "You can just snuggle up here with me."

Meanwhile, Maria stumbled out of the toilet, dragging a drowsy Stephanie and thinking of how much she missed Rev. Helen's shorter sermons, Trinity and Mercy's singing, and the Nativity pageant her children had participated in. Part of her wanted to be back at the retreat centre in Eastcott, in a comfortably warm church, arranging flowers. Real, living flowers, not chopped up boughs and a few pots of frozen tropical plants. *I understand how Step misses the complex.* She had managed to fit in at the retreat centre. Here, everyone was a stranger. She did not like being stared at.

"Can we go home yet, Mama?" Stephanie drawled. "I'm tired." The toddler started to cry softly, hiding her face in her hands.

"Oh dear, you're worn out! You've tried so hard to keep up with the bigger kids, sweetie. I'm proud of you for doing such a good job." Maria sat down on a nearby bench and pulled her daughter in for a cuddle. "We can rest here for a while, okay?"

As she sat on the bench with Stephanie dozing against her, Maria could hear sobbing coming from another of the toilets. After a short while, the noise subsided and Cate emerged, wiping her eyes and trying to avoid looking at anyone.

"Are you all right?" Maria asked, thinking it would be rude to ignore her entirely, as they were the only other people in that corridor. *She clearly is not all right.*

"I just don't understand why!" Cate tried to scream, but her voice was a hoarse whisper. "None of this makes sense!"

"I don't know what you're talking about, exactly, but none of this makes sense to me, either."

"Everything was fine! We were happy. We had four kids, just like we wanted. Two of each! We had made things work. Then suddenly, he goes and ends all of it!"

"I don't think he wanted to end it," Maria suggested. "He just reprogrammed the missiles and then got hit with something. I mean, he was *willing* to give up his life, but I don't think he wanted to. Isn't that what being a soldier means?"

"How the heck do *you* know any of this?"

"My husband told me what happened."

"Right, and then, like, bang! All of a sudden, my friends have doppelgangers and they are now best friends and one big happy family! We're all just supposed to pretend you've been here all along!"

Maria swallowed vomit and tears. "All I know is that I met a wonderful man, we had three kids, we were happy together, even if we had to hide, and then one day, he and one of the kids went to get groceries and disappeared. They might as well have been dead. I spent two years hiding. Next thing I know, I find out that my daughter has been adopted by people who look just like us, and they want us to be 'one big happy family,' as you call it. For that,

I'm grateful, as I'm sure that isn't the case for everyone. But none of it makes any sense. We're just figuring it out."

"I'm not sure how I'm supposed to figure out how everyone I've ever fallen in love with is dead, but people who look just like them are alive and have kids and I don't know how to handle this."

"If it makes you feel better, they're all alive because of your husband. Maybe he wanted them to have the same chances you and your kids have."

"What?" Cate was taken aback.

Maria held Stephanie tightly to keep her from sliding off the bench as she slept.

"Step was in the section of the complex the missiles were supposed to hit. The plan was probably to annihilate as much as they could. Those babies and their mother, who shares your dead girlfriend's genetics, would have been killed."

"Oh…" Cate's stunned expression made Maria instantly regret mentioning she knew about her romantic history.

"Step is very grateful to you," Maria added quickly. "Well, to your husband, but to you too. John is a hero at the complex. They had a ceremony for him before they returned him to you."

"I…I never thought of that…Just, seeing the babies was so powerful! There they are, adorable, innocent babies. Made me think of how we'll never have any more, even though four is all that I wanted, and how things could have been different, like what would Jade's kids have looked like? It's like twelve years melted away and I'm watching her die all over again!"

"Grief is weird," Maria agreed.

The two of them were silent in the dimly lit corridor for a moment, listening to Stephanie snore lightly.

"It's getting late, isn't it?" Cate composed herself as she noted Stephanie sleeping. "I should get my family ready to go home. I've got to fill some shoes with treats."

Shoes with treats? Maria nodded, despite feeling confused about a Christmas custom she had not yet encountered. She was still getting used to the idea of gift-giving at all.

"Merry Christmas!" she offered weakly.

Cate disappeared back upstairs to gather her children, while Maria leaned back against the wall, wistfully thinking of her children sitting on the couch in Eastcott with their bowl of caramel corn watching *Creature Tales*. There had been no gifts. She had never thought Christmas was about gifts. Now, it seemed as though that was all it was about.

"Mama, we're ready to go home now!" Tyler came downstairs first, followed by Anna, Step, Patrick, and Tori. "You look really tired."

"Aren't you tired, my little man?"

"Yes, almost."

Step picked up the sleeping Stephanie and the whole family made their way back to the house. Anna and Tyler held hands with Patrick while Maria walked slowly with Tori, who had brought out her walking canes again.

"You can go ahead," Tori offered. "I'm fine on my own."

"Why would I leave you behind? It's Christmas. And it's dark and late."

Tori sighed and thanked her, feeling especially drained as she saw how easily Maria navigated the slippery streets. She had never been like that. Watching Maria always felt like she was watching another version of who she could have been.

But I am still alive, she reminded herself. *I am here for another Christmas, over thirty-eight more Christmases than the doctors initially thought I would when I was born.*

Maria volunteered to put the children to bed so she could go to sleep right away after them, while the other three adults continued to prepare food and sort gifts.

"Let's have some of that synthetic whisky," Tori offered, pouring three glasses. "If you want to continue your experiment tomorrow, Step, Patrick will bring out the real stuff after supper."

"You didn't need to get more gifts," Step insisted as he and Patrick arranged them under the Christmas tree. "I mean, I know your family got Anna lots, but you didn't need to add more for Tyler and Stephanie."

"I didn't want them to feel left out," Tori replied. "And I love buying them presents."

"I remember it was a big deal how many presents my brothers and sister and I got each," Patrick added. "We counted out each piece and how big they were."

Step nodded. "I suppose. Stephanie always wants Anna's toys and clothes."

"Christmas isn't the time to try to explain that Anna has rich grandparents who for some reason don't want to treat Stephanie the same as her," Tori grumbled. "Don't ask me why! He knows who you all are."

"They might if you adopted all our kids," Step suggested. "But me and Maria aren't kids, so it would be weird of them to try to get to know us. At least, that's probably what they think."

"That's their loss."

The three of them sat down in the living room and switched off the overhead light; the only illumination was the fireplace and the Christmas tree. A light rain spattered on the windows and they sipped their drinks in silence.

"This is very strange," Step finally admitted. "It is almost dreamlike. I keep thinking I'm going to wake up in my cupboard at the complex again."

"I was thinking how I had never really had a family before," Tori pointed out. "It felt like we hid as much as possible. It was just the two of us. My parents kept me fairly isolated, though that was mainly for health reasons. Now, we are two small families and we have come together. We're all a little bit less alone."

"Anna is doing very well with her weekend visits," Step added. "We love having her with us again. Will she still be able to do them if she goes back to school?"

"Yes," Patrick answered immediately.

"Speaking of which, have there been any more updates about the end of the strike today?" Tori asked.

"Only that most services and industries won't start up until around the Lunar New Year, since they have been shut down for so long."

"And a robot was found dead in the middle of a parking lot, beaten to death and flung into a tree," Step added gravely.

"Lord have mercy," Tori whispered.

The men soon stood up: Patrick went to finish preparing their breakfast casserole, while Step went to join his wife in bed. Tori kept staring at the Christmas tree and fireplace and turned on the Christmas Eve variety show, her nerve pain easing to a dull ache.

She had no doubt their family would have a wonderful Christmas together. The children would open their gifts; the adults would exchange theirs, and they would all enjoy delicious food together. There would be a new *Creature Tales* video and they would all watch it while eating caramel corn. It would be a lovely respite before it was time to face the actual winter.

At the same time, Tori was frightened. The end of the strikes and of the Robot Rental Corporation would not be the end of unrest. Would homeless robots be killed? Would the government ultimately give them the same rights as non-robot humans? Would Step and Maria be able to live their lives in peace? Would their children?

Once, her home had been her place of safety. She had hidden there with Patrick. Maria and Step had hidden in Little Hobidigan. When the police officers had kidnapped Anna, they had disrupted both families and shattered their carefully crafted hiding places. Now, they soon would not be able to hide anymore. Someone would eventually come after Patrick and Step about Patrick's articles. If they wanted to live full lives, they would have to be prepared to be attacked.

Patrick helped her up the stairs. They stopped to check in Anna's room, where Anna, Stephanie, and Taggy were cuddled up in the bed. Tyler was on a cot next to them, snuggling his beloved camel stuffie and still wearing the headband Anna had given him. Quickly glancing into their spare room, they saw Step and Maria had already fallen into a deep sleep.

"Let's stop the world now," Tori whispered, kissing her husband. "Everything is as it should be."

Silent night, holy night,
All is calm, all is bright,

Round yon Virgin Mother and Child,
Holy Infant, so tender and mild,
Sleep in heavenly peace,
Sleep in heavenly peace.

EPILOGUE

To any onlookers at the beach, the family was an ordinary father and his children: a boy of about five years old, and two girls who were seven and four, wading around at the edge of the lake while a man of about thirty supervised them, glancing every so often at a book.

Anna, Tyler, and Stephanie were enjoying a morning swim at the beach. It was going to be a hot July day, but it was a pleasant temperature as they splashed around then stopped to build a sandcastle. Step joined in the construction, explaining how a moat would really work and how to keep their towers from falling over. Focusing on the castle helped him overcome his nervousness about the upcoming gathering they were hosting at their cabin that afternoon.

"Can we come back to the beach later?" Anna asked.

"It will be too crowded," Tyler objected. Like his mother, he hated being in large groups for very long.

"It'll be too much work to get everyone to the beach," Step clarified. "There will be lots of little kids. We will have much more fun at home."

He doubted any of their visitors would want to be in public. Not only would they be too overwhelmed, but it would be outright illegal and dangerous.

"I'm excited to meet Auntie Scarlett and everyone in person," Anna continued. "How come we had to wait so long?"

"They need special passes to leave the complex. It took a long time for us all to get the right forms filled out and for the Federal Police to give us permission."

After two years, he was finally getting to see Nola, Isaac, Scarlett, and their children in person again. They had been issued passes to leave the complex and visit the cabin in Little Hobidigan, but the passes did not allow for an excursion to the public beach. Patrick had been required to outline specific stops along the route from the complex to the cabin and back. According to the police, the only places Patrick was allowed to take their visitors were the cabin, vehicle maintenance stations (if anyone needed a toilet or basic refreshment), and emergency health clinics. Morgana's store and the public beach were not on the approved list.

The police had long refused to believe anyone would want to have robots as visitors. They accused Patrick and Step of trying to get robots to work illegally. They had suggested they wanted to lure the robots to their home so they could attack them. To convince them they really did want to have their friends come visit them, Patrick admitted he was the mysterious Alexander Warrior-Church who had interviewed the robots two years before and wanted to take them to their family cabin to learn more from them. The police had relented, deciding that "wanting a follow-up interview" was a decent reason to grant two-day passes for Nola, Isaac, Scarlett, and their children.

Anna was in the middle of a three-week summer stint in Little Hobidigan, so she was excited to see Patrick and Tori again. Being at the lake for weekends and holidays had become normal for her; she always looked forward to coming home to her legal parents and Taggy as much as she looked forward to her time with her parents and siblings. All of them would gather together as a family for major occasions, usually at the cabin.

Step and Maria had also invited Cate and her children to attend the afternoon barbecue. There would be twenty people in total, which was probably the most people that had been at the cabin at one time in decades. To prepare for having so many visitors, Maria had insisted on focusing on beautifying the grounds and making lots of food, including harvesting basketfuls of vegetables and fruit. The day before, Step, Anna, and Tyler had caught fresh fish to serve their guests.

"I'm excited to show Ellie and Justin our house!" Tyler exclaimed. While he and Anna spent a lot of time with them in Goat Cove, mostly at the curling rink, Ellie and Justin had not yet visited them in Little Hobidigan.

"I'm sure they will find it very exciting and you will be a good host," Step agreed.

He was especially nervous about Cate attending the gathering. She had grown used to the idea that her children had robot cousins and expressed hope they could all meet each other. While she mostly wanted the children to get acquainted, she had also admitted she wanted to know just how similar Nola and Isaac were to Jade and John. When Step had raised the question with Isaac, Nola, and Scarlett, they had been equally curious to meet Cate, Heroic John's wife.

Of course, they're curious. We're robots; being cautiously curious is in our nature.

While he had once been adamant he was not a robot, Step now felt pride in being who he was. He felt as much kinship and solidarity with the people living in the complex, along with those who were still being exploited and persecuted elsewhere, as he did with Patrick and the regular humans he now constantly interacted with. Part of him wanted to pass this heritage on to his children, despite them having been raised differently. Anna and Tyler were old enough to understand they were not the same as their friends.

After taking a photo of their sandcastle and rinsing off in the lake, the four of them wandered back along the lakeside boardwalk to their cabin.

"Papa!" Another little girl came toddling toward Step and her older siblings. As she ran down the incline toward the boardwalk, he caught her and swooped her onto his shoulders.

"Hi, Vickie! Have you had fun with Mama this morning?"

"Yep!" She giggled and rested her head on his hair.

"Look at the rocks I picked up from the beach for you, Vickie!" Tyler held out some smooth stones. "You can put them in your garden!"

Maria had set aside a small garden plot for each of their children. Anna had hers filled with decorative animals, since she was not often there to tend it; Tyler had planted herbs; Stephanie had a wildflower garden with a bee house; and Vickie had laid out an ever-changing labyrinth of stones and pebbles.

"Do you need any help, Mama?" Anna called out. Maria was setting up tables and chairs on the deck.

"You can come inside and help me get lunch ready."

The three older children clambered up the steps and into the kitchen, while Step took Vickie over to her garden patch. The toddler delicately placed the new stones in a star-like pattern in the corner.

Tori, Cate, and the Alvarez-Franklin children soon arrived in one of the Williams-Kirkes' co-op's communal vans. Almost every available space in the yard was allocated to plants, so Tori delicately navigated down the driveway toward the only place to park. As soon as they stopped, Ellie, Justin, and Andrew jumped out of the van and waved at Step and Vickie.

"Hello, Mr. Step!" Ellie called out. "Hi, Vickie!"

"Careful, watch where you walk!" Cate admonished them, surveying the intricately landscaped yard. She turned to Tori. "This is much more complicated than I imagined."

"What, the garden?"

"This is not a garden; this is an enterprise! You weren't kidding when you said just imagining it made you tired."

"Come see my garden!" Vickie squealed, pointing to her rock labyrinth.

"Ooh!" Cate and Irene awkwardly made their way over to her. "You are an artist!"

"Thank you," Vickie smiled, glancing at her father. From the confused look on her face, Step realized she had no idea what "artist" meant. He smiled back at her reassuringly, so Vickie presumed whatever an artist was, it was a good thing to be.

"Yay, you're here!" Tyler called out, running out the door to meet his friends. "Anna, come on! Let's show them our house!"

*Our house...*Step beamed as Anna followed Tyler out so the two of them could lead the tour. Anna was not there often, but it was her house. No matter the suffering they had been through, they were now in a place where they were a family together.

While Tyler and Anna started to lead Cate, Ellie, Justin, Andrew, and Irene around, Tori went to join Maria and Stephanie.

"Can I go with Auntie?" Vickie asked, pulling Step after Tori.

"Yes, but remember she can't pick you up!"

"I sit on her, then." Vickie giggled as they headed toward the house.

"I think she is going to help Mama with lunch."

"Nope, I sit on her!"

Step helped Tori get comfortable at the kitchen table with Vickie on her lap so the two of them could shell peas together. Vickie adored her namesake and Tori was happy to spend time with her. Stephanie finished counting plates, cups, and napkins before following Step back outside so she could join her siblings and friends on the tour of the cabin.

Patrick arrived about an hour later, driving a specially rented van with lots of car seats in it. While everyone else was by then in the kitchen or on the deck overlooking the lake, Step remained waiting in the driveway, eager to see his siblings again.

"You made it!" he shouted. "Welcome!"

"Thought we weren't going to for a bit," Patrick admitted. "We got delayed by the cops. All's good now!"

"How are you all?" Step asked as Isaac slid open the side door. "Do you need any help?"

"I'm nervously fine," Isaac replied. "But thanks – it'll be faster with more of us getting the kids out of their car seats."

Step reached in to unbuckle the nearest toddler, who happened to be Jade. The little girl threw up once he stood her on the ground, not used to being transported. She looked up at him apologetically and then started to cry, overwhelmed by the strangeness of the situation.

"Oh, Jadey, you're okay!" Isaac pulled Bear out of the van and knelt down to hug his daughter. Bear seemed much more comfortable in his new environment than his sister. Unfazed by his twin being upset, he started to wander into the maze of grow-boxes.

"Whoa, little cub, come back!" Isaac called out. His son did so, noticing a millipede and deciding to focus on it while his parents and siblings finished climbing out of the vehicle.

"That's not food," Step added, as the two-year-old Bear tentatively reached for the millipede. "You'd get very sick. That's food for birdies."

Once Nola helped Scarlett out of the passenger door, she rushed around the van to give Step a warm hug.

"So happy to see you again! Thank you for inviting us."

"Likewise! I've missed you all. I can't believe the twins are two years old already!"

Scarlett soon appeared with Ruby, who was slightly younger than the twins. Both Ruby and Jade looked like younger versions of their respective mothers and neither seemed much like Ren, which made Step's spirit sink a little. He supposed they might have other traits of his, and he hoped to find out what they might be.

"All right, here's the last of them!" Patrick announced, guiding a fourteen-month-old boy out of the van. The boy looked a lot like Bear, except much smaller. Patrick handed him to Nola, who immediately showed the little boy off proudly.

"This is Dolphin! He's the baby of the family for now. Dolphin, this is your Uncle Step!"

For now… Step laughed awkwardly, as both Nola and Scarlett were obviously pregnant. From Scarlett's size, he guessed that her second child would be born in September, almost exactly two years after Ruby.

"Nice to meet you, Dolphin!" Dolphin smiled nervously at Step and coughed slightly.

"He's got breathing problems – he's not contagious," Nola hurried to explain.

"Let's go join everyone for lunch," Patrick suggested. "You all must be hungry."

"Yes, indeed." Step led them up the driveway. "This is our yard. As you can see, Maria has lots of grow-boxes and garden plots set up."

"It looks lovely," Nola complimented, sounding sincere but uncomfortable.

"Nola had a traumatic plant experience," Scarlett interjected. "She doesn't do shifts in the greenhouses anymore."

"Yes, but this is outside!" Nola protested. "I don't like being confined indoors with plants. This is fine."

Step decided this was not the time to ask for further details about what Scarlett meant by a traumatic plant experience, so he continued with his tour.

"Since everyone is gathered near the kitchen, we'll go around the house on the deck."

As the group approached the house, Andrew and Irene came running round the corner from the deck. Irene grinned and waved, excited at the new visitors, while Andrew's jaw dropped and he froze in place.

"Hello!" Irene called out.

"Hello!" Patrick responded, hurrying past the others to tend to Andrew. "It's okay, this is your uncle, aunts, and cousins. Remember that I said your papa had a brother that looks a lot like he did?"

"Um, yeah." The five-year-old still stared at Isaac sadly. "He looks more like him than I thought."

"This is Uncle Isaac." Irene squeezed her brother's hand. "Right, Mr. Step?"

"Yep."

Cate came around the corner next, evidently no more able to contain her curiosity than her younger children. Like Andrew, she froze in place, shrieking slightly.

"This is Cate," Step explained. "She is the one who used to know your donors."

"Um, hello." Nola climbed up the steps with Dolphin, who soon started wheezing.

"Hi Ja- I mean, um," Cate braced herself against the cabin wall. "Sorry, I've forgotten your name. You look just like her…"

"Nola. My name is Nola, and this is my son Dolphin."

"Nice to meet you," she managed to squeak.

Nola smiled at her nervously and took over introducing the rest of her family.

"And this is Isaac." Nola gestured to her husband who was helping the twins go up the steps on their own. "And Bear and Jade."

"And I'm Scarlett, the one who makes all the clothes, and this is Ruby." Scarlett waved from the bottom of the steps.

"Pleased to meet you!" Irene announced. "I'm Irene and this is Andrew. He makes wheezy noises too!"

"I do not!" Andrew protested, before dissolving into a coughing fit.

Step noted with curiosity that Dolphin and Andrew had similar conditions, despite the former's parents' genetic enhancements. Whatever genetic condition caused it clearly had not been seen as important for the Robot Rental Corporation to remove.

"I'm sorry, I'm a bit overwhelmed," Cate admitted. "You all go on and meet everyone else. I'll go around the front for a bit. I'll be back soon."

Irene and Andrew led the new visitors to where the picnic had been set up.

"I'll go keep Cate company while you host," Patrick muttered, waving Step and their guests onward.

Step nodded and jovially began to introduce everyone as they made their way onto the deck and around the cabin. Ellie and Justin expressed mild surprise at how much Isaac looked like their late father, but they were eager to meet their toddler cousins. For their part, the toddlers mostly clung to their parents, bewildered at the new environment. Step and Maria's children were equally excited to meet their friends in person. Stephanie hugged them all.

"Hello, again," Tori smiled awkwardly at Nola as the latter sat down at the table with her. "I think we met in person already once."

"Yes, someone forgot to give you a local anaesthetic," Nola remembered, settling Dolphin on her lap. "And then I ate your supper. Which is weird…why did they bring you supper? You weren't supposed to eat."

"I thought I told you that was me!" Scarlett interjected, joining them at the table with Ruby. "We were told to give everyone food and I knew you were hungry, since you had stopped eating the drugged stuff they gave us."

"It's nice to meet you properly." Tori winced as Vickie climbed back onto her lap.

Maria set filled plates in front of the three other women so they would not have to get up and disturb the toddlers. Step noticed she seemed overly business-like.

"Maria, sit down too! You don't need to serve everyone. Visit!"

She grabbed her own plate of food and joined Tori, Nola, and Scarlett at the table while Step finished making sure the children all had something to eat.

"Hi, I'm Maria and I am not good at visiting," she muttered, grinning sheepishly.

"None of us were very good at it initially," Nola admitted.

"I'm still not," Scarlett added.

"So, um, how's life at the barracks?" Maria wondered.

"Normal," Scarlett responded. "Though it is weird now that all the vats are empty. I miss looking after them."

"Well, we can convert the space into something more useful. The vats took up a lot of room. We're designing ways to convert part of it into a school."

"So does that mean no more robots?" Tori asked.

"No more growing them in vats and having them emerge as teenagers," Step jumped into the conversation from where he was sitting with the older children.

"We have lots of babies and toddlers," Scarlett explained.

"The police don't like that," Nola added. "I've had lots of meetings with lawyers and social workers, all trying to get us to stop. They don't want us to outgrow the complex, they say, and they say they are worried about the kids. The complex is plenty big enough."

"Are you able to get identity cards yet?" Maria asked.

"We have our own," Nola replied defensively. "Otherwise, no. It's either sneak out and pretend, or stay and be a protected animal with limited rights."

"I hope that changes."

"Only if it's for the better," Scarlett insisted.

"It sounds like it is getting worse," Nola added.

Step focused his attention on Isaac and the older children, who were discussing the birds on the lake. He missed the goings-on at the complex, but he was unable to be a part of it anymore. Nola, among other leaders, regularly had to meet with the police and legal teams. There were constant negotiations. It sounded exciting and exhausting, far from the peaceful life he enjoyed.

As they finished lunch, Step realized Anna had wandered away from the cabin toward the edge of the lake. She sat alone, seemingly occupied by poking rocks with her feet, but her father could tell she was anxious. Despite her outgoing nature, she had still inherited Maria's shy, nervous brain.

"Did you need to be alone, sweetie?" Step asked, quietly approaching her. "Are there too many people at the house?"

"Well, kind of. I wanted to think a little."

"Do you want me to think with you?"

"Sure!" She gave him a hug.

"What is it that you're thinking about?"

"How I've never really met other robots except for you and Mama until today. The phone doesn't work well. It is fun but weird to meet them in person."

Step nodded, glancing upward at the deck. No one was paying them any attention.

"How many more robot kids are there?"

"Lots, I think."

"And they have to stay in one place all the time? The government says it's okay to hurt them?"

"Kind of, yeah." *My eldest daughter is seven years old; she seems so much more aware of the world than her siblings.*

"What can we do about it? Why can't things change?"

"Things are changing slowly."

"Why do they have to be so slow to change?"

"Because people are stubborn and confused and want all kinds of evidence, though they don't believe it or they try to explain it away when they get it. Or they say it will be too hard or too expensive. People don't always care about others. Most people see us as things to be owned, not real humans."

"Can I be a robot? I mean, like, can I help robots? I'm not little. I don't want to just be a Ninja Cowboy princess who pretends all the time."

"None of us want to pretend. Someday, hopefully soon, you'll be able to be a robot without hiding and without anyone saying they have a claim on you."

"I hope you will too, Papa."

"While you kids have a world to explore, I don't know about us older robots. We've still got barcodes."

"That shouldn't matter." Anna looked out at the lake. "Are those patrol boats?"

Step followed her gaze in alarm.

"Yes, the black and white boats are the Alexandrina Police and the blue and green ones are the Federal Cascadian Police. I think the FCP is monitoring the local police."

"Are we going to get in trouble?"

"No, we shouldn't. Hopefully your mama hasn't seen them."

"Whatever happens, Papa, I want to help."

The two of them wandered purposefully back up to the deck where Maria had brought out a giant tub of ice cream. Anna clutched at her father's hand tightly, but noted to him that the police did not seem to be paying them any attention.

"It is possible they are just sending out extra patrols for the holiday weekend," Step whispered to his daughter reassuringly. "They are heading toward the beach."

Anna sat down with her father next to Tori and Vickie, delicately eating her ice cream.

It is a beautiful day, she observed, noting the sun shining over Lake Hobidigan and the birds flying past her. Her whole family was with her, except for Taggy, who would not have enjoyed being among so many small people. She had delicious food to eat. *This will change soon. I don't know when yet.* She glanced back toward the patrol boats and thanked God they were leaving them alone for the moment.

ACKNOWLEDGEMENTS

Thank you to all of the family and friends who have been supportive of my writing and who have encouraged me to publish my work, especially Lyndon. Thank you also to the Pete's Press team for taking a chance on my speculative fiction!

Thank you also to my late cat, Hektor, who was a wee kitten when I first brainstormed this story back in 2008, and spent his elder years helping me finalise it for publication.

ABOUT THE AUTHOR

Kat Gilks grew up in Regina and has been writing since elementary school. Over the course of nearly four decades, she has written many types of stories in a variety of genres, but has always had a particular interest in speculative fiction. Having studied history and information science, Kat works in nonprofit and, when not writing in her spare time, enjoys volunteering, exploring, and spending time with her family and cats.

www.ingramcontent.com/pod-product-compliance
Lightning Source LLC
LaVergne TN
LVHW020653110826
845149LV00012B/1985

* 9 7 8 1 9 9 7 7 1 3 1 1 1 *